THE DEATH STORM

Starhawk saw the cloud swell with unbelievable speed. Then the oven heat of the storm surrounded them—the legendary desert storm that could strip their bodies and leave their clean-picked bones half-buried behind.

Flying gravel tore at Starhawk's face as she swung down from her saddle, trying to yell to Tazey, "We can kill the horses for a windbreak!" But she knew it was a last resort and nearly useless.

Her body aching already with desiccation, Starhawk squinted through the fog of smothering dust. She saw the girl's dim outline, walking into the storm, her hair flying back as she raised her hands. Tazey was stretching them into the wind, her fingers pressed together like a wedge. And the force of the storm curled back from her hands, leaving a wake of stillness.

Tazey—Princess Taswind, the King's daughter—was a witch!

By Barbara Hambly
Published by Ballantine Books:

DRAGONSBANE

THE LADIES OF MANDRIGYN

THE SILENT TOWER

THE WITCHES OF WENSHAR

The Darwath Trilogy
TIME OF THE DARK
THE WALLS OF AIR
THE ARMIES OF DAYLIGHT

The Witches of Wenshar

Barbara Hambly

A Del Rey Book

BALLANTINE BOOKS • NEW YORK

A Del Rey Book
Published by Ballantine Books

Copyright © 1987 by Barbara Hambly

All rights reserved under International and Pan-American
Copyright Conventions. Published in the United States of
America by Ballantine Books, a division of Random House,
Inc., New York, and simultaneously in Canada by Random
House of Canada Limited Toronto.

Library of Congress Catalog Card Number: 87-91135

ISBN 0-345-32934-1

Manufactured in the United States of America

First Edition: July 1987

Cover Art by Darrell K. Sweet
Maps by Shelly Shapiro

For Lester

AUTHOR'S NOTE

The word "witch" is a connotative and emotionally charged term. It implied different things at different places and times, and to different groups of people—and, for that reason, has been so used here.

The particular implications of the word as it is used in this story —specifically the different connotations of the words "wizard" and "witch" in the shirdane language—are drawn from the sixteenth/ seventeenth century view of witches and witchcraft, and from that view *only*. No more is meant by it than would be meant by my using various connotative words to describe persons of African descent, if I were writing from the viewpoint of a white Southerner in the 1920's. They do not represent my personal opinion or any blanket definition of witches (and indeed, have not been so used in other books of mine). Nor do they have anything to do with the implications of "witches" and "witchcraft" in medieval times, in the nineteenth century, in more conventionalized fairy tales, or at the present day.

What came to be known as European witchcraft was originally simply the worship of the old nature-deities, combined with the herbal medicine practiced by that faith's adherents, as seen through the distorting eye of a paranoid and intolerant medieval Church. The current Wiccan religion, whose devotees term themselves "witches," is a harking-back to this ancient faith, whose chief tenets were responsible use of white magic and love of the nature from which that power springs.

To those good-hearted and sincerely God-loving witches, I extend my apology. I hope I have made it clear in terms of the story itself that the word "witch" is only a word (like "love," or "god," or "Christian"): that it is in fact what people do with that word, or do because of what they think of that word, that causes good or ill.

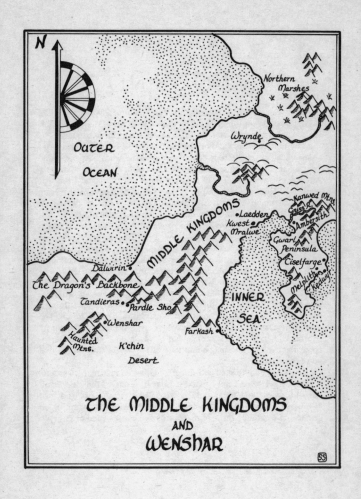

N

OUTER

OCEAN

Northern
Marshes

Wrynde

MIDDLE KINGDOMS

Kanwed Mtns.
Gnisi
Laedden · Ambersith
Kwest ·
· Mralwe

Gwarl
Peninsula
Ciselfarge

Dalwirin ·

The Dragon's Backbone

Melplith
Kedwyr

Tandieras ·   · Pardle Sho

INNER

· Wenshar

SEA

Haunted
Mtns.

K'chin

Farkash ·

Desert

THE MIDDLE KINGDOMS
AND
WENSHAR

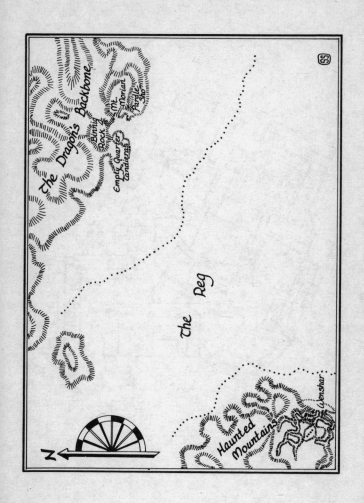

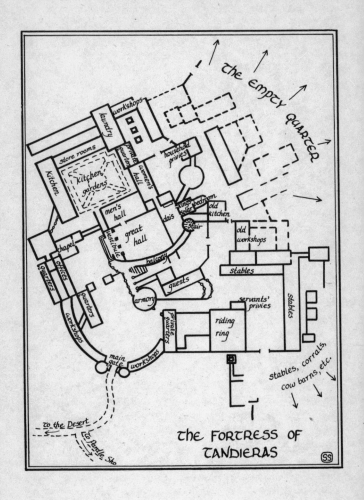

THE EMPTY QUARTER

workshops

laundry

store rooms

Kitchen

kitchen gardens

private quarter

women's hall

household privies

men's hall

dais

King's bedroom

solar

old kitchen

chapel

offices

quarters

vestibule

great hall

stair

old workshops

quarters

balcony

guests

stables

armory

servants' privies

workshops

private quarters

riding ring

stables

main gate

workshops

to the Desert

to Peolle Sho

stables, corrals, cow barns, etc.

THE FORTRESS OF
TANDIERAS

CHAPTER

—— 1 ——

*"Y*OU MAY BE A WIZARD, MY LADY," SUN WOLF SAID, tucking his big hands behind the buckle of his battered sword belt, "but you're also the biggest damn fool I've ever met in my life."

Every man has a gift, Starhawk sighed to herself. *Why do I choose to travel with a man whose gift is to be able to talk audibly with his foot in his mouth up to the knee?*

For one instant the sun-blasted garden with its small citrus trees and hard, clayey red soil was utterly silent. Beneath the sharp black lattice shadows of the bare arbor, the face of the Lady Kaletha, the White Witch of Wenshar, went rigid with an indignation which was three parts shock that anyone, let alone some roving barbarian in a dusty sheepskin doublet and scarred boots, would dare speak so to her. Her face paled against the dark red coils of her hair, and her protuberant blue eyes blazed, but for the first moment she was literally speechless. One of the little cluster of her ostentatiously black-

1

clothed disciples, misinterpreting, opened her mouth. Kaletha waved her silent.

"You barbarian pig." She had a voice like the clink of a dropped gold coin upon stone. "Are you slandering me out of fear of what I am—or jealousy of what I have?"

Behind her, her disciples murmured, nodding wisely to one another. The gardens of Pardle Sho were public, occupying the grounds of what had been the Governor's Palace back when the land of Wenshar had been ruled by the Lords of the Middle Kingdoms; across the vast open square of sand, two children chased each other through the zebra shadows of the cloister, their voices shrill as birds in the hot air.

After a moment Sun Wolf said, "I fear what you are, Lady."

She drew breath to make some final point, but he cut in over her words in a voice like the rasping of a rusted-out kettle. "What you are is an armed idiot—if you're not simply a liar."

Turning, he walked away. The dark lacework of the vine shadows rolled like the foam pattern on a wave along the lion-colored leather of his doublet, and the Lady Kaletha was left with the uncomfortable choice of giving him the last word or shouting her own rebuttal in an undignified fashion after his retreating back.

Thumbs hooked in her sword belt, Starhawk followed him down that hot, shaded colonnade and across the gardens to the street.

"You know, Chief," she remarked later, coming over with two tin tankards of beer to the intense gloom of a corner of the Longhorn Inn's common room, "sometimes your facility with words leaves me breathless."

His single eye, amber as a tiger's under a long, curling tuft of fading red-gold brow, flicked suspiciously up at her as she stepped casually over the back of the chair next to his and settled into it. The leather patch that covered the empty socket of his other eye was already scuffed and weathered to the same shade as his sungilded skin, but the telltale groove of years had not yet been worn across his forehead by its buckskin thong.

Starhawk's face, as usual, was inscrutable as she handed him his beer; features that would have been delicate, had not her original uncomeliness of a long jaw and a square chin been added to, in the course of nine years as a mercenary soldier, by a broken nose and three inches of whitening scar that decorated one high, fragile cheekbone. For the rest, she was a tall, rangy cheetah of a woman, dressed in a man's leather breeches, embroidered shirt, and sheepskin doublet. Her baby-fine blond hair was cropped short and, like Sun Wolf's thinning red-gold mane and faded mustache, bleached out by the sun of the K'Chin Desert, along whose northern edge they had been traveling for four days.

Sun Wolf grumbled, correctly suspecting that what lay behind those water-gray eyes was a deep and private amusement. "The woman is a fool." His voice was like the wheezy creak of an unoiled hinge, as if his vocal chords had all the flesh stripped from them, leaving nothing but bare wire.

Starhawk took a sip of her beer. It was bitter, like all the beer in the Middle Kingdoms, the color of mahogany, and very strong. "She's also the only thing we've seen that remotely resembles a wizard since we left Mandrigyn," she reminded him after a moment. "And since we can't go back to Mandrigyn . . ."

Sun Wolf brushed aside the reminder of his banishment from the city that was known as the Jewel of the Megantic Sea. "The Wizard King Altiokis lived and ruled for a hundred and fifty years," he growled. "He destroyed any wizard with even a guess of the power that might have challenged him. If this Kaletha woman has the powers she claims, he'd have destroyed her, too."

Starhawk shrugged. "She could have kept them hidden until his death. That was only nine months ago. Altiokis got much of his silver from the mines of Wenshar—it's a sure bet Pardle Sho and every little

mining town along the cordillera was riddled with his
spies. She has to have remained silent, like Yirth of
Mandrigyn did, in self-defense."

Sun Wolf wiped the beer foam from his thick, raggedy
mustache and said nothing.

Though the air in the common room was hot, still, and
strangely dense-feeling, not one of the half-dozen or so
miners and drifters there made a move to leave its indigo
shadows for the striped black-and-primrose shade of the
awning of peeled cottonwood poles outside. It was the
season of sandstorms, as autumn drew on toward winter.
In the north, sailors would be making fast their vessels
till spring opened the sea roads again, and farmers re-
chinking the thatch of their roofs. Throughout the north
and west and on to the cold steppes of the east, all life
came to a standstill for four months under the flail of
those bitter storms. Here in Wenshar, the southernmost
of the Middle Kingdoms on the borders of the desert,
even the few hardy herds of cattle grazing the patches of
scrub that passed for oases were chivvied in to closer
pastures near the foothill towns, and the silver miners
strung lines of rope from their dwellings to the pitheads,
lest the burning sand-winds rise while they were between
one point and another, and the darkness come on so
swiftly that they would be lost.

Deceptively idle-seeming, Starhawk scanned the
room.

Like half the buildings in Pardle Sho, the Longhorn
was adobe brick and about fifty years old. Its low roof,
thirty-five feet long and less than ten from side to side,
was supported by rafters of stripped scrub pine whose
shortness gave every adobe building in the town the appearance of a hallway. The older buildings of the town,
erected of stone when Pardle Sho was the administrative
center through which the Lords of Dalwirin ruled the
Desert Lords of the wastelands beyond, were spacious
and airy. According to Sun Wolf, who knew things like
that, the smallest of those stone houses fetched seven

times the price of any adobe dwelling in the town. Looking up at the blackened lattices of rafter and shadow over her head, Starhawk had to concede that the buyers had a point. Adobe was cheap and fast. The men and women who'd come over the mountains, first as slaves, then as free prospectors, to work the silver mines and eventually to wrest them and the land of Wenshar from those who had held them before, often could afford no better.

One of the first wars Starhawk had fought in, she recalled, had been some border squabble between Dalwirin, closest of the Middle Kingdoms north of the mountains, and Wenshar. She remembered being a little surprised that, approached by both sides, Sun Wolf had chosen to take Wenshar's money. She'd been twenty-one then, a silent girl only a year out of the convent which she'd abandoned to follow the big mercenary captain to war; a few weeks of defending the black granite passes of the Dragon's Backbone had shown her the wisdom of taking defense rather than attack on such terrain.

Sipping her beer, she remembered she hadn't had the slightest idea what to do with the prize money after the campaign. Sun Wolf, if she recalled correctly, had used his to buy a silver-eyed black girl named Shadowrose who could beat any warrior in the troop at backgammon.

She glanced across at the man beside her, his gold-furred forearms stretched before him on the table, picturing him then. Even back then, he'd been the best and certainly the richest mercenary in the length and breadth of the old boundaries of the fallen Empire of Gwenth. He'd had both his eyes then and a voice like a landslide in a gravel pit; the thin spot in his tawny hair had been small enough that he could deny its existence. His face had been a little less craggy, the points of bone on the corners of his bearlike shoulders a little less knobby. The deep silences within his soul had been hidden under the bluster of crude sex and physical challenge, which some men used to conceal their vulnerabilities from other men.

He sat now with his back to the corner of the room, as usual, his blind left eye toward her. She was the only person he allowed to sit on that side. Though she saw no more of his face than the broken-nosed profile against the brilliance of the open door, she could feel the thought moving through him, the tension in those heavy shoulders. "Face it, Chief. If this woman Kaletha doesn't teach you how to use your powers, who will?"

He moved his head a little, and she had a glimpse of the amber glint of his eye. Then he turned away again. "She's not the only wizard in the world."

"I thought we'd just established there weren't any at all."

"I don't like her."

"When you had the school at Wrynde, did the people who came to learn the arts of war from you need to like you?" When he didn't answer, she added, "If you're starving, do you need to like the baker from whom you buy your bread?"

He looked back at her then, a deep flame of annoyance in his eye that she'd read the truth in him. She drank off her beer and set the tankard down; her forearms, below the rolled sleeves of her blue-and-white embroidered shirt, were muscled like a man's, marked with the white scars of old wars. Across the common room under the glare of the bar lamps, a couple of women in the dusty clothes of miners were flirting with a lovely young man in brown silk, their voices a low mixture of sound, like a perfume of roses and musk.

"If you want to move on, you know I'll ride with you. You know I don't understand wizardry, or the needs of power. But you called Kaletha an armed idiot for having power and not using it wisely. What does that make you?"

Anger flared in that slitted yellow eye—she was reminded of a big, dusty lion baited in its lair and about to growl. But she met his gaze calmly, challenging him to deny what she said, and, after a moment, it fell. There was a long silence.

Then he sighed and pushed his half-finished tankard from him. "If it was battle, I'd know what to do," he said, very quietly, in a voice she seldom heard him use to her and never to anyone else. "I've been a soldier all my life, Hawk. I have an instinct of fighting that I trust, because it's been borne out in battle after battle. But I'm mageborn. Whether I like it or not, there's a wizard inside of me—not buried and whispering, as it is with the mageborn when their powers first stir, but grown and wild as a dragon. I passed through the Great Trial into the fullness of power without getting even the teaching that most mageborn managed to pick up in secret from the local grannies when Altiokis was alive and killing off wizards. It's like being born, not as a baby, but as a man—having no more mind than a baby, but wanting what a man wants."

Broodingly, he cradled the tankard between his blunt-fingered hands. Away from the lamplight near the bar, the shadows were darkening; the wind that ghosted through the door was cooler now than the trapped, stuffy-smelling heat, scented with dust and the wildness of the desert evening.

"There are times when the want consumes me. In the nine months since I came to the power, it's been like a fire inside me, burning me up. That patchwork of learning I was able to pick up in Mandrigyn before I was banished makes no sense to me. I have instincts shouting at me that mean nothing to me, and I don't know whether they're right or will lead me to a quick death and the Cold Hells. Sometimes I wish by all the spirits of my ancestors I'd been born like my father, just a great crafty beast; and other times..." He shook his head, with the nearest admission to helplessness Starhawk had seen from him in all the years since they had met.

Impulsively, she leaned across to him and put her hand on his; his fingers closed warm and rough around

hers, accepting a comfort neither of them would even
have considered a year ago. His hoarse voice was like
the scrape of blown sand in the gloom. "There's a vision
in me of myself, from long before I came to my powers
—one I had as a child, though I couldn't speak of it then.
But it's come back to me since I passed through the
Great Trial. It's a vision of looking at a great blazing fire
and wanting to grasp the core of the flame in my bare
hand, knowing it will hurt—but knowing that when the
flesh is all burned off, I'll be able to wield that core like a
sword."

Behind the long bar of sleeve-polished pine, the
owner of the Longhorn was lighting candles—dented tin
lusters throwing back a rancid light. Outside, shadows of
the spur-ranges of the Dragon's Backbone had covered
the town, the hem fringe of the garment of night. Miners,
townsmen, and those who rode herd on the tough, long-
horned cattle were coming in, dusty and cursing from
work. They were mostly the fair-skinned, blond, or red-
haired stock of the north, whence the Middle Kingdoms
had acquired their slaves, but with a fair sprinkling of the
dark-haired people of the Middle Kingdoms themselves,
and the black folk of the long, golden coastlines of the
southern Megantic. Among them, striking in their white
robes and head veils, were the swarthy shirdar, the
desert dwellers, who recognized not the King of Wenshar, but the Ancient Houses of the old Desert Lords.
Voices jostled in the warm dimness against the smells
of old sweat of work-soiled garments, of white or amber
liquor, and of the milky sweetness of beeswax. A round-
shouldered little black man in his sixties, the tracks of
some ancient battle overlying old ornamental scarring on
his face, his body hard as twisted ebony from work in
spite of the richness of his clothes, ordered drinks for
everyone in the place to thunderous applause.

As the owner's boy and girl began circulating with a
tray of beer and whiskey, the little man raised his hands.
Candle flame caught on his rings. Starhawk, though never

much of a looter in her years as a mercenary, had acquired a professional soldier's quick eye; she reckoned each of them at five gold pieces, a staggering sum to be carrying around on one's hands, particularly on the cordillera. In a voice several times the size of his tough little body, the man bellowed, "This drink is for the honor of the Princess Taswind! We'll serve it and we'll fight for it, come what may!"

Though Starhawk had no idea who the Princess Taswind was, she took a blunt pottery cup of liquor the color of henna from the tray the barboy offered her. Sun Wolf shook his head at the offer of another beer. After passing through the Great Trial, it had been months before he'd been able to touch alcohol at all. There was a chorus of cheers, some woman's raucous whoop riding up over them like a descant. Beside the bar one of the brown-faced shirdar warriors pushed back his head veils and raised his cup as the noise subsided a little. "And drink also to her lord and husband to be, Incarsyn of Hasdrozaboth, Lord of the Dunes!" Under the veils, black hair, long and thick as a woman's and braided against the dust, framed a hawk-thin face that was handsome, proud, and very young.

The three warriors with him—all young men *and none of them over twenty,* Starhawk thought—put aside their veils and lifted their cups. Their piercing cry rang against the sudden silence of the room like the discordant clatter of a dropped tray.

The silence in the room was so complete Starhawk could hear the jingle of bridle bits from the horses tied outside. The young man looked around him, his face scarlet with fury and shame. A few feet away at the bar, the tough little black man leaned against the railing, his brown eyes hard with derisive challenge.

Furious, the young man drank off his cup and hurled it at the wall behind the bar. The barkeep ducked aside —the cup itself, harder-fired than the adobe brick, did not even shatter. Silently, the four young shirdar stalked from the room, their white cloaks swirling against the jambs of the open doors as they vanished into the dusk outside.

"Norbas, one of these days you're going to buy yourself a shiv between the ribs," sighed a voice, deep and half-drunken, from the next table. The black man, stepping away from the bar, whirled in surprise. Then his scarred face broke into a blazing white grin as he saw the big man sitting there.

"What the hell are you doing here, Osgard?" He crowded his way over, followed by two or three others, wearing like him the clothes of wealthy townsmen: boned doublets and stiffened linen collars of gaudier hues than were considered good taste north of the mountains, breeches and boots rather than the more sophisticated long hose. The man at the next table was dressed the same way, though with the slight untidiness that spoke, like his slurring voice, of someone who had been drinking since just past noon.

"Can't a man slip out for a drink now and then?" Like Sun Wolf, the man Osgard was big, a thumb-breadth shorter than the Wolf's six feet, fairer than the Wolf and going gray. Like the others, under the richness of his clothes, his body was the body of a man who has both worked and fought. In his broad, unshaven face his green eyes glinted with annoyance. "Maybe I knew I'd meet you here. The match has been made, Norbas, like others before it. I tell you, let it be."

Norbas sniffed scornfully and stiff-armed a pottery cup brimming with the murderous white liquid known locally as Panther Sweat. "I never trusted those sneaky heathens and I never will," he stated flatly. "I bought the round to drink to Tazey's happiness, not to that of some barbarian she has to marry."

"You have a right to think as you please, but you'll come to grief carrying on about it in bars," the man Osgard said a little grimly. "It's for the good of the land;

I've told you that before . . ." And like the wash of a sea wave, the noise of other conversations covered theirs.

"It's a clever choice on somebody's part," Sun Wolf rumbled, half to himself, half to Starhawk. "It's sure as pox what I'd do if I ruled Wenshar." He contemplated the man Osgard for a moment against the blurred candle-light with a narrowed eye. "Most of the shirdar lords are fallen into decay—none of them ever ruled more than a couple handfuls of people in all their hundreds of miles of sand, anyway. With one mud-walled city, a string of oases, and a couple hundred goats and camels, Hasdro-zaboth's not terribly powerful, but it's ruinously old, like all the Houses of the Desert Lords. But it's an in to the kin network that Wenshar could call on if Dalwirin or Kwest Mralwe invaded them again from the north."

Starhawk nodded, accepting this information without inquiring how Sun Wolf knew it. Back in the days when Sun Wolf had been a mercenary captain and she his second-in-command, part of his success had been due to his minute knowledge of the politics and economics of every kingdom and principality likely to hire his troops. The habit had stayed with him—he gossiped like an old woman with every tale-telling merchant they'd met on the roads. His aim these days was principally to find rumor of a wizard to teach him to use the powers so suddenly arisen within him, but he managed to pick up a good deal of knowledge of other things in the process. Curious, she asked, "If they never had more than a couple hundred warriors, why do you say they're in decay? Decay from what?"

"From ruling the southern trade routes through the desert to the gold mines of Kimbu," he replied promptly. "The Lords of Wenshar—not the King now, but the An-cient House of the old Lords of Wenshar—ruled the whole desert, back when the Empire of Gwenth was still around in the north for Kimbu to trade with."

"Silly me," apologized Starhawk ironically, and Sun Wolf gave her a grin, half-embarrassed at his own sudden show of erudition, and squeezed the fingers still lightly clasped in his own.

They ordered dinner; through it Sun Wolf alternated between watching the increasing crowd in the tavern and particularly around the next table, where Osgard and Norbas were holding a sort of court for what looked like the wealthier miners, and relapsing into his own thoughts. By the look on his face, Starhawk thought he didn't care much for them, but she had learned long ago when to keep her silence. Full dark fell outside; Osgard and his friends departed singing; the local Children of Joy, youths as well as girls, began to make their appearance. Pergemis silks of rose and violet shimmered softly in the ochre lamplight, and painted eyes teased. When the tavern girl came to clear up, Sun Wolf signed to her to stay. "Where would I find the house of the Lady Kaletha? The wizard?"

The girl hastily sketched in the air the sign against evil. "She'll be up at the Fortress of Tandieras," she mumbled. "But if you need a healer or something, go to Yallow Sincress in Leatherworker's Row. He's . . ."

"Tandieras?" asked Sun Wolf, surprised to hear her name the fortress of the King.

The girl nodded, her dark eyes avoiding his. She was fourteen or so, gawky and plain, with the hawk features of the shirdar in the frame of her straight black braids. "Yeah. She's part of the King's Household." She gathered the pottery dishes with their vivid glazes of yellow and blue onto her tray and prepared to go. Sun Wolf dug into his pouch and dropped a quarter of a silver bit into the empty bread plate. The dark eyes raised to his, startled and shining.

"And where is the Fortress?" Sun Wolf got to his feet, readjusting the set of the sword at his hip.

"You're not gonna go *tonight*?" There was sudden, baffled fear in the girl's plunging brows. "She's a *witch*!" She used the shirdar word for it, and there was loathing in her voice.

"Funny," Starhawk remarked later, as they walked up Main Street, leaning into the steep slope of the hill upon which the town was built. "Most of the people we've met on the road figured wizards are something that died out a long time ago, if they ever existed to begin with. But she was afraid."

With the final sinking of the sun, the hot blast of the desert daylight had given way to dry and bitter cold. Dust hung in the air, the smell of it a constant with which they had lived for days; it blurred the lights of the inns and houses they passed, twinkling amber-gold in the ultramarine darkness. They'd added sheepskin coats to their doublets and still felt the thin lance of the desert night. They had left their horses behind at the inn—it had been a long journey, and the beasts were badly overridden.

Above them, thready moonlight touched the gilded turrets of the Cathedral of the Triple God, triumphant fingers stretching from the highest peak of the town. Higher still, the jagged peaks of the Dragon's Backbone loomed, massive granite domes and sugarloaves, with here and there unscalable plugs of black basalt—dry teeth goring at the stars.

Sun Wolf nodded thoughtfully as they turned along the face of the hill. Ahead of them, a mile or so from the town, the lights of the Fortress of Tandieras winked against the rocky bulk of the spur-range on which it was built. Like a moat, darkness lay before it where the road dipped from the flank of Pardle Hill, a long stretch of gully, boulder, and sand. From the dense shadows, the topmost twigs of a desiccated acacia tree reached up into the moonlight like crooked reeds above spring floods— for the rest it was pitchy dark. Starhawk's every nerve came alert. It was a patch of road made for robbers.

"There may be a reason for it," Sun Wolf said after a few moments. "But I'd fear Kaletha for different reasons. She's arrogant. She's young, Hawk, younger than you. I'm not saying no wizard that young can hold the kind of power she claims to hold, but, if one did, I think I'd feel it." The rock shadows loomed darkly around them. Starhawk's fingers touched the comforting hardness of her sword. Half her mind turned from the Wolf's scratchy wheeze to the soft whisper of shadow sounds. "She should still be a student, not claiming to be able to teach the secrets of the universe to a bunch of fatuous disciples."

"If she teaches you anything," Starhawk pointed out, "she'll have . . ."

Sun Wolf's hand tapped her shoulder for silence a split instant before she heard, faint and muffled, a man's cry and smelled the drift of kicked dust and blood on the night wind. Then there was the ringing whine of a drawn sword, and a voice thick with liquor yelled, "Rot your eyes, you scum-sucking swine . . . !"

The Wolf was already scrambling up over the rocks in the darkness.

Without a word passing between them, Starhawk knew what the plan was and moved forward at a soundless run toward the barely visible bend in the dark road. From the other side of the overhanging rocks, she heard the searing ring of steel on steel and a man's voice shouting, "Help! MURDER!" The scrub along the edge of the road would give more away by its noise than it would conceal in that pitchy dark; Starhawk felt, rather than actually saw, the wide bay between the boulders to her right, sensed violent movement somewhere in the Stygian blackness, and heard the sounds of struggle.

A white blur on the ground turned out to be the face and hands of a dead man amid a stench of spilled blood. She sprang noiselessly over him. Ahead of her, another man was backed to the gray-black front of a massive boulder—pale face, pale hands, the white V of a shirt visible through an unlaced doublet. Ill-defined forms danced before him. Starlight glinted on steel. Starhawk ran one of his black-cloaked attackers through the body before the man had time to realize what was happening.

He let out a gasping death scream, and the other assailants turned upon her in a body.

Then, from the top of the rocks, there was a berserker howl, and Sun Wolf was among them. Starhawk caught barely a glimpse of him as he dropped into the darkness. She found by instinct the shoulder of another dark form near to her, caught the thick cloth of his cloak, and shoved her sword up under his ribs as he turned toward the new threat. As she pulled the blade clear in a sticky gush of hot blood over her hand, she glimpsed the white robe beneath the cloak, already staining with the welling blood. Shirdar, she thought, turning and ducking the slash of a curved tulwar, cutting at breast level, and parrying steel that whined within inches of her face. The victim of the ambush had sailed into the fray, fighting like a drunken man with yells of fury. From the road behind them, hooves thudded and lanterns swayed in the darkness; reflected light showed Starhawk the gleam of a sword, and she cut in the darkness where the body would be. Her blade met nothing; the man had turned, and she heard the scrunch of his soft boots on gravel as he fled.

Beside her, the man they'd rescued was yelling, "Here! To me!"—with, Starhawk thought wryly, considerable optimism about whose side the reinforcements were on. A blue burst of witchlight flared in the darkness, the ghostly blaze turning Sun Wolf's craggy features and gore-slimed sword blade into a hashish vision of some barbarian berserker god. He had evidently decided that darkness was no longer to his advantage. By the faint St. Elmo's fire, Starhawk could see the last attackers fleeing into the shadows of the rocks, leaving their dead stretched upon the thin dust of the ground. Men and women in some kind of dark green livery studded with smoked steel were urging their horses down from the road, springing from their saddles to dart in pursuit, until their captain raised his hand and called them back.

"It's useless—don't get yourselves killed over it!" He reined up before Starhawk and the man beside her, the man she now recognized as Osgard from the tavern. The horseman stepped from his saddle with surprising grace for a man of his bulk. "Are you hurt, my lord?"

"By the Three, that was fighting!" Osgard flung an approving arm around Sun Wolf as he came up to them, the heavy sheepskin of his jerkin marked with a sword slash, but apparently unwounded himself. "You never saw the like, Nanciormis! This bastard had them running like rats—like rats!" Standing that close to him, Starhawk could smell, under the reek of the blood that smeared them all, stale alcohol in his sweat.

As tall as Osgard and Sun Wolf, the rider Nanciormis had the swarthy skin and aquiline features of the shirdar. What had once been a hawk-like beauty was blurred by a padded layer of fat. "My lord . . ." The other riders were closing in around them, and the torches they bore threw glints of gold on the clips that held back his waist-length black hair. "I've warned you before about going about the town so, unprotected and with no state . . ."

"State, hell," grumbled Osgard, bending to wipe his sword on the black robe of one of the fallen bandits and sheathing it at his side. His voice had lost its drunken slur—there's nothing like fighting for your life, thought Starhawk, to induce instant sobriety. "It wasn't state that got me crowned King of Wenshar."

Starhawk's glance cut sharply to Sun Wolf. She saw that he wasn't surprised.

"It was men like Norbas Milkom and Quaal Ambergados—miners and fighters, men who know the land. Men like . . ." Osgard turned and regarded Sun Wolf with an arrested eye. "I know you," he said.

Sun Wolf nodded. "Likely you do, your Majesty."

"Not just from the tavern . . ." The green eyes narrowed. "You're Sun Wolf. The mercenary of Wrynde. We hired you—what . . . ?"

"Last war but one with Dalwirin," Sun Wolf provided.

"Old Shilmarne was leading her forces down the passes..."

"By the Three, that was it!" The King slapped Sun Wolf enthusiastically on the back, then staggered. He'd taken a thigh wound, and blood was still tracking stickily down the leg of his breeches. Sun Wolf and Starhawk caught him as his knees gave way, Nanciormis springing belatedly to help.

Osgard made an impatient move to push them off. "I'm fine..."

"The hell you are," Sun Wolf rasped. He pulled from some inner pocket the silk scarf he'd long ago learned to keep handy and tied it around Osgard's leg above the wound. With the hilt of one of the hideout daggers in his boot, he twisted it tight. In the yellow glare of the torchlight, the King's face had gone suddenly waxen as the heat of battle died from his veins. "There a sawbones up at the fortress?"

Nanciormis nodded. "Can you sit a horse, my—"

"Of course I can sit a horse!" Osgard blustered furiously. "Just because I took a little scratch doesn't mean I'm going to go to pieces like some sniveling, weakling coward..." His sandy eyebrows stood out darkly against his gray flesh, and, like a candle being blown out, he fainted.

"Good," Sun Wolf grunted, as they eased him gently back to lay him on the sand. "With luck he'll stay unconscious and won't argue about his pox-rotted manhood all the way up to the Fortress."

The guards looked shocked, but, in the commander Nanciormis' eye, he caught the flicker of an appreciative grin.

CHAPTER

—— 2 ——

*I*N THE FORTRESS OF TANDIERAS SUPPER WAS OVER, THE
trestle tables in the Great Hall put away, and the chairs
and benches pushed back against the walls of the vast,
granite room which was the old castle's heart. Like the
Longhorn Inn, it was lit chiefly by wall sconces whose
polished metal reflectors threw back the soft beeswax
glow into the room, but here the height of the ceiling,
though it added to the cold, at least relieved the smoke.
In addition, a huge fireplace stretched along one side of
the feasting-dais at the far end, around which carved
chairs were clustered, and two chandeliers dangled—
unlit, massive, ominous iron wheels—in the dense
shadows overhead.

But Sun Wolf's first impression, as he stepped
through the triple archway that led from the vestibule
into the Hall, was one of color, gaiety, and movement.
Since it was the season of sandstorms, the big wooden
shutters that guarded the line of tall windows on the
room's southern wall had been closed nearly to for the

18

night. Servants in drab shirts and breeches, gently born retainers in colorful broadcloth and white ruffs, and guards in dark green leather were grouped around the sides of the Hall, clapping in time to the music of pipes, flutes, and the fast, heartbreaking throb of a hand-drum; in the center of the Hall, lit by hand-held lamps and torches all around her, a girl was doing a war dance.

It was one of the old war dances of the Middle Kingdoms, done these days for the sheer joy of its violent measures. A young man and a girl in guard's uniforms stood aside, sweat-soaked and panting, having clearly just finished their turn. As the dancer's shadow flickered across them, the blades below her glinted. They were using live weapons. But for all the concern on her face, the girl might have been dancing around and over a circle of wheat sheaves; her feet, clad in light riding boots under a kilted-up skirt, tapped at will, now this side, now that side, of the blued edges of the upturned swords. She looked to be about sixteen; her sand-blond hair, mixed fair and dark, caught the light on its thick curls; the torches were not brighter than her eyes.

Beside him, Sun Wolf was aware of Nanciormis striding through the arch into the room, his mouth open to call out the ill news. Sun Wolf caught the man's thick arm and said softly, "Don't startle her."

The guards' commander saw what he meant and checked, then blustered, "No, of course I wasn't going to." He signaled one of the pages to come over and whispered hasty instructions to the boy. The young face paled in the torchlight with shock. "Go on!" Nanciormis ordered, and the page went slipping off through the crowd toward the little knot of gentlemen-in-waiting who stood between the fireplace and the door that led from the dais to the King's solar beyond. Nanciormis glanced defensively back at Sun Wolf. "We can't let his Majesty remain out in the cold court!"

At that moment the music skirled to its circling conclusion; the girl stood panting and radiant in the tawny halo of the lights. A woman hastened down to her from the crowd on the dais, skinny and flustery, her narrow, white face framed unbecomingly in tight-pulled, black hair. She dressed in black, too; the harshness of the color triggered something in Sun Wolf's memory. She had been one of Kaletha's disciples in the public gardens that afternoon. She touched the girl's arm and said something. Stricken, the girl turned eyes wide with shock and green as absinthe toward the doorway; without a word she strode toward them, the black-clothed governess hurrying behind like a skinny ewe sheep who has fostered a gazelle.

"Uncle, is Father all right?" she demanded as soon as she got near enough to Sun Wolf and Nanciormis to speak. "Anshebbeth says—"

"Your father's fine, Tazey."

"You ought to send at once for the Lady Kaletha," the black-clothed woman panted, fussing up behind them. "She can—"

"We already did, Anshebbeth."

"I could go look for her—I know right where she is . . ."

"It's been taken care of." Nanciormis' voice was soothing. Anshebbeth's long white fingers clasped and unclasped nervously; her huge, dark eyes darted to Nanciormis' face, then to Sun Wolf's body—a look that was covert but unmistakable—then back again, her cheeks coloring slightly. Sun Wolf wondered whether the blush was because he was aware of the thoughts behind that look or simply that she was. Unaware, Nanciormis went on easily, "Captain Sun Wolf—my niece, the Princess Taswind—her governess the Lady Anshebbeth."

Guards were carrying the unconscious King into the hall. Gentlemen and ladies hurried to open the door through to the solar and to kindle lamps there; Tazey sprang after them, catching up her skirts as if impatient with their weight. Sun Wolf observed the lace trim of her petticoat and the slim strength of her calf in its soft boot before the sharp jab of a bony knee in his thigh made him look around; but Starhawk, who had materialized at his side, was looking around the room, innocently impassive.

Down in the hall, one of the underservants, a thickset hag with puffy ankles showing under a kilted-up skirt and black eyes glinting through a straggling pelt of gray hair, called out in a screechy voice, "Slow getting out the back window, was he, when the husband came home? Hard to run with his breeches around his ankles!"

Tazey didn't even check her stride, but Anshebbeth stopped, stiff with rage and indignation, torn for a moment between staying to take issue with the old woman and remaining with her nurseling. Then, as if she realized she would not come off the better in any battle of words, she spun and hurried after Tazey into the narrow solar door.

"Did you see who they were?" Nanciormis asked quietly, as he led Sun Wolf and the Hawk toward the carved chairs on the dais near the fire. A servant girl came up to take his heavy white cloak and returned his smile with a saucy wink; Sun Wolf, as he and Starhawk divested themselves of their scarred sheepskin coats, observed that Nanciormis drew the admiring eyes of several of the women of the Household. Though corpulent, he was a good-looking man still; but beyond that, Sun Wolf guessed he was the type of man whose vitality would attract women, no matter how fat he became. Even on short acquaintance and in spite of his carelessness about breaking into the delicate concentration needed for the war dance, Sun Wolf found the man likable.

He made a mental note to take that into account.

"Your people, it looked like."

Nanciormis checked his stride. His long hair, braided down from the temples and hanging in a loose mane of black curls behind, caught the sheen of the lamps as he jerked his head around.

"The shirdar—the desert folk," the Wolf went on.
"There was a little trouble at the Longhorn—four of 'em
proposed a toast to the Princess Taswind's prospective
husband—I take it the match is about as popular as mag-
gots in the beer hereabouts. A man named Norbas Milkom was the cause of it, though why they attacked the
King..."

The commander groaned, and all wariness fled from
his eyes. "I should have known. No, the match isn't a
popular one." He grinned ruefully and took a seat in one
of the chairs by the hearth—heavy ebony from the for-
ests of Kimbu in the south, recushioned with local work
of red leather. "Beyond a doubt, they attacked the King
because he was foolish enough to walk back alone—unlike our canny Norbas. It's known throughout the desert
they've been friends for forty years—if indeed they
were the same shirdar as the ones at the Longhorn."

A servant came up—the same who had taken their
coats—with an intricately worked brass tray holding
wine cups and dates in a hammered silver bowl. Sun
Wolf saw now that she, like Nanciormis and, he guessed,
Anshebbeth also, was of the shirdar, though without the
reserved dignity of their ways. Along the foothills, they
must have been living among and marrying with the ex-
slaves of the north for generations. When she thought no
one was looking, she mouthed a kiss at Nanciormis; he
received it with a suppressed smile and a dance of pleasure in his pouchy dark eyes.

He went on, "They may have been merely bandits—
there are a lot of them along the cordillera—or they may
have been operating by the same logic used by the men
of Wenshar when they kill Hasdrozidar of the Dunes or
Seifidar of the White Erg in retaliation for Regidar slave-
raids, not troubling to inquire the truth. All of our people
here are looked upon with mistrust by those who came
from the north of the mountains."

"With reason," a quiet voice said at his elbow. Sitting
with his back to a corner and his blind side to Starhawk,

Sun Wolf had seen the slender old man approach them—
he would, indeed, have been difficult to miss. He was
wearing what Starhawk irreverently described as the un-
dress uniform of Trinitarian bishops, and his scarlet surcoat and gold tabard picked up the torchlight on their
bullion embroidery as if the old man were netted all over
with a spiderweb of flame. Garnet and rock crystal
flashed from the worked medallions of sacred signs;
even the sleeves of his white under-robe were stitched
with tiny seed pearls. Under all that finery, the old man
would have been as pretty as a girl before he grew his
beard; full, slightly pouting red lips showed beneath the
silky white mustaches; the eyes with their snowy lashes
were the clear blue of morning sky.

In a soft, light voice, the Bishop went on, "It is fel-
lowship of worship that binds men together in trust,
Nanciormis. You have converted to the true faith of the
Triple God, but can the same be said of the shirdar in the
guards? It can not. They cling to their old superstitions,
their familial cults and wind djinns. How can any true
worshiper believe their oaths?"

"I'm sure they can't," Starhawk remarked, lying half-
slouched in her chair and regarding him with mild gray
eyes. "But the question's rather academic, isn't it, since
the Doctrines of Calcedus say that true worshipers aren't
obliged to keep oaths made to the followers of untrue
gods."

The old Bishop spread his hands deprecatingly. "We
are doves in the midst of serpents, Warlady," he explained. "We need such subterfuge to survive."

She studied the obvious wealth and power reflected in
those splendid robes and glanced over at Sun Wolf. "I
never met a Trinitarian yet who didn't have a good explanation for everything."

The Bishop inclined his white head. "It is because all
truths are revealed to us by Holy Scripture."

There was a stirring in the shadows beyond the fireplace; Sun Wolf had already, in his automatic identifica-

tion of every potential exit from the room, seen the narrow door half-hidden beside the blackened granite of the mantle. Now Kaletha stepped through into the light, followed by another one of her disciples, the only one that afternoon who had not, like her, worn black. Since what he did wear was the blue and gold habit of a Trinitarian novice, he was naturally taken aback when he saw the Bishop. He said, rather loudly, "As I told you, my Lady Kaletha, the King is in his bedchamber beyond the solar."

"Thank you, Egaldus." Kaletha inclined her head graciously and moved toward the dais in a queenly swishing of homespun black robes. After a second's hesitation, the young man, fair-haired and rather nervous looking, turned with clearly manufactured decisiveness and went bustling away in the other direction. Sun Wolf's glance slid to the Bishop, but the old man didn't seem to suspect anything; he was watching Kaletha's approach with a disapproving eye.

"A pity," he said, "that the only healer in the fortress should be a witch."

Kaletha paused on the outside of the ring of firelight, regarding them with an expression that could have nipped spring flowers in their buds. Sun Wolf, feeling that frigid glance pause for a moment on him before passing on, was suddenly conscious of the dust in his clothes and hair and the bruises from the fight that marked his face; Kaletha looked away, as if to say one could have expected to find Sun Wolf on hand in the aftermath of a brawl. To the Bishop she said, "We've been over it time and again, Galdron. It's scarcely likely that your condemnation of my powers one more time will cause me to go against what I know to be my destiny and my duty."

"It is scarcely likely," agreed the little man mildly, "but, as Bishop of Wenshar and, therefore responsible for the salvation of your soul from the sulfurous hells reserved for witches, I can yet hope."

The answer was so pat that Sun Wolf was barely able to stifle a snort of laughter; Kaletha's eye flicked to him, like a chilly draft, and then away again. *If wishes were horses*, Sun Wolf thought wryly, *there'd be hoofprints all over my hide . . .*

"Excuse me, Commander, Captain," the Bishop said, as Kaletha turned and crossed the dais to the doorway of the King's solar. "I should probably be present when she attends to the King."

"I take it she's the only sawbones you could get?" the Wolf asked, as the Bishop, like a glittering little doll, hastened to follow the tall, red-haired woman through the door. In the hall before them, things were quieting down. The gray-haired hag, in the midst of a gaggle of grooms and laundresses, was recounting some story to snickers of ribald laughter. The Trinitarian novice, Sun Wolf observed, had in truth had no other business—he was still hanging around the archways into the vestibule, talking with two others of Kaletha's disciples: a fattish boy of sixteen or so and a thin, worried-looking young woman, both dressed, like Kaletha and Anshebbeth, in black.

"On the contrary," Nanciormis said, sipping the wine the servant had left and offering Sun Wolf the hammered bowl of dates. "Kaletha's only recently come to that position, in the absence of anything better. Since she's decided she's going to be a wizard, she evidently considers it a part of her much-vaunted 'destiny.' But she's always been part of the Household."

"Has she?" the Wolf asked thoughtfully. *It would account*, he thought, *for that bitter defensiveness*. It was said that no prophet was without honor except in their own home village. Even he, when he'd announced to his former mercenary troops on his brief visit to Wrynde that spring that he'd become a wizard, had at least done so after going away and coming back. The Wizard King Altiokis had brooked no competition; Kaletha could not have so much as hinted at her powers while he was still

alive. She'd had to announce it cold, to people who'd
known her all her life. His too-ready imagination framed
the notion of claiming wizardy in the village where he'd
been raised, and his soul cringed from the thought.

Nanciormis shrugged casually. "She was lady-in-wait-
ing to my sister, Osgard's wife, the Lady Ciannis. When
Ciannis died, Osgard kept her on in the Household as
librarian, since she had a turn for it. It wasn't until news
came of the Wizard King's death that she declared herself to be mageborn and began to teach others."

He laughed, shortly and scornfully. "Not that anything's ever come of it that I've been able to see. Oh, she
claims to be able to teach magic, but who are her disciples? A lot of soured spinsters and frustrated virgins who
haven't anything better to do with their lives."

"You don't believe her power's real, then?" It must
have been the reaction of most of the people in the fortress.

Nanciormis waved a deprecating hand, chubby but
strong with its ancient rings of worn gold. "Oh, I'll admit
the woman has magic—perhaps some of those poor
fools who follow her do as well. But why pursue it?
What can it buy you that money cannot? It's been a
hundred and fifty years since the old city of Wenshar in
the desert was destroyed because of the witcheries practiced there, but, believe me, the local feeling toward it
hasn't changed."

Sun Wolf cocked his head a little, remembering the
way the girl in the inn had made the sign against evil. *But
she's a witch*, she had said. "Why is that?" he asked.
"What happened in Wenshar?"

The doors of the solar opened, and Tazey emerged
without her governess, looking anxious and preoccupied.
Nanciormis glanced at the dark doorway behind her and
said softly, "Least said of that is best. Have you paid for
rooms in town, Captain? Osgard will want to see you in
the morning, I'm sure. We can offer you bunks in the
Men's Hall..." He gestured toward a wide arched door

halfway down the Hall. ". . . and the Women's." His nod took in the narrow entrance beyond the hearth. "Or if you choose, we can give you a cell to share down near the stable courts, in the empty quarter of the fortress. It's mostly old workshops, kitchens, and barracks, but the closer rooms still have roofs and they're shuttered against storms, should one rise in the night."

Sun Wolf recognized by the inquiring gleam in the commander's eye that the offer was prompted as much by curiosity as by hospitality; he said, "We'll take the room out by the stables," and saw the big man nod to himself, as if he'd satisfied in his mind the relationship between the two partners and how he must deal with them.

From the solar door, the Bishop Galdron emerged, looking fastidious and disapproving; behind him came Kaletha, the gold lamplight deepening the lines of tiredness and disapproval on her fine-boned face, showing up her age, which the Wolf guessed at a year one side or the other of thirty. Anshebbeth fussed at her heels, as if Kaletha's comfort, not Tazey's, was her primary concern. But Tazey, standing near her uncle Nanciormis' chair, said nothing—evidently she understood her governess' discipleship. From across the room, the two other disciples hurried toward their teacher's side, only the novice keeping his watchful distance.

Pointedly ignoring Sun Wolf, the little group made for the doors.

Sun Wolf sighed. He had wanted to put this off until they were not in public, but his sense of timing warned him that to do so would only make the situation worse. There were some things which had to be done at the first available opportunity. He got to his feet and said, "Lady Kaletha."

Her step wavered. She was debating, he thought, whether to make him call out to her and follow her. *If she does*, he thought grimly, with a momentary vision of shaking her until her pearly teeth rattled . . . Then he let it go. Whatever she had, it was what he desperately needed. He would have to ask for it, in whatever fashion she dictated. *Stubborn, cake-mouthed female . . .*

Kaletha took another step, then seemed to change her mind, and stopped. She turned back, chin elevated, cornflower blue eyes regarding him as if he were a beggar.

He'd had runs up to enemy seige towers under fire that he'd enjoyed more. "My lady," he said, his raw, rasping voice neither loud nor furtively quiet, "I'm sorry. I had no right to say what I said to you today, and I ask your forgiveness for speaking stupidly." He forced his single eye to meet hers, aware of the stares of her disciples and of the others—servants, grooms, laundresses, guards, Taswind, and Nanciormis—in the Hall. He felt as he had during the Rites of Manhood in his village in the north long ago, stripped before the eyes of the tribe and obliged to take whatever abuse the shaman chose to give him. Only in that case, he thought dryly, at least those who watched him approved of what he sought to gain by the humiliation. That had been the last time, he realized, that he had ever asked for anything.

The chilly sweetness of her voice was as he remembered it from the gardens. "Do you say that because you are truly sorry," she asked, "or because you know that I will not share my wisdom with you unless you apologize?"

Sun Wolf took a deep breath. At least she had answered him, and spoken to him as if she would listen to what he said. "Both," he said.

It took away any possibility of an accusation of untruth and left her momentarily nonplussed. Then her blue eyes narrowed again. "At least you're honest," she said, as if sorry to learn of it. "That is the first thing you'll have to learn about the arts of wizardry, if you pursue them, Captain. Honesty is almost as important to the study of wizardry as is purity of the body and the soul. You must be honest—utterly honest—at all times, and you must learn to accept the honesty of others."

"You weren't too pleased about my honesty this afternoon."

She didn't miss a beat. "Those were not your true feelings. If you look into your heart, I think you'll find that it was your jealousy of me speaking what you wished to see, not what you actually saw."

With great effort Sun Wolf stifled the first words that came to his lips. *She can teach me*, he reminded himself grimly. *She's the only one I have found to teach me. The rest of it is none of my affair.* But he couldn't resist saying, carefully keeping the irony from his voice, "I expect you'd know more about that than I would, my lady."

From the corner of his eye he saw the impassive Starhawk put her tongue in her cheek, raise her eyebrows, and look away. But Kaletha nodded gravely, accepting his words on their face value and taking them as a deserved tribute to her clarity of insight. "It is something that comes when one has achieved a certain level of understanding." Behind her, her disciples nodded wisely, like a well-trained chorus. "You must learn to accept discipline, to understand self-control. They may be alien to you . . ."

"I've been a warrior all my life," Sun Wolf said, annoyed. "There *is* discipline involved in that, you know."

"It isn't at all the same thing," she responded serenely, and he bit back, *How the hell would you know?*

Patronizingly, she went on, "I've studied long and hard to achieve my power, Captain. It is my destiny to teach. With meditation and with spells, I can reach the deepest parts of the mind. The mind is all, if the body is pure—all magic comes from the purified intellect. I can wake powers in anyone, even in those who are not mageborn, if they are willing, honest, and pure." She cast another chilly look up and down his big, heavily muscled form, as if seeing through his dusty clothes and disapproving of what she saw. Her glance moved past him, touched Starhawk, and the lines of disapproval pinched a little deeper at the corners of her mouth. "That's something you'll have to learn to accept, if you wish to enter into your powers."

Anger heated in him, as she had no doubt meant it to; words crowded to his lips about frustrated spinsters who made a virtue of the fact that no man would tumble them on a bet. But, with a physical effort, he closed his muscles around those words like a fist. *To buy the bread*, he thought, *you couldn't insult the baker*—and in any case, what she thought about magic was none of his business.

But he'd be damn lucky, he thought dourly, looking at that pale, fine-boned face in the torchlight, if he didn't end by strangling the woman with her own long, red hair.

In his long silence, she studied him appraisingly. She had expected, he realized, some other reaction. After a moment she went on, "If you feel you have the strength and willingness to follow that path, come to me where I teach in the public gardens tomorrow afternoon."

She inclined her head with a graciousness that made Sun Wolf long to slap her and prepared to move off. Down in the Hall, the old laundress called out to her, "I'll bet you're pleased to have him join you—as a change from boys and women!"

Kaletha's face flushed with anger as she turned. Around the dirty old hag, the other laundresses and grooms were bellowing with laughter. As in the garden that afternoon, Kaletha was momentarily speechless with anger. In a flash of insight, Sun Wolf realized that, having no sense of humor, she was unable to slide from beneath this kind of indignity, unable even to understand it. And she must, he thought, have had to put up with it daily since she had announced her wizardry to the world.

All this went through his mind in an instant; as Kaletha drew breath to stammer some reply, he cut in over her words, "It's the sow in rut that squeals the loudest."

The old crone and her friends went into even louder

guffaws. "Come down to the laundry and see, you old boar!"

He gave an elaborate shrug. "I haven't got all night to stand in the line."

The laundress laughed so hard he could easily have counted her teeth, had she possessed any. He turned back to Kaletha and said quietly, "I'll be there tomorrow, my Lady, after I've seen the King."

As he and Starhawk walked from the hall, he was aware of Kaletha's speculative gaze upon his back.

The empty quarter of the fortress of Tandieras lay beyond the stables, a picked gray skeleton in the wan monochromes of dawn. From where he lay on the wide bed of waffle-crossed latigo and cottonwood poles, Sun Wolf could see through the half-open shutters of the window a broken labyrinth of crumbling adobe walls, fallen roofs, and scattered tiles—what had once been garrison quarters for the troops of Dalwirin, seige housing for the population of their administrative town, and barracoons for hundreds of slave miners. It was deserted now, covering several acres of ground; among the many things his father had considered unmanly for a warrior to possess had been an aesthetic sense, and Sun Wolf seldom admitted to anyone that he found such things as the stripped shapes of rock and wall or the sculpted dunes carved by the will of the wind beautiful.

Extending his senses, as he had learned to in the meditations Starhawk had taught him, he could feel life stirring in the ruins still. Somewhere desert rats scrabbled over crumbled bricks; somewhere snakes lay dreaming in old ovens, waiting for the sun to warm their cold blood. He felt the quick, furtive flick of a jerboa heading for its burrow. Though it was light enough now to make out the fallen bricks, the dun-colored walls with their drifts of piled sand, and the thrusting black spikes of camel-thorn and bullweed against them, there was not yet any sound of birds.

Traveling along the hem of the desert, he had grown familiar with all of them—sand warblers and wheatears and the soft, timid murmur of rock doves. The wells in the empty quarter should have drawn them by the hundreds.

He frowned.

Against his shoulder, Starhawk still slept, all her cheetah deadliness loosened and her thin face peaceful, her short crop of white-blonde hair ruffled and sticking up like a child's. The Wolf liked to think of his relationship with this woman whom he had known so long as one of equals, warriors of matched strength and capability. But at times like this, he was conscious of feeling toward her a desperate tenderness, a desire to shelter and protect, wholly at odds with their daytime selves or the lion-like lusts of the deep night. He grinned a little at himself—Starhawk was probably the least protectable woman he'd ever encountered.

I'm getting old, he thought ruefully. There was no fear in it, though a year ago it would have terrified him; he felt only amusement at himself. *Old and soft.*

Like the ruins, Starhawk's was a beauty of rocks and bones and scars. Moving his head a little, he kissed the delicate curve of bone on the outer corner of her eye.

Still there was no sound of birds.

His sleep had been unrestful, troubled by inchoate dreams. His anger at Kaletha had bitten deep; he realized that the anger was also at fate, at his ancestors, and at the fact that he'd had to go cap-in-hand to a woman and swallow her self-righteous insults, because only she could give him what he needed. In Wrynde, he remembered, it had been whispered that, like the mad God of the Bards, he had traded his eye for wisdom—he only wished that had been the case.

Yet he knew that Starhawk had been right, as she usually was. What angered him most about Kaletha— her arrogant assumption that she needed no teacher and that she herself was qualified to judge her own progress and that of others—was precisely what he himself was doing in refusing to accept her tutelage.

Beside him, Starhawk moved in her sleep, her arm tightening around his ribcage as if she found reassurance in the touch. He stroked her shoulder, the skin silky under his hand, and gazed out at the pink reflections warming the upper edges of the ruined walls. A stir of wind brought him the warm smell of the stables and the drift of baking bread from the palace kitchens.

Then the wind shifted, and he smelled blood.

Whether Starhawk smelled it, too, and reacted with the hair-trigger reflexes of a warrior in her sleep, or whether she simply felt the stiffening of his muscles, he didn't know, but a moment later her gray eyes were blinking up into his. She'd been in deep sleep a moment ago, but she neither moved nor spoke, instinctively keeping silence against any possible threat.

"Do you smell it?" he asked softly, but the wind had shifted again. There were only the scents of burning wood and baking bread from the kitchens. *So it isn't just the smell of chicken-killing for tonight's dinner*, he thought to himself.

She shook her head. All the childlike helplessness of sleep had dissolved into what it really was—his own fancies—and the woman who had curled so trustingly into his shoulder had a knife in her hand, ready for anything. Starhawk, the Wolf reflected with a grin, was the only person he knew who could be stark naked and still produce a concealed weapon at a second's notice.

"It's probably nothing," he said. "I heard jackals and pariah-dogs out in the empty quarter last night . . ." He frowned again and closed his eye, stilling his mind as he had often done scouting, listening as a wizard listens. The empty quarter was silent. No murmur of the doves that must nest there, no shrill cries of swifts, though it was time and past time when birds called their territories. Though the red trace of blood touched his nostrils again, he could hear no stealthy pad of jackal feet, no querulous snarls of scavenger rats. In the stables nearby a horse nickered softly over its morning feed; a girl began to sing.

Soundlessly, the Wolf rolled out of bed, found his boots and the buckskin trousers he'd worn down from Wrynde, his shirt and doublet, and his belt with sword and daggers. When Starhawk moved to join him, he shook his head and said again, "I don't think it's anything. I'll be back."

The cold was sharp on his face and throat as he stepped out of the little room, a cell in a line of low cells that could have been workshops, guest rooms or makeshift prisons along a narrow, sandy court just off the stables. A storm last week had drifted sand deep against the eastern walls; the adobe faces of the buildings showed marks where pebbles and flying chunks of stone had gouged the softer brick. The other cells of the court were deserted. A pack rat went flicking around the doorpost of one to the shelter of the shadows within.

Cautiously, Sun Wolf moved into the empty quarter. He found the place quite quickly, stalking through the silent maze of empty rooms and fallen beams, caved-in cellars and old wells shrouded thick in greedy vegetation. He had been expecting something, from the smell, but, even so, what he saw filled him with a loathing he could not explain.

The door of the little adobe workshop had been torn off years ago by the killer sandstorms of the desert; most of the roof tiles had blown away, though rafters barred the open, warming sky. The walls were streaked with years' worth of dove droppings, where they were not painted over with splashes of blood.

White and gray feathers were stuck in it and in the puddles on the floor that were still slick and only tacky-dry. From where he stood in the doorway, the Wolf could see the curled, pink feet and torn-off heads of the birds thrown into the corners, already half-invisible under swarming clots of ants.

He made a move to step into the room, but then drew back. There was something loathesome here, foul and utterly evil—a psychic stench that drove him back in fear, although he knew that whatever had done this was gone. He had sacked cities from the Megantic Sea to the Western Ocean and, when it was necessary to make his point, had cut men and women up alive. He did not know why that small cube of adobe-walled dawnlight and rafter-crossed sky, silent but for the persistent humming of flies, should turn him sick.

Only three or four doves were dead, less than he'd eat for supper. It was, he reminded himself, no business of his who had killed them, or why.

But he was a good enough tracker to see, with even the most cursory examination, that there were no footmarks, either entering the room or leaving it.

CHAPTER

—— 3 ——

"*D*AMNED WOMAN." *OSGARD ANTIVAR, KING OF* Wenshar and nominal Lord of all the K'Chin Desert, propped himself up on the low ebony divan and impatiently shoved aside the blue silk pillow from beneath his left knee. "Says she won't be responsible if the wound opens up again. Damn her, *I'll* be responsible! I'm not going to lie here like a maiden lady with the vapors all day!" The tray of silver-traced copper on the delicate, jointed shirdar camp table beside the couch contained a decanter of wine, but, pointedly, only one wine cup.

The King fished beneath the divan's pillows and produced a second one, which he slopped full. "Sit down, Captain, and drink up. You can, even if I'm not supposed to. Damned woman." Against the vivid reds and blues of the loose bed-robe he wore over shirt and breeches, he still looked gray from loss of blood, save for where the slight flush of fever colored his pouchy cheeks. "I could stand her when she was just the damn librarian. She kept her place, then."

Sun Wolf took the indicated chair—like the divan, of heavy, gilt-trimmed ebony—looted fifty years ago from the Governor's Palace and recently reupholstered in a local red wool. The King's solar was a big room, built out of the end of the Hall, and lined with windows on two sides. The ever-present storm shutters had been thrown open, and morning sunlight poured through, dazzling on the glass-smooth marble checkerwork of the floor as if on the sea. Like shaggy islands, the white pelts of mountain sheep alternated with black bearskins and scattered rugs of deep-desert work, bright, primitive mosaics of red and blue. It was a comfortable room for a King who'd worked in the mines as a boy.

"Kaletha tells me that tourniquet of yours probably kept me from being laid up worse than I am. Seems I have to thank you twice."

Sun Wolf shrugged dismissively. "I'd already gone to the trouble of saving your hide; be a pity to have wasted my time, after all." He slouched back in his chair, relaxed but watchful. Under his booming heartiness, the King was on edge; the wine, which Sun Wolf never touched at this hour of the morning, and the tray of white rolls, butter, honey, ham, and dates, which a noiseless servant now brought in, implied more than a man simply thanking another for keeping robbers from making pemmican of him. The King wanted something.

"That's what I like!" Osgard laughed. "A man who does what he has to without a lot of bother and fuss—a fighter, a man of his hands!" He threw a glance after the departing servant and refilled his wine cup. "They say you were the best mercenary in the West—at least you commanded the highest prices, back when we were fighting old Shilmarne and her troops. But by the Three, you delivered the goods! What are you doing ragtagging it like a tinker through the Middle Kingdoms, without the price of a roof over your head? You lose your troop?"

"I gave it up."

"Because of that?" Osgard gestured with his wine cup to the leather eye-patch.

The Wolf shook his head easily. "Just say I gambled high stakes with the gods."

"And lost?"

He touched the patch, the fire-seared socket beneath. "And won."

Osgard regarded him shrewdly for a moment, hearing in his shattered voice the echo of all those reasons and knowing that it was all of them that he would hear. He was silent for a moment, his big, work-knotted hands fidgeting with the stem of the goblet. His eyes shifted away, then back. *Here it comes*, the Wolf thought. Osgard said, "I want to hire you to teach my son."

Sun Wolf considered this for a moment in silence. It was the first he'd heard of the boy, for only the King's daughter had come flying to her father's side last night. The way word went around a small community like the fortress, there was no way the boy could not have heard. But he only asked, "How old is he?"

"Nine." The man's voice turned flinty. "Nanciormis has started him on sword and horses, but the boy's a sniveler. He'd rather run and hide than face his lessons like a man. His uncle has his own duties and can't go after him as he should. It's time the boy learned to be a man."

The tone of hard challenge made Sun Wolf remember his own father. Mistaking his silence, Osgard went on, "I'll make it worth your while, Captain. He's the Heir of Wenshar—the first born Heir in a hundred and fifty years, since the days when the Ancient House of Wenshar ruled this land. He's the foundation of my line, and, by the Three, I want him to be a King that knows how to wield a sword and hold his own!" He drank off his wine and set the cup crashing down on the bronze of the small tabletop, his wide, light-green eyes blazing with the intentness of a man who has always been able to strive for and win what he sought.

"I'm the fifth King of Wenshar since we threw out the governors and freed ourselves from slavery. I fought alongside my uncle Tyrill against the desert bandits and against old Shilmarne's troops and whatever you care to name. When Tyrill died, he named me his heir, the way Casfell Ghru named him, and old Kelden the Black before him. None of those men had an heir, barring Kelden's, who was killed in battle—they all chose the best man they knew as their successor. By the Three, it's kept the land strong!

"But it's different now. My uncle fell when I was young, and I married..." He hesitated infinitesimally, and when he spoke again, it was with a quieter note. "I married a lady of one of the Ancient Houses, the last Princess of the old House of Wenshar."

Sun Wolf cocked his head, curious. "Wenshar? From the old city out in the desert?"

"No." Osgard cut him off shortly, and his green eyes flickered for a moment with anger. Then, as if realizing he'd spoken more than he meant, he explained awkwardly, "That is—none of her people had been near there in generations. That city's empty, dead—the armies of the Middle Kingdoms destroyed it when they conquered these parts. But yes, her people used to rule all this country and much of the desert besides. Their house had no power anymore, but they were one of the Ancient Houses, nonetheless. And she was the kindest woman in all these lands and bore me the sweetest daughter a man could want, who's to marry one of the shirdar lords to seal their alliance with us... And she bore me a son." He sighed and refilled his cup again, the sunlight blinking hotly on the purple surface of the wine. "The boy's my heir. I want him to be the best man as well. He's got to hold what I've held, after I'm gone."

Sun Wolf sopped a piece of bread in the honey and said nothing. He was remembering the scene in the tavern last night, the little black man, Norbas Milkom, drink-

ing to the Lady Taswind's health, and not to her af-
fianced lord's.

"What's his name?"

"Jeryn." A little too loudly, after a little too long a
pause, Osgard went on, "The boy's not a coward. But he
needs discipline. He reads too much, that's all. I've put
that right, but he needs to be taught by a warrior, a man
who can think in an emergency—a man like yourself.
They say you used to run a school up in Wrynde for
warriors. Is that true?"

"It paid to know who I was getting in my troop."

The King grunted his approval. "And it pays me to
know who this country will be getting as King. Your
woman's a fighter, isn't she?"

"She was my second-in-command. She's gotten me
out of places so bad I don't even want to think about
them."

"You think she'd take a post in the guard here, if you
take it up to teach my boy?"

He paused in the act of smearing butter on his bread.
"Depends on what you'd pay her, probably."

Osgard laughed. "There's a mercenary talking," he
said with a grin. "A silver eagle every fortnight—and
you won't find purer coin anywhere in the Middle Kingdoms. Why should we water our silver? We dig it out of
the ground."

"Sounds good." Sun Wolf knew that as currency
went, Wenshar's was, indeed, one of the best. There
were cities in the Gwarl Peninsula where the silver content of the coinage varied from week to week.

"And the same for you, with board in the Hall and a
room here for the pair of you—and the knowledge that
you'll be helping a man who's worked hard and fought
hard all his life sleep easier nights."

The boy's got him worried, Sun Wolf thought, leaning
back in the gilded-ebony chair and considering the big
man before him, who pushed so impatiently at his bed-
robe and blankets. As a battlefield physician himself, he

was perfectly well aware that Osgard's steady consumption of wine would drive his fever up by nightfall; but he'd learned long ago never to attempt to separate a half-drunk man from his cup. If Kaletha had the nerve to attempt to do so, he had to approve of her courage, if not her judgment.

In many ways the King reminded Sun Wolf of his own father, though he was sandy instead of dark—a shaggy, roaring bear of a man, comfortable with the jostling give-and-take of casual friendship and unwilling to stir the mud at 'he bottom of his or anyone else's soul. A man who could fight all day, drink all evening, and fornicate all night—or who would die in the attempt to seem to.

A man, Sun Wolf thought, such as he himself had striven so hard to be, all those years.

"I'll talk to the Hawk," he said, "and meet your boy and decide then."

"And you, Starhawk?" Kaletha set down the pottery mug of coffee and looked at Starhawk in the buttercup sunlight pouring through the long south-facing windows of the Hall. "Will you, too, join our company, to learn the ways of power?"

Servants were moving back and forth from the service hatches to the trestle tables set up in the big room with its dark granite walls. There were few of them, as there were few guards—the underservants who ate at the lower end of the Hall fetched their own bread and butter and breakfast ale. Starhawk wondered a little about this. She could estimate within a silverpiece how much a place would yield in money and loot, and the fortress of Tandieras was undeniably rich. Ruling the largest chain of silver mines in the west of the world, they could scarcely be otherwise.

After last night's incidents, she was acutely aware that most of the underservants who brought grapes, cof-

fee, and clotted kefir porridge to the small table which
Kaletha had invited her to share were of the shirdar.

If Kaletha had expected surprise from her, she must
be disappointed. Away from the antagonism between her
and the Wolf, Starhawk's own reading of the woman's
character was that she preferred the company of women
to that of men, though not necessarily in bed. In her way,
Kaletha would have been pleased to show Sun Wolf up
by taking from him his lover's loyalty.

Nevertheless she gave the matter some thought before replying. "I'm not mageborn."

"That doesn't matter." Kaletha leaned forward, her
blue eyes intent. She was a beautiful woman whose
beauty, Starhawk guessed, had kept men from taking her
seriously—she wore her severeness like armor. But as
she spoke, she lowered her shield to show the woman
underneath. "Your Captain didn't believe me, but it is
true. I understand the secrets of power. I can raise that
power, bring it out of the depths of the souls of even the
non-mageborn. That is my destiny."

"It's true," Anshebbeth put in, hurrying over to them
from across the Hall. She had entered some moments
ago in dutiful attendance upon the Princess Taswind, her
own habitual, severe black gown contrasting sharply
with the girl's casual attire of boy's breeches, riding
boots, and a faded pink shirt. They had been chatting
comfortably, but, even at that distance, Starhawk had
seen Anshebbeth's eye rove quickly over the tables and
find Kaletha at her table, a little apart from the other
members of the Household. She had lost no time in
breaking off the conversation, taking her plate from the
High Table where Tazey seated herself alone, and has-
tening to Kaletha's side.

"Pradborn Dyer certainly isn't mageborn—he's one
of our company, a youth from the town—but Kaletha
has taught him, released the hidden strengths of his
mind, and he has begun to have visions and dreams,
which have come true. He can sometimes see things in

the dark and is led to find objects which are lost. And I myself, though I'm not mageborn, I have been studying with Kaletha, absorbing her wisdom, learning the secrets of her arts, for almost a year now. It has helped me, helped me enormously..." She glanced quickly sidelong at Kaletha, as if for approval.

If Kaletha was as annoyed as Starhawk at having her conversation intruded upon in this fashion, she didn't show it. She preened herself a little under the praise and gave a tolerant smile, retreating behind her schoolmistress facade.

Encouraged, Anshebbeth continued, "Do you know, it seemed that I knew for many years before the Wizard King's death what Kaletha was, though she never told a soul. But her power always shone out of her—"

"'Shebbeth—" Kaletha said, a little embarrassed now.

"It's true," the governess insisted eagerly. "Even Tazey—Princess Taswind—felt it when she was a little child." She looked back at Starhawk. "We've always been friends, Kaletha and I. She has virtually made me what I am today, has opened worlds to me I never dreamed of. Others felt it, too," she added, her dark eyes suddenly smoldering with venom. "Like that dirty hag Nexué, the laundress, with her filthy mouth and her filthy mind." She picked up a horn-handled tin knife to butter a roll, and her long fingers trembled a little with anger.

"Impure fornicators," responded Kaletha serenely, "see all things through the slime of their own impurity." She glanced a little nervously at Starhawk. For an instant, the Hawk saw again the human side of the woman, which interested her far more than the wizard and teacher did. "You mustn't be led to think..."

Starhawk shrugged. "It isn't any of my business."

Kaletha hesitated, not quite certain what to do with that answer. Anshebbeth, who had gone a little pink at the mention of impurity, was looking away. But, in fact, Starhawk had seen relationships like that of Kaletha and Anshebbeth before, among the nuns of the convent where she had grown up and, later, among the warrior women of Sun Wolf's troop; she knew that, in spite of the witlessly smutty remarks of Nexué and her tablemates, the two women weren't necessarily lovers. It was more than anything else a domination of the personality, based on Kaletha's desire to have a slave as much as Anshebbeth's need to be one.

Across the Hall, Nanciormis had just entered, wearing the plain, dark-green uniform of the guards and flirting with the two servant women who'd immediately found reasons to take them to that side of the room. Anshebbeth forced her gaze back to Starhawk, her mouth bracketed suddenly in hard little lines, and a stain of color lingering on her pointy cheekbones.

"It takes courage to follow Kaletha's path, the path of purity, the path of the mind. But I can tell, looking at you, that you have that."

"Not necessarily." Starhawk poured cream into her coffee and dabbed with her spoon at the swirls of dark and light.

Nonplussed, Anshebbeth opened her mouth, then shut it again. The smug self-satisfaction that had glowed from Kaletha in her disciple's presence faded, and her cinnamon brows puckered into a frown. "You've been a warrior a long time," she said after a moment. "That tells me you don't lack either physical bravery or the courage to go against what people expect of a woman. Do you have the courage to go against what *he* expects of *his* woman?"

Starhawk's attention remained on her cup. "It would depend on what was at stake."

"Freedom to do as you wish?" Kaletha pressed her. "To be first instead of second?"

"That's a tricky one." Starhawk looked up. "The fact is, I am best as a second—a better lieutenant than I am a captain."

"Is that what you truly believe," Kaletha asked, "or

only what it is more convenient for him that you believe?"

"Are you asking that out of genuine concern for me," Starhawk returned, "or only to get back at him by having me leave him?"

At this display of lèse-majesté, Anshebbeth almost dropped her spoon. But Kaletha held up a hand to silence her indignant indrawn breath; when her eyes met Starhawk's, they were rueful with the first admission of wrong the Hawk had seen from her.

At least, Starhawk thought, *she doesn't pretend she didn't understand what I asked.*

After a long pause, Kaletha said, "I agree. We both asked each other unfair questions. And I think we're each three-fourths sure we know the answers, both to our own and the other's . . . but only three-fourths." She looked down at the small plate of bread and kefir before her for a moment, then back at Starhawk, a spark of genuine warmth in her eyes. She held out her hand. "Will you join our company only for company, then? I, for one, would be pleased if you would."

The door on the dais that led through to the King's solar opened abruptly, and Sun Wolf emerged, followed immediately by Osgard himself. The King's face was mottled alcoholic red and pasty white, and he was limping heavily, but fended off Sun Wolf's single offer of assistance. Kaletha's brows snapped together; she got swiftly to her feet, black robe billowing as she strode towards him. "My Lord . . ."

He waved her angrily away. "I don't need your damned help, and I don't need your damned advice, either!" he roared. "I'm not a weakling! Hell, back when we were fighting Shilmarne's armies in the passes, I went through six hours of fighting with a shattered kneecap!"

Her voice thin, Kaletha said, "You were thirty then, my Lord, not fifty, and you hadn't been drinking."

"What's my age got to do with it, woman?" he bellowed back. "Or what I drink or how much I drink, for that matter? Where's that boy of mine?"

Frostily, she said, "Your son, my Lord, is not my responsibility."

"Well, you're supposed to be a damn wizard, you should know. Nanciormis..." He swung around in time to see the tall commander step easily up onto the dais. "You're supposed to have him for sword practice now."

Nanciormis shrugged. "I presumed other duties called him, for he did not come."

Balked of that prey, Osgard looked around for other and lighted on his daughter Tazey, who was consuming the last of her bread and posset with the swift care of one who proposes to escape unnoticed. "Where's your brother?" the King demanded, and Tazey, who had just taken a bite of bread, looked up at him, startled. "Hiding again, I daresay—in that damned library, most like. Send that..." He looked around again, and his eye lighted on Anshebbeth, down at Kaletha's table. Anshebbeth quailed visibly, and her thin hand went to her throat as he roared, "Why the hell aren't you up here with my daughter where you belong, woman? I don't keep you in my household to gossip with your girlfriends."

Tazey rose quickly. "I'll find Jeryn, Father."

"You'll sit down, girl. 'Shebbeth's your governess, and her duty is to keep beside you, not to go wandering off. Now go fetch him, woman!"

For one instant Anshebbeth sat rigid, her lips flattened into a thin line of anger and humiliation; then she got quickly to her feet and disappeared through a narrow door into the turret stair. She wasn't out of earshot when Osgard added to Sun Wolf, "Twitter-witted old virgin's enough to give any man the fidgets."

Starhawk buttered another hunk of bread as Kaletha came back to her, her blue eyes calm and contemptuous. "The man is a lout," the Witch of Wenshar said, "and is raising his son to be a lout as well. I had hoped that, along with weaponry, Nanciormis could teach him graciousness and polish, but I see he's taken the first opportunity to put a stop to that." She seated herself in a swish of heavy black skirts. On the bench at Starhawk's side again she said, "I hope you'll forgive my speaking honestly, but I scarcely find it likely that our future King will learn anything from that barbarian save the breaking of heads."

Starhawk shrugged. "Your opinion of the Chief has nothing to do with me."

"It's obvious that a man like that seeks out teaching in the ways of power simply to aid him in the killing of other men. The rest he disregards. He understands nothing about purity, nothing about the powers of the mind, from which all magic springs."

Starhawk dipped her bread in her coffee and took a soggy bite, far more amused than indignant. "And I'm sure you'll forgive my honest speaking when I say that you have a rather short acquaintance on which to judge him in such detail."

"I have eyes," Kaletha returned bitterly. In her glance, quickly averted, Starhawk read the contempt for Sun Wolf for having a mistress and at herself for being one. Curious, she leaned her bony elbow among the half-cleared breakfast dishes and waited. On the dais, Osgard was breathing stertorously; Sun Wolf, his massive, gold-furred arms folded, wore a closed expression of guarded annoyance. After a moment, Kaletha's stiff back relaxed. She turned back to the Hawk.

"I'm sorry," she said, the words sticking in her throat. "I've judged you, and I shouldn't have. Among people like yourselves, fornication is a matter of course, isn't it?"

"Oh, thanks!" Starhawk grinned, more amused than offended at the assumption of complete promiscuity— and indeed, she thought to herself, there was nothing to indicate to Kaletha that Sun Wolf hadn't lost his eye in a pothouse difference of opinion over some woman's favors, instead of a duel to the death with the greatest wizard in the world.

"About time," Osgard grunted, on the dais, as Anshebbeth came flustering back through the narrow door, which led to an inside stair. "Captain Sun Wolf—my son, Jeryn. Stand up straight, damn you, boy."

If Tazey, seated in apprehensive silence at the High Table behind them, was clearly her father's daughter, with the King's height, his athletic grace, his streaky blond hair, and absinthe–green eyes, then Jeryn was just as clearly a shirdar woman's child. He had the thin, hawklike features, though his unwashed, black curls were cut short and his olive skin was paste-pale from staying indoors. At this distance, Starhawk couldn't see the color of his eyes, for they were downcast, sullen, and shifty, guarding secrets and resentments under puffy lids. He dressed in the formal clothes of court, short trunks and hose, which bagged around his skinny knees; he wore them without pride and looked shabby and unkempt, an orphan who has dressed himself from a prince's ragbag.

"What do you think, Captain?" Osgard's tone had turned bullying. "You figure you can do anything with this boy?"

Jeryn said nothing, just held himself braced in a way that spoke worlds about the kind of treatment he expected from his father. And it was hardly, Starhawk thought impersonally, a fair question. There were enough people left in the Hall that Sun Wolf's refusal would be widely interpreted as an admission that he couldn't make a warrior of the boy, either through his own fault or through Jeryn's. Osgard had undoubtedly meant the scene to hinge on Sun Wolf's pride in his ability to teach. Though the Hawk knew this would not have applied, she also knew that putting Sun Wolf to the choice now, in public, would work because he would not openly reject the boy.

After a long moment, Sun Wolf said, "I said I'd have to talk to my partner."

It was a way out, but Osgard wasn't about to give it to him. "Well, hell," he said genially, "there's no trouble about that, is there?" He turned, and held out his hand to Starhawk. "You got no objections to a post in the guards, have you, Warlady? A silver eagle every fortnight, board and bed? Pardle Sho may not have the fancies you'll find north of the mountains, but there's money aplenty here and places to spend it, if you're not too finicky in your tastes. It may not pay like the mines do, but there's more honor to it and less labor. How can you say no to that?"

Sun Wolf's eye had the angry smolder of a man who has been gotten around in a way that he could not fight without looking like a boor. Starhawk, aware that Sun Wolf had no objections to looking like a boor and was on the verge of making an issue of it, rose, hooked her hands into her sword belt, and said casually, "I can't say no till I've tried it for a week."

It was something the Wolf had taught her—when in doubt, play for time.

In a week, she reasoned, anything could happen.

And, in point of fact, it did.

Starhawk wasn't sure just what woke her. *A dream,* she thought—a dream of three women in a candlelit room, their shadows moving over the painted walls, giving the grotesque images there a terrible life of their own. She could not hear their words, but they sat close together around the candles, combing their hair and whispering. The room had no windows, but somehow Starhawk knew that it was late at night. The scene was an ordinary enough one, yet something about it—the way the shadows flickered over those frescoes whose designs and motives she could not quite make out, the way the candlelight glowed in the dark, liquid eyes—frightened her. She had the feeling of being a child, listening to an adult discussion of smiling hate, a sense of something hideously wrong whose form and nature she could not understand. Though the wavering light pene-

trated to all corners of the little bedchamber, with its
curtained bed and its delicate, jointed shirdar furnishings
—though that nervous illumination showed nothing but
the three women, with their long black hair and robes of
white gauze—she knew they were not there alone.

She woke up sweating, knowing there was something
with her in the room.

The moon outside was full. By the angle of the bars of
silken light streaming in through the window, she knew it
was late in the night. A band of it lay across the bed,
palpable as a gauze scarf; she felt that, had she dared
move, she could reach across and pluck it up. Beside
her, the bed was empty. Sun Wolf would still be with
Nanciormis and the King, nursing his beer and telling
war lies. She herself had been less interested in getting to
know them than she was in going alert on morning duty.

She did not move, but, from where she lay, she could
see almost the whole room under the brilliance of the
inpouring desert moonlight.

It was empty.

There was something there.

Her eyes touched every black pocket of shadow,
every angle of that ghostly radiance, from the spread of
the cracks of the floor—like an arcane pattern of
unreadable runes—to the hard spark of the buckles on
her doublet and jacket, which lay thrown over the
room's single chair. The night cold was icy on her face,
the smell of the dry mountains filled her nostrils with a
clarity too vivid for dreaming.

She wondered if it was watching her and what movement she could make that might do any good.

Years of war had given her an instinct for danger.
Whatever was in the room with her, she had no doubt
whatsoever that it was utterly evil.

She lay on the inner side of the wide bed, under a
black bearskin and two quilts against the freezing night
of the desert foothills. In her fear there was none of the
child-terror that wants only to pull the covers over the

head, secure in the knowledge that the evil will not violate that sanctuary; her fear was adult. To reach the door, she would have to roll across the width of the bed; to reach the window, she must dive over the foot. The sense of evil strengthened, localized; there should have been a shadow there, crouching just beyond the foot of the bed where the moonlight struck the brightest, but there was none.

Outside in the stables, the dogs began to howl.

She felt a tweak and a jerk and saw the blankets move.

Then clear and distant, she heard Sun Wolf's voice, like metal scraping in the cold, still night; and Nanciormis' rich laugh. Nothing moved, nothing changed in that terrible still life of empty moonlight, but she felt the stir and shift of air and heard a sound no louder than the scratch of a cockroach's hard claws on the granite lump of the threshold. Through the open door, she saw dust swirl in the court outside, though no wind stirred the camel-bush just beyond.

She rolled from the bed, pulling the topmost blanket off and around her body. Automatically, she caught up her sword, knowing it would be useless. The court outside was drenched in liquid–silver moonlight that shadowed every pebble, every stone of the little well-head, every leaf of the camel-thorn and sedges clustering around. Not even an insect moved, but the dogs howled again, desperate, terrified; from the stables, she heard the stamp of frightened hooves. She forced herself still, hidden in the shadows of the door. Across the court, an adobe gate made a pale blur in the shadows surrounding the Hold—across that granite monolith, a line of shuttered windows marked the Hall like a row of sightless eyes. Above them, a balcony ran the length of the building, every arched doorway looking onto it rimmed in the silvery glow of the moon. In the checkered maze of shadow between Hall and gate, Sun Wolf's voice echoed on the stone, bidding Nanciormis good night. Though she could clearly see there was nothing by the moonlit gate, still terror filled her. She stepped into the fragile splendor of the moon, cried out desperately, "Chief, look out!" and her voice echoed against the high wall of the silent Hold.

Hating to, but knowing if the Wolf were in danger she must be closer, she gripped her sword and ran forward into the court—and stopped suddenly.

There was nothing beside the gate.

Of course, there never had been anything beside the gate—but it was gone, now.

Slowly, not trusting her instincts, she moved again, her naked sword in her hand, her other hand clutching tight the blanket wrapped around her. Her heart was thudding in her chest, the air cold in her nostrils against the warmth of her breath, the dust chill beneath her feet.

She stood beside the gate. There was nothing there, nor anywhere else in the night.

The soft scrape and rustle in the shadows made her turn sharply, in time to see Sun Wolf drop over the low wall that bounded the empty quarter, some distance from the little gate. He hesitated for a moment, and she signaled him to come. Her arm, where it held the blanket over her, was a mass of gooseflesh—she was trembling, though not entirely with cold.

He had his sword in hand, the moonlight bitter as frost on its edge and point. "What is it?"

She hesitated, not certain what to say. "I—I don't know. I didn't see anything, but . . ."

But what?

He studied her white, sharp face in the moonlight, with her baby-fair hair, flattened by the pillow, sticking in all directions, her gray eyes alert and watchful as a warrior's, but puzzled, troubled. "Tracks?"

She shook her head. She sensed that she ought to feel foolish, like one who had wakened screaming from a nightmare about hens or rabbits, but she didn't. The danger had been real, that she knew. And the Chief, may the Mother bless his balding head, accepted it as such. They had fought shoulder-to-shoulder for a long time and knew that, while their observations might be inexplicable, they were at least not inaccurate. He looked around him at the deserted court, as if scenting the air for some trace whiff of evil, his single yellow eye gleaming almost colorless in the ripe moonlight. The aftershock was coming over her with the memory of the fear; she was conscious of a desire for him to hold her, for the rough, knobby feel of sword hilt and belt buckle through the blanket, crushing against her flesh. She told herself not to be stupid. In an emergency that kind of activity tied up one's sword arm. Her instincts told her the danger was over, but her mind and the habits of a lifetime of war refused quite to trust.

"Come on," he said softly. "Whatever it is, it seems to be gone." He began to move toward her, then stopped himself and led the way back down the stony path, a sword-length apart, like scouts on patrol. Starhawk felt surprised at how sharply the rocks in the court cut her bruised feet. She had not even noticed them, before. She and the Chief flanked the dark slot of the cell doorway, entered—ready for anything—though both were almost certain that there was nothing inside. And there was not.

While Sun Wolf was checking the room, Starhawk turned to look back over her shoulder at the gate. It stood innocent under the blaze of moonlight, no shadow touching its sand-worn pine lintels, nothing moving the weeds around it. Something white drifting along the balcony of the Hold made her raise her eyes; she could see a figure there, the crystal glory of moonlight glinting in the gold clips that held his long black braids. He was gliding from archway to archway, as if seeking a room— she remembered he and the Chief had been drinking and remembered, also, the telltale tracks of broken veins that at close distance marked the commander's elegant nose.

But even though he seemed to have trouble finding which room was his own, he moved with his usual steady grace. He pushed aside the curtain within one dark arch, and Starhawk thought she heard the soft, startled cry of a woman's voice from within. But no scream followed it; he stepped through into the darkness, and the darkness hid him.

CHAPTER

—— 4 ——

*S*UN *WOLF'S TERM OF EMPLOYMENT AS INSTRUCTOR IN* manliness to the Heir of Wenshar lasted slightly less than twelve hours—something of a record, even for Sun Wolf.

He had the weedy, sullen boy slathered with herbed grease to protect his virginal skin from the sun, and protesting all the way, out of the fortress between dawn and sunup, running on the lizard-colored ranges of scrub and camel-bush that spread out below the black granite knoll of Tandieras. The blue dawn periods between the freezing cold of night and the breathless daytime heat were brief; though, as autumn advanced, they would lengthen. *As it was,* Sun Wolf thought disgustedly when Jeryn stumbled to a gasping halt after a quarter of a mile, *they were more than lavish.*

"This isn't safe, you know," the boy panted sulkily and jumped aside, lashing his hand at an inquisitive bee. He wiped at the sweat tracking through the grease; stripped to a linen loincloth, with dust plastering his scrawny legs and snarly hair, he was a sorry sight. "If a sandstorm came up now, we couldn't get back."

"True enough," the Wolf agreed. And indeed, three days ago, on the ride in from the distant coast, he and the Hawk had been trapped in a cave in the black cliffs of the Dragon's Backbone by a sandstorm. He had felt it coming—the breathless rise in temperature and the throbbing in his head—long before the Hawk had, and that had saved them, allowing them to reach cover in time. From the moment the cloudy line of white had become visible on the desert horizon until all the world had been swallowed by a screaming maelstrom of wind-driven sand had been literally minutes. After the blinding brown darkness had passed, they'd found the desert littered with the ruined corpses of prairie dogs and cactus owls, the flesh literally filed from their bones by the pebbles and sand in the wind. In Tandieras it was said that even wearing the protective white head veils of a desert rider, a man could be smothered and dried to a mummy in a drift of superheated dust within half an hour.

"But I can read the weather; feel the storms before they hit, before they even come into sight. I know there's nothing on the way."

The boy shot him a look of sullen disbelief from black eyes that looked far too big for his pointy white face and retreated again behind his wall of silence. Sun Wolf had already found that, protest though he might, the boy would never ask for help. Perhaps it was because he had early learned that doing so would only worsen any situation with his father.

Jeryn tried again. "Nanciormis never made me do this."

"And that's why you got winded after two minutes of exercise." Sun Wolf pushed back his long hair—he had barely broken sweat. "We're going to do this every morning at this time, and it's going to be hateful as hell for about three weeks, and there's nothing I can do about that. Let's go."

"I'm still tired!" the boy whined.

"Kid, you're gonna be tired for months," the Wolf said. "You're going to run back to the fortress and lift your weights and work a little with a stick with me, sometime before breakfast this morning. Now you can either do it fast and have time to do other things you'd like, or slow. It's up to you."

The boy's full, soft mouth pursed up tight to hide the resentful trembling of his lips, and he turned furiously away. He began to race back toward the Citadel at an angry, breakneck pace *calculated,* Sun Wolf thought, following with a hunting lion's dogtrot, *to exhaust him before he'd gone a third the distance*.

He couldn't say that he blamed the boy. Since yesterday, he had his own frustration and resentment to chew at his soul.

Kaletha's method of training was entirely different from the brief, exhausting exercise in memorization he had undergone with the witch Yirth of Mandrigyn and from the dogged routines he had worked out for himself. He had learned to meditate from Starhawk and did so dawn and dusk, but Kaletha's instructions in meditation were more complicated and involved her frequent intervention. "You must learn to change the harmonies of the music of your mind," she said, kneeling before him in the latticed shade of a corner of the public gardens of the town, and Sun Wolf, to whom meditation had always been a matter of inner silence, again fought the urge to slap that smug look off her face.

As an exercise, it seemed unbelievably trivial. But the White Witch's other students didn't seem to think so. In their various shaded niches along the colonnade at the top end of the public gardens where they usually met, they were all meditating with faces furrowed in either concentration or ecstasy—*both,* Sun Wolf suspected irritably, *for their teacher's benefit*. Starhawk meditated alone and had taught him to do the same. The few times he had seen her at it, she had seemed relaxed, almost asleep. *But then,* he thought wryly to himself, *it took more than communion with her soul to disturb the Hawk's marble calm.* He had known her for nine years and was still trying to figure out what it would take.

He could see her, down across the blasting afternoon sunlight of the open court in the indigo arches of shade beyond, talking to the grizzled Norbas Milkom, owner of the Golden Vulture Mine. The black man's scarred face split with a laugh; by their gestures, they were discussing the mountain campaign of eight years ago.

In the afternoons, when the heat of the day had begun to burn itself off and the people woke from their siestas, half the population of Pardle Sho ended up in these gardens. The three acres of rambling walkways—under arbors of grape, jacaranda, and phoenix-vine, or of bare, sandy squares where occasional ancient orange and cypress trees stood but more often simply native cactus—covered the last footslopes of Mount Morian where the land was too irregular for even the builders of Pardle to put houses. Before the Revolt, the gardens had originally belonged to the governors of the slave-worked mines, and the ruins of the Palace formed their southern boundary. But now they were the favorite promenade of the town, where people came in the afternoons to talk, hear gossip, meet their friends, flirt, transact personal business, or listen to the singers who sat in their shaded corners, caps full of pennies before them. It wasn't unusual for itinerant teachers to meet with their students there; at the other end of the colonnade Sun Wolf knew one brisk little man could always be found teaching engineering to a class of one or two.

Kaletha's voice came to him, measured as if each word were a precious thing to be cherished by its lucky recipient. "Purity of the body is the greatest necessity of magic," she emphasized for the third or fourth time that day. She was speaking to Luatha Welldig, a fat, discontented-looking woman of forty or so, dressed, like all of them except the Wolf and Egaldus, the Trinitarian novice, in severe and unbecoming black, but her glance flicked to Sun Wolf as she spoke. "Without purity of the body—freedom from spiritous liquors, from overindulgence, from the crudities of fornication—" she was looking straight at him as she emphasized the word, "—the mind remains a prisoner in the maze of the senses. The body must be pure, if the mind is to be free. All magic rises from the mind, the intellect, the reason."

"That isn't true," Sun Wolf said, looking up.

Kaletha's pink lips lost their curves and flattened into a disapproving line. "Naturally, you'd prefer not to believe so."

He shook his head, refusing to be angered. Slowly, stammeringly, not certain how to explain and oddly conscious of his scraped-out croak of a voice, he said, "The intellect may learn to guide magic, but it doesn't spring from the reason, any more than water is generated by the pipe it flows through."

"Nonsense," Kaletha said briskly. "Reason and the ability to control the base passions are the sole province of humans, and humans are the only living creatures to possess magic."

"But they aren't."

The dark red brows climbed. "Oh? Are you telling me that camels can turn sandstorms? Or house cats can read oracle-bones? Or do you believe in funny little people we can't see who hide in cellars and clean up the kitchens of deserving goodwives?"

Sun Wolf felt the anger stir in him, and with it a deep unwillingness to argue the point. He felt in his heart she was wrong, yet lacked the technical expertise to prove himself right—and lacked, still more, any desire to pick and unravel at the smoky whole of his instincts.

Into his silence, Anshebbeth said timidly, "Kaletha, when you speak of purity—surely there are different sorts of—of physical love." She spoke as if she could barely get the word out of her throat. Sun Wolf stared at her in surprise, startled that she would defect from her

teacher's slightest utterance, much less do so to take up
his side of the question. In the harlequin sunlight of the
vine's shade, her thin, white cheeks were blotched with
embarrassed red. "Can't—can't true love be—be freeing to the soul as well as to the body?"

Kaletha sighed. "*Really,* Anshebbeth." She turned
away.

The governess fell silent, her thin hand stealing up to
touch her throat in its high collar, as if to massage away
some dreadful tightness.

Sun Wolf considered her thoughtfully for a moment.
She had surely had little to say to him, falling in obediently with Kaletha's contempt. But he remembered
the look she'd once given him: covert lust plunging
immediately into scalding shame; he'd seen her, too,
hungrily following Nanciormis with her eyes. He wondered how that sharp, tense white face would look if it
relaxed into laughter, and what the masses of tight-
braided black hair would feel like unraveling under a
man's caressing hand. But her gaze had already gone
back to Kaletha, and she leaned to catch what the
White Witch was saying to Egaldus. *No man,* he realized, *would stand a chance of gaining Anshebbeth's
undivided attention if Kaletha were in the room—supposing that he'd want it.*

Manlike, he had simply considered her contemptible.
Now, realizing what she had all her life given up for the
sake of this woman's bare approval, he saw her as pathetic.

Across the court a kingfisher glitter of brightness
caught his eye. The Bishop Galdron had joined Norbas
Milkom; the two men talked gravely, the white-bearded
patriarch with his glittering gold tabard and the tough,
scarred mine owner, the diamonds from his rings flashing. Starhawk had left them. A moment later he saw her
walking along the colonnade with Nanciormis. Both the
Bishop and the mine owner watched the big Guards
Commander disapprovingly. If Nanciormis was aware of

their looks or their disapproval he didn't show it; he moved like a king, serene and elegant in his slashed red-velvet doublet and flowing desert cloak, his dark hair knotted up on the back of his head against the afternoon's heat.

During their drinking bout last night, Sun Wolf had observed that, although Nanciormis, like most of the men of the desert, tended to treat women with a combination of courtliness and patronage, he recognized the women of his guard as colleagues in the arts of war and only flirted with them with their tacit permission. He wasn't flirting with the Hawk, Sun Wolf could see. Flirtation was an art Starhawk had never understood. She would still occasionally give Sun Wolf a blank look when he complimented or teased her, which amused him. Beneath that lioness facade, she was in some ways a startlingly innocent girl.

And yet . . .

Last night came back to him, the sharp fear in Starhawk's voice as she'd called to him from beyond the moonlit gate. She was not a woman to run from shadows. Her fear had not been the timidity of a woman asking a man's reassurance, but a warrior's fear of a very real danger. There had been neither tracks nor marks in either the yard or the little cell they shared.

Starhawk had not had any explanation, but, with a shiver, he recalled the dead doves.

A shadow fell across him. He looked up to see Nanciormis. "I see you've joined the would-be Summoners of Storm." The big man braced one thick shoulder against the arbor post with its twisting of thick, scraggy vines and looked genially down at Sun Wolf. "A useful skill for a warrior to acquire, now that there's no Wizard King to hunt you down and kill you for it—but your time could be better spent."

"If I were looking for skills to augment war," the Wolf replied, "I don't doubt it. But I have quick-and-dirty wizardry already."

"Have you?" The coffee-dark eyes narrowed thoughtfully. "I know the servants all say you do. I only thought that meant you'd managed to impress the Lady Kaletha in some fashion—not easy, I'll admit. What then do you seek here?"

Sun Wolf was silent for a long time, looking up into that fleshy, handsome face with its high cheekbones and aquiline nose already flecked with broken veins. The dark eyes, with their shadows of pouches and wrinkles, were both wise and cynical, but there was no dismissal in them.

After a few moments he said, "I don't know. If I knew, it would be easier. A man can learn to fight in the streets and taverns, but against a warrior, trained and disciplined, he's no match in a long fight; and he can't use that knowledge for anything else."

Nanciormis' brow puckered. He clearly did not understand. Sun Wolf had guessed already, from the sloppiness with which Jeryn had been trained that he would not. Sun Wolf guessed that in Nanciormis' younger days—and he couldn't be much above thirty-five now, though his portliness made him look older—he had been a notable warrior. But his very abilities, like his natural charm, had spared him from having to learn discipline. Never having had to learn anything beyond what he already knew, he was a man who lived on the surface of things—adept but unimaginative. Having never been defeated, he operated on the unconscious assumption that he never would be. A professional would destroy him.

There was a small stirring among Kaletha's disciples now, as she moved across to speak to Starhawk. Beyond her, Sun Wolf could see Egaldus fade unobtrusively into the shadows. A little to his surprise, he realized the novice was using a cloaking-spell, a means of nonvisibility, to avoid the notice of his master, the Bishop, on the other side of the garden. It was one of the first magics Sun Wolf had learned to use, and the young man did it with considerable skill. Only by concentrating could the

Wolf keep him in sight; the shadows of the twisted grape-vines lay like a blind over the bright hair and the embroidered blue and white of his robes. Anshebbeth, too, the Wolf noticed, had grown very quiet, gazing down at her thin hands.

Nanciormis beckoned him, and the Wolf rose to follow down the shaded aisle of cracked and uneven tiles. The commander glanced back at Starhawk—leaning against a gnarled wisteria vine, her head a little on one side as she talked to Kaletha—then across at Milkom and the Bishop again. "I'd advise you to be a little careful who sees you here," he said softly. "Witches have a bad name in Wenshar, as I told you last night. Whatever you think Kaletha might give you may not be worth what you'll have to pay for it."

That morning, across the speckled range land, Sun Wolf had seen the dark, jagged line of the Haunted Mountains, guarding the secrets of the ancient city of Wenshar. But Kaletha had grown angry when he'd asked her about it and had spoken of other things. It struck him now that though, with the decline of the day's heat the gardens were filling up with off-shift miners, cattle herders, and young people of the town, no casual strollers came up this far from the gardens below. He had enough experience with human nature to realize that this was not from tolerance. If fear had not kept them away, he thought, they'd be gawking and heckling like bumpkins at a fair.

Fear of Kaletha? he wondered. *Or—of what?*

"I see you managed to catch my nephew for sword practice this morning," Nanciormis went on, his eye trailing appreciatively after a fair-haired girl strolling down the colonnade on the other side of the court until the shadows at its end swallowed her. "What do you think of him?"

What Sun Wolf thought of him was that he'd been very poorly taught. But he only said, "You can't tell anything on the first day. They're always eager to impress you with how much they already know." That applied to himself, he thought ruefully a moment later, as well as to Jeryn.

Nanciormis laughed. "If you do as well tomorrow you'll be lucky. The boy has a certain quickness, but he's lazy and, I suspect, a coward. I've tried to push him into courage, or at least put him in situations where he'd be forced to master his fears, but he's clever at hiding. He can disappear for hours when there's something afoot he doesn't want to do. I've tried to get him onto something a bit more manly than that pudding-footed slug of a pony he's had since he was a toddler—Tazey rides other horses with no trouble, but he won't. And as for venturing even a few yards out onto the desert . . ."

"Has anyone ever taught him to survive in the desert?"

"How, when he won't poke his nose outside the library?" demanded Nanciormis, amused. "In any case, he's so afraid of going out there that he's not likely to need the knowledge. If you can do anything to increase his nerve, we'll all be grateful—his father most of all. His father's never had much use for him."

"Even though he's the first heir born to Wenshar since the Ancient House of Wenshar failed?"

The dark eyes slid sharply sidelong to him, then flicked away. "Osgard's always been in an ambivalent position about Jeryn. He is, as you say, the heir, and Osgard has enough pride in the realm that he wants the boy to be able to hold it after him. But Ciannis died bearing him. I'm told it was a bad pregnancy, and she nearly lost him twice. Osgard saw then and sees now that in some fashion he was obliged to trade a woman he loved for a child who was like a sickly rabbit in his infancy and who turned bookish the minute he learned to read. Book learning is all very well in a ruler, but there are other things, as there are other things besides war— not that the citizen-kings, the war-kings before Osgard ever understood style, beauty, or respect for the ancient ways. But Jeryn's sneaky and furtive as well as cowardly."

"I expect, if my father drank himself maudlin and hated me for killing my mother, I'd be sneaky and furtive, too."

Nanciormis gave him a sharp look. "Osgard never used to drink himself sodden that way before Ciannis died."

"No," the Wolf said, "I don't expect he did." They had reached the end of the colonnade; the lengthening of the afternoon light had shifted the shade of the trellises overhead, and bars of puma-colored light sprawled across the worn tile of the walkway. Across the court, he could catch the faint burring of a mandolin badly played and a nasal voice singing snatches of a popular song. In an hour he'd have to locate Jeryn again for another lesson before dinner and he had the feeling this wasn't going to be as easy as this morning had been. The novelty had definitely worn off.

He glanced back in Kaletha's direction. The Bishop of Pardle having taken his leave, Egaldus was standing at her side, listening to her conversation with his heart in his sky blue eyes. Kaletha asked him something. He gestured with the grace of one trained to the theatrics of Trinitarian liturgy and plucked a ball of greenish light from the air. It shone softly against his fingers in the shadows. Kaletha laid a hand on his shoulder and nodded approvingly. Anshebbeth looked away, her thin lips pursed.

"What about his sister?" Sun Wolf asked. "It would do him good to have a sparring partner. I think she's a sensible girl, and she's enough older than he that he won't feel belittled if she beats him. She looks as if she'd be good, too. I watched her in the war dance. She moves like a warrior."

Nanciormis grinned. "She should. When she was a little girl there wasn't a boy in the town she couldn't trounce in either a fight or a ball game. She can ride anything with four hooves and dances like a bird on the wing. I'm afraid it wouldn't do, though."

"No. The boy doesn't like her?" Sun Wolf guessed.

"Worships her—or at least he did, up until a year or so ago. He tolerates her now, as boys do with older sisters." A gust of swallows swirled down into the central court, perching on the stone rim of the nearly dry fountain there to drink. Bees were coming out as well, dipping down to the water that was fed by springs welling from the harsh stones of the Dragon's Backbone. Sun Wolf guessed there would be water in these fountains year-round.

Nanciormis went on, "No, it isn't a problem with Jeryn. But as you know, Tazey's going to be married to Incarsyn of Hasdrozaboth. He'll be here tomorrow for the final negotiations. And while among my people there is the occasional warlady, it certainly would not do for their lord to marry one, or for Osgard to—shall we say? —foist one off upon him as a wife. Nor would Incarsyn want such a woman—certainly his sister would not and she's the true ruler of the Dunes. The marriage is a political expedient to tie these—" He paused, catching himself up over some epithet he had been about to apply to the sons of slaves imported from the north to work the silver mines, who had taken the best of the foothills land from the Desert Lords and pushed them deeper into the wastes of the K'Chin. Then he concluded the phrase. "—these new realms to the Ancient Houses, even as his own was. But, as with Osgard's marriage to my sister, there can be romance in it as well. Incarsyn is young and comely, but he is a man of the shirdar and not apt to take to a woman who is too adept in wielding a sword."

Sun Wolf glanced along the colonnade. Like sheets of opaque gold, the sunlight lay between the arbor pillars now, blinding and stiflingly hot where it struck. The contrast with the twisted shade of the vine-sheltered bay where Kaletha and her small group of students sat was dazzling. Their dark robes blended with the shadows, the faces only a white blur like cutouts from paper. Ka-letha was speaking to them all, her voice a soft, hypnotic drone, whispering hidden secrets of magic and power. Beside them, leaning on the pillar, Starhawk stood listening, the shearing brilliance of the sunlight lying dappled over her square shoulders and close-cropped hair like wind-scattered petals.

He smiled a little to himself and said simply, "That's his loss."

"Captain."

Sun Wolf, whose single eye was good enough to distinguish in the polished brass of a shield on the armory wall the reflection of the man who stood in the doorway shadows said, "My Lord?" before turning. "Keep at it, boy," he added, as Jeryn automatically lowered his sword. "An enemy's not going to give you time to rest your arm, so neither will I."

The red-lipped little mouth tightened angrily, but the boy turned back to the ironwood hacking-post. His strokes against it barely splintered the wood. Down, backhand, forehand—down, backhand, forehand—each blow with its laborious windup and finish was a separate action, with no carry-through of momentum from one blow to the next. Sun Wolf turned to face the King.

"I'd like a word with you."

"You're paying for my time," the Wolf responded, walking over to the broad arch of the door. The faint, uneven *tup . . . tup . . .* of steel on unyielding wood echoed softly in the stone vaults of the round room with its high-up ring of windows, a muted percussion behind the words they spoke.

"Damn right I'm paying for your time," Osgard said. He stood foursquare, his shoulders broad in their straining doublet of dull bronze, the wide gold chain over his shoulders catching little chips of light on its S-shaped links. As usual, the King's neck ruff was undone and lay in limp disorder under his chin; also, as usual, he smelled faintly of stale wine. "And what I'm not paying for is to have it said that my son's being taught by witches."

Sun Wolf hooked his thumbs over the broad leather belt of his war kilt. Salty droplets of sweat hung from the ends of his thin, wet-dark hair and trickled down through the gold rug of hair on his back. His rusted voice was soft. "Who says this?"

"Are you denying it?"

"No. I'm just curious to know who says it."

"I have that carrot-headed bitch in my Household out of respect to my dead wife and because I'd rather, if we do have a witch in Wenshar again, that she was under my eye rather than scheming in the pay of the shirdar lords or the Middle Kingdoms. But I've told her to keep her distance from my children. I'm not having talk start about them, and, God knows, there's been talk enough, with that sleek little tomcat Egaldus sneaking here from the Bishop's palace and Galdron all in a snit over it. Well, I won't have it, I tell you!"

His face was scarlet with its mottled network of broken veins; his voice, in the stone vaults of the room, was like thunder. The chop of sword against wood had ceased.

"Nobody in my life ever asked me what I'd have or I wouldn't have," Sun Wolf replied, his single eye narrowing, "and I'll lay odds nobody ever asked you, either. Now, you can push your son into being what you want him to be, but what I am and who I spend my time with is no affair of yours."

"I'm not pushing anyone!" Osgard roared. "Don't play the sophist with me! I get enough of that from Kaletha and that damned Bishop! My son is my affair, and my Household is my affair, and I won't have it said there are witches teaching the Heir of Wenshar!"

Goaded, Sun Wolf snapped, "I'm teaching him swordsmanship, rot your eyes, not poxy divination—I couldn't teach him divination if I wanted to!"

"I'd better not hear of you keeping company with that damned woman again . . ."

"If you don't want to hear of it, then you'd better stop gossiping with your laundry women!"

The guess was evidently correct, for the King's face went redder, if that were possible, and Sun Wolf set himself for a side step and a blow. But the King only drew deep ragged breaths, his thick, liquor-scarred face working with rage. "Get out of here."

Forcing down his own anger, Sun Wolf turned in silence and went. Aside from the fact that it was a stupid quarrel, he knew that calm acquiescence would be more annoying to Osgard than reciprocated wrath—and he was right. As he walked past him into the trapped heat of the stone corridor, Osgard bellowed, "GET OUT OF HERE!" The shout rang in the groins of the roof like beaten steel. A moment later he heard the singing clatter of metal and knew that the King must have strode to snatch the boy-sized sword from his son's hand and hurl it in rage against the wall. But he did not look back to see.

In the little adobe room on the edge of the empty quarter he left a note: *Gone to the hills.* Then he singled his own dappled gelding from the palace cavy, saddled up, and left Tandieras as the sun touched the broken edge of the Dragon's Backbone like a phoenix settling to rest.

CHAPTER

—— 5 ——

*F*OR HER PART, STARHAWK WAS NOT UNDULY DISCON-
certed by Sun Wolf's disappearance. She had long experience with his habit of storming off in a rage to be by
himself for hours, days, or sometimes a week or more—
and she had her own suspicions about where he had
gone. From the open watch-station on the highest tower
of the Citadel of Tandieras where she stood guard duty,
she could look across the flatlands to where the isabel-
line scrub country faded into the vast plain of blackish,
pea-sized gravel called the reg—treeless, waterless, lifeless, stretching away to join the ergs, the dune seas of
the south. Though the sun had barely cleared the
shoulders of Mount Morian, the desert had already
begun to shimmer with the heat. Through the wavering
air could be seen, like the dark spine of a half-buried
skeleton, the Haunted Range, which guarded the dead
city of Wenshar at its feet.

With Starhawk this morning was Taswind of Wenshar, the dry wind flicking at her tawny hair as it stirred

70

in the turban of white veils that Starhawk, like the other guards, wore to protect her head from the desert sun. Instead of her usual boy's riding clothes, Tazey wore a gown of rose-colored wool; following the girl's absent gaze, Starhawk could guess why. Around the tower, the Citadel lay spread out like a peasant's counterpane of blackish grays and maroons and a dozen faded hues of homespun buff, stitched here and there with the dull green of dusty bullweed and cactus. The square block of the Hold lay almost directly underfoot—the Hall, the King's solar and his bedchamber beyond, the long balcony which connected the rooms of his Household, the sprawl of Women's Hall and Men's, and the brighter quadrangle of the kitchen gardens.

From up here, Starhawk could see the small cell where she and the Wolf had stayed and the little gate that led from the empty quarter to the dark, granite courts beneath the balcony of the Household. The empty quarter beyond lay like a picked skeleton—a jumbled chaos of adobe walls, five and six feet thick, decaying back into the mud of which they were formed, a tangle of shadows over which doves stirred like windblown leaves.

Starhawk, neither sentimental nor concerned about proving her courage to herself or anyone else, had slept last night in a bunk in the Women's Hall with the laundresses, scullery maids, and female guards, and had slept well.

Where the stables ran into the vacant quarter there was a harshness of new yellow wood and unweathered tiles. A row of old shops and halls had been converted into stabling for the white horses of the shirdar lord, Incarsyn of Hasdrozaboth, and quarters for his servants and guards. Elsewhere, more repairs marked the rooms where he himself was housed. A scrap of red bunting from yesterday's welcome stirred in the tepid morning wind like a strayed hair ribbon. It was to these rooms that Tazey's eyes were drawn.

"New earrings," Starhawk commented after a moment, not adding that Tazey had also done up her hair differently to complement the tiny, lustrous teardrop stones. "Were they part of his groom-gift?"

The girl's face went pink like a deep-desert sunset. "No," she said, and shyly met the Hawk's eyes. "He sent these to me this morning all on his own, not because he had to—I mean, they weren't heirlooms of his house or anything. He bought them new in the market, just for me. They're sand-pearls."

Starhawk studied the odd, pearl-like stones found so rarely in the wasteland stream beds. "And, if you'll forgive me for being crass," she said, "not cheap."

Tazey blushed still pinker, recognizing that Starhawk understood the compliment their cost implied. The Lord of the Dunes had arrived yesterday with his retinue, and, in the ensuing twenty-four hours, Starhawk had seen Tazey undergo a transformation from an unselfconscious girl to a young lady who knows herself to be not only wanted, but desired. It was a role she was not used to, but the very novelty, at the moment, gave her a sparkle of untasted delight. Whatever else could be said about Incarsyn of Hasdrozaboth, at least he knew the proper way of dealing with a bride who had been given no choice of her groom.

The girl shook her head, took a deep breath, and met her eyes. "Warlady, listen," she said. "I—I need to talk to you. I think I need help, but it can't get to Father. Will you promise?"

"No," said Starhawk calmly, and saw the girl's tanned face fall. She looped back a trailing end of her white veils. "Your father pays me for my loyalty—I can't promise not to tell him something I don't know, when it might touch the safety of his realm. But I do promise I'll give you as much as I can."

Tazey looked relieved and nodded, understanding the distinction. Starhawk had time to think obliquely, *She isn't pregnant and she hasn't learned some invasion plan of Incarsyn's* ... before the girl said, "It's Jeryn. He's gone."

"When?"

She shook her head. "This morning—maybe last night. I don't know. You know Father had a fight with Captain Sun Wolf."

Starhawk shrugged impatiently, "The Chief fights with everyone he works for. It's nothing. He'll be back."

"Jeryn..." Tazey hesitated. "Jeryn asked me the night the Chief left if he'd gone for good. He said he didn't think so, since you were still here. And I said, I—I thought he might have gone to the old city of Wenshar."

Starhawk's eyes narrowed. "Why did you think that?"

The absinthe green gaze avoided hers. "It's the sort of place he might go if—if he were interested in magic and wasn't afraid of the stories." Her face still averted, she hurried on, "And then this morning, I went to Jeryn's room because—because he'd been upset yesterday. Uncle Nanciormis said something to him at his lessons yesterday—you know Uncle's back teaching him? I think he called him a coward..." She looked back at the Hawk, grief and hurt in her face at what she could neither control nor repair. "And he isn't a coward, really he isn't. Only... Anyway, his bed was empty. And I'm afraid he's gone after the Captain."

Starhawk considered this in silence for some moments, wondering how much of the obviously fabricated tale was based in truth. Tazey's gaze had fallen—she was an appallingly poor liar. Her hands, long and slender like Nanciormis' and presumably her mother's, though they were burned brown as a cowhand's by the sun, pleated nervously at the silk-fine folds of her skirt.

"You realize it's far more likely he's hiding somewhere because it's time for his lessons? Especially if your uncle's been calling him a coward."

Tazey's face flushed, and she shook her head emphatically. "I—I've looked in all his usual hiding places. He's not in the Fortress. I know it."

Starhawk forbore to ask her how she knew, knowing she would only get another evasion. She glanced out across the reg toward the crumbling black line of the Haunted Range, hiding behind its curtain of heat dance, then back at the girl. "I'm not free until after breakfast." By the angle of the shadows that lay across the face of the Binnig Rock, the giant granite half-dome which loomed above the jumbled shoulders of the Dragon's Backbone where they crowded close to Tandieras knoll, that would be fairly soon. "After this long, I don't think an hour either way will make much difference to Jeryn." She added, "You know it can't be just you and me."

The girl swallowed apprehensively. "I go riding all the time without 'Shebbeth."

"That's not what I mean and you know it," the Hawk said, her voice gruff. "Could you trust Incarsyn?"

There was a long silence while Tazey struggled between what she knew to be true and what she wished to believe about the man she was required to marry. Then she shook her head. "He wouldn't understand." She groped for a way to phrase the fact that the Prince, who, she wanted to think perfect, in fact had very little in common with her. "He wouldn't think it proper that I go. I mean, that I ride a horse..." Miserably, she added, "Among his people, noble ladies all ride in litters."

She broke off, looking away again, fighting off the tightness in her throat that was not in keeping with the romance of the Prince's ardent wooing. *The worst of it was,* Starhawk supposed, *that Incarsyn would never understand.*

But there was nothing she could say; to avoid anything worse, she stuck to the matter at hand. "We'll find some of the guard who'll keep their mouths shut. You probably know them better than I. Be thinking about that between now and breakfast."

"All right." Relieved not to have that open wound sympathetically prodded, Tazey smiled, gathered up a handful of skirts, and picked her way carefully down the ladder to the tower room below. A few minutes later, Starhawk could see her as a foreshortened oval of rose pink and straw, hurrying from the door at the tower's base towards the Hall.

A good and dutiful daughter, she thought, with ironic pity, doing her best to meet halfway a bridegroom whom she had no choice but to accept. And what choice *had* she? She had not even the freedom to choose, as Starhawk had once chosen, the solitary mysticism of the convent over a life as some man's cherished brood mare and bedmate. The alliance with some Desert Lord not quite powerful enough to be a threat had to be made— the dowry had already been paid. Had the girl been able to make one good, cogent argument to her father against the match, she might have had a chance. But she could not, even to herself, allow the joy of her own freedom as a reason. Why give up a man who bore all conventional resemblance to the prince of your dreams on the grounds that you would never be able to ride again?

Starhawk shook her head. The inconvenience of believing in the Mother—or the Triple God of the Trinitarians, for that matter—was the belief that events had some kind of universal meaning. Sun Wolf, at least, was secure in the knowledge that the spirits of his departed ancestors were no more able to control the random events of this world than he was—though, being dead, they could see them coming. She herself had long since given up trying to guess good from ill and let them all move in the Invisible Circle as they would. But her heart hurt for the girl, nevertheless.

Starhawk saw Prince Incarsyn an hour and a half later, when she came to her late breakfast in the Hall. A few years younger than she, he was dazzlingly handsome, with the graceful vitality of a man who thinks with his body rather than his intellect. The clothing of the desert added to the feral beauty of his movements— loose trousers and half-boots, a tunic of dark indigo silk, thick with gold embroidery, and, over all, the flowing

white cloak of the shirdar. Like all the folk of the desert,
he had a complexion of sun-dyed bronze and black, curly
hair, clubbed back from his temples in jeweled pins and
falling almost to his waist behind. He paused in the act of
handing Tazey graciously down from the dais to bow to
Starhawk as she entered, and Tazey wavered, her hand
still in his, torn between excusing herself from him to
speak to Starhawk and prolonging his attentions to her.

It didn't help, of course, that Incarsyn had absolutely
no doubt that she would accompany him.

Starhawk said, "Let me get my breakfast, and I'll see
you in a few minutes," and the girl nodded, grateful to be
spared the awkward choice. Feeling Tazey to be shy as
he conducted her toward the Hall door, Incarsyn chival-
rously carried the weight of the conversation, clearly
attributing her confusion to himself. His soft, well-
modulated voice was lost among the other mingled
voices echoing in the high ceiling of the Hall as Starhawk
made her way to Kaletha's small table.

"I don't like it," Norbas Milkom was grumbling at
the High Table beside the King. He reached into the dish
of ham before him, a splash of rainbows dancing from a
diamond the size of a rabbit's eye on his gnarled black
finger. "I told you before and I'm here to tell you again
—I don't like it, and the miners don't like it. This marrying into the tribes! Why can't the girl be let to wed her
own kind, eh? One of my boys or Quaal Ambergados'
son. The Three Gods know we're as wealthy as any Desert Lord skulking about the sands with his handful of
followers and goats—money we came by honestly, digging it from the ground with our hands, not plundering it
from traders."

Nanciormis, sitting at the King's other side, said
nothing, but his pouchy eyes glinted at this slight to his
people. Starhawk saw Anshebbeth—in hovering attendance on Tazey and her betrothed, but close enough to
the High Table to be eavesdropping as usual—turn and
glare back at Milkom with smoldering indignation.

Was her anger for the sake of the shirdar—Anshebbeth's own people, though she worked in the King's Household and had given up going veiled as the deep-desert women did? Starhawk wondered, *Or could it be for Nanciormis' sake?* It had not been lost upon Starhawk that, while she should have been keeping an eye on her charge, Anshebbeth's glance kept straying to the commander's broad, green velvet shoulders.

"Kings must marry their own kind, Norbas," Osgard said patiently. "If she did not wed one of the Desert Lords, it would have to be the son of one of the Lords of the Middle Kingdoms."

"Why must it?" Milkom demanded, the old tribal scarring on his face flexing with his frown like braids of rope. On Nanciormis' other side, the Bishop Galdron leaned forward amid a glitter of bullion embroidery and jeweled sleeve borders.

"I confess to a certain apprehension for the welfare of the Princess Taswind's soul," he said in his mellifluous voice. "The shirdar are pagans, remember, worshiping the djinns of the desert. As a woman of an Ancient House, she will have to be initiated into the cult of the women of the family. There are evil influences there..."

"The old beard-wagger sees evil influences under his chamberpot." The voice spoke almost in Starhawk's ear. She swung around, startled, to the place she'd thought vacant at her left—*dammit*—she'd turned her head a moment ago and *seen* it vacant. The novice Egaldus sat there, a cup of coffee cradled between his well-kept hands, smiling in discreet triumph at her and Kaletha's astonishment.

"Not bad, eh?" he grinned, eyes dancing like the boy he still mostly was.

Kaletha's back seemed to lengthen. "Scarcely a seemly use of your powers."

"Kaletha..." He reached across Starhawk, to put a hand over the Witch's cold, white fingers. Kaletha made as if she would draw away, but did not. "I'll have to be in

attendance on him this afternoon. Perhaps if I came
later?" The bright blue eyes were ardent with hope. Kaletha averted her face, but her hand remained where it
was. "I have power—you raised it in me," he coaxed
softly. "You're the only one who can teach me. Please."

He certainly knew how to ask, Starhawk thought,
amused. *No wonder Sun Wolf annoyed Kaletha.*

Old Nexué's voice croaked out, "Well, it's her Little
Majesty!" and Starhawk glanced up to see Tazey had
come back into the Hall. "Been giving you a wee taste of
the wedding-night beef?" Tazey, blushing furiously, hurried over to where Starhawk sat as the old woman and
the gaggle of laundresses with her, hooting with lewd
glee and making gestures and comments as old as woman
and man, pushed their way out the kitchen door and
back to their work. The King and his party had risen and
left; the High Table was empty now save for Nanciormis,
who sat alone, long fingers stroking the silver wine cup
before him, his dark, curving brows pulled together in
thought. Anshebbeth, lingering on the dais in some private reverie, jerked about at the old woman's first cackle
and stamped her foot, calling furiously after her, "Stop
it! How dare you, you filthy hag!"

But by that time, Nexué had gone.

"'Shebbeth, don't," pleaded Tazey, though her own
cheeks were red as if burned. "She didn't mean any
harm."

As she and Starhawk climbed the dark inner stair to
her rooms so that she could change to riding clothes and
head veils, she added "She—and Kaletha, who just
burns up inside about it—should know by now that
Nexué *always* gets worse about something if you show
you're upset over it."

At the corrals they were joined by two young guards
named Pothero and Shem, who, Starhawk guessed, had
been childhood friends of Tazey's. As they came near,
Shem, who was the taller of the two and black, said,
"Jeryn's pony, Walleye, is gone."

Tazey flinched, startled, then recovered herself and nodded. "Yes, I—I know," she stammered—but she hadn't known. *If she had,* Starhawk thought, adjusting her veils, *she'd have brought it in as evidence. She knew he was gone, but wasn't about to tell me how.* With the uneasy sense of edges not matching, she mounted the stringy yellow dun the boys had saddled for her and followed Tazey through the Fortress gate and down the knoll, swinging through the steep rocks and out onto the desert floor. The two young guards brought up the rear, head veils fluttering in the dry mid–morning heat.

The stillness of the air increased Starhawk's disquiet. The horses' hooves were a swift splatter of sound, like thrown water on the hard, dusty earth; the electric quality of the air prickled against her exposed cheeks. It was autumn, the season of the killer storms—the season of the Witches, they called it in Wenshar. She knew there was no telling when such a storm would strike. They were riding across the open palm of fate.

"Why do you think Jeryn went seeking the Chief in Wenshar?" she asked, as the jutting, dark mass of Tandieras knoll, the Fortress, and the looming, eroded shoulders of the Binnig Rock dwindled to ragged darkness behind them. Ahead, the ground lay hard and speckled dun, studded with widely spaced tufts of wiry grass and an occasional waxy-leaved camel-bush. In spite of the nearness of the winter, it was still stiflingly hot; heat dances, turned the air to water, concealing the broken line of dark, glazed sandstone mountains far ahead. "And don't say you don't know," added Starhawk quietly, and Tazey bit her lip.

For a while, the girl only concentrated on the barren landscape before them, her gloved hands sure and steady on the reins. Then she ducked her head a little, as if ashamed.

"As I said," she murmured, "Wenshar is where a mage would go. Because of the Witches."

"Who?"

Her voice was barely audible over the soft thud of hooves on stone-hard earth. "The Witches of Wenshar."

Starhawk urged her horse up beside the girl's thick-necked bay, so that they rode knee to knee. "I've never heard of them."

"Father doesn't like them talked about." Tazey glanced nervously at Starhawk, then away. "There used to be a saying—there still is, in the town—'Wicked as the Witches of Wenshar.' Only sometimes it's 'Wicked as the Women of Wenshar,' because all the women of the Ancient House of Wenshar were witches. Their souls were damned because of it, the Bishop says. They could summon the sandstorms, or dismiss them; they could part the winds with their hands, or call darkness in broad day just by combing their hair, or summon the dead. They were cruel and evil and they ruled all these lands along the foothills of the Dragon's Backbone, before the Lords of the Middle Kingdoms came and took the lands away and dominated the other Desert Lords. I suppose it's why Father was so angry when he found out any teacher of Jeryn's was mageborn."

"Because of the reputation they gave the mageborn in Pardle Sho?" Starhawk asked, puzzled.

Tazey turned to look at her, green eyes wide in the gauze frame of rippling veils. "Because of Mother. She was the last Princess of the Ancient House of Wenshar. Father is afraid—has always been afraid—that people would say the evil is in our blood. And it isn't," she added earnestly, as if worried that Starhawk would think so, too. "Jeryn can't stand Kaletha. I—"

Starhawk raised a hand, silencing her, and reined in. "Stay back," she ordered the others sharply, already swinging down from the saddle as Tazey drew rein beside her. "Don't foul the ground."

"What is it?"

They had reached the harsh, stone plain of the reg, a landscape that made the desolate scrub closer to the foothills seem a pleasure garden. Here nothing grew, nothing lived. The seeds which slept elsewhere in the desert soil, awaiting rain, had long ago died in their sleep; the eternal carpet of pebbles lay hot, black, and utterly lifeless underfoot. Starhawk felt the burn of it through the soles of her boots, through the buckskin knee of her breeches where it touched the ground, and through her gloved hands. The storms could turn the reg into a flaying hail of rock—the riders had stopped twice already, to pick the small, vicious stones from their horses' feet. Now Starhawk picked up a small stone and held it to the hot afternoon sun. On its upper edge was a faint smudge of blood.

She smelled it, then wet her finger and touched the dried patch of brown. "Last night, it looks like." She tossed it down.

"Look, here's more." Pothero sprang down a little further on. The smudge on that stone was smaller, barely a fleck.

"Not drops." Starhawk squinted out over the bleak, stony carpet of the reg. In the heat-shimmer, eroded columns of sun-blackened stone rose from the barren pebbles, some singly, others in ragged lines. Tsuroka, the shirdar called them—guards posted by the desert djinns to keep watch on the dead land. "How much did Jeryn know about horses, Tazey?"

The girl shook her head. "Not much. He hated riding. He always got sunburned because he'd never do it enough, and it made his bottom sore. And Father and Uncle Nanciormis were always making him ride horses too strong for him—to build up his courage, they said."

Starhawk cursed without heat.

Tazey went on, "Walleye used to be my pony; he was just a fat, old slug Jeryn could ride on when he was about five. But he always liked the pony best because he wasn't afraid of him."

"*Is* he afraid of horses?"

The girl hesitated, thinking about it. "Not horses in general," she said after a moment. "But of the horses

Uncle gives him, yes. And they are pretty high-spirited."
She smiled. "This one I'm riding is really his."

"Your father," began Starhawk, looking at the jittery,
restive bay. Then she sighed, and let the observation go
unmade. "Fan out," she ordered the guards. "Looks like
poor old Walleye picked up a stone. See if you can find
any more traces."

There was more blood, further on. When, a mile and a
half later, they came to a wide patch of gray sand left by
last week's storm, even the eternal sweep of the desert
winds had not been able to eradicate wholly the marks
which indicated that Jeryn had still been riding his pony.
Starhawk cursed again—the visceral oaths that only
worshipers of the Mother can contemplate.

"He doesn't know any better," Tazey pleaded unhap-
pily.

"Then he shouldn't have charge of a defenseless
brute," Starhawk retorted. "He probably thought the
poor thing's gait was out because of the gravel."

She straightened up, to scan the hot, southern horizon
for the fiftieth time that afternoon. But the earth lay silent. The dividing line between black and blue was sharp
and clean as if cut with a knife and a rule. The shadows
lay over toward the east, kohl-dark and lengthening.
They had come nearly twenty miles from the foot of
Tandieras Pass, with nearly ten more to go toward the
shallow inward curve of the eastward cliffs of the
Haunted Range where the City of Wenshar had lain.

Uneasily, Shem said, "We're not going to find Jeryn
in the ruins before dark."

Beneath his veils, Pothero's dark eyes shifted.
Stories, Tazey had said. *What stories, concerning a city
a century and a half dead?*

"He'll know we'll be looking for him," Shem offered
encouragingly. He unwound his veils a little to take a
drink from one of the waterskins. His teeth flashed in an
uneasy grin. "Hell, he'll probably be waiting for us on
the edge of the ruins, or be starting back, lame pony or

no lame pony. He won't want to be in that place when night comes any more than—"

"If he made it that far." Starhawk walked a few paces forward and picked up something from the ground—a single thread of white muslin, but bright as a banner against the leaden gravel. She held it up. "He must have torn up his headcloth to tie around the pony's foot. That's worse than stupid—he can't have known he shouldn't let the sun get to his head—but it's my guess he'd make for the nearest shelter." She glanced up at Tazey. "He isn't stupid, is he? Just ignorant as hell."

The girl nodded wretchedly.

"Those rocks?" Shem pointed toward the north, where a weathered gray flatiron of rocks broke the sand like a beached ship half-heeled over in heavy seas.

Starhawk considered them, then looked away to the southeast, where, some five miles off, stood three tsuroka, crumbling, cinder-colored columns dyed maroon by the afternoon glare. "I think he'd have turned back first, figuring he could make it back to Tandieras. By the time he realized he couldn't, he'd be closer to those. You boys ride north—we'll check south. Send up a smoke if you find him."

It was Starhawk who found him when her horse whinnied as they neared the decaying heaps of talus and rubble that surrounded the tsuroka and was answered by a faint, neighing reply. Jeryn was curled in the long purple shadows of an overhanging boulder. His bare face was sunburned red and blistered in spite of the coating of the Wolf's sunburn grease, tear-tracks cutting the dust and slime like water runnels on the desert's face. He was asleep, but woke up, crying, when Tazey called his name and came scrambling down the rocks to him; brother and sister clutched each other desperately, and Starhawk could see the boy was dehydrated and feverish from the sun. He kept sobbing, "Don't tell Father! Promise not to tell Father!"

"We won't," Tazey whispered reassuringly, as the

hot, desperate hands clutched at her shirt sleeves and veils. "We're all sworn to secrecy, you know we are . . ."

"I didn't make it," Jeryn sobbed. "But I'm not a coward—Uncle said I was a coward not to fetch him back, if I didn't like the way Uncle was teaching me. But I'm not—I'm not. Is Walleye going to be all right?"

Starhawk, aware of the priorities, had already checked the miserable pony's split and bleeding hoof. She caught the beast's hanging head and dumped most of her spare water down its throat, knowing that, though Jeryn might have remembered to take water for himself, he had undoubtedly forgotten that horses drink, too. "I don't know," she said roughly, still angry about the pony's suffering. "He'll need one hell of a farrier to fix that hoof."

"I did as best I could," the boy sobbed miserably, still huddled in his sister's arms. "He can't die. . . . It's all my fault . . ."

Starhawk opened her mouth to deliver some well-chosen words about ignorance which had in times past raised blisters on the hides of toughened mercenaries, then shut it again. Whatever else could be said, Jeryn, having gotten his poor pony into this mess, hadn't left him in it; and considering how frightened the boy must have been, there was a good deal in his favor for that. So she only said, "If we can get him back to Tandieras, he should be all right."

She glanced back out at the hot, black flatness of the reg, then at the two children, the boy sobbing, his burned face pressed to Tazey's shoulders. "And I think your uncle deserves to be horsewhipped, and your father as well. This wasn't brave—it was criminally stupid."

"Uncle didn't mean—" began Tazey, more frightened by the mercenary's perfectly level, conversational tone than by all her father's roaring bluster.

"Your uncle," returned Starhawk, with quiet viciousness, "never means much of anything by what he says or does. Most people who sow harm don't. He's like a nearsighted man, seeing clearly only what he wants and not much caring to think about the rest." She scrambled out of the shadowed cleft, the rock burning through her boot soles as she returned to the horses and collected a broken handful of mesquite and acacia branches tied to the back of the saddle. She'd gathered them at the edge of the reg, knowing that, if a signal was needed, out there she would find nothing to burn. *It is just soldier's luck,* she thought, hunkered over a handful of bark peelings and cracking flint and steel, *that the sun is just past the strength required to use a burning-glass.*

When she'd coaxed the spark into a smoldery thread of smoke, she looked back. Tazey had pulled off her veils, soaked them from the waterskin and wrapped them around her brother's swollen face. "You know your father will be searching by now."

The girl nodded miserably. Jeryn, clinging to her waist, broke into frightened, half-delirious sobs. Starhawk checked the southern horizon again, gauging the tiredness of the horses, her recollection of the look of last night's moon, and the state of their water. The skyline was clean, unblurred by the telltale line of dust, but her hackles prickled at the sight of it. Across the reg to the north, the sun gilded a plume of dust as Shem and Pothero rode back toward them.

"Come on," she said softly. "We've pushed our luck already. It's a long way back."

The storm appeared on the southern horizon when they were seven miles from the rocks. Starhawk had sensed the growing uneasiness of the horses, the heat, and the close, pounding feeling in her head and had turned her eyes, again and again, to the blank southern quarter of the sky. Now she saw it, a deadly glitter like gold tumbling in a hopper, darkness and lightning underneath. Her horse flung up its head, terror overriding its weariness. She twisted its face back into the wind, and heard Shem cry out and the clatter of retreating hooves even as she yelled, "Make for the rocks!" Through a blur of dust and the wind-torn ends of her veils, she saw he'd been thrown. The cloud before them swelled with unbelievable speed, the oven-heat of the storm surrounding them, and brown darkness began to fall.

The horses were frantic, even the lame Walleye fought to escape and run before the storm, though they could not hope to outrace it. Pothero tried to pick up Shem, and his piebald gelding threw them both and went galloping north amid a stinging whirlwind of flying sand and stones.

The air was laden with dust, hot and smothering. Flying gravel tore at Starhawk's face as she wrenched her horse to a stop. Electricity tightened like a vise around her skull—in the howling fog of approaching darkness, she could see the dry lightning leaping from earth to sky. She swung down from her saddle, trying to yell to Tazey, "We can kill the horses for a windbreak!" knowing it to be a last resort and nearly useless. The scream of the winds ripped her words away. She dimly saw Tazey's horse rear, overbalanced by the two children on its back. Something black and huge, the flying trunk of a deep-desert acacia tree, she thought, came whirling out of the gloom like a malevolent ghost and struck the horse broadside. They toppled, Tazey dragging her brother clear. In panic Starhawk's horse jerked its head, snapping the reins in her hands. Then it, too, was gone.

Darkness covered them, a black wing of death. An uprooted cactus came flying out of the darkness to strike her, the spines tearing through the steel-studded leather of her doublet as if it were silk. But worse than that was the heat and the dust, winding them already in a baking shroud that would drain the moisture from their bodies and leave them mummified. Shem and Pothero stumbled to her, heads wrapped in their veils like corpses, blind with dust. Jeryn grabbed her from out of the darkness, sobbing something about Tazey...

Her head throbbing unbearably, her body aching already with desiccation, Starhawk squinted through the

flying black fog of smothering dust. A flicker of dry lightning showed her the girl's dim outline, walking into the
storm, her unveiled hair flying back as she raised her
hands.

For the first instant, Starhawk thought it was to protect her eyes from the dust. But a second burst of
ghostly light outlined Tazey's hands as she stretched
them into the wind, fingers pressed together like a
wedge. And, as if they had been a wedge, the winds
parted around them.

In her first, bursting glare of enlightenment, Starhawk's chief thought was, *So that's how she knew where
her brother would be.*

The force of the storm curled back from Tazey's
hands like waters breaking over a rock, leaving an ar-
rowhead wake of stillness. In that eerie wake, only tiny
puffs and eddies of wind touched Starhawk's face, but
she could see the dust on either side in heaving curtains
and hear the screaming keen of flying sand over gravel.
The two young guards stared, dumb with shock and horror, at that blade-slim figure in the choking gloom; but
when one of them opened his mouth to cry out something obvious, Starhawk, Jeryn still clinging to her waist,
strode over to him and said quietly, "Don't say it."

The young man stared at her, blood from blown gravel
and debris trickling down his face, staining his veils.
"But—"

"You break her concentration, and we're all dead."

Starhawk had dealt with wizards before; the two
youths had not. They turned horrified eyes back to the
girl they'd grown up with, as if she had been transformed
before them into some dreadful monster. Like theirs, her
face was scratched and torn, matted with dust. In the
ghostly darkness, Starhawk could barely distinguish her
features—her eyes shut, her lips moving occasionally,
her hair tangled with blown twigs and gray with dust, her
outstretched hands bleeding. She seemed locked in some
dreadful trance, focusing all her mind, her soul, her life,

upon turning the winds, as she had been told witches could do. The pony Walleye, reeling like a drunken thing, had staggered into the wedge of stillness behind her and collapsed. The young guards, staring at her, seemed to waver between doing the same and taking their chances with the storm.

Seeing the horror on their faces, Starhawk added grimly, "And you had damn well better keep your mouths shut about this afterward as well." She turned and led the stumbling Jeryn back close to his sister. After long hesitation, the two young guardsmen followed.

It was almost dawn before they returned to Tandieras, but nearly the whole of the Fortress was grouped by torchlight around the gate. Runners from the search party that had found their small fire after the storm died had carried rumors as well as demands for water and medical attention. Starhawk, her body hurting from dehydration and sheer weariness, saw from afar the carpet of firefly lights against the charcoal bulk of the Fortress knoll and cursed.

She reined the horse she had been given by the searchers over close to Tazey's makeshift litter. Jeryn, in exhausted sleep, stirred fitfully in her arms and sobbed, "I promised not to tell...I promised...don't tell Father..." Starhawk tightened her grip around the boy's scrawny body and reflected, with calm anger, that, beyond a doubt, some officious fool *had* told his father.

The men of the search party had all been very quiet. Tazey herself, though she had seemed only very dazed after the passing of the storm, had not spoken at all and now, under the light of the searchers' torches, seemed to have drifted into a vague sleep. Starhawk remembered how, once during the past summer, Sun Wolf, driven by frustration and rage at his own impotence to tap the wellsprings of his power, had worked at calling the lightning throughout one northlands storm. Perhaps he had thought that, like the physical skills of which he was such a master, the power could be increased with violent and steady use—and perhaps, if the wielder knew what he was doing, it could. He had lain in a fitful half-trance of black and hopeless depression for days, as if his soul as well as his body and his power had been drained.

Rest would cure it, the Hawk thought. *If, that is, she were allowed to rest.*

The crowds by the gate were very still, as the rescuers had been, when Shem and Pothero whispered of what they had seen.

In the cold dawn light, the yellow torch glare altered the faces of the crowd—awed, frightened, confused. Starhawk saw the Bishop Galdron, lips pressed in arctic anger, as if Tazey had chosen to be mageborn instead of desperately hiding her suspicions about her powers. Beside that small, glittering figure, Egaldus was keeping his thin face carefully expressionless, but he radiated barely concealed triumph and glee—glee that on Kaletha's face was transformed into smug satisfaction as she tried to push her way forward through the crowd in the broad court before the steps of the Hold. Starhawk, knowing Kaletha saw herself already as Royal Instructress in Magic, felt a twinge of weary anger. Anshebbbeth, closely buttoned as usual despite the earliness of the hour, wore a tight expression, her genuine concern for Tazey's injuries fighting with naked jealousy, as if what the girl possessed had been taken away from her.

Between the torches that flared on either side of the doors into the Hall, Osgard, Nanciormis, and the handsome young Incarsyn stood, their faces a study in shocked noncommitment. Incarsyn, particularly, looked simply confused, as if struggling to select the most appropriate emotion out of a rather small natural stock.

Starhawk dismounted. None of the guards seemed eager to go near the litter, so she helped Tazey to stand. Dusty, scratched, her blond hair hanging like a dried broom around her scorched face, the girl wavered unsteadily on her feet, and Jeryn, stumbling, staggered to support her other side. In dreamlike weariness, they moved through the haze of torchlit dust toward the steps, where a bloodshot, tear-streaked Osgard waited, his untidy doublet smeared with liquor stains. The silence was absolute, but Starhawk could feel it around her, worse than the weight of the storm.

Then into that silence, old Nexué's voice cawed like canvas ripping. "A witch! She's a witch!"

Tazey raised her head, her green eyes transparent with horror. "No," she whispered, pleading for it not to be so. Then her voice wailed, crackling *"No!"*

Kaletha had started to bustle forward, but Nexué pushed before her, skinny finger pointing. Tazey could only stare at her, blank with shock, a rim of white showing all around her pupils in the torchlight. There was triumph and distorted glee in the old woman's face, as if the damnation and ruin of the Princess were some kind of personal victory. "A witch! A—"

With a kind of calm rage Starhawk turned and backhanded the old woman across the mouth with her closed fist, knocking her sprawling to the dirt. She was too late. Tazey whimpered again, "No . . ." Covering her face with her hands, she slowly collapsed. Osgard, Nanciormis, and Incarsyn all hesitated to step forward, and it was Starhawk who caught the fainting girl in her arms.

CHAPTER

—— 6 ——

*F*ROM THE WINDOW OF THE TEMPLE, SUN WOLF COULD
see the lights bobbing in the canyon below.

He had seen them last night, when he had looked out
into the black violence of the killer winds. Later, when
the rock-cut palaces of the vanished city, carved from
the very sandstone of the canyon walls, had lain cold and
colorless under the ghostly moon, they had been there
still. They flickered at him now from empty doorways,
from black eye sockets of wide square windows, and
from the shadows of the peach-colored columns of the
carved facades. The whisper of their bodiless voices
braided into the wail of the desert winds.

He knew what they were.

In the north, as a child, he had seen demons, the only
person he had ever known who could do so. His father,
he remembered, had beaten him the one time he had
spoken of it—for telling lies, he'd said. Sun Wolf wondered now whether it had actually been for telling what

91

the old man did not want to accept as truth. He had wanted a warrior son.

In all his years of hearing tales about demons, the Wolf had never heard that they could hurt people much. He knew their thin, whistling voices called from the hollow places of the earth, luring men to their deaths in marshes or over gullies in the dark of the moon. But they fled men and bright lights. No man who knew what and where they were should be in danger from those cold, incorporeal spirits.

Yet he knew himself to be in danger, though danger of what he did not know.

He had scribbled in the dust of the rose-hued sandstone temple he had taken for his quarters the few patchy demonspells Yirth of Mandrigyn had taught him and drawn all the Runes of Light on the doorpost and on the sills of the great upper window.

And still he did not feel quite safe.

They moved below him through the monochrome darkness of the canyon, faint lights that shone but did not illuminate the smooth pillars, the filigree turrets, or the winding stairs cut at intervals in the fantastically eroded rock faces of the canyon wall.

The City of Wenshar had been built where the tawny sandstone cliff–face of the Haunted Range— black with the baked mineral patina of the scorching sun—curved inward to form a shallow plain raised above the level of the desert and sheltered from the cruelty of the winds. There, three small streams flowed out of the broken mountains to lose themselves in the farther desert. On the raised plain, the City of Wenshar had spread out around its gardens of date palms and cypresses—until the invading armies of the Middle Kingdoms had crushed the Ancient House of Wenshar and taken its lands and its mines.

Time and sand had nearly destroyed the few walls war had left standing. But up the three canyons lay a twisting maze of wadis and cuts—of square, isolated blocks and towering stone needles, valleys as wide as a street or so narrow the Wolf could span them with his arms—lit only by bright ribbons of sky three hundred feet above. Here the wealthy nobles of Wenshar had carved gem–like palaces and temples from the living cliffs themselves. Sheltered from the sun, their fantastic sandstone facades had not been darkened by the desert heat. They shone peach and amber and rose, softly banded yellows, citrine, honey. Here, time had ceased, dammed behind the enchantment of the stone.

Sun Wolf had always loved rocks, their strength and the personality of their shapes. On the road and in Tandieras, he had missed having a rock garden in which to meditate and spend time. Hearing nothing more of Wenshar than its evil reputation, he had been awestruck by this fairy-tale beauty.

Yet from every shadow, in every niche and doorway, he sensed the presence of demons. The city crawled with them, big and little; in the three days he had wandered here, he had felt them watching him. Sometimes it seemed to him that he had only to press his hands to the ground to hear their voices. But that was something he feared to do.

By day he never saw them, though occasionally, in those palaces cut deeper than a single chamber into the cliffs, he heard their flitter and murmur, like dry leaves blowing over stone floors that neither wind nor plant had touched in generations. But two evenings ago, in the shadows of the central canyon, he had glimpsed them, no more than a flicker out of the corner of his eye, massing in the shadows before him as he tried to leave. He had doubled on his tracks to take a narrow wadi that rejoined the main way lower down—the mountains here were split into great, free-standing blocks in places, which enterprising ancient nobles had hollowed into whole palaces. But the demons had been waiting for him. The sun had disappeared by then from the brilliant stream of blue overhead, its rays only edging the topmost rim of the rocks. He could sense a soft, evil chittering in the shadows.

When he'd doubled back again, he'd realized he was being driven.

There was no lore of demons in any of the jumble of things Yirth had taught him, nor had he ever found any in his search for wizards. He knew they rose out of rocks and swamps, out of water sometimes. If they were in this land, the magic of the old Witches of Wenshar would have held them at bay until, with the Witches' destruction, they had seeped forth like oil from the ground.

They had no strength. Being bodiless, he doubted they could physically hurt a man much. Nor could he think of a reason they would want to, needing no sustenance. Yet in places the canyon floors were heaped with broken piles of animal bones, mouflon sheep and gazelles, driven to their deaths from the ledges above even as men were lured into marshes by the demons of the north. The bones lay whole and undisturbed.

Standing there in the growing azure dimness of the evening, listening to the crooning whisper of the demons massing like lightning bugs in the shadows before him, he had suddenly wondered why.

He had turned again, seeking a way out. The canyon had widened before him into a long space where a line of eroded stone needles, narrow columns as high as the canyon walls, towered gilt-tipped against an opal sky. Twisted cypress trees, a recollection of vanished wells, stood about the needles' bases, gray trunks weathered and contorted as if they sought to swallow their own branches. Entirely across the rear of the canyon stretched the longest palace facade he had yet seen. Amber steps led up to level upon level of peach and salmon columns, fragile turrets, and strange spires, all glowing in the last of the light. But as Sun Wolf stood in the black shade beneath the undead cypresses, he'd heard voices crying out to him from the dark arches of that vast edifice, sweet as the voices of children who live upon human blood.

He had been afraid then, unreasoningly, and had fled back down the canyon, heedless of the whistling gibber in the shadows through which he passed. He had gone to his own temple headquarters in the westernmost canyon and scrawled the ghostly scrim of runes, invisible to any eyes but his own, over the windows and doors behind him. He had no way of knowing whether they would, in fact, keep the demons from passing. He had sat awake through that night and every night since.

Outside, they moved in the darkness still. Faint, deformed bodies drifted in shells of light, seeping in and out of the rocks, floating in the air like drifts of vagrant mist. He knew that what he saw was their true being, as a mirror will reflect the true being of a wizard cloaked in illusion, and what frightened him was that he could not tell whether they were ugly or beautiful. He could hear them whispering to one another in their piping, little voices and knew that, if he allowed himself to, he would understand—or think he understood. But that, too, he feared to do.

Why did he feel that they would come if he bade them?

Why this strange sense, in the inner corners of his heart, that he knew their names?

They had tried twice more to drive him into that open space at the end of the central canyon where dark cypresses grew at the feet of the needles—tried to drive him into the cantaloupe-colored palace that lay beyond. He had gone there once, the day following the first attempt, curious as to what they wanted of him. He had chosen the hour of noon, when the burnished sun beat straight down on the gravel that covered the carved roadways and dry stream bed—the one hour when he felt safest.

From the top of the steps he had looked into a shadowy hall, a huge, square space whose walls were covered to the height of his shoulders in places with the fine gray sand that drifted between the columns of its open facade. The room went back far deeper than any he had previously seen, its nether end hidden in shadow, and, unlike any other he had seen, its walls had once been plastered and painted. The dim shapes of the frescoes there were almost unrecognizable, yet something about their posture, the activities implied in the stiff, shadowy outlines which were all that remained, troubled him. To his right he could see a small black rectangle of shadow, an inconspicuous door to some inner chamber from which no window opened to the outside. And from that dark door, softly and distinctly, he had heard Starhawk's voice say, "Chief?"

After that he had not dared to go into the central canyon at all. In the heat of noon he slept; in the few morning and evening hours he searched the city, looking for any sign, any book, or any talisman that the Witches of Wenshar might have left, searching for some trace of their power among the crowding mazes of rose-colored cliffs. Only that day he had heard the desperate, feeble crying of a baby and had followed the sound to the entrance of that central canyon. He had stood there a long time, listening to that starved wailing before turning his back and walking away.

By night he watched, and the demons watched him.

Two nights ago, while the storm had screamed overhead and the canyons had been filled with a ghostly haze of hot dust that stirred with eddying winds, they had gathered hundreds thick outside, drifting close to the window where he stood, heart pounding, to stare at him with empty, glowing eyes.

Now the sky above the canyon rim was paling. In an hour it would be safe for him to sleep. He prepared himself to meditate, for it was for this as well as for other things that he had come here. But as he settled his mind into stillness—sharp and clear and small as in a dream —he became aware that Starhawk had entered the city.

Like an echo in his mind, he seemed to hear the strike of hooves along the crumbling walls that spread out beyond the canyons. As he sometimes could, he called her to mind and saw her sitting her horse amid the faded tesselations of the old market square's broken pavement, the stir of dawn wind moving in her white head veils and the horse's flaxen mane. Then he saw her turn her head sharply, as if at some sound.

Very quickly, Sun Wolf descended the curved flight of buttercup sandstone steps to the wide room below. Beyond the spell-written doorsill, the canyon was filled with blue silence; the hush of the place was unnatural, for, in spite of the water in its few stone tanks, birds shunned the place. His feet scrunched on the drifts of sand and gravel as he hastened down the old road. In the hours when the demons still walked, it was too dangerous to take his horse.

As he'd hoped, Starhawk's good sense had kept her in open ground. She sat a sorrel nag from the Palace cavy at the mouth of the narrowest of the three canyons, turning her head cautiously, listening for sounds. The first light of the desert dawn lay full over her, glinting in the silver mountings of her dark green guards' doublet and jerkin and on the steel of sword hilt and dagger. Even as Sun Wolf saw her among the scattered ruins of waist-high walls and fallen pillars of shattered red porphyry, she leaned forward in the saddle, as if trying to catch the echo of some faint cry up in the canyon before her. Nearby, there was a sharp cracking noise, like stone falling from a great height upon stone, and her horse flung up its head, rolling a white, terrified eyed, and tried to bolt.

Starhawk was ready, and the Wolf guessed it wasn't the first such incident since she'd entered the ruins. She reined the frightened animal in a tight circle at the first skittish leap. Framed in the white veils, her sunburned face was impassive; but even at this distance, she looked stretched and taut, as she did when she'd been on patrol too long. As soon as she had the horse under control, he stepped from the shadows of a dilapidated archway and called out to her, "Hawk!"

She looked up, started to spur in his direction, then reined again. Holding in the nervous horse with one hand, she fished in her jerkin pocket for something, and the new light flashed across glass as she angled the mirror in his direction. Only then, satisfied, did she nudge the horse and trot through the drifted sand and bull thorns of the street to where he stood.

"What is it?" She would never, he knew, have come seeking him without reason.

"It's Tazey," Starhawk said quietly. "You'd better come."

"So she's been in a coma since then." Starhawk held her horse in, fighting its not unnatural eagerness to put large expanses of the reg between itself and the harsh, maroon-black cliffs of the Haunted Range's outward face. "Kaletha tried to get in to see her last night. Osgard won't hear of it, and it was all Nanciormis could do to keep him from throwing Kaletha out of the Household entirely." There was no change in her soft, slightly gruff voice as she added, "I think she's dying, Chief."

He glanced sharply over at her. The cuts on her face from the sand and rocks of the storm still glared red and ugly; her gray eyes were fixed ahead of her on the dark notch of Tandieras Pass, barely visible across the lifeless plain of black gravel. Nine years of fighting other peoples' wars for money had taught them both that it is difficult to ride or fight while in tears. Tears were for later.

Sun Wolf squinted with his single eye at his horseback shadow on the pea gravel underfoot, calculating the angle of the sun. "What time did you leave there?"

"Midnight. Osgard and Kaletha were still fighting."

"Wonderful." He pulled the end of his veil up over his mouth against the dust. "I can tell he's going to be thrilled to death to see me."

The shadows had turned and were beginning to

lengthen again when they rode up the trail to the dark
stone gatehouse of the Fortress on Tandieras Pass. "No
sound of mourning," was Sun Wolf's laconic comment.
Starhawk nodded. They were both thinking like warriors
of the next thing at hand—a cold-bloodedness they
understood in one another. Sun Wolf felt no obligation to
express his genuine fears for the girl, of whom he'd become fond in the few days he'd known her—nor did he
assume Starhawk's enigmatic calm to spring from un-
concern. If Tazey died, there would be time enough for
grief.

After three days of parched silence in the Haunted
Range, it seemed strange to him to see people moving
around and to smell water and cooking meats, stranger
still to realize he could believe in the reality of what he
saw. As they rode in under the gloom of the gatehouse, a
small, waiting shadow caught his eye. He reined in, letting Starhawk precede him into the dust-hazed confusion
of the stable yards. The shadow stepped forward, piti-
fully small and thin in his dark doublet and hose and the
sorry white ruffle at his neck. The pointy white face
looked pleadingly up at him through the gloom.

"How's your sister?" the Wolf asked quietly.

For a moment he had the impression Jeryn would run
away. Then the boy ducked his head and mumbled,
"You've got to help her. What's wrong with her is magic,
isn't it?"

"It is." Sun Wolf dismounted and stood looking down
at the skinny, furtive little boy. "And I'll do whatever I
can do—but only if *you* get yourself back into bed. The
Hawk tells me you caught one hell of a sunstroke coming
out to fetch me."

Jeryn colored slightly. "I'm better."

Sun Wolf put his hand under the boy's chin and forced
the head up to look critically into Jeryn's face. "The hell
you are," he replied evenly after a moment's study of the
too-white countenance under its short black curls. "A
man who doesn't rest his injuries isn't just a fool—

he's a liability to his commander, because they'll never heal properly and, sure as pox and blisters, they'll act up when he's needed most." He passed his hand roughly over the boy's hair, as if patting a dog. "I'll take care of your sister."

"Captain..." Jeryn hesitated, then swallowed hard. "I—I'm sorry. It was all my fault to begin with but—but Uncle Nanciormis said I was a coward for not standing up for you to Father. He said if I didn't like the way he taught me I should have tried to keep you here. And I—I'm *not* a coward," he insisted, with the wretchedness of one who knows he will not be believed. "It's just that..." He stopped, his lips pressed tight. Then, embarrassed to show his tears, he turned to flee.

"Jeryn."

Though it spoke so quietly, the rusted voice stopped him. He turned, fighting desperately not to cry.

"I never needed proof you were brave," the Wolf said. In the white frame of veils, his face seemed dark in shadows, with its unshaven jaw and single, panther—yellow-eye. "And I never saw any reason to think you were a coward. What's between your father and me is something you don't have to concern yourself with. It has nothing to do with you."

"No, sir," Jeryn whispered. "I'm sorry, sir."

The boy turned and started to run away when Sun Wolf asked, "Your dad with Tazey?"

He stopped again and turned back. "Yes, sir," he said. Then, matter-of-factly, "He's drunk, sir."

Sun Wolf nodded. "Fighting drunk or passing-out drunk?"

"Fighting drunk, sir."

"Wonderful." The Wolf sighed. "Thanks, Scout. Now you get to bed."

"Yes, Captain." And the boy was gone like a shadow.

"You have to hand it to the King for stamina," Sun Wolf grumbled, unwinding his head veils as he and Star-hawk climbed the sand-drifted path up from the stables toward the black, square towers of the Hold. "A man's got to be tough to stay fighting drunk for over twenty-four hours without moving along to the passing-out stage."

"I used to work for a man who could do it," Starhawk commented, as they mounted the outside stair. Sun Wolf checked his step as if she'd pinked him with a dagger in the back.

"That was different!"

"*Different* was one word for it," she agreed mildly.

Sun Wolf growled, "That's the damn thing about falling in love with your second-in-command," and resumed his stride up to the balcony with its row of arched doors, Starhawk unsmiling at his heels. "They are with you too long and they know you too well."

"Yes, Chief."

Jeryn and Taswind occupied the last two rooms along the balcony shared by the King's Household. The brazen sun slanted along the dark granite curve of the building's southern face, hurling the shadows of the two partners like an inky scarf into room after room. Anshebbeth, sitting in one of them, sprang up with a nervous cry, her hands reaching out, her face pale and hollowed with sleepless strain. When she saw who it was, she sank back and resumed twisting her hands.

Even out on the balcony, Sun Wolf could hear Osgard's braying voice.

"I won't have it, I tell you! That foul-mouthed nag Nexué's been all over the town, and there isn't a man who isn't saying my daughter's a witch!"

"Although I take exception to the connotations of the word *witch*," Kaletha's caustic voice said, "you cannot deny that what happened has proved that Taswind *is* mageborn."

"The hell I can't deny it!" He turned to loom furiously over Kaletha as Sun Wolf pushed aside the patterned curtain that led into the outer chamber of Tazey's rooms. "She's no more a witch than her mother was! A sweeter, dearer, more obedient girl never walked the face of the earth, do you hear me?"

Kaletha only stiffened and looked down her nose at the bloodshot, unshaven, sweaty giant before her. As usual, her dark red hair was pulled back in braids and loops as intricate as potter's work and her plain black homespun gown spotless; her very fastidiousness a scornful rebuke. "She is mageborn," she insisted stubbornly. "You owe it to her to let me teach her the ways of power."

"I owe it to her to keep her the hell away from you! I won't have it said, and I'll personally take and thrash you if you go near her with your sleep-spells and your weather-calling, and your filthy, stolen books! What man's going to want to marry her, Desert Lord or no Desert Lord, if lies like that go around?"

Her protuberant blue eyes blazed. "They are not lies, and there is no shame attached to it."

"You uppity hag! She'd die of shame before she'd be what you are! Get out of my sight, before I—"

"If you will admit me instead of that useless, whining Bishop—"

"To have her be your student?" Osgard roared, losing what little remained of his temper.

"She needs a teacher, and as I'm the only one—"

"What my daughter needs is a husband! I'll have the man crucified who says she's a witch—or woman, too! I tell you this—she'll never be a student of yours! Now get out!"

The inner door curtain moved, its woven pattern of reds and blues like a wind-stirred garden where the edge of the sunsplash hit it. The Bishop Galdron stepped through, white hands folded before his belt. Though minus his brocaded ceremonial tabard, he still reminded Sun Wolf of an overdressed doll, robe and stole and surcoat all worked with a blazing galaxy of jeweled hieratic symbols. His cold blue eyes touched Sun Wolf and the Hawk, still standing in the arched doorway, then moved to Kaletha. Sternly, he said, "Yes, go. You have done harm enough by your mere presence. Better Taswind had died than had damned her soul with witchery."

"She's no witch!" Osgard roared, livid.

"She is a witch." The old man's red lips folded taut within the silky frame of mustaches. "And as a witch, she is damned . . ."

"Get out off here, both of you!" Osgard's face was scarlet, a tear-streaked mess of graying stubble and broken veins. "You should talk about witchery, you stinking hypocrite, when your own acolyte has been keeping company with Kaletha for months!"

Galdron turned, startled and deeply shocked, and Kaletha could not repress a smile of smug and vicious triumph at his discomfiture. Then she swept past Sun Wolf and out onto the balcony. Galdron, face pink with anger, hastened at her heels. The curtain swirled in the backwash of their wake, then settled over the folded-back storm shutters once more.

Sun Wolf remained, facing the King.

"You . . ." Osgard's voice was thick and slurred. "You —it's your fault. My son ran away to see you . . ."

"Your son ran away because he was too scared of you to speak for me, and your daughter was too scared to ask your help." Sun Wolf folded his arms, his whole body relaxed into battle-waiting, a deceptive, hair-trigger readiness. "Now will you let me save her life, or are you going to have her die to prove yourself right?"

Osgard's face went white with speechless anger; Sun Wolf wondered clinically if he would suffer a stroke on the spot. Then, with a bellow like an exploding furnace, he roared, "I'll have you crucified for that! Guards!" In a swirling gust of stale wine fumes the King sprang for Sun Wolf's throat.

Reflecting in the split second between the King's attack and his own reaction that his father had been right when he'd cautioned him, in the name of all his ancestors, never to mess with magic or argue with drunks, Sun

Wolf sidestepped the attack. He blocked the outstretched hands with a swipe of one forearm and used the other hand to deliver a neat, straight punch to the stubbly jaw that the King walked directly into.

Osgard went down like a felled tree.

Sun Wolf stepped back from the unconscious King just as Nanciormis and half a dozen guardsmen came bursting through the door that led down to the inner stair from the Hall. For a moment the Wolf and Nanciormis faced one another across the slumped body, the guards clustering at his back and clutching their sword hilts in readiness for anything. Then the commander turned to the guards and said gravely, "His Majesty is fatigued. Take him to his room."

He stepped aside as they bore the King out past him and down the stairs, watching inscrutably until they turned the corner down into the Hall. Then he glanced back at Sun Wolf.

"I see I was wrong about the uses of magic," he said quietly. "Do what you can for her. I'll see you're left alone."

"I'd call that magnanimous of him," Starhawk remarked softly, as the commander passed through the wide arch out onto the balcony and thence, presumably, to his own room down at its farther end. "Except that he waited until he was damn sure nobody was around to hear him say it."

"Maybe." Sun Wolf watched thoughtfully as the vast curtain settled back to stillness once more against the hard glare of the arch. "He's a politician, Hawk—and as a politician he deals with the way things are, not how they're supposed to be. Whatever else can be said about him, he's enough of a shirdar lord to know that magic has nothing to do with the Bishop's threats of Hell."

He turned for the inner door to Tazey's room, and Starhawk said quietly, "'Shebbeth should be here."

He stopped, a little surprised, knowing she was right. For all she was a soldier, the Hawk had a woman's acute sensitivity to social usages. "If you think she'd be of any use, you're welcome to go look for her," he said. "Though it's my guess Osgard turned her out—and no wonder."

Starhawk paused, remembering the governess' tear-streaked face and hysterical hand-wringing, glimpsed through the balcony door, and said no more on the subject.

The windows of Tazey's small bedroom faced northwest, toward the harsh chaparral desert and the rugged mountains beyond. At this time of the day, the room was flooded with sunlight and, with the windows tightly shut in accordance with good medical practice, unbearably hot and close. The air was heavy with the smells of burned herbs, sickly after the dry movement of the desert air from which Sun Wolf had come. Tazey lay stretched out on her narrow bed; but for the movement of her young breasts under the sheet, she might have been dead already. Her tan stood out like a bad coat of paint against the underlying waxiness of her flesh; from the corners of her shut eyes ran the dried tracks of tears wept in her sleep.

Hesitantly, Sun Wolf knelt beside the bed and took the girl's hand in his. It felt cold. He counted the pulse, when he found it after long search, and it was leaden as a stream choked with winter ice. A lifetime on the battlefield had given him a certain skill at rough-and-ready surgery; later, Yirth of Mandrigyn had shown him the spells to hold the failing spirit to the flesh until the flesh had time to respond to medicines. But this was not a matter of the flesh at all. The symptoms resembled, if anything, those of freezing and exhaustion.

He had no idea where to start. He had healed warriors with warriors' means, but this was different. In the last nine months, he had done a very little healing by means of the few spells Yirth had taught him and had always been astonished when they worked. He looked down now at the girl's browned face against the pillow, the scattered, sun-streaked hair, and the blue smudges of exhaustion that shadowed the tensed eyelids. For the first time, he released his hold on a warrior's readiness and felt grief for her, grief and a terrible pity for what had befallen her.

He remembered her in the war dance—the light, buoyant strength of her movements, the joy in her eyes at being only what she was. In the few days he'd been in Tandieras he'd become fond of her, with a virile middle-aged man's affection for a young girl, that odd combination of paternalism and a sort of nonpersonal lust. But she was, he understood now, a wizard like himself, perhaps stronger than he. And she would be as terrified of her powers as he was of his. *The sweetest daughter a man could want,* her father had said of her. No wonder she was terrified to find herself, against her will, the thing he most wanted for her not to be. No wonder that knowledge drove her power inward, until her very soul was eating her body with guilt and grief and shame.

He let go of her hand and rose to open the casements of the windows, letting in the dry smell of the desert—the comforting mingle of stables, sage, and sky. Voices drifted to him—Kaletha's short and defiant from the courts below, the Bishop's full of querulous rage. Closer, he heard Anshebbeth's sobs, muffled, as if against bedding or a man's shoulder. Taking a stump of chalk from his pocket, he drew on the red-tiled floor around the bed one of the Magic Circles, a precautionary measure against evils that Yirth, when she had taught him this one, had been unable to define clearly. After a moment's thought, he also traced the runes of wizardry, of life, of strength, of journeys undertaken and safely completed— marks that would draw to them the constellations of influences and could help to focus his mind. It was all done by rote—he had never used them before and had no idea how to do so, but went through the motions as he would have undertaken weapons drill with an unfamiliar piece of equipment. There was no sense neglecting his teaching simply because it meant nothing to him yet.

He returned to the bed and took Tazey's hand.

He wondered if it was imagination, if it felt colder than it had. He drew three deep breaths and settled his mind to meditation. Clumsily, hesitantly, he pushed aside all the crowding worries and resentments, the random thoughts that the mind flings up to disguise its fear of stillness. He gathered light around him and, as if sinking into deep water, he sought the Invisible Circle, where he knew he would find Tazey hiding from herself.

She woke up crying. For a long time, she lay with her face turned away from him, sobbing as if everything within her body and soul had been torn out of her—*as indeed,* Sun Wolf thought, almost too weary for pity, *it had been.* He himself felt little but an exhaustion all out of proportion to the short time he felt he had meditated. Then, gently making her roll over, he rubbed her back as he had seen market women rub babies to soothe their wordless griefs.

Only after a time did he notice that the room was cool. The air outside the broad window had been drenched with light and heat when he had sunk into meditation; it was dark as pitch now. Listening, he tried to determine from the sounds in the building below how late it was, but that was difficult, for Tazey's illness had cast a pall of silence over the Citadel. Someone—Starhawk, probably—had kindled the two alabaster night lamps that rested on the carved ebony clothes chest, and molten lakes of light wavered on the ceiling above.

He felt weak and a little strange, as if he had swum for miles. His legs, doubled up under him, were stiff and prickly as he shifted position. For a long time, he was content to remain where he was, only rubbing the girl's back to let her know she was not alone. He had found her in the desolate country that borders the lands of death, wandering, crying, in darkness; he knew, and she knew, that she had not wanted to come back with him.

After a long time she turned her head on the pillow and whispered, "Is my father very angry?"

She was a mage like himself now, and he could not lie to her. Moreover, in the shadowlands of the soul there is always a bond between those who have sought and those who have been found. He said, "Yes. But you can't let that rule you anymore."

She drew in a quick breath and held it for a few seconds before letting it go. "I didn't want this," she said at last, her voice very thin. She lifted her face from the pillow, ugly, swollen, cut up with the violence of the sandstorm and crumply with tears. Her absinthe–green eyes were circled in lavender smudges, the eyes of the woman she would one day be. "I tried . . ."

"Jeryn knew enough to ask you where I was."

She nodded miserably. "I used to find things when I was little and he was just a baby. Once when he got lost in the old quarter of the Fortress I found him just by—by shutting my eyes and thinking about him. That's how I knew you were in Wenshar and how I knew he'd gone after you. But later I—I tried not to do it anymore." She sniffled, and wiped her reddened nose. "Does this mean that I'm damned?"

"It means that Galdron will say you are."

She was silent for a time, digesting this distinction, then said, "I didn't want this. I don't want to be a witch. Witches are . . ."

She paused and looked up at him.

"No one's asking you to decide right now," Sun Wolf said quietly. "But I, for one, want to thank you, with all my heart, for saving the Hawk's life. You saved Jeryn, too, and your friends Pothero and Shem."

"But they're afraid of me now," she murmured, and another tear crept down her puffy cheek.

"Probably," he agreed. "But I don't think Jeryn is, and I know the Hawk's not—so it isn't everybody."

Her voice was distant, wistful, as if she already knew she was speaking of someone else. "I don't want to change. I mean—I might not like what I'll become."

Tenderly, he brushed aside the snarly rats of her dust-laden hair. "Then don't change tonight," he replied. "You can't change at three in the morning anyway, nobody can . . ." Her sob caught on a laugh. "Sleep now."

"Will you . . ." She swallowed, embarrassed. "Do you think you could—could stay with me for a little while? I had dreams. . . . When I was asleep, before you found me, I dreamed . . . awful things. The Witches . . ."

"I'll be here," he reassured her softly, weary as he was from the long day's ride and from last night's watching. (He had been known to sit for longer than this in all-night watches on some enemy camps.) He held Tazey's hand, large and strong and warm now in his own, while her soft breathing evened toward dreamless sleep. Detachedly, he studied the smudgy, chalked circles around the bed—the Circle of Light, Yirth had called one, and the Circle of Darkness, though why they were so called she had not known. He shook his head. *Kaletha was right,* he thught. *She would have to be taught,* and he knew that neither he, nor, he suspected, Kaletha, was equipped to do it.

Another thought crossed his mind, and he frowned, wondering why it had not occurred to him before—not only for Tazey, but for himself.

Tazey murmured something, stirred in her sleep, and then lay quiet again. Though she still slept lightly, he could see no dreams tracking her discolored eyelids. Soundless, as if on patrol, he climbed stiffly to his feet and crossed to the curtained door.

"Hawk?" he said softly into the dimness beyond.

There was no reply.

He stepped past the curtain to the candlelit outer room. Muted radiance played over the carved wooden armoire, the oak chairs with their red leather seats, and the little round corner fireplace. On the polished sideboard, a couple of candles in silver holders shed soft rings of brightness. The heavy curtains had been drawn over the archway to the balcony—a stray gust of dry wind stirred them, a ripple of reflected flame danced along their gilt borders. There was no one there.

He walked to the other doorway, which led to the inner stair down to the Hall. Through it he could see torchlight and shadow from the hall below playing across the stone vaults. A muffled clamor of voices came to him, rising and falling, agitated but unintelligible. *If Galdron's making more trouble for her,* he thought grimly, *or Nexué . . . If Kaletha's carrying on again about her poxy rights . . .*

A shadow swept across the red glow from beneath, and a moment later he heard a cat-soft stride on the stairs that could only be Starhawk's.

"What is it?" he asked when she appeared in the doorway.

Her face inexpressive, she said, "Nexué the laundress."

Sun Wolf's single yellow eye glinted dangerously. "What's the bitch been up to now?"

"Not much," said Starhawk calmly. "She's dead."

CHAPTER

—— 7 ——

WITH QUIET VICIOUSNESS, ANSHEBBETH SAID, "I can't say I'm surprised to hear it. Sooner or later someone was bound to wring that filthy old woman's neck." She stared into the fire with dark eyes that smoldered like the logs crumbling there.

"Don't talk like that." Kaletha shot her an angry sidelong glance; in her black homespun lap, Sun Wolf observed that her hands were shaking.

The governess looked up at her, hurt at the rebuke. "You—" she began, and Kaletha cut her off.

"Hatred is an impurity of the soul as foul as the fornications of the body," she said too quickly. "If I've taught you nothing else, you should have learned that."

Her dark eyes filling with wounded tears, Anshebbeth nodded, her hand stealing to her tightening throat as she mumbled that she had not meant it. Annoyed, Kaletha looked away. Egaldus, talking quietly with Nanciormis, the Bishop, and two shaken-looking guardsmen down near the door, raised his head at the shrillness of her

words; but after a moment's hesitation, he stayed where
he was.

Quietly, Sun Wolf moved to the wine cabinet at the far
side of the dais from the dim glow of the hearth where
the two women sat, and filled two silver goblets of wine.

"That's your answer to everything, isn't it?" demanded Kaletha as Sun Wolf's shadow fell over her.
"Drink—like that pathetic sot Osgard . . ."

"My answer to everything is having you relax,
woman."

"I am relaxed, and I don't need your wine, nor does
'Shebbeth." Anshebbeth stopped her hand in mid-reach
for the goblet, then obediently folded it with her other in
her lap.

Nanciormis left the little group beside the arched vestibule doors and strode the length of the Hall to the dais
to put a gentling hand on Anshebbeth's shoulder. In the
wavery glow of the sconces on either side of the hearth,
his curving black brows stood out sharply, as if, beneath
the bronze of his tan, he had gone pale at what he had
heard.

"Perhaps Anshebbeth should go up and sit with Lady
Taswind," he suggested softly. "I need to speak with the
Captain alone for a few moments." To Sun Wolf, in private, he had made any number of crude jests at the governess's expense, but part of his charm lay in his
knowing when to say the right thing.

Shebbeth's anxious glance shifted from Nanciormis to
Kaletha, but Kaletha, still irrationally annoyed with her
subservience, looked away in pointed disgust. That she
would have been still more annoyed had Anshebbeth not
immediately agreed with her, as she had done in the public gardens when the subject of physical love came up,
evidently had no bearing on the matter. Anshebbeth,
with the tight misery on her face of one who knows she
can do no right, gathered her dark skirts and hastened
away up the winding stair.

"At least that gets *her* out of our hair," Nanciormis

murmured, taking one of the goblets from Sun Wolf's hand and leading him away from the carved bench where Kaletha now sat alone. "How is Tazey?"

Sun Wolf shook his head. "Sleeping all right, now," he said softly. "She'll live—but I tell you right now, she won't be the same."

The commander let out his breath in a sigh. "Dear Gods—" He used the shirdar word for gods. "Never in a hundred years would I have thought Jeryn would try to go after you. Frankly, I didn't think the boy had it in him—but it was a stupid thing to say, nevertheless."

"What did you say?" The Wolf paused in his step and regarded the commander curiously under the harsh doubled light of a pair of torches on the wall.

The gold rings that held his braids flashed as Nanciormis shook his head. "I no longer remember exactly, though I should. He'd been whining all afternoon—that Sun Wolf hadn't made him climb ropes and Sun Wolf hadn't made him do tumbling and Sun Wolf hadn't made him lift weights—which I knew perfectly well you had. At last I lost my temper and said that if he preferred your teaching, he should have had the nerve to stand up to his father for you. That's all. I *never* meant that he should go after you." He took a quick gulp of the wine; some of the color was returning to his heavy cheeks. "And now this . . ."

Sun Wolf glanced along the Hall to the guards, still grouped in a whispering cluster around the dark archways to the vestibule. "What happened?"

Nanciormis took another drink and shook his head. "It must have happened sometime late last night," he said quietly. "Whoever did it has to have been tremendously strong. Nexué was literally hacked into pieces. I don't know what they used—an axe or a scythe, perhaps . . ." He swallowed, still shaken by the memory.

He had seen war, Sun Wolf thought. *This was different.*

"A strong man can do a lot of damage with a sword."

He turned his own untouched cup in his hands, watching the torch-glare flash on the dark wine, but not drinking. He had eaten nothing since their nooning stop at the edge of the reg, and he knew his capacity for wine was not what it once had been. "And this happened last night?"

"Or early this morning. She was found in one of the old workshops in the empty quarter—by the blood trail, she'd been pursued there . . ."

"What was she doing down there?"

Nanciormis let out an ironic bark of laughter. "There's a servants' privy near the wall—by the look of it that's where she was bound, though she could have been going anywhere. Nexué was a sneak and a spy as well as a gossip—there wasn't much going on in the Citadel she didn't know about. The empty quarter's been used for assignations before this."

"And she wasn't found until *tonight*?" Sun Wolf's tufted eyebrows plunged down over his nose, making the worn eye patch shift.

"What with . . ." Nanciormis hesitated. Even with Osgard snoring in his bedchamber, he was treading softly. "With the uproar over Taswind, no one noticed her absence until this evening when the wind turned."

"What about the dogs?"

"Dogs?" Nanciormis looked blank.

"There are dogs all over this Fortress. You're not telling me they weren't at the corpse."

The commander frowned suddenly, seeing the anomaly. "They weren't," he said after a moment. "Nor were the raverns, now that you speak of it, and there are always a few of them hanging around the kitchen middens. Now why . . . ?"

"I'd like to have a look at the place."

Nanciormis nodded. Sun Wolf glanced back—Starhawk was sitting on the bench beside Kaletha with her arm around those slender, bowed dark shoulders. The

Bishop being out of the room, Egaldus was hunkered down before the White Witch, holding her hands and speaking soft words of comfort to her. Kaletha sat rigid, shaking her head stubbornly again and again.

Though Sun Wolf said nothing, Starhawk looked up at him and, with a final, gentle pat, rose from Kaletha's side. As she joined him and they began to walk toward the door of the Hall, Sun Wolf paused and looked back at Nanciormis. "Osgard know?" he asked.

The commander's full-lipped mouth quirked with scorn. "Would it do any good if he did?"

"You'll have to be gone by daybreak," Starhawk said as she and the Wolf wound their way through the small courts around the Hold's long southern side toward the little gate that led to the empty quarter. "Osgard gave me the word I could stay—apparently they really need guards because working in the mines pays twice what the King does—but he made it damn clear I'd better not mention how I happened not to get killed by the sand-storm."

"What's his alternative explanation?"

She shrugged. Even with the moon on the wane, its light was strong enough to cast shadows beneath the small adobe gateway. Looking back at the Hold, the Wolf could see the glow of the night lamps in Tazey's rooms, turning the curtained arch to a dully glowing gold like a banked oven. He didn't remember who all else those rooms belonged to, save for the one with the rose reflection of candlelight, which must be Jeryn's. He paused in the small gateway, looking down at the sloping path across the little court beyond, and an odd shiver went down his spine at the sight of the black door to the cell he and the Hawk had shared.

Matter-of-factly, Starhawk went on, "I don't think he has one, not even for himself."

"He'd better," the Wolf growled. "She's got to be taught."

She glanced up at him in the ivory–yellow moonlight. "Who taught Kaletha, I wonder?"

He grinned. Starhawk might not be mageborn, but she understood more about how magic had to work than anyone the Wolf had ever talked to. "It occurred to me to wonder that myself when I was up with Tazey. I've been thinking Kaletha sprang her 'destiny' on the other people here in Tandieras cold, but... There has to have been somebody, even if he never declared his own powers for fear of Altiokis. Beyond a doubt, he or she is dead now, because we haven't heard of any other wizard—but there could have been another student. If we can find out who that wizard was and back-trail him..."

"I don't know," the Hawk said doubtfully. "I've listened to her teach. Now, when you taught back at the warrior's school in Wrynde, it was always, 'My father always said...' or 'The captain of Queen Izacha's bodyguard showed me this...' But she hands it all down as if she'd invented it."

Sun Wolf paused, realizing what it was about Kaletha's teaching that had rubbed him the wrong way. "In other words, she wouldn't say." He leaned his wide shoulders in the broken adobe of the gateway. The moonlight, where it touched his hair, turned it to wan and faded gold. Across the court a pack rat slipped from the door of their cell, ran a few paces, stopped to sit up, sniffing cautiously at the cold air, then dashed in a tiny skiff of thrown sand to the camel-bush beside the old well. "She's close with her power," the Wolf went on slowly. "She wants to stay the teacher, to hold her disciples to her—she likes the power it gives. If there is competition for the post, she's not going to let anyone know. But in a place like this, you can't hide the kind of relationship teacher and student have to have. It takes years to learn, Hawk—if she'd been that close to someone that long, somebody would know."

"'Shebbeth," Starhawk said promptly. "She's been

here at least ten years. Jealous as she is of anyone who's Kaletha's friend, you bet she'd know."

"And she'd probably tell," the Wolf said, "if only to run them down." He looked back over his shoulder to the amber warmth of the archway at the top of the outside stair. "She'll keep," he said. "She's with Tazey now and shouldn't be leaving her. Come on." He shoved himself off the wall with one shoulder and moved out into the cold moonlight of the court, the sandy gravel scrunching under his boots. "There's a lot to do and not much left of the night."

They found Nexué's tracks easily—Starhawk could have done so herself without Sun Wolf's ability to see in darkness. Even the scrubby, wire grass and camel-thorn cast frail shadows by the brilliance of the westering moon. The path to the servants' privies out beyond the stable hugged the wall, but, since the storm, no one had crossed the little court itself. A single line of smudgy marks veered sharply away from the packed earth of the path, first back toward the gate, then away past the cells into the empty quarter.

"She must have seen someone standing about there in the shadows of the corner of the wall," the Wolf guessed, studying them. "Or heard something . . ."

"Heard, most likely." Starhawk picked her way carefully through the drifted sand left by the storm. "There are no marks in that shadow."

Sun Wolf grunted to himself. He could see where Nexué had changed direction and run, not back toward the gate, but across the court to the mazes of crumbling adobe walls and barred black moonlight of the empty quarter. Circling, he kept his eyes to the ground, moving cautiously so as not to foul other marks. But even with a wizard's vision in darkness, he saw no print, no mark, no reason that would have caused the old woman to do so.

Someone on the path, perhaps? In the ensuing twenty-four hours between the incident and its discovery, scores of servants had taken this route to the privies. *Still* . . .

Drift-sand from the storm lay deep in the court, poured in little dunes through the door of the abandoned cell. Nexué's tracks were only a desperate shuffle—her run must have been slow and scuffling, with sand and pea gravel kicked back in sloppy crescents behind her. If someone had run in her tracks, the footmarks were only blurred dents, tangled with hers.

Yet something made the Wolf uneasy. The empty quarter lay silent as death around him as he stalked the trail to its obvious and pitiful conclusion—the first drippy smattering of blood, where some swung weapon had made its contact with flesh, then the hand mark where Nexué had stumbled, caught herself, and fled desperately on through the parched, empty courts. The blood had dried during the intervening day, but the old dye shop where she had finally fallen reeked of it still. Looking around him at the dark stains lying like shadows where no shadows should be, Sun Wolf felt a kind of thankfulness that it was now the coldest part of the night and there were no insects.

Nexué had been a gross and dirty-minded old woman, he thought, *but still . . . By the amount of blood, she must have run about here for a long time.*

What was left of the body had been taken away. The ground was a scuffed muck of confused tracks of the guards, Nanciormis, and the Bishop. Impersonally, Sun Wolf cursed them all.

"Not a single damn killer's track," he muttered as he and Starhawk retraced their route back through the empty courts and the walkways whose roofs had been stripped away by decades of autumn storms and whose shattered rafters slanted down amid the sand drifts to impede their steps. Somewhere in the stillness an owl hooted; there was the swift skitter of sand, a shadow passing soundlessly overhead, and a faint squeak of pain. Sun Wolf's boots slid heavily in the drifted sand between two walls, then ground on the harsh gravel beyond. "And if they had the wits to run along the tops of the broken walls, they could have gotten clean away without leaving so much as a mark. There's a dozen dry wells and pits where a weapon and bloodstained clothing could have been dropped..." He paused, frowning, his single eye glinting like transparent amber in the zebra shadows. "I don't like this, Hawk."

She nodded, understanding what he meant. Around them, the empty quarter was silent as death.

"Could you have done it?"

"Physically?" She shook her head. "Oh, maybe with one of those big two-handed swords like Eo the Blacksmith used to use—the kind that, even if she hit you with the flat of it, would break your back. But there wasn't room in some of those corridors to use something like that, and you sure as hell couldn't do it running. No." She folded her arms, looking around her at the silent mazes of sand and half-fallen adobe. "I can understand someone wanting to kill her to shut her up about something—the Mother knows she was a spy as well as a gossip and spread her filth around like a monkey. But —they found her literally in pieces, Wolf. Someone chased her through those courts and walls for nearly a hundred yards. What they did to her was more than just murder—and I can think of only one person who was big enough and strong enough to cut her up that way and who wanted to shut her up."

Sun Wolf nodded. Before them, the bulk of the Hold was mostly dark now as the final commotions of magic and murder lapsed into exhausted repose. The light still burned in Tazey's room at one end of the long southern balcony. At the southeastern end of the jagged block of crenelated granite, another rectangle of wine gold showed where a lamp still glowed in the King's solar.

The Wolf said slowly, "We can't know he was the only one, Hawk. There could have been others, for other reasons or maybe for the same reason. But yes—I'd sort

of like to know where Osgard was around this time last
night."

When Sun Wolf ascended the stair that curved up
over the Hold's southern face, the rooms along the balcony were silent. Below and around him, the velvet
darkness had turned to ash; eastward, the slag-colored
bulk of Mount Morian loomed against the first stains of
dawn. Like candlelight caught on a needle's tip, the spire
of the cathedral below glinted with wakening gold. Pin-
pricks of light across the mountain's feet showed where
men and women were already rising to breakfast in darkness before going on shift in the mines. Standing on the
balcony, the Wolf sensed all the furtive movements of
the night winding to a close—foxes and coyotes in the
empty mile between town and Fortress trotting back to
their burrows in the rocks, licking the last dabs of blood
from their whiskers, wrens and wheatears waking to
whistle their territories in the dark.

In Tazey's room, the candles still burned. Sun Wolf,
hidden in the fold of shadow and curtain, softly called
Anshebbeth's name, remembering how sound carried
against the long southern face of the Hold, but got no
reply. Stepping soundlessly across to the inner chamber,
he saw Tazey tossing restlessly in unquiet sleep; there
was no sign of her governess. He cursed the woman for
leaving her and crossed to the bed to lay his hand over
the girl's fingers. They felt hot. Her face looked flushed
and swollen, as if with fever; when he bent over her, she
turned her head away, whispering desperately, "I won't!
I won't!"

With a touch astonishingly light for such massive
hands, he brushed aside the snarly hair from her face.
"You don't have to, Tazey," he murmured, though he
could tell she was deep asleep.

She gave a little sob and quieted; he remained kneeling beside the bed, where he had spent so many hours
that afternoon, until she appeared easier in her dreams.

It seemed incredible to him that this was part of that same night.

When her breathing had settled into evenness again, he got to his feet and moved softly through the outer room once more and out to the balcony. As Tazey's governess, Anshebbeth should have a room near hers, though privately he suspected she was with Kaletha, wherever Kaletha was. 'Shebbeth was genuinely fond of her charge, but he'd seen her abandon Tazey any number of times, when she should have been playing chaperone, to go scurrying to the Witch's side. *And overwrought as she had been down in the Hall earlier,* he thought, *Kaletha just might have asked it of her.*

But he was wrong.

The curtains were drawn shut over the next arch, but a strip of roseate light lay like a petticoat hem on the tiles beneath. He listened for a moment, but heard no sound, then gently pushed the curtain aside.

Anshebbeth startled up from the divan. "My love, what . . . ?" she began, seeing his dark shape against the night; then, as he stepped into the light, her sleep-flushed face scalded crimson, then drained white. She hastily pulled her unfastened gown across her narrow breasts, shaking fingers tangling with the unbound swatches of her black hair as she clutched the collar up to her throat. Her shoes lay separate, fallen, on two sides of the divan; the warm air redolent with the pungence of sex.

His whole mind one giant, astonished question, Sun Wolf only said, "You should be with Tazey. She shouldn't be alone."

"No—of course not—" she twittered inaudibly, fumbling at buttons, her huge dark eyes cast down. "That is—I came in here to—to lie down. I was so tired—the news about Nexué . . ."

He looked from the rucked cushions of the divan to her narrow white toes, peeping, somehow obscene, from beneath the crumpled skirts. Starhawk, he thought, would be vastly interested, as he was himself—it came to him in a burst of enlightenment why 'Shebbeth had spoken out in favor of carnality and called down Kaletha's scorn on her head.

"It's none of my business," he said quietly. "But I have to be gone from here at dawn, and there's something I want to ask you."

She turned back, her narrow face suspicious as she finger-combed her thick hair back, her black eyes darting over the tiled floor in quest of hairpins. They were strewn everywhere, as a man's plucking hand would leave them scattered. Sun Wolf picked up two and walked over to give them to her. He had never considered her a pretty woman, though physical beauty meant less to him that it once had; more than her thin, pointy plainness, her obsessive clinginess repulsed him. The cruel jests Nanciormis made of her were not entirely unjustified. She took the hairpins from his hand without touching his fingers; her eyes did not meet his. "What?" she asked.

He did not sit on the divan, knowing she would have shrunk from him. "It's to help Tazey," he said gently, and she relaxed a little and looked up into his face. "And she's going to need help."

Anshebbeth drew in her breath and let it go in a tense sigh. She was taut as wet rope, as if holding herself in. Sun Wolf fetched a chair from against the wall and sat opposite her; he saw her relax a little more, now that his physical size did not tower over her. Shrilly, she said, "Kaletha is more than willing to help. But that—that pathetic sot of a father of hers won't let her." She brought out Kaletha's words pat. "He'd rather see her die than admit she was born with the power."

"I know," said the Wolf. "That's what I need to talk to you about. Tazey's father and Kaletha don't get along—I think that's one reason he's refusing to accept her help or the help of any of her students."

"He's just being unreasonable," she returned, speaking rapidly, still not meeting his eyes. She pushed one hairpin in, but dropped the other nervously. It glinted in her sable lap with the coppery gleam of the lamp. "He's a stubborn old drunkard who won't see Kaletha's power, her skill, her destiny—"

Sun Wolf held up his hand. "I know that. But neither you, I, nor Kaletha, can help what he is."

"He can admit he's been wrong..."

"But he won't."

"He should," she insisted stubbornly, and Sun Wolf felt a surge of sympathy for Nanciormis' cruel jokes.

"And he may—but maybe not early enough to help Tazey." Anshebbeth started to make a comeback to this, and he went resolutely on. "All we can do is deal with the situation as it is. Osgard doesn't believe Kaletha, doesn't credit her power, I think partly because he's known her all her life. But another wizard might have a chance."

"It's Kaletha's right to be her teacher." The thin white hands clenched in her lap as she leaned forward. "It's her destiny."

"Maybe," said Sun Wolf, wondering how Anshebbeth could go on championing the cause of a teacher who he had seen treat her like an importunate dog. "But if there's a fight over it with Osgard, it's Tazey who's going to suffer."

Anshebbeth's mouth tightened, as if she would protest Kaletha's rights in the matter yet again, but she did not. She looked down at her long, thin hands, turning the fallen hairpin over and over again in her lap, and said nothing.

"Who was Kaletha's teacher?"

She raised her eyes at that and answered immediately, pride in her voice. "Oh, she didn't have one."

Sun Wolf frowned. "What do you mean, didn't have one? You don't just...just make up spells. Someone has to teach you."

The governess shook her head, the expression on her face the smug, proud look of a girl who is friends with the prettiest girl in school. "Kaletha didn't need a teacher. And, in any case, there was no one—since the destruction of Wenshar, there has been violent, unreasonable prejudice against the mageborn throughout these lands. Her destiny led her to books of magic, lost for centuries, but she had the power before then. I knew it even when she was just a young girl and I first came here to be Taswind's governess. It glowed out of her, like the flame in an alabaster lamp." Her face changed as she remembered that imperious red-haired girl; soft eagerness suffused her voice. "She was seventeen, beautiful, proud, and pure—even then—as if she knew her destiny. And there were many men who—who—who would have dishonored her purity, if they could. But she was strong, disdaining such abasement..." Her voice faltered, and color mounted again in her pale cheeks. She hastened on, "Right from the beginning, though I am the elder, it was she who was my teacher, not I hers. She—"

"What books?" He had heard her on the subject of Kaletha before. Osgard's words came back to him, *your filthy, stolen books* . . . "Where did she get them?"

"She would never say." Her hand fidgeted nervously at her throat, but she looked glad to speak of something other than Kaletha's idea of purity. "I never saw them, myself. But if it had not been the books, she would have grown in her powers in some other way. And it is much harder," she added nervously, "to achieve that kind of skill simply from books without a teacher. All that she has, she has striven for herself—with meditation, self-denial, and—and her own mind. She is one of those people who cannot help but be great. I..." Her voice trailed off. Nervously, she stroked the disheveled cushions of the divan, her black hair spilling down, all wrinkled from its braids, to curtain her crimsoning face. "I will never be great. My honor is—has always been—to help her. She knows this. We understand one another."

She understands you, anyway, the Wolf thought, with

cynical pity. *You poor deluded bitch.* But he only said, "Where are these books?"

But Anshebbeth would only shake her head, unwilling—or unable—to say.

Starhawk was waiting for him at the bottom of the stairs. He tried to think when she must last have slept, before riding out to Wenshar to fetch him—and, that, after the sandstorm and all that had happened since. But as usual, she gave the impression that, if he had suggested immediate and bloody battle, she would only have asked in which direction the enemy lay.

He sighed. He himself felt utterly weary, the tiredness coming on him suddenly, like the rising tides of the distant sea. Daylight and darkness memories telescoped together: bluish lights wavering among pillared shadows upon which they cast no brightness; Osgard's thick, slurring voice raised in anger; and a single line of desperately stumbling footprints through the drifted sand of an empty, moonlit court. The moon stood now over the Binnig Rock, a baroque pearl on the gray silk sky.

"You'd better go." Starhawk leaned her elbow on the smooth granite of the balustrade, the line of her body reminding him of a lioness in its easy strength. He saw now she'd washed and changed clothes at some time during the night; she was always as clean as a cat when she wasn't up to her elbows in other people's blood. "They tell me you can make a pretty decent living as a miner—the pay's twice what guards get."

Sun Wolf looked up at the line of dark archways on the balcony above—the balcony where he remembered Starhawk saying she'd seen a man slip into one of those rooms, and heard a woman's startled cry, on the night he and Nanciormis had come walking back from drinking with the King. He remembered, too, Starhawk's voice that night, calling out to him from the frosted moonlight of the court, warning him of danger whose existence she could not prove.

Then he glanced back toward the dove-colored bulk

of that gate. Nexué had passed through it, on her way to what had turned out to be her death. He wondered if the birds in the empty quarter had been silent that morning, as they had been when he had found the slaughtered doves.

"I don't think I should leave, Hawk," he said quietly.

Her tone was judicious. "King's gonna be sore when he sees you in the Hall for breakfast."

He didn't take up her jest. "Smuggle me some. I'll be a couple of courtyards into the empty quarter." Even as he said it, he felt a shiver, remembering again the blood-splattered adobe, the sifted gray dust untouched by tracks. Beyond the little gate he could see the maze of walls and rafters and courtyards filled with drifted sand and broken tiles—the unburied corpse of a fortress. The woman beside him straightened up and tucked her hands into her sword belt, a stance she had picked up over the years from him. The first glow of dawn glinted like cold steel dew on the studding of her jerkin. She regarded him with eyes the color of the gray-winter sky, not surprised. But then, the Hawk was never surprised.

"Why ever Nexué was killed, that butchering wasn't the act of a sane man. And maybe it wasn't the act of a man at all. There's a stink about this, Hawk, a stink of evil. I don't know who's going to need protection, but somebody sure as hell will."

CHAPTER

—— 8 ——

*T*HROUGHOUT THAT DAY AND THE NEXT, SUN WOLF
lay hidden in the empty quarter. When he went to earth
there in the dawn after the finding of Nexué's body, it
was with a certain uneasiness, but he slept dreamlessly
in one of the long dormitories, which still retained its
roof. He took the time to scratch the Circle of Light and
the Circle of Darkness in the dust around him, not
knowing whether they would work against a supernatu-
ral danger and not knowing what that danger might be. It
was only an edge, a possibility—like covering his tracks.
Waking with the noon sun glaring through the holes in
the roof where, over the years, storms had blown tiles
loose, he saw a camel-spider the size of his out-spread
hand trundle determinedly over the uneven curves of the
dirt-covered floor, stop at the edge of the outer Circle,
then skirt it as if it were a pool of water.

During the day, Sun Wolf remained indoors and under
cover. Too many windows and battlements of the Fortress overlooked the sprawl of those decaying walls. In

his heart, he did not really fear Osgard's threat to have him crucified if he ever showed his face in Tandieras again . . . but that was Osgard sane.

Someone had cut Nexué to pieces, and Sun Wolf was not about to make the mistake of thinking that drunken yelling was all the King might do in his rage.

When darkness fell, he moved out of the few roofed buildings and looked for tracks. Even in a desert climate, adobe structures decayed very rapidly once they lost their roofs; the maze of the empty quarter consisted of many walls only a few feet high as well as cells, chambers, and dormitories, whose roofs had but recently fallen but still retained their semblance of being rooms. Drifts of sand, gravel, and broken roof tiles lay everywhere, stitched with tracks: the ladderlike marks of sidewinders, the feathering of lizard tracks, light bird prints like the ancient shirdar runes he had seen carved in the butter-colored sandstone of Wenshar. The adobe walls were five feet thick and more—it was easily possible for a human killer to have run along the tops of them, leaving no marks on the sand below. But nowhere around the blood-splattered dyer's workshop did he find signs of a man's weight having passed along the top of the walls.

Like the foxes that slept in their holes all day, Sun Wolf prowled the maze of shadows in the checkered moonlight. In the northern courtyards he sensed a trace of magic, the uneasy scent of spells in the darkness. As he had when scouting beneath the walls of an enemy city, he sank close to the ground, putting himself below a standing man's line of sight, aware that the indigo velvet of the shadows would be no concealment from mageborn eyes. He followed the magic, like a thread of perfume. Oddly, he sensed no danger, but a moment later saw a scorpion, barbed tail held high, veer suddenly out of its way and go scurrying off in another direction. He remembered again how the birds had fallen silent the morning he had found the dead doves.

Cautiously, he slipped forward; as he looked over the sill of a decapitated wall, he heard a woman moan.

The man and woman in the cell beyond lay twined together, the moonlight that poured through the broken roof covering their legs from the thighs down like a cast-back silken sheet. Where it struck the clothes on which they lay, Sun Wolf could see the glitter of bullion embroidery against black homespun, the tabard written over with the holy runes of the Trinitarians. In the shadows, his wizard's sight picked out the soft surge of the full breast and the young man's arm, white as the body of the woman he clasped. Gold hair tumbled, mingling with unraveling coils of smoky red.

It was none of his business, he knew, as he moved back with all the silence of those hundreds of night-scout missions. But it did occur to him to wonder whether, after all her talk of purity, Kaletha had ever seen Nexué spying on her here.

For Starhawk it was an interesting time. She had always enjoyed watching people, taking a deep and satisfied delight in seeing her friends behave exactly like themselves, whether for good or ill. She had always done this, and it had never earned her popularity. Neither her brothers and their sweethearts, the nuns in the Convent of St. Cherybi where she had grown up, nor the other mercenaries of Sun Wolf's troop had felt particularly comfortable under the nonjudgmental gaze of those calm gray eyes. Perhaps this was because, as an outsider, she was frequently amused by what was going on and, often at the same time, felt deep and genuine concern.

In two days of quietly standing guard and attending Kaletha's lectures in the gardens of Pardle Sho, she sometimes had the impression of lying on the bank of a water hole, watching from a blind as the animals came down to drink.

Tazey remained in her bed, for the most part only lying and looking at the ceiling, though occasionally she wept. It had cost Starhawk little to leave her family and enter the convent, but she still remembered with agonizing clarity the single long night she had spent trying to decide whether to remain there quietly among women she had known all of her short life or to follow the dark and violent path of a man she had spoken to only once, a man who had touched off in her soul a powder keg of longings which, in her heart, she knew could never again be quenched. Her greatest fear, she remembered, had been that she would turn into someone she did not want to be—someone she would not even want to know. But she had known, from the first moment she understood that Sun Wolf would admit her into his troop, that there was no way back. She would either go, or know forever that she had not gone.

Whatever lay beyond the silent wall that guarded the future, Starhawk's heart ached for the girl and her lonely choice.

It would help, she thought with impersonal anger, *if they would simply leave Tazey alone*. But of course they did not. Her father came, sober, grave, his sweat smelling of last night's liquor in the dense heat of morning, and talked gently to her, calling her his little girl. Tazey agreed with what he asked her but when she was alone, she wept hopelessly for hours. The Bishop Galdron put in his appearance, too, speaking in measured, mellifluous tones about the Nine Hells and predestined choices. Starhawk, meeting him on the stairs coming down from the balcony of the Household, informed him that if he ever spoke so to Tazey again she would personally slit his nostrils.

"The man is a bigot and a hyporcrite," Kaletha said primly, folding her hands amid the jagged sun-splashes that fell through the arbor onto her black homespun knees. "He cannot possibly sincerely believe that the use of one's wizardry automatically condemns one to eternal damnation. But even so, a threat of physical violence, however much you may not have meant it, reflects badly on us all."

Starhawk shrugged. "If I were a wizard, or even wanted to be a wizard," she said evenly, "you might have a point—always supposing I accepted your right to judge my conduct." Kaletha started a little, but hastily got her first reaction in hand and did her best not to show her surprise that any one in her company would not automatically accept her dictates. *In her more human moments,* Starhawk thought obliquely, *Kaletha has the grace to realize the hubris of that assumption.* Around them, the public gardens of Pardle Sho were somnolent under the heat; its few spiky cacti and dark boulders, which were all that graced this particular high court, reminded her for some reason of the Wolf.

Starhawk went on, "And yes, I did mean it. Tazey has to make her own choice in this. Whether she decides to turn her back on her father and a potential husband or hurt for the rest of her life pretending that sandstorm never happened, it's *her own choice*, and Galdron has no business waving Hell under her nose. Either way, she's going to have enough hurting to do as it is."

"The man is a boor..." Anshebbeth began, looking up from a meditation upon which she had clearly not been concentrating.

"No," Kaletha corrected. "He's very civilized—it's what makes him dangerous."

"It makes him believable, at any rate," Egaldus added thoughtfully. He was seated on the granite bench in the latticed shade beside Kaletha; the bench was only large enough to seat two comfortably, but Anshebbeth had crowded onto the end of it under the pretext of needing to speak to Kaletha and had gone into her meditation there rather than moving to another bench. It automatically included her in any conversation, and Starhawk, having watched her find reasons to follow Kaletha from where they had formerly been sitting, guessed that changing seats again probably would not shake her.

The young novice's face settled into a curiously adult line as he went on, "My Lord Bishop has the gift of always having a plausible answer, always having some alternative possibility. You know he's coming up to the Fortress tonight, with a scheme for sending Tazey to an outlying nunnery in the foothills near Farkash on the coast. Disinheriting her, in effect, but also exiling her."

Kaletha's face flushed with anger. "He can't! In any case, sending her away from any possibility of being properly taught won't make her any the less mageborn!"

"No," Egaldus said drily. He stood up, the sunlight tipping the thick masses of his fair hair like a soft, sparkling halo around his face. "But it seems to be Galdron's current panacea." His blue eyes looked gravely down into those of the woman before him, and he sighed. "He's talking about doing it to me as well."

As if her throat had been cut, the White Witch's high color ebbed to wax. Not quite aware of what she did, she reached out to take his hand.

The young man went on, "He's learned about . . ." He glanced at Starhawk, Anshebbeth watching them with devouring black eyes, and the other students—Pradborn Dyer, Luatha Welldig, and Shelaina Clerk—meditating or chanting quietly to themselves on other benches along the uneven, latticed walk. "About my being your student," he finished. "He speaks of sending me to Dalwirin or even to Kwest Mralwe."

A little numbly, Kaletha said, "He is your mentor. You told me yourself he looked upon you as his chosen novice, his eventual successor."

Egaldus nodded. "That's what he can't forgive. That after he's favored me, I'd dare find the spark within myself and come to you to kindle it to flame. It's why I have to learn from you all I can before I go, if I'm to be on my own."

Her face changed at that. Starhawk felt it, almost like a physical cooling of the air as Kaletha's hand slipped away from his, and her body settled back just a fraction on the bench. Egaldus felt it as well. His blue eyes had an odd, calculating glint as he regarded her, his head tilted a little to one side. Very softly, he asked, "Or are you still going to keep it all to yourself?"

Turning, he walked away.

He had gone five or six paces when Kaletha started up. "Egaldus..."

"Kaletha..." Anshebbeth's timing as she turned and laid her hand on the younger woman's arm was far too precise to be accidental. Egaldus rounded the corner at the end of the walkway. The brazen sun seemed to ignite his embroidered tabard in gold and azure fire against the parched sand as he strode down the garden. As if oblivious to all that had passed before, Anshebbeth said, "Since I *will* be able to speak to Tazey, perhaps if you told *me* what to say to her, or gave me some instruction to pass along to her..."

In a voice like watered poison, Kaletha said, "I'm afraid you'd scarcely be qualified."

The older woman's mouth pinched tight. A blotch of sunlight, falling on her face, caught the sudden twist of wrinkles around her hungry eyes. "Perhaps if you spent as much time teaching me as you do teaching Egaldus..."

"Egaldus is mageborn."

"You said before, you could make me mageborn, too." Anshebbeth's shrill voice cracked. "You said I—"

Crushingly, Kaletha said, "That was when my teachings—my efforts to release the powers hidden within the human mind—were your first priority, Anshebbeth. That was when you were willing to devote yourself to purity of the body and exercises of the mind. I'm not sure that's true anymore."

Anshebbeth was still holding onto her arm. Kaletha turned her wrist to shake off the possessive clutch of those long white fingers and walked after Egaldus, her voluminous black robes billowing behind her in the glare of the autumn sun.

* * *

"That wasn't exactly fair."

Kaletha averted her face, pretending to be looking out across one of the smaller courtyards near the bottom of the gardens. This one was well watered, with a couple of orange trees pregnant with fruit in its center. The smell of them mingled thickly with that of the roses growing in little craters of packed gray-brown earth at the four corners, the ever-present harshness of dust, and the sticky warmth from the vendor of cinnamon buns on the opposite walkway.

"If she'd quit hanging onto me, maybe she'd be pushed away less."

Starhawk had spotted Kaletha alone here on her way out of the gardens to return to her duties. Anshebbeth was still looking for her higher up. Whether Kaletha had overtaken and spoken to Egaldus or not, Starhawk guessed the result was pretty much the same. She leaned her shoulder against the coarse, shaggy wood of the arbor and looked down at that white profile beneath its auburn swags of hair. "If you pushed her all the way away," she remarked, "she would have gone."

"You don't know 'Shebbeth." Kaletha remained resolutely staring into the garden, the harsh light showing up the small wrinkles in the delicate skin around her eyes. Above the tangle of bare wisteria vines and old walls, the shadows had begun to slant across the face of Mount Morian and to dye black the eastern cliffs of the distant Binning Rock. "She elected me as her mentor and teacher and someone to tell her what to do and be when I was seventeen. And the Mother knows she needed it—an awkward half-caste provincial from Smelting with enough shirdar nobility in her background to get her parents to send her to finishing school in the Middle Kingdoms and make her discontented with everything around her. Neurotic, whining, clinging . . ."

"But you've known her for a long time."

Kaletha paused. The beautiful shoulders under their

black gown tensed as she presented the back of her head
to Starhawk's unemotional gaze. Then she sighed, seem-
ing to read in the Hawk's uninflected voice the unspoken
observation that, had she truly wanted Anshebbeth
never to bother her again, she'd had ample time to say
so. Some of the stiffness went out of her. "I know," she
said.

She looked up at Starhawk, the defenses of the one
whom she made herself to be in front of her disciples
lowered, hesitantly, like the shield of a warrior who
doesn't quite trust the cry of "friend." "And I was...
unfair. But—I don't know."

"Well," the Hawk said judiciously, "I admit that when
someone walks around all day with 'Please don't kick
me' written on their back, the temptation to kick them
can be almost overwhelming."

The White Witch started to stiffen with indignant de-
nial of any sentiment so unworthy of her, then caught the
glint of understanding in those calm eyes, pale in the
sunburned face.

Starhawk went on, "And her timing wasn't the best."
She came around and sat on the other end of the bench,
facing Kaletha in the hot, spotted shade. "But it's still no
reason to be cruel."

Kaletha sighed again and nodded. With a gesture
oddly human after her rigid, self-controlled serenity, she
pressed her fingers to her eyelids, smudged brown with
sleeplessness. Her face looked suddenly older, with the
struggle not to admit, even to herself, that she was jealous, that she was frustrated by the King, and that she
could not quite control all those around her. "Maybe it's
for the best," she said wearily. "Egaldus being sent away,
I mean—if he *is* going to be sent away. He might have
just said that to..." She paused, then changed her mind
about what she was going to say and went on with something else, her tone calm as a frozen lake. "He is very—
eager. Too eager, like your friend, though of course his
teaching is far more advanced than Captain Sun Wolf's

is, and I believe he has more potential because his mind is better disciplined. He's like a man trying to pour water into a basin which isn't dug deep enough. He doesn't understand when I try to tell him that some of it's going to spill on the ground."

Are you going to keep it all to yourself? he had asked. Starhawk leaned her back to the arbor post behind her and remembered Sun Wolf's words about Kaletha and her power. Looking across at that pale, controlled face, Starhawk wondered suddenly how much of Kaletha's desire to teach Tazey stemmed from the fear that she might be surpassed in power by a girl younger than herself. A couple of young girls strolled past them, each with a miner on either arm, the girls all done up in bright cotton and glass-bead finery, flowers and sweet grass braided into their long hair.

For a moment Kaletha's lips hardened in a disapproving sneer. Then she went on, still behind her wall of pedagogical calm, as if Egaldus was truly the issue. "It takes years of preparing the mind, of disciplining the body. I know, I studied in silence, in darkness, for years . . ." She stopped again and looked quickly at Starhawk, as if remembering her closeness to Sun Wolf. Then, bitterly, she twisted on the bench and looked out into the dry garden again, keeping her secrets clenched close within. "All magic springs from the mind," she said after a moment. "How can power spring from a dirty and undisciplined place? It requires study and purity . . ." She hesitated over the word.

"Not to mention," Starhawk said softly, "the Great Trial."

Startlement broke Kaletha out of that rigid mold. There was genuine puzzlement in her voice. "The what?"

"She'd never *heard* of it?"

Starhawk shook her head. She had come down to the empty quarter as soon as it grew fully dark. It was a restless night, full of the movement and dry, electric whispers of the wind. Far out on the desert Sun Wolf could sense a storm, but it was traveling elsewhere, and the foothills would only feel its farthest hem fringes. The moon hung over the black hump of Mount Morian like a trimmed coin.

Last night Starhawk had not come to him, knowing it was possible that she would be watched. Before they had become lovers, Sun Wolf had occasionally wondered about his second-in-command's habitual self-contained calm—off hand, soft-voiced, capable of an animal's logical cruelty. He had trained with her and fought sword-to-sword with her too often not to suspect fire lay under that gray ice. It was her vulnerability which had surprised him. It was good, beyond anything he had known, not to have to hide the needs and fears of his soul from her behind an unbreakable wall of strength.

They coupled in fierce silence in the cell that had been theirs, close enough to hear the music that drifted from the Hall. Afterward, spent, they lay in the darkness, warming one another under the meager blankets Starhawk had left for him with last night's food, taking pleasure only in the touch of one another's skin. It seemed like half the night before they spoke.

"She asked me what it was," Starhawk said from the hollow of his shoulder where she lay. "I told her. I have a feeling she meant to go through it in secret, so no one would know she hadn't done it already, until I told her how it was done."

Sun Wolf shivered. The hallucinatory poison which could bring a wizard's powers to fruition invariably killed the nonmageborn—*and perhaps,* he thought, *some of the less strong among the mageborn as well.* The old man who had whispered of it to Starhawk once had spoken of preparation for the Trial, but no one knew anymore what that preparation had been. He himself had only survived it because he had a trained mercenary's physical strength. The agonized screaming was what had destroyed his voice. The memory of the pain would follow him to his grave. He knew down to the depths of his heart that if he had not been given the poison for other reasons—if he had known he would have to take it to achieve a mage's full powers—he would never have had the courage to do it.

But then, like Tazey, he had never wanted to be a mage.

"Tazey will have to go through it."

Starhawk's short, baby-soft hair moved against his chest. "I know."

"She'll need a hell of a lot of teaching first."

She nodded again. "You know the Bishop and Norbas Milkom have come up here to try and talk Osgard into sending her to a convent," she said. "The Bishop because he's afraid for her soul—I think Norbas Milkom because he sees it as a good way to break up her marriage with a shirdar lord and maybe later, just coincidentally, talk her around into marrying one of his own sons."

"They'll never do it." Sun Wolf's hand smoothed the skin of her shoulder absently, yet delighting in the feel of it, like silk under his palm, broken by the delicate trapunto of an old knife scar. "It hinges on Osgard admitting that Tazey's mageborn—that she isn't the perfect little princess he's always wanted. Galdron's going to be lucky if he gets away from the palace without a flogging for even bringing it up."

But evidently the Bishop went unflogged, for three hours later he came, in silence, to the base of the outside stair that led up to Tazey's lighted room. The night had grown cold, the terrible electric quality of it ebbing as the distant storm died away over the desert. The music had long since ceased from the Hall, but the light in the King's solar continued to burn, and an occasional soft-footed servant had come and gone from the curtained archway of Tazey's room. The curtains were orange and scarlet desert work; with the lights in the room behind them, they rippled like a rainbow of fire. A reflection of that dim and far-off luminescence sparkled on the Bishop's embroidered cloak as he gathered up his robes like a lady's skirts, glanced surreptitiously around him, and started to ascend the stair.

"It's a bit late to be going calling, Galdron," said a soft, even voice from the shadows of the stair.

The old man stopped with an apoplectic snort. Midway up the stair, a rawboned figure unfolded itself from the shadows; the sinking moonlight brushed a few ivory strands of short-cropped hair and the glint of steel studding on a green leather jerkin such as the guards wore. The Bishop blustered, "They said that the Princess sleeps ill of nights and that, if she was still awake, I might speak with her." But like her, he kept his voice low. A sharp word spoken anywhere between the stair and the little gate that led from the court to the empty quarter would wake every sleeper on that side of the Palace.

"They probably didn't mean at three hours before dawn."

"I have been speaking with the King," the Bishop replied with dignity. "I thought..."

"You thought you might be able to talk Tazey into wanting what you want for her? Give her a few choice nightmares to think about before she sees her father at breakfast?"

"Whatever nightmares the witch's guilty conscience might visit upon her," Galdron said sententiously, "they are well spent if they will save her from the eternal nightmare of Hell by causing her to repent."

"Repent what? How she was born? Saving four people from dying? You have a beautiful voice, Galdron; you can probably persuade people into believing anything." The dark figure began to descend the stairs toward him, and there was a sudden flash of moon-silvered steel as a thin knife appeared in her hand. "I think it would be a whole lot less persuasive with your nose slit clear back to the sinuses."

Galdron backed down the stairs so hastily that he nearly tripped on the flowing satin of his crimson robe. He stammered, "I shall call—"

"Call whom?" a rich, deep voice asked softly from the courtyard shadows. The Bishop looked back irritably over his shoulder. In the shadows, eyes gleamed white in a dark face above the pale blur of a collar ruffle. "The guards, and tell them you tried to talk your way around Tazey when her Daddy had already told you no? I told you it was a fool idea. Let's go back to town."

Galdron hesitated for a moment. In the moonlight Starhawk saw his face purse with frustration. Then he looked up at her where she stood on the stairs, his white beard like streaks of ermine among the dark fur of his cloak collar. "Don't believe that I have given up," he said, still softly. "The girl's soul is in danger. I have told her father so, though that..." He hesitated and glanced at Norbas Milkom, who had materialized beside him in the shadows. He amended, "... though her father will not believe me. There is too much witchery in this Palace already. She must be removed, or evil will come of it."

And turning, he vanished into the night. Laughing softly to herself, Starhawk slipped her knife back into her boot and went up the stairs.

The following morning Tazey was pronounced well enough to make her appearance in the Hall at breakfast.

Sitting in her usual place at Kaletha's table, Starhawk eyed the girl worriedly, as Tazey was ushered in by her father and her uncle. Her dust-blond hair artificially curled, her broad, straight shoulders framed in a profusion of cantaloupe-colored silk ruffles, she looked washed out and miserable, hopelessly distant from the gay and beautiful girl who had so joyfully danced the war dance. Years of friendship with Sun Wolf's various concubines had given Starhawk the ability to spot make-up carefully applied, in this case to cover the ravages of sleeplessness and doubt. The King, in puce damask that accentuated the broken veins in his nose and cheeks, held his daughter's hand with possessive pride, his weary, bloodshot green eyes darting over the faces of the unnaturally large crowd at breakfast, daring any to speak.

None did. *However and whyever Nexué's strident gossip had been silenced,* Starhawk thought, *the silencing had been effective. There was a good chance that the whole affair would be scotched.*

And what then? she wondered. *The gorgeous and somewhat wooden-headed Prince Incarsyn would marry Tazey and carry her off in splendor to his jewel-like little city deep in the dune seas of the south. She would eat candied dates, ride in palanquins, bear his babies, and try to forget what it felt like to part the winds with her hands.*

As the King conducted his daughter to her place at the High Table, Anshebbeth came hurrying down to where Starhawk and Kaletha sat. The governess, in her high-necked velvet gown, looked as if she, like Tazey, had spent a night either sleepless or ravaged by hideous dreams; her thin hands twitched as she kept glancing back toward the King. Though her place was with her charge on what was clearly an official occasion, she perched nervously on the chair at Kaletha's other side.

"They came last night," she fretted. "The Bishop and Norbas Milkom..."

"Starhawk was telling me," Kaletha replied, a little spitefully, as if to lay emphasis on Anshebbeth's exclusion from the prior conversation.

The governess threw a hunted look up at the High Table where Osgard was irritably ordering Jeryn to sit up straight. The boy, just up from his own bout with sunstroke, looked like a lizard in molt, wan and exhausted and peeling, his white hands with their bitten nails toying listlessly with his food. Her voice sank to a whisper, "Do you think he will—will proclaim your banishment?"

"*Your* banishment?" Starhawk asked, surprised.

Kaletha's lips compressed with barely stifled irritation. Anshebbeth explained hurriedly to Starhawk, "We were told, Kaletha and I, that the real reason Galdron and Norbas Milkom came last night was to demand that —that Kaletha be sent away! Only because of her power, only because her excellence would be a temptation to the Princess—only out of spite, and jealousy, because of Egaldus becoming a wizard! They hate her, Galdron and Milkom . . ."

"Stop it, 'Shebbeth!" Kaletha said, embarrassed.

"It's true," the governess said eagerly, trying too hard to make up yesterday's lost ground. "You know they hate you."

Kaletha pushed at a forkful of beans on her plate. Still without looking up, she said, "I wish you'd stop taking every backstairs rumor your lover whispers into your ears as sacred truth."

At the viciousness in Kaletha's voice as she pronounced the word *lover,* Anshebbeth's pale face turned the color of paper, her hand clutching nervously at her throat.

Coldly, Kaletha turned to face her. "You don't think I know you've been playing the slut with Nanciormis? The man gossips like an old woman and sneaks and spies worse than Nexué did. No wonder I've never been able to raise the smallest powers in you, as I have in Egaldus. All you think about is yourself."

Not at all to Starhawk's surprise, Anshebbeth hung her head. There were tears perilously close to the surface as she whispered, "I—You're right, Kaletha. I have —I have thought too much of myself—not enough of your welfare, or that of others. If I haven't achieved power yet, I realize it's my own fault . . ."

Kaletha opened her mouth to say something else, but Starhawk, realizing that nothing encourages cruelty so much as subservience, broke in with, "I think you'd better get back to the High Table, Anshebbeth, or Osgard *will* think about banishing Kaletha."

The governess started, throwing a stricken glance up at Osgard's irritated face. She gulped, hastily wiped her eyes, and gathered up her flowing skirts, to scurry back and take her place at the bottom of the High Table, dropping flustered curtseys to everyone there, even as a stirring around the Hall door marked the entry of Incarsyn of Hasdrozaboth, Lord of the Dunes.

He looks, Starhawk thought, *his usual gorgeous self in the full panoply of the shirdar lords*. He had all Nanciormis' grace and beauty, unblurred by the lines of sensuality and indulgence which had long ago eroded the commander's handsomeness. In his white cloak, his baggy trousers and soft boots with their stamp-work of gold, his flowing surcoat, and strings of scarlet and blue amulets, he looked like a young and graceful hunting cat; whereas the commander, though he had the same hawk-like shirdar features and the same thick braids of black hair, more resembled a somewhat spoiled tabby who has long ago decided that mousing was beneath him.

Osgard rose, leading Tazey by the hand. The girl's face had the set, desperate look it had worn, Starhawk realized, when she had first stepped forward to face the darkness of the storm.

With slightly rehearsed grace, Incarsyn bowed and smiled. "It is better than you know, my Princess, to see you well again."

Tazey took a deep breath, released her father's hand, and stepped forward. Reaching up, she removed the small, gleaming droplets of the sand-pearls from her ears. Her voice was small and steady and like the clink of a dropped dagger in the enormous silence of the Hall.

"Thank you." She faltered for one instant, glanced desperately back at the King, then went on. "You've been too good to me for me to want to pay you in false coin. What you've heard is true. I'm mageborn." And she put the sand-pearls into his hand.

In that hideous instant of silence, Starhawk's interested glance took in all the faces at the High Table—Osgard's engorging with blood as his hand came up involuntarily as if he would strike her, and Jeryn's dark eyes blazing to life with the first expression of soaring joy Starhawk had seen in them at his sister's courage; Nancioromis was smiling. *Why smiling?* Beside her, she was aware of Kaletha smiling, too, with triumph at having thwarted the King and with anticipation at being, after all, Tazey's teacher.

For one shocked instant, Incarsyn looked as taken aback as if Tazey had confessed to selling her favors in the Pardle bazaar.

The silence seemed to last for minutes, though Starhawk calculated it was in fact twelve or thirteen seconds. Then Osgard found the breath to gasp, "You—"

Incarsyn lifted a stilling finger. Reaching forward, he took Tazey's hand, turned it over gently, and replaced the sand-pearls in her palm.

"It is a poor lover," he said softly, his liquid voice carrying to all corners of the Hall, "who abandons his betrothed because she cuts off her hair, or changes its color, or decides that she will learn to play the war pipes. What you have told me is no more than this. If you will have me, Lady Taswind..." Graceful as a panther, he sank to one knee and, closing her fingers around the pearls, pressed a kiss upon her knuckles. "...I will still be your true lord."

The applause rang like a thunderclap in the rafters, shouts of approval and toasts in weak breakfast wine. Osgard, stayed in his stride forward to shake Tazey until her teeth rattled, stepped back, his broad face wreathed in a smile of startled surprise at this magnanimity. But Tazey, Starhawk saw, looked stunned, shaking her head in confusion as a tear tracked down her hollowed face.

"I think it was beautiful," Anshebbeth sighed dewily, coming to join Kaletha's table a few minutes later.

"Do you?" Nanciormis walked quietly up behind her, a half-drunk vessel of wine in hand, pressed there by the King to toast the betrothed couple. His pouchy eyes glinted with cynicism which could not quite conceal furious anger.

Anshebbeth flustered, confused about what she might have said wrong and even more confused by Nanciormis' presence, *as if,* thought Starhawk, *she can not make up her mind whether to stand next to him or Kaletha.* "Well—that is—after what people have been saying... though of course there's nothing wrong with it... But Incarsyn—"

"Incarsyn," said Nanciormis bitterly, "would have said the same thing were she a humpbacked leper and still the daughter of the King of Wenshar. I know." He looked somberly at Kaletha, and even her cool reserve relaxed a little, under his warm brown gaze. "I met him late last night, coming back from the brothels in town. 'Does it matter to me if the girl's a witch-bitch?' he said. 'I rode north to marry her whatever she looked like; if she boils toads and couples with snakes for her pleasure, what is that to me? It could be worse—she could play the war pipes.'"

Anshebbeth went white with shock and disillusionment. Kaletha's nostrils flared in anger, but there was no surprise in her face as she threw a bitter glance at the High Table, where Tazey, rigid with desperate composure, listened to the Prince's light glow of blandishments that spared her the effort of stammering a reply. "So he'll take her away with him after all," she said bitterly. "And her father will be spared having to think about her 'disgrace.'"

"It's what he came here for."

With soft and bitter violence, she whispered, "Men,"

and turned her head suddenly, going back to her breakfast in arctic rage.

After a moment's hesitation Anshebbeth gathered up her long skirts and sat beside Kaletha, offering the comfort of her presence, but she threw one look quickly back over her shoulder at Nanciormis, as if asking his permission. Nanciormis said nothing, but his dark eyes warmed for a moment with complicity; with that Anshebbeth smiled, uneasily content.

"Then it's been a sham all along?" Starhawk asked quietly, looking up at the commander.

"By no means." Nanciormis shrugged, started to drink from the cup in his hand, then grimaced, and put it down. "She's a beautiful girl, after all. But she's my niece—I care about her happiness." He looked back toward the High Table, a very real anger in every line of his thick shoulders beneath their snowy cape. He was a politician, as Sun Wolf had said, for all his relatively minor post as commander of the guards; Starhawk knew him to be skilled in dissimulation, seldom showing his true thoughts. But his anger in this situation was genuine—*and so it might be,* thought Starhawk. She herself had never seen that side of Incarsyn—in fact, had never seen him being other than a shirdar gentleman: not very imaginative, but doing his best within his limits to be kind.

Nanciormis went on bitterly, "He cares less for her than he does for his horses—I've heard him say two or three times that he wouldn't trust any woman on them..." Kaletha's back stiffened at that, and she turned from her barely touched plate to look up at him again. "He despises the mageborn—I won't repeat to you some of the things he's said about you, Kaletha, and your followers. But he has better sense than to say them to a girl who can get him related to the mines of Wenshar and maybe out from under the control of that sister of his. But of course, I can't say so to her."

"Since she had no choice in the matter," Starhawk remarked softly, "what would be the point?"

Down at the end of the High Table, a sudden movement of red and black caught her eye, and she saw Jeryn sit up, looking toward the doors with sudden brightness lighting up his thin face for the second time. At the same instant, she knew that Sun Wolf was looking for her; turning, she saw him standing in the archways that led to the shadowy vestibule, scanning the crowd.

As if she had called out to him across the great, sun-shafted hall, he turned his head and met her gaze.

Perhaps because they had been together last night, she felt for one split instant the strange tangle of her love for him pull her daytime mind—a passionate caring that was both physical and maternal, a need for his happiness that was so deep it shamed her . . .

And then, between one eyeblink and the next, the soldier in her realized he wasn't supposed to be there.

But he was walking foward toward the dais, and so happy was Osgard with his alliance with the shirdar secured that he lofted his cup in greeting and called out, "Hey, Captain!" before he remembered why he'd ejected the Wolf from his court.

A look of truculent suspicion clouded his face, and he stood up. Starhawk had already begun to move toward the Wolf, reading in his silence, the way he held his body, that there was something very wrong. Under a layer of dusty beard-stubble his face looked drawn, as she remembered it looking sometimes when he would look on things that had been done in the sacking of a city, in the cold light of the following day. His leather eye patch was blotched with moisture, his faded hair sleek and wet, as if he had dunked his head in a horse trough to clear his mind. Starhawk thought, *If he tries to stop the match now, we're going to have to fight our way out*, touched her sword hilt, and gauged the best route to the closet window.

Osgard must have been thinking the same thing, for he demanded roughly, "I thought I told you to stay the hell away."

"You did," the Wolf said. "I just came to tell you the Bishop Galdron and Norbas Milkom are dead."

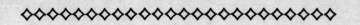

CHAPTER

—— 9 ——

"*W*HEN DID YOU SEE GALDRON?*"*

Starhawk held tight to the reins as her horse tried to throw up its head, made nervous by the stench of blood. "About three hours after midnight." The sun, already well above Dragon's Backbone at breakfast time, was now hot; the air in the little clearing among the boulders where she and the Wolf had first rescued Osgard from the disgruntled shirdar seemed alive with the low buzz of insects. Used as she was to day-old battlefields, the place made Starhawk's stomach turn. "Milkom was with him. I got the impression they were heading straight back to town."

Standing beside her near the little cluster of horses at the road's edge, Sun Wolf nodded. "They must have been. I was wakened by something about two hours before dawn, but all I heard was every coyote in the hills howling. It wasn't till daylight that I smelled the blood."

From the mouth of a little wadi that wound away back

into the rocks stumbled one of the band of Trinitarian priests who had met the posse from the Fortress at the place; he was an oldish man, bareheaded even in the rising heat, his robes like an incongruous bouquet of orchids against the lead-colored rocks. He leaned against a boulder and vomited as if he had been poisoned. Even at this distance, Starhawk could see the rim of scarlet along the hem of his robe.

Sun Wolf scratched his moustache and continued, "I went on into town to the Cathedral and got Egaldus and a bunch of the priests to come out here to keep an eye on the place, but I had a look around, first. You see anything odd about this?"

She looked around them at the small space of open ground. In places dark mud had dried to crusted puddles, soaking into the dust; she noted automatically that the ground underfoot was dust and pebbles, not sand, and covered like a lunatic quilt with back-and-forth stitching of tracks—the priests', the posse's, those of the onlookers that had already begun to gather and were being held back, rather unsuccessfully, by Nanciormis and a couple of his guards back on the road.

"You mean, besides two men and two horses dismembered?" she remarked, glancing back at Sun Wolf.

"Besides that," he agreed, folding his arms.

She scanned the road: the gravelly dip and the surrounding rocks; Egaldus with his blond hair like a thick halo in the hot sun, speaking with gentle authority to the older priest; and Osgard, some distance away, sitting on a boulder, his face buried in his hands. Softly, she said, "I'm trying to picture how it was done, Chief, and I can't. The area of the kill's huge—it starts over there where one of the horses came down..." She pointed to a churned-up patch of black mud on the slope down from the road. Tracks zigzagged frantically away, passing within feet of them—pointed-toed slippers. She'd noted them on Galdron, pearled tips poking coyly from beneath the crimson hem of his robe. One of them, with the foot still in it, lay halfway under a boulder near the mouth of the wadi, swarming with flies. So far the priests had missed it. "Milkom's body was over in those rocks there, but the first blood starts only a few feet from here." That, by the look of it, had been an artery. She was astonished the little man had been able to run so far. "Two trained assassins on good horses could have done it, *maybe*. But . . ."

Her glance slipped back to the Wolf. His sunburned face looked dark against the white frame of his head veils; his single eye, yellow as a lion's, was narrowed in thought. Knowing his answer already, she said, "There weren't any tracks, were there?"

"No," he said.

For a time they were both silent. Across the open ground, Osgard's voice rose in a despairing shriek to no one in particular, "I'll have the bastard crucified! I'll have the skin flayed off him and leave him for the ants! I'll get whoever did this—I'll get him!" Nanciormis came hurrying down from the road toward him, leaving the guards to deal with the gaggle of neck-craning miners and cattle herders. Incarsyn, standing closer to the King, holding the bridle of his own horse—one of the famous white mares of the desert—didn't move. He looked dazed and shaken, like the man in the legend who had bargained with the djinns for his worst enemy's head in a box and, opening it, had found his own.

After a little while Starhawk said, "While I was getting ready to ride with you, 'Shebbeth came to me, in tears because Galdron had never liked Nanciormis, and she was afraid people would think he had something to do with it. She said Nanciormis was with her last night . . ."

"Was he?" Sun Wolf asked, more out of curiosity than anything else.

"Oh, yes." She nodded. "I was on the balcony for

at least two hours after I saw Galdron. Nanciormis came sliding out of 'Shebbeth's room close to dawn."

Her dark brows twitched together for a moment as she remembered the narrow, rather gloomy confines of the Women's Hall, with its unmade beds, abandoned by the underservants when they went to see Tazey's reinstatement at breakfast, and the grayish shafts of filtered light that came in through the windows that overlooked the wide quadrangle of the kitchen courts. Anshebbeth had clutched desperately at her hands, her face skull-like, sleepless, and her hagridden eyes huge, begging the Hawk not to tell anyone. She would be ruined, utterly ruined, if the King found out. Starhawk, knowing the standards of propriety necessary in a Princess' chaperone, had to agree with her there. But she would testify to anyone, she said, if necessary, that Nanciormis had not been abroad that night . . .

She looked across at the commander now. He was kneeling on the ground before the King, graceful as a tiger in spite of his bulk, every gesture he made lambent with beauty and power. For this man, poor Anshebbeth was risking not only her reputation—no small thing in a community as tight knit as this one—but her position, Tazey's reputation, her friendship with the person dearest to her, and her own hopeless dreams of sharing Kaletha's magic; and for thanks, Nanciormis tumbled her as he casually tumbled the laundry women, making jokes about her behind her back.

It was all none of Starhawk's business, but she was conscious of a wish to see the commander prey to some kind of comprehensively disfiguring skin disorder for a number of weeks.

Quietly, she went on, "The damn thing is, it would be nice to have to worry about it being Nanciormis, or Osgard . . . or anyone."

Sun Wolf nodded. The wind turned, blowing a little skiff of dust over the dark splatterings of the blood trails; Egaldus and two of Incarsyn's shirdar bodyguards emerged from behind the rocks, carrying something between them wrapped in a blanket. One of the horses whinnied and shied. Overhead, the vultures rode the thermals, curious but staying unnaturally high.

Like the hoarse, stripped scrape of metal, Sun Wolf's voice went on. "I had a feeling about Nexué's death, and this time, I'm sure. Whatever killed those poor bastards, Hawk, it was nothing human. I think the time has come for me to have a little talk with Kaletha."

"You have no right to ask me about my power!" Kaletha almost spat the words at him, like an angry cat. In the slatey shadows of the small chamber just off the Women's Hall, her face was like a white mask, floating above the dark, heavy folds of her gown.

"The hell I haven't, woman! Two men have been murdered, and a woman also, if I'm right. You're a wizard . . ."

"Just because you can find no sign of a killer, you accuse me?"

Sun Wolf's eye narrowed. "I'm not accusing anyone. But you have books of magic that could tell us—"

"So!" The word came out like a trumpet of bitter laughter. "I thought we'd come to them, sooner or later. You'll take any excuse to get your hands on them, won't you? You are greedy, like Egaldus, but without Egaldus' discipline and respect."

Sun Wolf held his temper with an effort, but his harsh voice was thin. "I don't give a tin damn if your way of holding power over your students is to deny them knowledge—"

"Power has nothing to do with it! I *share* my knowledge!"

He didn't take that bait, but went inexorably on. "—but right now we need to know what killed those men, what *could* have killed them. You're the wizard around here. I know there are demons in Wenshar.

There could be other creatures in the desert as well, creatures we know nothing of . . ."

Kaletha scoffed, "Who told you that old tale? That old tattler Nanciormis?"

"I've seen them, dammit!"

"More lies," she said, her voice cold. "No one has ever seen these so-called demons—nor, for all the superstitions about them, has anyone ever been hurt by them. They're tales to keep children good and to give men an excuse for punishing wives who meddle. But magic is entirely the product of the human mind, purified by self-sacrifice and reason . . ."

"If it's entirely the product of the human mind," said the Wolf, "then it has to be fouler than a cat-house latrine."

"Don't you use language like that to me."

"Don't you understand?" Sun Wolf took a step toward her, and the tall woman fell back before him, hate and resentment in every rigid line of her body. Through the wide window that overlooked the kitchen garden, doves could be heard, and the soft chatter of women walking the paths between the dusty herb beds. The smoke of the kitchen fires, already heating up for that evening's dinner, drifted like an acrid whiff of far-off battle on the shift of the wind. "Magic is born in us, because we're children of the earth. It isn't we who produce it. Its presence doesn't make us better or holier people. Magic can be as pure and true as a man giving up his life for people he doesn't even know—may his ancestors help the poor clown—or as foul and petty as the things lovers say to each other when they tire of love."

"That's another lie!" The smoky red braids swung against her cheeks with the sharp turn of her head.

"How would you know?" he demanded. "What do you think the Great Trial is? What do you think it does? It breaks open the crust we grow over our souls because we can't stand the sight of what's down at the bottom. It makes us see and understand."

"That may be true of your magic, may the Mother help you," Kaletha said, her voice shaking, "but it isn't true of mine. Don't play the wise man with me, giving yourself airs because you thought some barbarian rite of passage would give you all you wanted. You can see it didn't. You have neither wisdom nor purity—every word you say makes it plainer to me that you should never be allowed to touch the books of power that are in my custody."

"Who put them into your custody?"

"Fate!" she lashed at him. She strode from him, diagonally away across the small, sparsely furnished stone room, with its virginal bed in its niche and the tall-legged reading desk beside the open window. Beside the desk in the slanting bar of yellow light, she swung passionately back.

"They are mine." The blaze of her intensity could be almost physically felt where he stood near the door. "Magic has all but died in the hundred years of Altiokis' tyranny and repression. It has become soiled and filthy with superstition, dirtied from the handling of men like yourself, who see it only as a tool to further their own greeds and lusts."

Softly, he said, "You're quick to say what kind of a man I am and what I want."

"My power has made me quick." Contempt dripped from her voice like honey from a rotting tree. "And it is up to me to teach magic, to refound it among the worthy and the pure."

"Like Egaldus?"

Her breath caught, her nostrils flared, and her lips clamped shut as if sealed. For a moment there was no sound in the room but the hiss of her breath in her nostrils. Even the passing tread of feet in the garden outside had ceased.

He went on, "Now, I don't care if you couple with

him in the empty quarter—hell, it wouldn't matter to me if you had him in the Hall at breakfast time. But don't try to tell me what I am. Don't look down on me for loving the Hawk, nor on the Hawk for loving me."

Stiffly, she said, "That isn't the same. Your love for her is founded in the flesh alone and debases you both. But mine for Egaldus grew first from our purity, from his admiration and regard. Only later did it...blossom. Though I don't expect you, or anyone else, would understand that it is different from the loves of other people."

"So it's like demons," Sun Wolf said softly, "that I can see and you can't. I need to see those books, Kaletha."

"No." Her voice was flat as baked clay.

He walked over to the window, to stand near her in the rectangle of the light. "Don't you understand?" he said, his voice quiet now, without anger. He looked across into those beautiful blue eyes, hard with suspicion beneath the cinnamon lashes. "If the killer was a—a being, a ghost or a devil—" Her lip curved with scorn. "—they might contain some mention of it, some way to track it, to fight it..."

"Something *you* might believe," she returned. "They contain the usual superstitions, the interpretations of those ignorant of the true sources of magic."

"All right," he said. "If the killer is a wizard, using magic, at least we could trace him or her. Where did you get the books, Kaletha? Who wrote them? What other wizard gave you your knowledge? You can use your power to find the true culprit."

"You think I haven't thought of that?" She swung away from him, scorn jeering in her voice. She paced, a restless red eagle caged in the narrow room. "You think just because I'm not a soldier like your precious mistress I have no brains? Yes, I'm going to use my power to find the true culprit—my power, yours, Egaldus—the latent powers hidden deep in the souls of Luatha and Pradborn, 'Shebbeth and Shelaina. Haven't you, with all your wisdom—" the word rolled caustic from her tongue, "—seen the obvious means of finding the culprit? I'm going to ask the Bishop Galdron."

Sun Wolf stared at her, shocked and cold as if she had unexpectedly driven a dagger of ice into his heart. For a moment he couldn't think of anything to say. In the silence, he heard the clink of Starhawk's spurs on the tiled walk outside, her voice asking some question, and Anshebbeth's answering.

He finally whispered, "Galdron's dead."

Kaletha's nostrils widened a little at the obviousness of the remark. But she only said, "He and Milkom died late in the night, a few hours, at most, before dawn. It has not yet been one full cycle of the sun. When we call his spirit, it will answer."

"That's necromancy." The horror he felt went deeper than his memories of his childhood—of the village shaman making his stinking conjurations with the fetid remains of enemies' hands and ears—deeper than conscious thought.

Kaletha said calmly, "It has been called so, yes."

"You tell me I'm an evil magician," the Wolf said, stunned that Kaletha would contemplate such a thing, "and then you stand there in cold blood and tell me you're going to conjure the spirits of the dead..."

"Of the Bishop of Pardle," Kaletha corrected him. "It is not the same thing. I will conjure him because, for all his hypocrisy about magic, he was pure in both mind and body. We should have nothing to fear from the spirits of the pure."

Sun Wolf's voice was hoarse. "The dead are dead."

Her lips pursed up like a nursemaid's at the stubbornness of a stupid child. "No more than what I would expect," she said, "of a barbarian. Your superstitious dread of the dead, like these 'demons' you claim to see..."

"Would you stop calling me a barbarian?" He took a deep breath. "Yes, I'm a barbarian, and yes, I fear the dead, and yes, I fear demons, and with good reason. They're things you can't tamper with."

"Only if your magic is impure," Kaletha responded evenly. "You do well to fear, Sun Wolf—it shows prudence. But I assure you it has been done before, safely —even routinely. Men like yourself misunderstood it, fearing and hating. They slandered those who had the power to do it. But those who understood what they were doing came to no harm. Tonight, when we make the conjuration, you will see."

"I'll see nothing, Lady." Sun Wolf stepped back, filled with a loathing fear that a lifetime of bloodshed had never brought to him.

"Don't be silly," she snapped. Carnelian glints flickered in her eyebrows as they snapped together. "I need all the power I can raise. There must be seven of us."

"You can find your seventh elsewhere. And if you don't, better still."

"Now who's obstructing whom in finding the killer?"

"I don't know." Sun Wolf backed toward the door, fearing, and not even much caring that she clearly thought it was her that he feared. "But if you summon enough power to call the spirits of the dead, the killer may not be what you find."

Later, when he went up to the library, Sun Wolf wondered what it was about the idea of summoning the dead that filled with with such unreasoning horror. Yirth of Mandrigyn had warned him against it— scarcely necessary, since among her spells and incantations there had been no means of doing so. He could see her stern, narrow face again now, with its jade-cold eyes and the disfiguring birthmark like a smutch of thrown filth over her mouth and chin. Low and soft as a rosewood flute, she had said, *As for the calling of the dead, they say that no matter how good the purpose of the callers, nothing but evil has ever come of it* ...

Behind that memory, the images of his childhood

swam—the shaman of his village in the bitter north, Many Voices, laying out by firelight the Circle of Bones to summon the voices of the ancestors. Even then, the hair had prickled on the back of his neck, for fear that he might see pupils gleam once more in the sockets of those dead, smoke-stained skulls.

Of course he hadn't. Many Voices had been a thoroughgoing charlatan, but the best the village had possessed at the time. The little man had shown signs of living to a ruinous old age—so perhaps he was up there still.

At least, Sun Wolf thought, as he entered the first of the several quiet, shadowy rooms above the solar, with storm shutters folded nearly to and black ranks of books sleeping in the dimness, *Many Voices had been harmless.* He had made his conjurations against the storms that had regularly soaked the village, *cast his curses against cows which had continued to chew untroubled cuds in the meadows* which lay like deep pockets of velvet among the rocks of the cold moors, guarded closely the secrets of his ignorance, and never promised to do anything of critical importance. *Kaletha . . .*

Sun Wolf frowned into the dimness of the room. *Kaletha.*

Her books had come from somewhere, he thought. *If wizards enjoyed such a foul reputation in Wenshar, it would be no surprise that, Altiokis aside, some earlier mage had kept quiet about his or her power. Even now, that mage's other pupils might be abroad.*

To help? he wondered. *Or is it one of them whom we're looking for, casting this magic at us from afar? Or . . . What?*

He remembered the demons in Wenshar, the bluewhite gleam of their skeletal light, and the sense of terror, of danger. Danger of what? No one had ever heard of demons physically harming a man, and Milkom and the Bishop had been literally ripped to pieces.

Without any real hope of finding anything, he began
to walk along the doorless cabinets of blackened oak,
looking at the books within. By the shape of the cabinets
he guessed that this room had been the original library
and archive of the Fortress. The chamber beyond, with
its wide, south-facing windows looking out over the desert, had clearly always been a scriptorium. The books
had undoubtedly been mostly ledgers then, paybooks
and quartermasters' reports, stacked on their sides behind locked cabinet doors, along with paper and ink. He
could see the holes in the oak cabinet fronts where the
doors had been removed and the marks where the height
of shelves had been altered, to stand the books upright in
the new fashion; he saw also where new shelves had
been added to accommodate acquisitions over the years,
first here and then in the scriptorium and the other small
room to his left. There were both new and old books
there—enormous tomes of yellowed parchment, reeking
of dust and lanolin, their crackling leaves scattered with
illuminated capitals, as if someone had spilled a flower
basket over them—and dense, cramped volumes of
paper, printed on smudgy new presses like the ones they
had in the universities of Kwest Mralwe and the Gwarl
Peninsula.

He took one of the old books off the shelf and opened
its worn and dirty red leather covers. It was a treatise
upon the divine interrelationships between the Three
Gods, at unnecessary length, in the queer, intricately in-
flected dialect of the realms of the eastern steppes
beyond the Tchard Mountains. Further along he found a
romance in the florid old style of the Megantic Bight.
Sun Wolf could read most permutations of the old language of Gwenth, though he could write only the choppy
book hand of the north and the runes of his own childhood tongue. He replaced the romance, after running a
quick, critical eye over its pages:

So evil was the countenance of the creature
that Wintessa did faint, and Grovand held her
in his arms and, despite the danger of the
monster leaping at them, was lost in the beauty
of her curls that lay like a river of spun gold
upon his breast, and her lips pale as sea shells
in the shining moon of her face . . .

*I'd have dropped the silly bint, spun-gold curls and
all*, Sun Wolf thought dourly, moving on. He tried to picture Starhawk fainting in his arms at the sight of a monster leaping at them, no matter how evil its countenance.
She'd probably have grabbed a broom handle and
tripped the thing while he, Sun Wolf, was still unsheating
his sword.

He picked up a small, black-bound book from a table
and found it in a tongue unknown to him—even the let-
ters like nothing of the alphabet of Gwenth.

"That's in the shirdane."

Turning sharply, he saw Jeryn leaning in the doorway
of the smaller room to his left. He tried to remember
when he'd seen the boy last—a glimpse of him, slouched
in his chair at the High Table at breakfast that morning,
when Sun Wolf had broken the news of the Bishop's and
Milkom's deaths.

"The shirdar were never in the Empire, so they never
read and wrote the way everyone else does. People talk
about them as if they were barbarians, but they're not,
you know." The boy hesitated in the doorway, a fat book
tucked under one scrawny arm, as if unsure of his welcome.

Sun Wolf folded his book shut. "I know," he said. He
looked around him at the dark ranks of silent knowledge.
"These seem to be from all corners of the world."

Jeryn nodded, his dark eyes looking wide in his
pinched, thin face above its formal little ruff. "I didn't
know you could read, Chief."

"Well, people talk about me as if I was a barbarian, too."

The boy grinned, a little embarrassed, and ducked his head.

Sun Wolf leaned back against a corner of the shelves, turning the volume over in his big, scarred hands. "How well do you know the books in this place?"

Jeryn shrugged. "Pretty well." Finding his ease again, he came in and took a tall-legged, spindly stool from a writing desk to climb up and unerringly replace the tome he carried on a high shelf. "I can read most of them, but some of them are hard—the writing's little, and they talk about things I don't understand. But this one's one of the good ones," he added, holding up the volume before he slid it back into place. "It's about rocks and jewels and smelting gold. Did you know that, instead of breaking up the silver rock with hammers, they could probably make a machine to do it, and run it off a mule-treadmill?"

"And to think they want to waste your brains turning you into a dumb warrior." The Wolf sighed. "Is there any other place in the Fortress where somebody could hide books?"

The boy thought for a moment, then shook his head. "I don't know. In their rooms, maybe. How many books?"

Sun Wolf glanced at the shelf near him. The smallest volumes would have hidden under his hand, the bigger ones were longer than his forearm. He had taken a quick glance around Kaletha's cell-like room—it had been bare as a nun's. "I don't know."

"I bet we could find out." Jeryn climbed down from the stool again and pulled ineffectually at his black hose where they twisted around his skinny calves. Sun Wolf estimated it was the time when the boy should have been at afternoon sword practice, but didn't say so. He was no longer a teacher, so it wasn't his business. Besides, from what he'd seen of Nanciormis' teaching, he guessed the boy was better off as he was. Having no talent for dealing with children, the Wolf simply treated Jeryn as he would have treated another man—in this case a man who had knowledge of the libraries of the Fortress.

"They have a record of the books here." The boy led him into the small chamber from which he'd come —like the original library, dim, close, and smelling of paper, ink, and the dust of storms, which had been left to accumulate on the thick granite of the window sills around the joints of the shutters. "They write everything down. They have to," he added, pulling the fat ledger from the shelf and glancing back at Sun Wolf. "If you don't write everything down, you'll never know if it disappears."

Sun Wolf grinned. "You should try keeping track of a troop of mercenaries during the winter, if you want practice writing things down so they don't disappear." He set his book on the corner of the table as Jeryn opened the ledger, and leaned over the boy's shoulder to look. "We want books of magic—books of power. I don't know where they came from, how many of them there were, or when they came in, but it was at least a couple of years ago, probably more. But they came in from somewhere, and I think Kaletha got her hands on them and stashed them someplace."

"The empty quarter of the Palace?" Jeryn suggested promptly, keeping his place in the long, cramped columns of titles with one delicate forefinger as he glanced up.

"I would have thought so," the Wolf said, after a moment's consideration. "But most of those buildings are pretty unprotected. The ones with the roofs off are decaying badly already. And people go there sometimes, looking for lost chickens or a quiet place to fornicate . . ." *Oh, well,* he thought a half second later, as the dark eyes flicked up to him and then away, suddenly a boy's again and startled to hear a grownup just come out and say it. "I don't think she'd risk it."

"There are cellars under the empty quarter, you know," Jeryn said after a moment. "Cut down into the rock, some of them. They used to store grain and things down there during the season of storms, back when this was the Fortress and they were under seige all the time. Most of 'em are real dirty," he added fastidiously, and went back to perusing the cramped columns of book hand before them.

"Black Book of Wenshar?" Sun Wolf squinted down at the unfamiliar handwriting. "Sounds promising."

"They only call it that because it's got a black cover," Jeryn supplied. "It's a big book with the family trees of the Ancient House of Wenshar, one of the books Mother brought with her in her dowry. It says here, 'Writ in the shirdane.'"

"Well, that won't do us much good."

"Oh, I can read the shirdane," said Jeryn. "Kaletha taught me, back before she became a wizard and started teaching magic. Later some of the scribes helped me. That book there..." He pointed to the little black-bound volume Sun Wolf had set down, ruinously old with its crumbling pages in slanting, flowing characters, their ink faded almost to nothing, "It starts out..." He opened it, studied the last page for a moment, then explained, "The shirdar do their books wrong way 'round. This says, *A Treatise on the Use of Cactus and...and...*" He struggled with the word, then said, "I don't know this one. Cactus and something, anyway, *in Healing.*"

"Aloe, probably," Sun Wolf guessed, looking down at the boy with a kind of admiration. "Does your father know you read this?"

Jeryn fell silent at the mention of his father. After a long moment he said, "I don't think so. I told him I could, once, and he—he said I shouldn't waste my time."

Sun Wolf stared to say, *A man who spends twelve hours a day pickling himself in brandy has a lot of room to talk about wasting time*, but shut his mouth on the words. The boy had enough troubles without being reminded of what was undoubtedly as great a shame to him as his bookishness was a shame to his father. Instead he simply said, "Well, I'm telling you it's not a waste of time—not in a King who's going to have to deal with the shirdar all his life. Was this part of your mother's dowry?"

"I think so," said Jeryn, turning the small volume thoughtfully over in his hands. "She brought a lot of books, and some of them were pretty old."

Sun Wolf scanned rapidly down the list before him. "This one isn't listed here, though—not in your mother's things."

"That's funny," said Jeryn. "Because I thought all the shirdane books were Mother's. In fact, I know they were, because it doesn't say anywhere else that they're in that language."

"So there are books here that weren't listed." Sun Wolf weighed the alien herbary in his hand, remembering something Starhawk had told him Tazey had said, an idea slowly taking shape in his mind. "Where are the others in the shirdane?"

Jeryn hurried back out to the larger room, to one of the cabinets which still retained its door. As he unlatched and swung it open, he said, "They keep them all together, because nobody can read them except a couple of clerks."

Some were almost new, others ancient and filthy, their leather covers blackened with smoke and dust and the oily grip of hands long turned to clay. Sun Wolf counted them—there were twenty-five. "And there were only seventeen on your mother's dowry list." He turned back to the boy, his single eye glinting in the hazy gleam of evening sunlight that diffused through the half-closed shutters. Reaching up, he took one of the oldest looking and balanced it on the edge of a shelf for the boy to look at.

"*The Book of the Surgeon*," Jeryn read out the scrolled, faded symbols laboriously. "Oh, look, there's a skeleton!" he added eagerly, opening a few leaves in.

"And not a very good one," Sun Wolf added, gazing down over his shoulder. "His elbow bends the wrong way—look. I don't remember this on the list, either."

Jeryn shook his head, puzzled.

"Is there an inventory of things that were here when the Fortress was taken over during the rebellion?"

"There should be," Jeryn said slowly. "I mean, if I were a rebel captain and took over an enemy fortress, I'd want a list of what was there so I'd know how to use it against the enemy."

By the time they located it, the sun had long since sunk behind the mountains; all three still, dust-smelling rooms had gone pitch dark, and both searchers were smutched from head to foot with the stirred grime of ages. Sun Wolf ws objectively conscious that he was both tired and hungry. In the furor over Milkom's and the Bishop's deaths, Osgard had not had time to order the Wolf from the Fortress, but he'd missed breakfast and wasn't sure if his welcome would hold for dinner— always provided there was anything left by the time he and Jeryn got down to the Hall. But all weariness faded beneath an unaccustomed, scholarly elation as he and Jeryn sat cross-legged on the book-scattered floor, surrounded by the blue-white pool of magelight that illuminated the crackling pages of the old ledger that rested on Sun Wolf's knees.

"Here it is." His hand cast wavering cobalt shadows over the faded page as he pointed. "Thirty volumes of accompts, six large skins for the working of covers and forty skins of parchment . . . dried ink . . . ink pots . . . *twenty-six Books of the Witches of Wenshar*. I thought as much, when Kaletha talked about the summoning of the dead."

"Twenty-six," Jeryn said, his small hand resting lightly on Sun Wolf's shoulder as he looked around his arm at the page. "And if Mother brought seventeen," he said, "and there's twenty-five there now. . ."

"That means that somewhere in this Fortress are eighteen books," Sun Wolf said, his voice low and his single eye gazing thoughtfully into the darkness, "written by the Witches of Wenshar."

CHAPTER

—— 10 ——

DARKNESS LAY OVER THE FORTRESS OF TANDIERAS; hiding in corners from the yellow torchlight in the Hall, but walking, alive and sniffing, through the empty quarter. Pale starlight rimmed the broken tiles of the old weavers' courtyard with frost, but did not touch the sable blackness inside the long building there. By the wavering sulfur glow of the requisite seven bowls of fire, Kaletha gathered her followers for the summoning of the dead.

Clear and silvery, her voice lifted in the invocation to the Mother. "We ask her aid, having done all that we can . . . We have purified ourselves with fasting . . . We have cleansed this room with fire and herbs and water . . ."

Standing between Anshebbeth and young Pradborn Dyer, Starhawk flexed her aching hands. She hadn't swept floors since her convent days.

". . . We have circled ourselves with Darkness and with Light . . ."

A spurt of gold flame from one of the bowls made the deep-scratched lines of the pentacle seem to bend and lengthen. It sprawled over the earthen floor like a dead bird; the smell of the dry ground where it had been cut mingled with that of the adobe walls, of must and crushed herbs, of the cloying incense, and the electric dustiness of the wind. A gust groaned through the walls of the empty quarter which lay just beyond the court, making the flames shudder; Starhawk could not repress a quick glance over her shoulder, to the darkness that seemed to wait just outside.

Wreathed in smoke and incense, Kaletha moved from point to point of the pentacle, taking care never to step across its lines. She touched, in turn, the water in the dishes at its valleys and passed her hands above the bowls of fire; the shadows of her fingers caressed the faces of those who stood in the narrow zone between the inner pentacle and the outer Circle of Light.

"We have drawn the Circle of Light about us, to ward off all creatures of darkness; we stand before you defended against all that would do us harm..."

Except ourselves, thought Starhawk, as the cold hands of those on either side shut around hers. *Except ourselves.*

"I don't like it," the Chief had said, when she'd spoken to him earlier that evening down in the Hall.

She hadn't asked, 'Why not?' If he had anything to go on but his animal instinct for danger he would have said as much. Instead she had asked, "How dangerous can it be?"

"I don't know. I don't know how powerful Kaletha is or what kind of magic she's learned from those books of hers. I don't know how much power she'll be able to raise from those of her following who have power of their own—Egaldus and Shelaina." This had been a few hours ago, when Starhawk had come down to the Hall and found Sun Wolf and Jeryn devouring a belated dinner of fried cheese and porridge. Their hair and faces

glistened from what looked like a hasty wash in the nearest horse trough, and their shirts and doublets were gray
with old dust and cobwebs. "According to everything
I've heard from Tazey and Nanciormis, the power of the
Witches of Wenshar was just about always used for evil.
It wasn't a question of some of them being good and
some of them evil—they were all a bad lot, no matter
how good they were to start with."

When Starhawk looked doubtful of that, Jeryn put in,
"It's true." The branch of candles, used at supper and
relighted by the errant pair as they'd come from their
mysterious investigations in the library, shone in his dark
eyes as he looked up at her. "It's why Tazey was so
scared—why Father's so angry, too. It isn't just that
Tazey didn't want to turn into a witch and be damned.
She didn't want to turn into someone who'd deserve to
be damned. And they did."

The supper things had long since been cleared away,
and the folk who remained in the lower end of the Hall,
sewing or mending harnesses or sharpening weapons,
talked in muffled tones. Beneath the door of the solar, a
thread of light was visible. For a time, Osgard's pacing
shadow had crossed it, back and forth, back and forth,
as if he imagined he could outwalk pain and loss. Some
time ago this had ceased. Now there was only the muted
clink of a solitary wine cup on the little bronze table.

Starhawk had frowned, her gaze going from the big,
lion-colored barbarian with his eye patch and his scarred
forearms under their tangle of sun-bleached hair, the
brass of his grimy doublet winking softly in the candlelight, to the fragile boy beside him, his black curls
mussed and usual shabby primness thrown to the winds.
"Is that possible?" she'd asked. "For magic to be intrinsically evil?"

"It shouldn't be," the Wolf had said. "But then, by all
rights, it shouldn't work at all. But it does. We still don't
know *why* magic works, Hawk, any more than we know
what lightning is or what life is, for that matter—why a

woman should be able to bring another human being alive out of her belly, a person who never existed before and who could raise empires and ride the wind...Why women?"

"They're smarter," Starhawk replied promptly and with a straight face.

The Wolf had grinned back—it was an old jest between them. Then he'd sobered and said, "We don't have to understand a thing, or even believe in it, to be killed by it, Hawk. And after going for years believing magic had nothing to do with me, I'm not about to start thinking I understand it. I *don't think* magic should—or could—automatically corrupt those who wield it; but on the other hand, there's a certain amount of unreliable evidence that in this case it *did*. And in any event, I've been warned against necromancy before. Kaletha may not need to intend evil for evil to come of it."

"She needs seven," the Hawk had said slowly, propping her boot on the bench beside him, her elbow on her thigh. "I'm the only other person she trusts. And in an odd way—I don't exactly trust her, because she's irresponsible with her power and with her influence over other people. But...in a way I understand her."

He had looked up at her for a moment from his half-devoured meal, puzzled, as if he had not quite expected her to form a friendship or a liking where he had none. Not that it was against his will or even his expectations —merely, that he had not thought about the possibility since they had become lovers.

Finally he'd asked, "Pox rot it, Hawk, don't you feel it?"

"I feel there's danger, yes," she'd said. "But I also think one or the other of us should be there. And if she's going to call power out of whichever of us it is, it should probably be me because I don't have any."

He had nodded, accepting her logic. But the sense of danger came back to her now, a nervous prickle; a warrior's indefinable awareness that the situation, for reasons she could not precisely define, stank like carrion. She had spent the hours between her talk with Sun Wolf and the approach to midnight meditating, and perhaps it was for this reason the night around her seemed alive, and the darkness filled with half-coalesced entities, waiting only to be named.

She was the only one in the Circle who neither was nor wished she had been mageborn. As they joined hands and Kaletha formed the final link in the glowing ring of human energy between Circle and pentagram, she looked at the faces of those around her: Luatha, her fat face creased in concentration, which did not quite eradicate the lines of sullen discontent around her mouth; Shelaina, wraith-like and withdrawn, looking at Kaletha with her face transfigured by the half-trance in which, under Kaletha's guidance, she could light fires from cold wood; and Pradborn, his eyes tight shut and his lips moving as he muttered to himself one of Kaletha's spells of self-hypnosis. Beside her, Starhawk was aware of Anshebbeth, her whole thin body tense as the fist of a frightened amateur around a knife hilt, her face a white mask with its sleepless, dark-circled eyes. Through her palms, clasping Anshebbeth's long, cold finger bones and Pradborn's chubby flipper, she felt the stir of power, an almost palpable crosscurrent of moving energy, different from the deepening stillness of the Invisible Circle in which the nuns of St. Cherybi had meditated. Or perhaps, the practical part of her mind said, it was only her knowledge of the tensions which divided that little band.

At Kaletha's signal, Egaldus' musical tenor rose to lead the chanting. The words were unfamiliar to Starhawk except for one earlier rehearsal, an ancient invocation whose hypnotic sonority numbed the mind. Kaletha's eyes were shut. Outside, the wind muttered distant rumors of storm.

We are children of Earth, thought Starhawk, her mind beginning to sink under the drone of the voices and of her own participation in the archaic ritual, her thoughts slipping down beneath the weight of the incense toward the point at which they would be completely stilled. *Deny it though the Trinitarians might, our minds are born of our bodies, clay informed by living fire; from this comes the power of what we are, not what we do.*

As her mind blended with the chant and the drug-like sweetness of the smoke, the part of her that remained a warrior tingled like a cat at sunset with the sense of power growing in the darkness beyond the protective Circle of Light.

By starlight, the empty quarter of the Palace had the disjointed appearance of a beast's skeleton, rib and femur and tibia tracing where the walls had lain, amid a scattering of random vertebrae. The fragile whiteness picked out bleached edges and corners of wall and stone and the silken curve of miniature dunes whose crests frayed in the searching wind. Shadow swathed empty doors and windows and filled the mouths of a hundred courts and alleyways like black curtains of cobweb. The air was livid with electricity and the sulfur stench of power.

If he struck flint, Sun Wolf thought, standing in the sand-strewn court just inside the gate, the ether itself would explode.

Methodically, he began to quarter the ruins.

He carried no light, nor did he summon the fox fire of the mages, not wanting to confuse his eyes with what they saw in light and shadow. He was aware that it would be difficult in any case to see what he sought. Kaletha would have concealed the place from the casual eye, casting spells around the entrance to the cellar—if cellar it was—that would cause the glance to slip over the place, as it habitually slipped over so many things in common life. From his experience scouting and using scouts, Sun Wolf was well aware how few people could name every item in a room or tell whether a door opened outward or inward; most people, if asked, would

be surprised to learn of the door. He had learned also
how easy were the spells to make this happen.

So he walked through the empty courts carefully,
marking with a little scribble of light each empty doorway through which he passed—temporary marks, which
would fade with the sunlight and be gone. He counted on
his fingers the four corners of every roofless cell he entered—old workshops with desiccated shards of benches
tumbled where the sandstorms had left them along the
walls, *their corners deep in sand and shattered roof tiles,*
the dark rafters overhead murmuring with the voices of
sleeping doves; what had once been kitchens, with
foxes' messes in their round little fireplaces; and roofless
stables and byres filled with a whispering harlequin of
shadow and the furtive scurry of nervous desert rats.
The ones farther in had roof beams fallen down across
them; nearer the inhabited portions of the Fortress, the
beams, scarce in that treeless country, had been taken
away. Even in the rare rains of the foothill winters, the
thick walls, five and six feet wide at the base, were beginning to melt to shapeless lines of mud.

He made himself walk to every corner and touch the
drifted mats of wood chips and sand there, knowing how
illusions could make him think he had seen each shadowed corner look like every other. He knew that it was
in the minute and singular checking of every detail that
good siegecraft and good generalship—and, incidentally,
good magic—lay, so only those with a certain methodi-
cal patience could master them.

Yet through it all, he was conscious of the magic
moving in the night. The air seemed to grit upon his skin,
as if all his body were a raw wound; the magic-laden
silences picked and chewed at his taut nerves until even
the sliding of his long hair over his scalp in the movement of hot, restless desert winds was enough to make
him start. He could sense Kaletha and her disciples
raising power from the bones of the earth, calling it forth
from the ambient air; he knew that his own magic par-

took of it, drawing strength from the strength that walked free and restless in the darkness. He had visited the dyer's workshop with its shallow, crumbling vat pits, where Nexué's body had been found the day after her murder. But now, when he walked its four corners again, looking with particular care at the hideously stained stones of its fallen walls, he could feel the echoes of the malice and horror that had been enacted there still lingering in the ground. The bass strings of a harp will speak if the wind passes across them; so crumbling ghosts of magic vibrated around him there as he passed, a shadowless shadow in the night. In another place he felt it again, like a weak afterwhisper of sound. It took him a few moments of gazing at the black stripes of rafters overhead against a blacker sky to realize that it had been in this cell that he had found the massacred doves.

Hand knit to hand; flesh to flesh. Starhawk was aware, through the strange sparkling darkness of what was almost like meditation, of the power passing through the meat and sinew from the innermost marrow to the innermost marrow of the knotted bones within. She had never before partaken of this pooling of power, but she could sense the energy moving around the circle, greater than Kaletha's power, or Egaldus' fast-growing strength. It seemed to her that the flames that burned over the herbs and the incense had sunk, that shadow moved over the faces of the seven, that the lines scratched in the earth to define the pentacle and the Circle were faintly glowing, and that the faces themselves, which she had known throughout the last ten days, had changed, different and yet not unfamiliar, as if she had always known what they looked like underneath the skin.

She was chanting, repeating over and over the meaningless syllables of the unknown rite, the sound itself washing over her mind like the rhythm of sea waves; she

was aware they had all begun to sway with the movement. She had no idea how long they had been chanting,
nor did she care; as when she meditated, it seemed to
her that time had settled and stopped, and she would
have been neither surprised nor upset to walk outside
and discover that the stars had not moved at all or that
the sun was rising. But in meditation, she was conscious
of all things, like the silence of deep water. In this, she
was conscious only of the chant, the steady beat of its
strength in her mind, and the scarcely controlled power
slipping from hand to hand. It was like sleep, but moving
sleep. The mind was released, she thought dimly—the
mind that lay like a shield over the dark well beneath,
from which the power came.

And just before her own mind surrendered to the
chanting, she realized why all of the victims had been
attacked when they were. *But if that's the case . . .* she
thought, and fear hit her as suddenly as if she had
stepped off a cliff.

Like the whisper of wind, she heard Kaletha's voice,
though whether inside her skull or outside she could not
be sure. "Don't break the Circle . . . Don't pull your mind
from the power . . ."

The others were relying on her. For a panicked instant
she wanted to release the hands she held, flee to the
empty quarter and find the Chief, tell him, warn him . . .
But the disciplines of meditation were strong. She let her
thoughts sink back into the nothingness of the chant,
and, as if she had opened her hand, the knowledge rav-
eled away into the dry flicker of the night wind.

Sun Wolf put his hand on the loose dune of sand-cov-
ered rubble, which dissolved before his eyes into insub-
stantial shadow. He saw almost at the same moment that
his fingers touched it, the iron of the grillework that the
spell had concealed, and he jerked his hand away in terror, as if burned. He fell back a step, the muttering dryness of the desert wind making cold the sweat that

suddenly stood on his brow, his heart slamming like a smelter's hammer...

But there was nothing to be afraid of.

His mind told him that, even as his breath raced from his lips. *Not even instinct,* he thought, *no clue, no sign. Just fear itself.*

His father's harsh teachings had managed to make him forget for nearly forty years that he had been mage-born, but it had never quite eradicated his curiosity. The old man had said a hundred times, "You're too nosey for a warrior, boy," usually followed up by a clip on the ear. He stepped forward again.

He could see the spell marks now on the iron. That delicate frieze of signs, invisible to the human eye, could only have been written by Kaletha. In the living horror that whispered in every shadow of the night, he still felt fear of them and of this place, a deserted kitchen in the midst of the old quarter; but he was aware now that not only the grille, but the remains of the tiled floor and the crumbling adobe walls, had been written with fear-spells. The power that walked the night picked them up and made them resonate in his mind like the ghastly images of nightmares.

He wiped the sweat from his palms and fished in his doublet pocket for a wax writing tablet and stylus. It was only the spells of the night, he told himself, forcing his hand steady as he copied the signs as well as he could, to study them later. There was no danger...

Or was there?

He clicked the tablet closed and pocketed it once again. Just because his fear was induced by a spell didn't mean that there was no reason to fear.

Kaletha would be on the lookout for a spell mark near her hideaway; but, at a guess, she had no woodscraft. He marked the corner with three bricks, to find it again in case of some spell that confused the memory of directions, and walked out into the court.

The fear lessened as he stepped beneath the broken

door-lintel. Outside, the wind was stronger—not the hard, tearing forerunner of the storms, but the shifting whisper of dry voices, playing tag among the ancient stones, like the demon voices in the canyons of Wenshar. In a corner near a dry well, he found a couple of dusty cottonwood saplings, seeded in a wet year from the old tree in the next court. They were half-dead, and it was no difficult thing to tear one of them up by its shallow roots. His nape prickling like a dog's at the queer, rising tension of the night, he pulled his knife from his belt and began stripping the sapling into a pole, listening all the while, though for what he did not know.

He wondered if Kaletha would be able to summon the voice of the dead.

More than any artificial spell of hers, laid on this place to keep intruders away, the thought terrified him.

Cautiously, he reentered the darkness of the ruin.

The sapling was nearly seven feet long, brittle as only dry cottonwood could be. He worked its end through the metal of the grille and levered sideways. The metal grated on stone; like the swish of silk on dust, he heard something move sharply in the pitchy darkness underneath.

The iron was heavy, but no earth had settled around it—it was nearly clean of rust. He tipped the grille out of its sunken bed and reached gingerly over to topple it aside. Then he looked down into the hole beneath and felt the skin crawl along his scalp.

The pit below was alive with snakes.

Most of them were the brown-and-gray desert rattlers. When his body bulked dark against the night above them, they set up a dry buzzing as they raised their horned noses skyward. In the darkness, he could see among them the slender lead-colored rock asps and, like gross, flat-headed slugs, the big cave mambas, as long as his arm and half again as fat. Even as he watched, he saw another one slither forth from a hole in the wall of the pit, to fall with a soft, sickening plop to join its brethren. The sandy floor of the cellar below seemed to glitter with black, watching eyes.

They must have been drawn by Kaletha's spells from all over the empty quarter, he thought, *since first I came near the place.*

He felt a sudden rush of sympathy for the local attitude toward the Witches of Wenshar.

Well, pox rot you, he thought. *Two can play that game.*

He hunkered down on the rim of the pit, sapling pole in hand. The vicious buzzing of the rattlers rose again; in the darkness he could make out sinuous movement and the dozenfold flicking of forked, black, questing tongues.

Reaching out with his mind, he felt the prickling of those stupid alien angers, a shortsighted rage to strike at warmth and the smell of blood. Never taking his eye from the snakes, he caressed the cottonwood pole with his big, sword-scarred hands, as if to work magic into it as he would work a lotion. He imparted his smell to it, the heat of his flesh, and the shadow of his bulk against the night. The darkness all about him seemed charged with power, intensifying in his mind the smell-feel of the reptile instincts below that woke such disturbing echoes in his own thoughts. He could feel the spells that worked on them, that had drawn them there, and that would turn them to attack a man. Those spells, too, he worked and turned into the wood, while taking into his own body the illusion of coldness and stasis and the smell of the ancient stones.

He addressed a brief prayer to such of his ancestors as might be listening and flung the pole down into the corner of the pit below.

It bounced; at the movement, the snakes were upon it, striking again and again at the spell-written wood. There was absolutely no time to lose and none to think, but it did cross Sun Wolf's mind, as he lowered himself by his hands and dropped the few feet remaining to the sandy floor of the pit, that it was perfectly possible for

him to have gotten the first part of his spells right and
muffed the second.

No, he thought. His body bloodless, smelling of stone
and dust was cold to the tongues of the snakes. He was a
dead thing; it was the pole that was alive and must be
killed.

They continued to strike the pole.

The cellar was clean, about a dozen feet square, and
low-roofed, smelling of earth and stone and of the dusty
fetor of the snakes. The air there was dry and still. No
dust drifted its corners—the walls above sheltered its
entrance from the prevailing winds. A short ladder lay
along one wall, where it could be lowered and dropped
from above. In the darkness, Sun Wolf could make out a
table, a reading stand, and a tall-legged stool. Beyond
them, a niche was cut out of the far wall, a low ceiling
beam sheltering a sort of hollow there. Deep inside it he
saw two small chests of iron-bound leather, neither of
them larger than a woman could carry by herself. There
were no lamps. To nonmageborn eyes, even by day, the
place would be dim and shadowy, and by night, a Stygian
pit.

But even in the darkness, he could see the skittery
movement swarming along the lids of the chests.

He threw a quick glance back at the crawling heap of
loathsomeness around the pole. His instincts told him
that wouldn't last much longer; it was a fight to keep his
concentration on the illusions that kept them attacking
the wood and blocked their awareness of the heat of his
own veins. He understood then why meditation was so
essential, strengthening and freeing the concentration.
He knew he could maintain two illusions at once, but
never three.

The lids of the chests were crawling with scorpions.

Slow with loathing, his hand went to the pocket of his
doublet for his gloves. But even as he did so, movement
caught his eye on the overhanging beam and on the earth
and stones it carried. He'd have to duck his head under

it to reach the chests. Even as he watched, a scorpion dropped down from the beam into the niche—one of the big, shiny brown ones, long as a man's hand, whose stings could pierce all but the toughest leather. The sweat was cold on his face as he passed his hand nervously across the back of his neck, and he understood then that he couldn't do it. The boxes were locked. Given time, he could force a lock, but he could not pick up a trunk that size, filled with the weight of books, without crawling halfway under that lintel.

Kaletha had defeated him.

Anger and resentment surged up in him, but the sensible part of him, the strategist that had come more and more to the fore as he grew older, told him not to be stupid. He had been in situations where he would rather have died than admit that a woman had defeated him, but the stupidity of the acts to which he had let himself be driven in that kind of rage had never been worth it. She had power. Though he could feel that his own powers were heightened with the sorcery stirring through the night, something told him not to push his luck.

His hyperquick hearing picked up the stir and swish of movement behind him. Turning, he saw the snakes had finally realized that what they bit was dead wood. For the most part they were still milling, but a mamba as big around as his leg was crawling toward him like a swollen, dirt-colored worm.

Snakes would strike at sudden movement; he glided away from the chests, glancing everywhere and cursing his blindness on his left side. It might have been the heat of his anger at Kaletha that shivered the wall of illusions that covered him, merely the cumulative pressures of maintaining the spells, or the uncanny power that filled the night like hallucinatory flame—he did not know. But other snakes swung their heads toward him, tongues flicking. He flipped the ladder cautiously over with the toe of his boot, and a single scorpion—the small, whitish-gray kind whose sting was no worse than the sting of a bee—darted to safety in a corner. He jerked his foot aside as the mamba struck at his boot heel and he shoved the ladder into position. If he panicked, he knew the spells would crumble. Before the snake could strike again, he was scrambling up out of the pit, to the wind and shadows above.

When he reached the top, his hands were shaking so badly he could barely push the ladder down through the hole again and replace the grille.

"And when was that?" asked Starhawk, her voice quiet in the gloom of the little cell beyond the stables.

Sun Wolf shook his head. They lay together in the makeshift bed of pine poles and faded quilts, flesh against chilled flesh, but neither had moved to make love. Their kisses had been those of comfort against fears and thoughts neither could quite define, and they held each other, not as lovers do, but like brother and sister, frightened of the dark. "I don't know. I came back here; it was at least an hour before you did." He moved his head, to look down at the browned, delicate face in its short frame of ivory hair, where it lay on the hard pillow of his pectorals. "Why?"

Her gray eyes seemed transparent in the thin glow of the magelight that burned like a lamp around the tip of one bedpost. "Because I—I'm not sure, but I think that's when there was a break in the power of the Circle. It's like—I can't tell what the Circle was like. Like a tug of war, maybe, or—or rising to the climax of lovemaking. I don't know. But there can be no break in it, no slacking. The power has to feed on itself."

Sun Wolf nodded, understanding. "What you may not be strong enough to get from yourself, you can achieve by combining many minds—if you can get those minds to pull together. Yes. But if one stops pulling, they all slack."

"And they all did," said Starhawk. "It was like a har-

ness trace breaking, or like falling out of love. Kaletha
tried to recover it, but . . . we never did, completely."

She moved her weight slightly against him, hard muscle and hard bone, the ridges of scars breaking the silk of
the flesh.

He asked, "Did Galdron come?"

Starhawk shook her head and moved again, pressing
closer to him under the mottled, sand-colored homespun
of the worn quilts. By the witchlight, he could see the
deepening of the scratchwork of fine lines around her
eyes; through his arm around her body, he felt the tension of her muscles.

"What is it?"

"I don't know." She shook her head again, and Sun
Wolf, sensing not only her fear but his own, drew her
tighter yet against him. "The concentration broke, or it
never peaked. Nothing. But I could feel it—" She looked
around her at the darkness crowding onto the blue
witchlight and the velvet night beyond the window, charcoal black and still with the predawn drop of the wind, as
if all the world held its breath. "And I feel it still."

"I know," the Wolf said softly. "So do I. And I'm
wondering why. Power was built up, Hawk—it's still
here, hanging over the empty quarter like a miasma.
Something . . ."

She frowned suddenly, as some word of his tugged at
her mind.

"What is it?"

"I don't know. Something you said . . . Something I
thought during the summoning . . . it was important, but
damned if I can remember what it was or why. Only . . ."

Something beyond the windows snagged the corner of
his vision. His head whipped around, and the Hawk,
feeling the sudden flinch of his muscles, was silent, as he
killed the blue glow of the witchlight and they lay together, staring out of darkness into the dark.

There was movement in the empty quarter.

He rolled silently out of bed and walked naked to the

window, holding to the velvet density of the shadows around the wall. The air was freezing on his flesh. Like a ghost, Starhawk joined him, the quilt thrown over her shoulder, carrying her sword.

Neither spoke. Around them the power was palpable in the night, the hideous tension that had grown, not lessened, as those who had formed the Circle had sought their beds.

Sun Wolf was not sure, but he thought he saw the bluish flicker of demon light among the labyrinth of skeleton walls.

Silently he turned away and found his boots, war kilt, and sword. As he pulled them on, Starhawk joined him, locating her own clothing as she had located her weapon by touch in the dark. By the time she was ready, Sun Wolf had gone to the door and was looking out across the little court toward the empty quarter. He was sure of it now. There were demons there.

This is none of my affair, he told himself. But he felt his heart quicken with the same fear he had felt in the carved canyons of Wenshar, a fear unlike—deeper than —a man's fear of death or harm. *Fear of what?* the calm, detached portion of his mind wondered impersonally. *It has nothing to do with me.*

But in a queer way he knew that it did.

His hand tightened around the greasy old hilt of his sword. The Hawk was like an armed shadow behind him as he moved silently across the starlit court.

In the labyrinth of the old courtyards, the presence of the demons was stronger. He could sense them, feel their malice prickle along his skin, and hear their thin, piping voices calling to one another among the stones. *Why here?* he wondered. *Why tonight?* Did they follow the smell of power, gravitating to this place for the same reasons that they haunted the ruins of Wenshar? Was that what they wanted of him when they had hovered through those moonless canyon nights outside the window of the rock-cut temple, waiting for him? Was it the revived power of the old Witches that drew them now, like vultures to the stink of dying things?

He could hear their voices, sometimes little piping cries or a low crooning, like a child singing over and over to itself the only line of a song that it knew. For an instant it crossed his mind that it *was* a child, lost somewhere in the mazes; then he shook his head and thrust the thought aside. Like their voices, it was only bait in a trap.

What kind of a trap? he wondered. *A trap for whom and why? Except for the occasional biting-demon, they couldn't harm humans—could they?* As in the ruins of Wenshar, he felt cold with fear of them, fear not for his body, but fear of he did not know what. He wondered suddenly about the Witches of Wenshar and about what had become of those who had refused to use their power for evil—or if they had ever had a choice.

Faint and confused among the walls, he heard a voice calling, "Kaletha! Kaletha!" *Egaldus,* he thought ... *or a demon's voice that sounded like his. Had Kaletha run to check her cache, as soon as she could rid herself of her disciples? Was that why the concentration of the Circle had given way when she had somehow felt his spells against her snakes?*

"Kaletha!" he bellowed, and the echoes mocked him, *Kalethakalethakaletha* ... "If you can hear me, stand still and call!" *call ... callcall ...*"

"Kaletha!" came the other voice, like a desperate echo.

Sun Wolf strode forward, his eye sharp along the ground before him, the tops of the walls, and the few remaining buildings on all sides. They crossed through what had been a stable court, then hurried down a roofless colonnade where the sand drifted knee-deep along the back wall. Through an eyeless window gap, he saw the flicker of something bright and moving, a discarded insect-chitin of light, save for those greedy, unhuman eyes ... then it was gone. He realized that he still had his sword ready in his hand and that Starhawk did, too, though neither weapon would do them the slightest good. The very air seemed weighted with evil, ready at a word to take shape . . .

Why did he feel that, in the back of his mind, he knew that word?

"Kaletha!" he roared. "Egaldus!"

Farther off now, but recognizable as the young acolyte's, the voice called out, "Kaletha? Kal . . ."

And then the word turned to a scream.

CHAPTER

—— 11 ——

"*T*HE DEMONS WERE THERE. *I* KNOW, *I* SAW THEM."

"Are you saying you think they did it?" Incarsyn
asked from his place on Osgard's left.

Nanciormis sneered, "Don't be an ass, man."

Osgard's bloodshot green eyes narrowed. "If you saw
them, they couldn't have been demons, Captain.
Demons are . . ."

"Invisible," Sun Wolf finished, slouching back in his
black oak chair at the fireplace end of the High Table and
studying the three men facing him across the length of
the dark board. "I know." Through the line of tall southern windows the sun slanted in hard bars of horizontal
gold, but around them, the Fortress of Tandieras was
unwontedly quiet. Not until sunup would any man or
woman of the guards venture into the empty quarter to
fetch forth Egaldus' remains, but the rumor had swept
the place like a chaparral fire after a dry summer. Sun
Wolf could hear the murmur of it, breathing like wind in

the corners of the servants' halls; he could feel the silence as he or Kaletha passed.

He went on, "I don't know why I've always been able to see them, but I have. It may come of being mage-born . . ."

"Kaletha can't," Nanciormis pointed out promptly. "Nor, to the best of my knowledge, can . . ." He just barely broke off the word *Tazey* at a furious glare from the King.

"It is said among my people," Incarsyn put in, "that those who can see demons do so because they are themselves demon-spawned."

"That's rubbish," the King snapped.

"So there are those among you who can do it?" Sun Wolf asked thoughtfully, raking the Lord of the Dunes with his single golden eye.

The young man nodded, but he didn't look comfortable about the whole subject. Since yesterday, he had the pale, shaken appearance of one in the grip of some heavy and unaccustomed thinking.

At Osgard's invitation, the Lord of the Dunes had come to this council, but Sun Wolf, feeling the subpulse of politics between the three men, sensed that the request had been a false one. He had sat there through Sun Wolf's recital of his second investigation of the empty quarter last night and of the finding of what was left of Egaldus' body, looking handsome and exotic and a little puzzled in his gold-stitched tunic and snowy cloak. Neither Nanciormis nor Osgard had much to ask him—he was there simply, Sun Wolf guessed, to remind him that he was still pledged to become Osgard's son-in-law, no matter what afterthoughts might be now churning through his mind.

Nanciormis said, "In any case it's foolish to believe it was demons. They are incapable of harming man."

"Not necessarily," the Wolf said. "There have been biting-demons, stone-throwers . . ."

"But certainly none capable of doing that kind of damage."

Incarsyn folded one white hand upon the other and appeared to study for a moment the circle of glinting fire thrown by the facets of his ruby ring. Then he looked up again. "Among my people, it was said that such things happened to those who ran afoul of the Witches of Wenshar."

"Old wives' tales!" Osgard's voice was harsh as the crack of a whip in the warm blaze of the morning heat.

"Were they?" Sun Wolf asked softly and turned to look at the young Lord of the Dunes. "Tell me, Incarsyn, were all the Witches of Wenshar evil? Was there none among them who used her power for something other than selfishness and lust?"

The young man frowned and shook his head. Obviously the concept of a good witch had never crossed his mind. Perhaps in the shirdane in which he thought, such a concept was linguistically impossible. In the crystalline brilliance of the morning sunlight after the sleepless alarms of the night, his youth and hardness contrasted even more sharply with Nanciormis' slack cheeks and double chin—the more so because of the racial similarity of those two hawk-boned sets of features framed in the flowing darkness of their braided hair. "None," he said simply and then smiled a little, lightening up his face. "They were, you understand, women. A woman will, by nature, put first in her considerations, the things that immediately affect her whether they be material goods or satisfaction." He spoke as one who forgives a simple-minded child for soiling itself, and Sun Wolf suppressed an unexpected urge to get up and knock his handsome head against the wall.

He started to retort, but Osgard's heavy voice drowned them both. "The Witches of Wenshar have nothing to do with it!" he thundered. "It's clear as daylight what happened! Egaldus was tampering with heresy and magic last night with that bitch Kaletha, trying to

raise spirits, they say, and got what was coming to him.
They both had every reason to wish Galdron ill, since
the old hypocrite was threatening to exile him—"

"And so he raised up a spell that backfired on himself?" Sun Wolf demanded. "Talk sense, man."

"Kaletha and Egaldus were lovers," Nanciormis
added scornfully, but his dark eyes, regarding Sun Wolf,
were narrow with thought. "She'd never have harmed a
hair of his golden head."

"Which isn't necessarily true," remarked Starhawk
later, when the Wolf was sitting cross-legged on the parapet of the watchtower, a hundred feet above the granite
courts of the Hold, peeling an orange. "Just because you
love someone doesn't mean you can't fear and hate and
resent them as well."

"People couple for all kinds of reasons." In the stifling
stillness of the desert air, the orange's perfume was
shockingly sweet. "You can lie with someone you hate, if
it gives you a chance at them."

"True, but that's not what I mean." Starhawk turned
her gaze from the brazen emptiness of the desert.
Framed in the white veils, her face had a stripped look
—bones, scars, and ice-gray eyes like a man's—but for
the softness of the lips. "Love isn't an easy thing to define. You can resent people you love—enough to want to
kill them, or at least hurt them badly. People do it all the
time. Not the least reason is because they hold that
power over you."

Sun Wolf was silent for a moment, thinking about that
and wondering if the Hawk spoke from personal experience on that score. He offered her a segment of the orange, and she shook her head—she never ate on duty, he
remembered, even if it was only watching the dead landscape of the desert for motion that never came. From up
here, the Haunted Mountains were visible, a stained and
broken knife blade over the heat shimmer of the reg.
Had she resented him—hated him, even—in the years
she'd been the second-in-command of his mercenary

army, loving him and watching him bed a steady parade of eighteen-year-old concubines? In those days he had seldom thought of her as a woman. Perhaps neither had she.

But looking up, troubled, he met the smile in her eyes, so he asked instead, "You think Kaletha resented Egaldus enough to kill him?"

"You're a teacher." The Hawk made a sweeping scan of the desert horizon, then turned her eyes back to him again. "Would you train a student who was strong enough to defeat you? Not just to give you a good fight —but to whip you, crush you, kill you maybe?"

Again Sun Wolf fell quiet for a time. The sun, warm on his own loose-draped veils and the leather of his shoulders and thighs, had lost its summer intensity, but the air still felt thick and electric, charged with storms. At last he said, "I never have done so. I don't know." He hesitated, then added truthfully, "I'd like to think I'd have more pride as a teacher than I would have vanity as a warrior, but . . . I don't know."

Starhawk smiled a little and resumed her steady watching, presenting him with the smooth line of her profile, somehow delicate in spite of the high cheek-bones and too-strong chin. "And you're forty now and a wizard," she said. "I can lay you money you wouldn't have when you were twenty-eight. Would you have trained me to be able to defeat you?"

The words were slow and hard to say. "I'd like to think you could." But even as he said them, he knew he didn't, not really.

You are greedy, like Egaldus, Kaletha had said. And to her Egaldus had said, *You still wish to keep it all to yourself*. He had held Kaletha in contempt for doing it—it wasn't a particularly pleasant thing to realize about himself.

"But you're pretty sure I wouldn't," said Starhawk, her voice gentle. "I understand Kaletha, Wolf. And in spite of herself, I rather like her. I think she's wrong to be hoarding the books of power, but I can understand why she's doing it—why she keeps her disciples under her thumb the way she does—maybe why she let Egaldus seduce her. She knows she's never had proper teaching; she knows now about the Great Trial, which she didn't know about before. Whatever she says about it, she knows you've gone through it and she hasn't. She's fighting to hang onto her power—over you, over them, over Egaldus."

"You think she'd have killed him to keep him away from the books?" Then he frowned, his blunt fingers pausing in mid-motion, sticky with red orange juice like droplets of blood. "But I went after the books, too. Hell, I went down into the pit. Nothing happened to me."

"It may not have been an impersonal trap," Starhawk said quietly. "Whatever destroyed Egaldus..." She turned back to him, dark, level brows tugging down over her nose. "*Could* Kaletha have summoned up that kind of power, specifically? Or...?"

"I don't know!" Sun Wolf swung his hand in frustration. "Incarsyn said the Witches of Wenshar did, but..." He looked up and saw the woman's face suddenly puckered with a far-off look, as if she listened for some sound beyond the range of hearing. "What is it?"

She shook her head. "I—I can't remember." She leaned on the battlement, a rangy cheetah-shape of dark green leather and white shirt sleeves against the endless speckled dustiness of barren scrub land. "It's on the edge of my mind, something about how the power was summoned... I don't know." She made a wry face. "I'll remember it in the middle of the night sometime." Even those words seemed to catch a loose thread in her memory, and she paused again. Then her eyes turned back to the desert, and all concentration on dreams or half-memories vanished in sudden sharp alertness.

Sun Wolf slewed around on his precarious perch on the battlement to follow her gaze.

On the hard desert horizon a gray plume of dust floated, glittering in the morning air.

"It can't be a storm." Tazey shaded her eyes and gazed out over the desert. She was still dressed, as her father had ordered, in girlish ruffles and curls for the benefit of her suitor; pinks and lavenders that looked garishly incongruous around the strained and hagridden face.

"Of course it can," Kaletha snapped, glancing sidelong at her. "I have sensed one on its way since morning..."

"If it's a storm, it's got a damn narrow base." Sun Wolf turned, as Starhawk and Nanciormis appeared on the thin flight of stone steps that led down to the courtyard below the gatehouse balcony where they stood, both with brass spyglasses in their hands. "The winds won't hit till this evening."

Kaletha's nostrils flared with tired loathing at this contradiction of her words. Like Tazey, she looked rather white around the mouth, though Sun Wolf could not see from her eyes if she had been crying. She looked haggard, as if the magic that had weighted the air last night had been drawn from her veins. Sun Wolf found himself remembering that Egaldus had died calling her name.

The Witches of Wenshar, he thought, and realized that the three of them standing there on the gatehouse, gazing off across the desert toward the advancing column of dust, were the only witches in Wenshar now.

Starhawk handed him his spyglass, made by the best instrument-maker in Pergemis; he unfolded it with a snap as Nanciormis extended his own and set it to his eye. In the dust and heat haze, the shapes of horsemen and dromedaries were clearly visible, as were the white burnooses of the shirdar and the brightly dyed curtains of a swathed litter. He took his eye from the glass at the sound of footsteps on the stair behind him in time to see

Osgard, Incarsyn, and Anshebbeth hurriedly mounting the stairs to crowd onto the gatehouse platform.

Anshebbeth hurried straight to Kaletha. "You shouldn't be out here," she fussed. "You should be resting, you've had a terrible shock."

Kaletha shook her off impatiently. Snubbed and hurt, the governess turned to Tazey. "And you, dear—You were awake all night, practically..."

"*Please*, 'Shebbeth..."

Nanciormis handed his spyglass to Incarsyn and said, "Is that who I think it is?"

The young man stood gazing like some beautiful statue, the loose sleeves of his crimson tunic flattened to his arm muscles by the hot eddy of wind which rolled the knot of curls at the nape of his neck. A crease of consternation appeared on his brow. "The Hasdrozidar," he said at last. "My own people." He lowered the spyglass from his eye, the curves of his mouth set tight with apprehension.

Nanciormis said silkily, "They will be led, I believe, by your sister, the Lady Illyra."

Even at this distance, Sun Wolf could now make out unaided the swaying shape of the great litter in the midst of its circle of mounted outriders. They were moving fast. Either they, too, sensed the onset of the storm that would hit the Fortress a few hours after nightfall, or they simply had the desert dweller's instinctive uneasiness about being in open ground in the season of witches. Beside him, he was aware of the look of sick fright on Tazey's face and of the slow flush of anger to Osgard's.

Incarsyn's voice was tight but steady. "So it seems." He hesitated for a moment, as if figuring out what his next action should be, then turned and placed a comforting hand on Tazey's shoulder. "Have no fear, my Princess. She is only a woman. She cannot separate me from the wife that I will have." He bowed with his usual lithe grace, then strode away down the stairs.

Osgard rumbled, "She'd damn bloody well better

not," and followed after, his white surcoat billowing in the hot winds that had begun to shift along the Fortress's parched granite walls.

Tazey still stood looking out across the desert, her face like something boarded against storms worse than that which she had parted with her hands. Her fingers, where they rested on the parapet, where shaking.

"Only a woman," Nanciormis quoted derisively. At a glance from him, Anshebbeth fell back from her protective hovering at Tazey's side. The big shirdar lord's voice was soft, but carried clearly to those who remained on the parapet beneath the tall shadows of the Hold. "When that young man decides he wants the alliance with Wenshar's silver mines, there isn't much that shakes him. Don't be deceived, Tazey. He knows your esteem will only pave his way."

"Let her alone," Starhawk said quietly.

Nanciormis glanced at her, impatient. She had stood where the shadows fell most densely, without saying anything, her hands tucked behind her sword belt—it was easy to forget she was there. "I don't want my niece deceived into something she'll regret," he said roughly. "Incarsyn cares less for her than he cares for his horses. He's told me that."

Tazey did not look at him, but Sun Wolf could see in the burnished sun-glare the swim of tears in her eyes. "I haven't been deceived," she said in a small, steady voice. "I've been pushed and bargained for and cozened and threatened with everything from a good beating to eternal damnation..." Her voice shivered, but did not break. "The only thing that's helped me to bear it is that he's been kind enough to try and deceive me."

"In Pardle Sho," her uncle retorted with smooth brutality, "there's a woman who raises rabbits for meat. She goes out every morning when she feeds them, picks them up, pets them, cuddles them, and calls each by its own name, so that they will come to her and she doesn't have to chase after them at slaughtering time."

Tazey swung around, looking up at the tall bulk of the man beside her. The sun glimmered in the tear that lay on her face and on the pink opalescence of the sand-pearls dangling from her ears. She whispered, "I hate you." Turning, she gathered up her absurd, ruffled skirts and ran after her father down the narrow steps.

The sun slanted over toward evening; the wind began to rise. It talked to itself in thin, whistling sneers around the corners of the Fortress, in and out of the thick, de-caying adobe walls of the empty quarter; it smelled of sand and electricity and burned the sinuses with dust. Tempers shortened as the grip of the drying air crushed brains and nerves; people too often spoke their minds or acted without considering consequences; small hatreds and angers flared. In the courts of the cordillera towns, a storm was considered mitigating circumstances in cases of assault and murder.

The caravan from the far-off oasis city of Hasdroza-both had arrived. Its hundred or so lean, sun-hardened riders had stabled their horses and camels in the hastily fitted dormitories on the edges of the empty quarter and joined to crowd the bodyguard, already formidable, of their Lord. From his little cell near the stables, Sun Wolf could hear them talking to one another in the lilting sing-song of the shirdane and smell their cook fires and the spiced greasiness of their meals as he unrolled his armor from its wrappings.

"She'll know if you aren't at supper," Starhawk said quietly. She folded her arms and looked out past the half-furled window shutters to the sulfurous light in the little court. A man dressed like a groom, his black, curly hair proclaiming him one of the shirdar—though he had, like most of the Wenshidar, cut off his braids when he had gone to work for the new rulers of the land—passed along the path from the gate, heading for the privies. Starhawk saw him glance nervously at the parched, si-lent walls of the empty quarter and hurry his steps.

"It's the only time I can be sure where she'll be." In the long heat of the afternoon they had made love and slept, though in his dreams Sun Wolf had seen again the cold, bodiless eyes of the demons. A little uneasily now he unrolled the shirt of chain mail he hadn't worn since the seige of Melplith a year ago and checked the buckles and leather. The weight of it was strange in his hands after so long, the harsh, musical jingling of its rings both foreign and familiar to his ears. There was a bright patch where it had been mended on the breast—a sizeable rip, but he could not for the life of him remember what had done that or when.

"If she can kill at a distance," Starhawk said, "that might not matter." Behind her, a dust devil scampered across the court; a chance gust of wind groaned around the walls. From the stables nearby, Sun Wolf could hear the horses stamping nervously in their stalls. "Always supposing Kaletha is the killer."

Sun Wolf nodded, not surprised. That thought had crossed his mind as well. "You think there might be someone else. Someone who's hiding the fact they're mageborn. Someone who might, at some time in the past, have had access to the books."

"Something like that." She braced her shoulders against the window frame, the slice of light angling through, shining white against her hair. "A witch would have to be awfully stupid to go around killing people by magic in a community where there aren't lots of witches around, but we've both seen stupider things. Remember that apothecary in Laedden who poisoned his neighbors' wells? It might almost be—I don't know—some kind of elemental force, like a beast, killing at random. It's hard to picture someone inflicting that kind of butchery deliberately."

"I found it hard to picture a couple of boys killing their own mother to get the family savings to buy their way out of a besieged city," the Wolf remarked. "We live and learn. They sure as hell offered me the money to let

them through the lines at Melplith." He pulled the heavy
leather chaps he'd borrowed from one of the horse
wranglers from beneath the bed, laid them alongside the
mail shirt, studied the ensemble, and tried to judge
whether the protection offered would be worth the limi-
tation of his movements. The chaps would certainly protect him from the snakes if he moved fast enough, as the
thick leather gloves he'd acquired would protect his
hands from the scorpions. As for meeting anything else
...they might keep him from being hamstrung and
brought down on the first slash, but after that, nothing
would prevent the whirlwind violence that had destroyed
Egaldus and that had scattered pieces of the Bishop Galdron and Norbas Milkom over a dozen square yards of
sand from shredding the flesh from his bones.

"Do you think you can keep Kaletha busy for the next
few hours?"

If he was attacked, he reflected, hefting the stiff
guards in his hands, there would be nowhere to run anyway. Feeling Starhawk's silence, he looked up.

"Chief," said Starhawk slowly, "I'd rather not."

Once, he knew, he would have demanded why, quick
and rather indignant. Now he let the silence lie; after a
long moment she sorted out her words.

"I'll watch her if you want and try to stop her or get
word to you if she comes into the empty quarter. But I
won't use her friendship with me—her trust of me, in
spite of what she knows about me and you—against her.
I want to keep her friendship with me separate from my
love for you."

Her voice was, as usual, calm and uninflected, giving
nothing to anyone, not even to him. But in the years he
had known her, and especially since they had been
lovers, he had come to listen beneath its cool tones. He
remembered her on the tower, saying, *But you're pretty
sure I wouldn't*, and he realized he had asked her, un-
thinkingly, what he had no right to ask.

In the first half second he felt anger at himself and

annoyance at her for doing that to him . . . and a little, he realized, for choosing Kaletha's rights over his whims. That pushed him back to sanity, and he nodded. "All right," he said. And then, though he saw no change in the gray eyes still resting on his face, he added with a kind of stiff unfamiliarity, "I'm sorry. I shouldn't have asked you that."

She concealed her relief and her somewhat unflattering surprise equally well and only said, "I'll do what I can."

As it happened, the entire question became academic anyway.

Starhawk left him to look for Kaletha; the night drew on. The groan and mutter of the winds fell still, the silence even more terrible, hot and thick over the fortress on its knoll and the dusty town beyond. The night was pregnant with storm. Sun Wolf, sitting on the splintery wooden doorsill of his cell waiting for darkness, watched the shutters being put up in every window of Tandieras. The sun sank, turning the Binnig Rock to the color of old blood and flashing like threads of fire on the spires of Pardle Cathedral. He knew there were lamps being lighted in the Hall and in the line of archways on the balcony of the Household, but not even a sliver of brightness illuminated the dark bulk of the Hold. It seemed to him a dead fortress, silent as the rocks. Even the birds were hushed, seeking their own hiding places. The stillness was eerie, too like that of the dead City of Wenshar.

He tried to relax and center his mind, tried to keep it on the spells he knew he would have to work, but it strayed again and again to Starhawk. It had startled him that she would refuse to go against one of her other friends for his sake, and he was aware that he felt miffed about it, as if she should feel loyalty to no one but himself. It was unfair to Starhawk, and he knew it.

He sighed and shook his head at himself. His ancestors would die of shame. Going soft, his father would

say—yielding where he should grasp tighter for his own
survival. He had survived forty years by hanging on. His
life had been a fist which let nothing go. It was difficult
to open it to other things.

As a warrior, he had known what he was. Here, in
this baked landscape of black rocks and demons' whispers, he was seeing what he might become; and like
Tazey, he found that it terrified him.

The hardness of that dreadful, motionless sky softened to a scrim of dove-colored silk. The smell of the
storm was in his veins, pricking and hissing at his mind.
It was not quite dark, but if he was to finish, it was best
that he go now. With all the windows of the Hold shuttered, it was good odds no one would see him. He carefully closed up the windows of his own little cell and, in
the semi-dark, stripped off his leather doublet, the chill
startling against his ribs through the worn homespun of
his patched shirt.

It wasn't until the approaching footfalls were very
close to the doorway that he realized it was not Starhawk returning. He looked up as a shadow blotted what
was left of the light. Against the dusk he saw two of the
white-robed shirdar, their hands on their sword hilts,
motioning silently for him to come.

"So you are Sun Wolf." The veiled woman's hands
moved on the arms of her jointed bronze camp chair.
They were strong hands, white, like Incarsyn's, moiréd
with a lace of shadow in the shuttered chamber's flickering dusk. "The barbarian mercenary."

"My Lady." He inclined his head and felt the scrutiny
of those remarkable dark eyes. "And you are the Lady
Illyra, chief of the people of the Dunes."

Her mouth was hidden beneath the indigo veils which
shrouded the faces of all deep-desert women, but the
heavy lids of those dark eyes lowered. At their corners
he saw the brief crinkle of appreciation at what he knew
to be considerably more than an idle compliment. But

she said, "It is not the way of our people that a woman should rule. It is my brother who is Lord of the Dunes." Her voice was low and harsh, and in it was the authority of one who had never asked any man's leave. By the dry, leathery folds of skin around her eyes, Sun Wolf guessed her age at close to his own—forty. Since her teens, according to rumor, she had ruled for her baby brother Incarsyn, commanding the armies of Hasdrozaboth without ever removing her modest veils. The thin, dark fabric puckered with her breath as she went on, "The women ruled Wenshar, and there was nothing but grief for the shirdar, for all the years of their ruling and for all the years after. I speak merely as ambassador for my brother, who has heavier tasks at hand."

Sun Wolf considered her for a moment—the tall, rangy body, muffled in robes and veils of black and indigo, the nose that crested out beneath the gauze of the veil, and the brilliant eyes, cold as a rattlesnake's, on his. He wondered whether she were beautiful or ugly beneath those layers of gauze and knew that it did not matter, neither to her nor to anyone else. He said, "Matters like courting a woman of Wenshar?"

"He will not marry her."

"He said that he would, knowing what she is."

There was scorn in the deep voice. "He does not know what she is. He thinks magic is what the women do with feathers and herbs, to make this man or that love them or to make barren the other concubines of their husbands. He thinks it is an amusement, like dancing or zhendigo, the arts of touch, and practiced for the same reasons—to please men." The movement of her body breathed a musky perfume which mingled with the pungence of the incense-scattered charcoal in the braziers behind her and the sting of dust stirring from the shutters of the windows. "So think all men, when first they say, 'I will take to me a woman who knows magic.' For this is all the magic that they will allow women in the desert. I know," she went on softly. "I have ordered the death of more than one witch among my people."

She took a bell from the table at her side and rang it, a tiny, piercing sound in the gloom. Sun Wolf, relaxed but battle-ready and still not certain where this interview would lead, moved a hand casually to his sword hilt as a slave came in, a good-looking young fellow with the beardless chin and soft fleshiness of a eunuch. Kneeling, the slave laid a cushion of red, embroidered wool by Sun Wolf's feet. As he settled upon it, sitting on his knees after the fashion of the desert, Sun Wolf automatically checked all possible entrances to the room. Most of them had been curtained against drafts, which lifted the hangings uneasily, like the dark shrouds of passing ghosts. He was particularly aware of the one directly behind his back.

"Why?" he asked her curiously. "You know what it is to be a woman and to fight for power."

"For that same reason," she replied. "I know what I did to win the power I hold. Our ways are not the ways of the north countries, Lord Captain. The desert is harsh. It does not forgive even well-meant errors. Our ways have lasted for a hundred generations of men. They work. When one crosses a desert, one does not leave the straight path from water hole to water hole, even though people cry, 'There is water over that dune there.'" A gust of wind bellied a curtain in the shadows beside her and stirred at the gauze veils covering her face and hair. "To change the old ways is to risk becoming lost. So the Witches of Wenshar proved."

"Tell me," Sun Wolf said, "about the Witches of Wenshar."

"The rumors that brought me here to halt this match of my brother's," she said, "noise that you are a witch yourself. Is this true?" The word she used, with its dialectical inflection, lacking in the less formal speech of Wenshar, tugged at something in his thoughts.

He nodded slowly, unwilling to use that word, that inflection, for himself. "It is."

"Good." The lines around her eyes flexed again, though he had the feeling that, beneath her veil, the smile on her lips would not be a pleasant one. "Very good. Listen to me, Captain Barbarian. My brother is anxious to make this match with the daughter of the King of Wenshar, because we are a small people among the Lords of the Desert. We have never been great among the tribes, and some of our neighbors are very powerful. Particularly, we, like all the tribes, are threatened by the great lords of the north, the Middle Kingdoms beyond the mountains. They have told me that the Wizard King who held all the world in subjugation is now dead, and I have lived in the desert long enough to know that, when the great lion dies, there is much fighting among the jackals for his flesh. My people have need these days for strength."

Sun Wolf remembered all the petty wars which throughout the spring and summer had wracked what was left of the Wizard King's empire. "This is so."

The hands, long and strong with their hooked nails, folded around the chair arms. The Wolf found himself wondering whether this woman had ever been married, as all women of the shirdar by custom must be, and if so, what had become of the poor bastard.

"Yet I say that my brother will not marry a witch, even though she is the daughter—and will be the sister—of the King of Wenshar, and that King, her brother, a sickly boy of no great strength. It I let the marriage go forward and permitted her to live afterwards, she would grow in strength, not having learned, as all our women do, to speak softly and in fear of men. In time she would challenge my powers, and those others who object to me would gather around her. Whether I was right or I was wrong, there would be dissensions in our people, and for those dissensions many, perhaps all, would die. If she married and died soon after, that would be worse, for her father, her brother, or her uncle, who casts his eyes on the power in Wenshar, would take it as a reason to ride against us, and again many would die."

"And if she married and did not die in spite of your best efforts," added Sun Wolf, "the situation would be worse still."

The slow smile once again shivered the corners of her eyes and crept like poisoned syrup into her voice. "I see we understand one another."

"I understand you, woman," said the Wolf. "But I still don't understand what you want of me."

"No?" The level, dark brow tilted at one end, vanishing under the low band of dark silk. "Without this girl, my people still need some power, some weapon against those who threaten us. Indeed, as a witch, if she weds one of these sons of slaves who make up what passes for nobility here, we shall need it still more. And like my brother, I would not be averse to having a mage among our people, particularly one renowned in the arts of war."

Sun Wolf's mouth twitched a little beneath his ragged moustache. "Just so long as he's a man."

She nodded equably. "Just so. You would be no challenge to me, Captain. They say, even in the deep desert, that you are a man who is loyal to those who pay him and not a whore to take pay from this man and that, not caring. You are a fighter and a wizard, not a ruler of men—for if you were a ruler of men, you would have found men to rule ere this."

Sun Wolf was silent for a time. He could feel the storm very clse now, like the edge of a knife against his skin. Dimly, he heard men calling to one another outside and the snorting and stamping of the prized white horses of Hasdrozaboth, against the rising groan of the wind. After some moments he said, "I do not know what I am, Lady. When I hired myself to others to do their fighting for them, I knew what I was selling. I don't know that anymore. I can't say, 'I'll do this' or 'I'll do that,' because magic . . ." He paused, knowing that whatever he could say about magic, she would not understand, because he did not understand it himself. He shook his head. "Tell me about the Witches of Wenshar. What is it that walks in the ruins of Wenshar?"

Illyra rose from her chair and paced around behind it, her big hands resting on the small, flat circle of its back. Behind her the embroidered red-and-blue hangings over the windows had begun to belly and ripple with a continuous movement, as if evil things scurried invisibly behind them. Sun Wolf felt the electricity in the air crackle along the hair of his arms and begin to pound in his temples. Illyra considered him for a moment with wise, dark, cruel eyes.

"You have been there, then?"

"Yes."

"And what did you see?"

"Demons," Sun Wolf said. Resting easily on his folded-up knees on the red wool cushion, he looked up at the veiled woman before him. "The demons that rise out of the earth."

"That was all?" she asked, and he nodded.

The woman sighed and paced a few feet from him, then turned back. "In the desert," she said, "all the men revere and fear the djinns of the sand and the sky, the spirits that dwell in the rocks. But the women of the Ancient Houses have their own cults, each to its House. Each cult guards its own secrets. So with the Women of Wenshar." Her hands rested like a vulture's claws over the chair back, pale against the dark knurling of the grain.

"It was a poisoned cult, they say. They handed its secrets down generation after generation. They chose whom they wished to marry to their sons and brothers, to bring into the cult, and took what men they would to couple with, as men take concubines. It is said that they called up demons out of the earth and coupled with them as well. They practiced necromancy and called the spirits of the dead. Any who opposed the Witches were torn to pieces, as they say were the Bishop, the King's friend Milkom who hated the shirdar, this priest who was the White Witch's lover, and the old washerwoman who slandered her. They say also that any woman who betrayed the cult met a similar fate. Certainly it fell upon any man whom they hated."

"And did this magic corrupt any who touched it?" asked the Wolf.

Illyra studied him curiously, heavy lids masking her eyes, as if asking what lay behind the question. A gust of wind took her enormous veil, swirling it so that its end nearly brushed Sun Wolf's face where he knelt before her chair, and made the flames of the brazier twist like snakes seeking to escape the incense-strewn coals. When they subsided, the room seemed darker than before.

"So they say." Her voice was hard and bitter. "Any girl who, seeing the rites of power, refused to embrace them, perished—but it is said that such was the skill of the Women of Wenshar in choosing and guiding their initiates that few refused.

"Thus they ruled all of Wenshar and much of the desert round about through fear. And thus it was that, when the Lords of the Middle Kingdoms rode down over the passes to destroy Wenshar and slaughtered these women with fire and sword and magic of their own, none of the Desert Lords would help the Witches, for all had suffered by their arrogance, greed, and senseless destruction."

She began to pace again like her brother, moving with a leashed, animal grace. "The fools. They let their enemies pour out the wine that they themselves had to drink. The northern lords held the passes of Wenshar, and from there it was a simple matter for them to conquer the desert as well." The anger in her voice was as harsh as if the women who had wronged her had done so personally and were still alive, not generations dead and turned to ash. "And so the Witches brought ill upon us all. And even when the northern lords were destroyed, it was not the same as it had been before. Their power was taken by the sons of slaves, the scum of the mines, who know nothing of this land and care less—dispossessing us, the shirdar, from our rightful rule. They only want its silver, like a man who buys a horse, thinking only to eat it and not of the grace of its legs, the softness of its muzzle, or the speed of its shadow over the land. They are pigs, their noses flat from pressing them to piles of gold . . ." She turned back to him, somber eyes dark with ancient rage. "And they hire what armies they will, to destroy what is good and beautiful and turn it only into money, which is all they understand. There is not a shirdar lord who does not feel this at heart—for they destroyed not only our power, but the order of things as they should be."

As if suddenly aware of how far her anger had brought her, she halted in her pacing and looked down at him again, cold and withdrawn once more. "So I tell you this," she finished quietly. "My brother will never marry the seed of that doubled evil, the offspring of witches and slaves. Not for all the alliances in the desert, nor all the silver which they can grub from the ground."

Her eyes narrowed, returning to him. "And you, Sun Wolf," she said. "If you do not serve me, whom then will you serve?"

He shook his head and said, "Lady, I do not know."

CHAPTER

—— 12 ——

WITH THE FINAL SINKING OF THE SUN, THE WIND had risen to nearly gale velocities; Sun Wolf had to fight his way along the rope stretched across the court of the shirdar, his hands and face torn by sand and flying pebbles like stinging insects. Even in the shelter of the small courts and pillared colonnades on the west side of the Hall, visibility wasn't much better, the thick haze of hot, gray dust adding to the blackness of the night. Ghostly flashes of dry lightning illuminated the murk, but gave no clear light.

In the Hall, most of the Household was still at supper or lingering over its remains. The moment he entered the big, shadowy chamber, Sun Wolf felt the tension, the smell of barely masked fear—the sense of being in a plague city, where no man knew which neighbor's chance touch might end his life. Torchlight, blurred by the dust in the air, skittered over the faces of guards and servants, retainers, gentlemen, and ladies-in-waiting who, in ordinary circumstances, would long have retired to their rooms. To this and to the keyed-up tension of the storm was added also the baking dryness of the air. Men were drinking more heavily than usual, and their voices grated against the uneasy hush in the Hall.

In spite of the unusually large number of people in the Hall, the gap around Kaletha's table was noticeable. The White Witch sat, staring ahead numbly, a plate of untouched eggs and greens before her. Anshebbeth, at her side, was talking gently to her, trying to draw her out of herself with a patience the Wolf would scarcely have expected from the twitchy old maid. With a mercenary's usual practicality, Starhawk was downing her dinner, but Sun Wolf didn't deceive himself into believing her oblivious to those covert glances and fearful whispers all around.

Kaletha looked bad—drained and shaken and ill. *She might have killed her lover to preserve her pride and her power*, the Wolf thought unwillingly, *but she had loved him.* Some of the Hawk's words came back to him, and he wondered what it would do to him, to lie, against his better judgment, with someone, not out of caring, but solely in order to keep his power over them—to make, in essence, a whore of himself for power. Would he then kill the person who had done that to him?

Could she? Starhawk had asked.

He now knew what he had formerly only suspected, that indeed she could. And, moreover, if the magic of the Witches somehow corrupted those who used it, she very likely would.

As Egaldus had done when the Bishop had sat at the High Table, Sun Wolf cloaked himself in shadow and illusion to cross the Hall. As he did so, he wondered obliquely whether Kaletha would have killed Galdron to protect Egaldus, if she were already jealous of Egaldus . . . or if, when dealing with love, any logic mattered.

Starhawk looked up at him in surprise when he sat beside her. Since Kaletha and Anshebbeth were far too wrapped up in one another to do so, she spooned him up

stew from the common dish and poured him some ale,
which he drank thirstily. At the High Table, Osgard took
no notice.

This was hardly surprising, since the big man had obviously been drinking all afternoon and showed no signs
of letting up now. His harsh, blustering voice boomed
out over the frightened murmur of muted conversation
around him: "... white-livered little coward. He lied
about you, Nanciormis. D'you know what he said? What
the hell's gonna come to this country with a lying little
coward for a King?"

Nanciormis, fastidious and elegant in his pearled
black doublet and lace ruff, turned his head slightly to
regard his brother-in-law with veiled disgust and contempt. Beside the sprawling, wine-soaked giant, Jeryn
sat in crushed silence, his unwashed hair and untidy
clothes a sorry sight. The Wolf remembered Illyra's
scorn for the sons of slaves and wondered suddenly
whether Nanciormis, last scion of the Ancient House of
Wenshar, felt it, too. Tazey, on her brother's right, put
down her small fan of ornamental feathers to reach
across and touch the boy's arm, as if to tell him he
wasn't alone.

In the unvoiced whisper scouts use on night missions,
Starhawk murmured, "What did you find?'"

The Wolf shook his head. "I didn't go. Had an assig-
nation with a lady instead."

"I hope she bit you. You want some bread?" She
broke a loaf and handed him half. It tasted faintly of
dust—there was a skin of dust over the head on the ale,
which gritted in the Wolf's moustache.

"If she had, I'd be the rest of the night cauterizing the
wound. Anything happen that I should know about?"

"Two fights between guards and Incarsyn's shirdar,
one between a laundress and a scullery maid, and rumors
of a strike down at the Vulture Mine in Pardle Sho."

"It could just be the storm."

"No. They say the miners are afraid to go down the

pithead, for fear of meeting whatever's been doing this killing. Yes, it's stupid—but this business is going to come to blood fast, Chief." She wiped her fingers neatly on a piece of bread and reached for one of the oranges in the yellow pottery bowl on the corner of the table. On her other side, Anshebbeth's gentle, comforting voice ran on. Against the shadows, Kaletha's ravaged profile was motionless, white as carved bone.

Quietly, the Wolf said, "It's just a question of whether the right person's gets shed." In a soft voice, he told the Hawk of his interview with the Lady Illyra. "Incarsyn may talk as if women are nothing in the shirdar—and maybe they aren't, in the things the men lay claim to, like riding and dancing and worshiping the wind—but it's damn certain *some* of them can hold power."

"Maybe," Starhawk said quietly. "If you've been raised to know how to finesse for it and if that kind of power is what you want."

A gust of wind from outside made the torch flame swirl and leap and the massive shutters rattle as if in shock. There was a commotion around the outer doors of the Hall; in the dark arches from the vestibule, Incarsyn stood framed, dust streaming in gray threads as he unwrapped his veils. His white-cloaked warriors were like a silent company of sand djinns behind.

"My Lord." Osgard heaved himself to his feet and gestured with his cup to the empty place on Nanciormis' left. "We feared we'd not see you." His bass voice drawled with wine.

Lithe as a puma, the shirdar lord made his way among the benches. Anshebbeth started unwillingly to rise from her place beside Kaletha to be with Tazey as propriety demanded. But Incarsyn stopped short at the foot of the dais and inclined his head, his braids swinging forward like gold-bound velvet ropes.

"My Lord," he said. "It grieves me much to say so, but my esteemed sister has brought me messages of great urgency from my people. It is necessary that, as soon as the storm subsides, I and my men make immediate preparations to return to them as quickly as may be. Please forgive us this unpardonable breach of civility and rest assured that the memory of your hospitality will remain with us, as the memory of campfire light upon a night of cold."

In the long moment of silence, the King's red face flushed still deeper crimson. There was no one in the room unaware of what the young Prince had really said. Osgard's voice thickened with an intoxicated rage that knew no diplomacy. "And my daughter?"

The movement of Tazey's feather fan froze, her brows stood out black on a face suddenly ashen.

Without a word between them, Sun Wolf and Starhawk slid to their feet and began to make their unobtrusive way to the dais.

Once more Incarsyn bowed, but he did not meet Tazey's eyes. His voice was unwilling but still smooth. "I fear that the messages that my sister has brought have made it impossible for me to wed your beautiful daughter, my Lord."

Osgard surged to his feet. "You mean you won't have her—is that what you're saying?" he bellowed. "*My* daughter, the Princess of Wenshar..."

"Father..." Tazey began pleadingly, and Nanciormis, alarmed, started to get up.

Face purple with rage, Osgard hurled his chair aside. "You louse-picking, pox-rotted, djinn-worshiping horse kisser! My daughter..." He lunged for the young man, hands outstretched to kill. Nanciormis, taken entirely by surprise, leaped after him and caught him from one side, as Incarsyn stepped back, his hand going to his dagger hilt. Sun Wolf and Starhawk got the King's other arm just as Nanciormis buckled from a booted kick to his thigh that nearly broke the bone. As he stumbled back, Sun Wolf grimly held onto the heaving, swearing drunkard, reflecting that all the commander's fighting had obviously been done, sword in hand, on battlefields. He himself had gone through more tavern brawls than he could count and had dealt with enough drunks to constitute a more formidable army than many small cities could have mustered. He and Starhawk dragged the clawing, cursing King backward over the ruins of the chair toward the door of the solar, which Jeryn, the only person at the table who seemed to have retained his wits, dashed ahead of them to open.

The minute they were out of sight in the darkened solar, Sun Wolf pulled a hand free and slugged Osgard a hard blow to the jaw to knock him out. It took him three tries and left both him and Starhawk covered with bruises, spilled wine, and fingernail scratches, before they shoveled the King's inert body onto the divan.

"Mother!" Starhawk swore, as Sun Wolf flexed his bruised hand. "I've seen you coldcock a *horse* for a bet, Chief..."

"It was a sober horse," the Wolf growled. Still shaking his knuckles, he turned disgustedly to the door. When they emerged from the solar, the dais seemed to be jammed with people: servants all talking excitedly and guards looking at one another, wondering whether they should arrest Sun Wolf for lèse majesté. Nanciormis was standing with Incarsyn, who had not moved from his place before the High Table; his beautiful voice, too low for them to catch the exact words, was smooth and rapid, every beautifully wrought gesture speaking of conciliation and apology for a father's very real, though regrettable, anger for what he felt, however wrongly, to be a slight upon his daughter...

"And he was picked as King by his predecessor?" Starhawk wondered quietly, glancing back at the sodden, snoring form in the chamber behind them. "It's a wonder they haven't been at war continually for years."

Sun Wolf shook his head. "Drinking like that grows on them, Hawk," he said softly. "He probably hasn't been like this for more than a year or so. I'd bet a week's pay it takes less now to set him off than it did, and he'd tell you himself he's had more reason these days..." Still rubbing his aching hand, he glanced down to see Jeryn at his side within the solar door. "You always that quick, Scout, or you been in tavern brawls before?"

Jeryn gave a cracked laugh and looked away so Sun Wolf wouldn't see him sneak a hand up to wipe his eyes; the Wolf dropped a casual hand to the boy's quilted velvet shoulder. At the foot of the dais, Nanciormis seemed to be making headway. Sun Wolf caught the shirdane word for storm. Around the clustered backs of shirdar and green-clothed Fortress guards, Incarsyn could be seen to be nodding, unwilling but mollified. In the strange dust haze of the lamplight, Anshebbeth was at Tazey's side, holding the girl's hand, furiously protective and nearly in tears herself. Tazey, fan trembling in her shaking fingers, looked gray around the mouth, as if she were about to be sick.

Again he caught the word for storms in the babble of the shirdane and the phrase, *the season of witches*. Glancing down at the boy beside him he asked softly, "How's your etymology, Scout?"

Jeryn looked up at him, surprised.

"Can you tell me the difference between a wizard and a witch?"

"Sure," Starhawk remarked. "A wizard is what they call you when they want to hire you, and a witch is what they call you when they're getting ready to run you out of town."

Nanciormis and Incarsyn made deep mutual bows. The Lord of the Dunes turned away. Her face set and white, Tazey rose from her place, handing her fan to the startled Anshebbeth and slipping through the crowd toward the two Desert Lords. In the grimy orange torchlight she looked older, haggard, and shaken; when she stopped before Incarsyn, Sun Wolf could see by the tremor of her girlish gown how badly her legs were shaking.

She began, "My Lord Incarsyn..."

The Lord of the Dunes turned away from her without meeting her eyes. With his retainers behind him, he strode the length of the smoky, silent room and out the door. The wind swirled in their white cloaks, tearing at the torch flames. Then they were gone.

Only then did the noise rise again, the muted voices like the *hrush* of the sea.

Nanciormis walked over to his niece and put a comforting arm around her shoulders. She jerked away from him, the color that had flooded her cheeks an instant earlier bleaching away again, her eyes filmed with blinding tears. After a moment's stillness, she, too, walked from the room.

"Having met the Lady Illyra," the Wolf remarked softly in the brown gloom of the shadowed dais. "I think Tazey's well out of it."

Starhawk rubbed the bridge of her nose, as if seeking to crush out the dry ache within her skull. "She was always well out of it," she replied. "She never wanted it."

Beside them, a sharp, tiny noise and a gasp of pain made them turn. Anshebbeth stood staring down at her bleeding palm, where the furious clench of her hand had broken the delicate ivory sticks of Tazey's fan. With a muffled sob of embarrassment, the governess fled the room, leaving the broken fan lying on the floor, its feathers dabbed in blood like a slaughtered bird.

"You've got to admit," Sun Wolf said later, "that Incarsyn did the most tactful thing he could. The business about 'messages from my people' was all my granny's second-best mail shirt, but as a reason for leaving, it would pass. If Osgard hadn't been damn drunken fool enough to push it, people would have gotten used to the idea in six or ten months that he wasn't coming back to wed Tazey, without ever having to insult Tazey by saying it out loud." He picked up his cards. "Isn't there anything in that deck below a nine?"

"Stop complaining; you dealt this hand."

"Bloody Kaletha's taught you how to hex decks."

"Yeah. And if you'd hung around with her long enough, you'd have learned it, too. How's that for a crib?"

"Damn Mother worshipper."

"At least I don't worship sticks and old bottles, like some barbarian ex-commanders of mercenaries I could name but won't, because they're present. Fifteen two, fifteen four, and a pair is six plus those are all the same suit . . ."

"I see 'em."

" . . . and two for thirty-one . . ." She moved the peg neatly around the cribbage board in the flickering ochre firelight.

Sun Wolf grumbled again, "Damn Mother worshipper."

It was growing late, but few people had left the Hall. The storm still howled around the walls; the hot air was thick with dust and electricity and heavy with the unventilated stinks of torch smoke, cooking, and stale sweat. Underservants had taken up the trestle tables, but at least half of those who had eaten supper were still there. Now and then their voices would rise, sharp and angry, as the crackling air shortened tempers and made speech careless. Then silence would fall again as they all realized once more their unwillingness to leave, and the wind would moan among the rafters like the grieving damned.

It would be a long way, Sun Wolf reflected, down those dark corridors to rooms where they'd lie alone, listening to that wind and wondering whether Nexué and Egaldus had seen anything of their killer before they died. Even the lower servants and guards, whose dormitories opened off the main Hall, clustered still around the hazy pools of muddy torchlight, perfectly prepared to wait out the storm. Contrary to custom, the doors of both the Men's Hall and the Women's stood open. Upper servants—the chief cook, the dancing master, musicians, and clerks—who had their own chambers, nodded sleepily over games of cards and backgammon; the chief scribe was curled up, unabashedly asleep in a gloomy corner.

Sun Wolf stared moodily out past his unsatisfactory collection of fives, sixes, and unmatched royalty, wondering if it was the same in those halls on the fringes of the empty quarter which had been given over to Incarsyn and his retinue. He'd sized them up when he'd been taken through to Illyra's quarters and knew them as hardened warriors who feared neither man nor the desert's cruelty.

But this was different, this death which could be neither fought nor fled. The demons of Wenshar returned to his mind, the moony, phosphorescent forms that had flicked in the corner of his vision in the silence of the empty quarter, and the way those cold, glowing shapes had clustered during the storm, thick as bees at swarming time, beneath the windows of the temple in Wenshar.

He wondered where Kaletha was and exactly when in the confusion she had slipped from the Hall.

Starhawk was looking inquiringly at him over her flat-folded hand of cards, the slight crease of pain more marked on her forehead. He laid his own cards down quietly. "I'm going out to have a look around. The storm's fading," he added, as she started to protest. "The heart of it's off south, anyway."

"Be careful." She said it casually, but in her eyes he saw she didn't mean the storm.

He shook his head. "I feel—I don't know. I don't sense any danger—not like last night. In any case, it's not midnight yet, or anywhere near. The other attacks were all between midnight and dawn. I won't be long."

"I seem to remember hunting you for two or three months after the last time you said that," Starhawk remarked, collecting the cards and shuffling them competently. "But have it your own way." She was laying out a hand of solitaire as, cloaked in shadow and illusion, he drifted for the vestibule.

The wind nearly jerked the great outer door from his hands as he opened it a crack to slip through. Outside, the bulk of the Hold and the courts and walkways around it offered him some protection; but even so, the force of the gale made him stagger. Like a man fighting to wade through a riptide, he thrashed his way to the pillars of the colonnade and, wrapping his arms around the nearest one, held his body tight against it. Sand-laden wind clawed his long hair back from his face and ripped at his skin with talons of gravel. The hot dust clogged his nostrils and the electricity in the air throbbed in his brain.

He could sense the moon riding high over the roiling wall of dust and chaos. With his eye squeezed shut against the savagery of the storm, he let his soul dip toward the silence of meditation, listening—seeking the Invisible Circle in which he would be free to walk everywhere in the tempest-torn citadel.

Slowly he became aware of the various currents of the searing wind streaming like water around the towers, of the weight of stone and tile on the balanced stars and chevrons of the roof beams, of nightlamp shadows beneath them, and of the open eyes of two royal children staring awake at the raving darkness. He felt the lightning flare off the Cathedral's dry, glittering spikes and die between the Binnig Rock and Mount Morian. He sensed how the hurricane savagery ripped and swirled around the walls in the empty quarter. Sand was scouring the broken tiles of the floor, the dust was burying the smells of decaying blood there, the snakes in their holes were dreaming of ophidian hates, and the doves in their crannies were dreaming of nameless, walking fear...

Above the wind, he heard a scream.

The sound wrenched him from his contemplation. Even as it did so, his sense of it was lost, swallowed up in the demented fury of the winds. His warrior's instinct told him to rush back at once to the Hall for help—the wizard in him forced him back into the silence of his meditation, casting through the wind-scoured halls for the direction of the sound.

Another scream and another, above him and to his right. The balcony of the Household.

He swung around and ran for the Hall door.

As he fought it open, he heard the scream as men would hear it, surging in terror over the howling of the fading storm, directionless, from nowhere, terrifying in its uncertainty. Rising like an echo behind it, he thought he heard a second scream of horror and despair; but with the wind hammering in his ears as he heaved the door to, he could not tell. By the time he crossed the vestibule, Starhawk, sword in hand and a dozen scared servants at her back, was halfway up the interior stairs.

The little hall that ran behind the upper rooms of the Household was a vortex of winds. He flung a glowing ball of blue light before him, and it showed him all the doors tight shut. He was aware of others clambering up the narrow flight behind him: Osgard, in night clothes stinking of stale wine and vomit; two guards, ashen-faced with fear; the chief cook with a cleaver; and Incarsyn, naked under a silken bedgown, sword in hand. A door jerked open near him, and Anshebbeth ran out, fully dressed, her black eyes wide with horror, clutching the black billows of her skirts. She gasped, "On the balcony! I heard . . ."

Sun Wolf leaned into the wind as he plunged through her room and out through the open shutters to the darkness and storm.

Up on the long balcony, the violence of the storm was terrific. Had it not been for the crenelations of the wall, the Wolf would have been swept from his feet; but feeling himself skid under the sweep of the powerful blast that scoured the south wall, he dropped to his knees and grabbed for the stone of the wall. After a moment, he put forth his strength against it, turning the main force of the

blast enough to struggle to his feet. The dust in the air
threw back most of the witchlight, but he could make out
which of the archway shutters had been forced open
from within. The great inner curtain flapped like a torn
sail in the slip stream. Staggering to the parapet, he
looked down.

The dark, irregular lump of a body could just be made
out, huddled at the foot of the wall. Eddies of the storm,
broken by the courtyard walls, rippled at the dark sprawl
of bloodied robes and stirred the black, half-unraveled
braids of the jeweled hair.

"Did you see it clearly?" Osgard handed Nanciormis a
cup of wine.

The commander hesitated for a long moment, dark
eyes traveling from Osgard's face to Sun Wolf's. Then he
shook his head and gasped as Kaletha rinsed down the
abraded wound in his arm with a scouring concoction of
wine and marigolds. "But believe me, I didn't stay for a
close look."

Sun Wolf folded his arms and leaned his back against
the tiled mantel of the solar. The last, spent whispers of
the storm were dying down. In the silence, Anshebbeth's
sobbing was jarringly loud. When they had carried the
unconscious Nanciormis inside, she had collapsed into
hysterical screams. Kaletha, appearing out of nowhere,
her carnelian hair streaming disheveled down her back,
had struck her disciple across the face and cursed her,
from jealousy or impatience or merely the burn of the
storm along her overstretched nerves. Ignored and hurt,
the governess now whimpered wretchedly in a corner.

While Kaletha was ascertaining that Nanciormis was
in fact still alive—due to his falling first to the roof of a
small colonnade and only from there to the ground in the
shelter of the wall—Sun Wolf and Starhawk had run
lightly back up the inner stairs and along the narrow corridor to Nanciormis' room. Not surprisingly, they had
found nothing there. A chair had been overset, and the

jointed bronze table thrust violently aside. An open book
sprawled on the floor. Sun Wolf picked it up; it was a
treatise on falconry. Against the stone wall, a burned
patch and a ring of amber shards showed where the lamp
had been hurled, the flame killed almost at once by the
dust-laden violence of the wind. Dust and debris were
everywhere, from when the shutters had been opened.
Sun Wolf had closed and locked the door behind him,
and only Starhawk's presence at his side had prevented
him from glancing repeatedly back over his shoulder at
the darkness until they were in the torchlight of the solar
once again.

"I don't know what made me look up," Nanciormis
was saying quietly. "I couldn't sleep, though, on the
whole, storms don't bother me. But there was something—some sense of evil in that room . . ."

He glanced quickly up at Sun Wolf again and then at
Kaletha, silently tidying up her poultices and dressings.
A frown creased his brow.

"What is it?" the Wolf asked, and Nanciormis looked
quickly away.

"Nothing," he lied. Even having his heels sniffed by
death didn't seem to have shaken his sangfroid. He
looked pallid and bruised from his plunge over the parapet; but in the frame of his half-unraveled braids and
dusty, open shirt collar, his fleshy face had already regained its usual sardonic lines.

Incarsyn, standing beside Osgard, his unbraided hair
hanging like a woman's to his waist and their earlier
quarrel passed over now in this crisis, asked softly, "Did
it speak?"

The commander looked up at him, his dark eyes half
puzzled, as if searching for the right words for a memory
of terror and chaos. "I—I don't exactly know. I
think . . ." He passed a hand over his mouth. "It—when
it moved toward me I realized—I knew I was in danger
but it was like a nightmare. But when it moved I flung
the lamp at it . . ." He hesitated, glanced at Sun Wolf

again, then away. Having seen Nanciormis' slowness to react to Osgard's drunken attack on Incarsyn, Sun Wolf was a little surprised that the commander had gotten away at all and mentally noted that whatever it was— spell, demon, djinn—evidently it did give sufficient warning to escape, if there was anywhere to escape to.

Anshebbeth, rocking back and forth, covered her eyes with her hands and whispered, "Oh, dear Mother..."

"Anshebbeth, *shut up*!" Kaletha's voice cracked. Sun Wolf observed with interest that, although Nanciormis had quickly recovered, Kaletha's hands were shaking uncontrollably. She dropped the scissors and picked them up again, her eyes downcast.

"How did you know what to do?" Osgard poured himself another cup of wine, but it was only an automatic gesture; his face was pale with shock, and he looked cold sober and ill.

"The last scion of the Ancient House of Wenshar," Incarsyn said softly, "would know."

Kaletha glanced sharply at Nanciormis, who only shook his head. "I—I don't know, exactly." He pulled up his white silk shirt once more over the bandage. Under it, the muscle of his body was still discernible, like rock half-buried in soft mud. "But yes, the stories I had heard said that—that men had escaped the Witches by running out into the storms. They were often killed that way, too, of course; it was only chance that I fell on the sheltered side of the wall."

Sun Wolf frowned, sifting this in his mind. He guessed that Nanciormis' account might not be entirely trusted, yet saw no reason for the commander to lie about his escape. He was, as Incarsyn said, the last scion of the Ancient House. The Wolf wondered what the commander was hiding.

Osgard wiped his stubbly face. "You'll sleep the rest of the night here," he said. "It—it doesn't seem to strike when people are together..."

"It struck Galdron and Milkom together," the Wolf pointed out, leaning one arm along the tiled mantelpiece. "Though it may only have been meant to kill one. But it's also only happened between midnight and dawn before. Now it's getting earlier. And we have no guarantee it won't have a second try. It's a long way yet till day."

Anshebbeth groaned and covered her face with long, skeletal fingers. Kaletha began *"Really..."* Starhawk, with a glance at her that would have frozen a millpond, went over to rest comforting hands on the governess' shoulders.

"I can't stand this," Anshebbeth whispered brokenly. "I can't stand it..."

"Now, Anshebbeth," Nanciormis began, looking embarrassed and uneasy at the prospect of another full-blown bout of hysterics. *And well he might,* Sun Wolf thought sourly. *A man might be bedding a woman in secret and still shrink from openly admitting it, particularly a woman as unprestigious as Anshebbeth.* For her part, desperately as she might need comfort, the governess clearly knew better than to seek it publicly in his arms. "Perhaps you'd better go back to your room and get some sleep."

"No!" 'Shebbeth wailed. "I want to stay here."

"It might be better," Starhawk put in tactfully, "if you stayed with Tazey." She glanced at the King. "We should probably move Jeryn in there for the rest of the night as well. I'll keep guard."

Anshebbeth looked desperately at Kaletha for comfort, but she, too, was looking the other way, hastily gathering her things to depart. As Sun Wolf followed her more slowly out into the Hall, he heard Nanciormis say to the King, "I think I'd better have a word with you, Osgard..."

The wind still sobbed in the narrow stair as Sun Wolf ascended. The noise almost masked the slithery swirl of a silk nightdress around the turning above him and the sticky pat of a bare foot on cold stone fleeing into darkness. When he reached Tazey's room, the lamp flames were still shuddering with the wind of a body's hasty passage, but the girl lay on her bed, rigid and pretending sleep, her hands pressed over her face.

Sun Wolf walked the darkness of the empty quarter until dawn. He sensed no evil, no danger there, yet his every instinct of a warrior prickled that there was something amiss. In the shifting sand drifts among the broken walls, he sought for signs of Kaletha's passing, but found none. That meant nothing—the nervous after-eddies of the storm would have eradicated them. Kaletha had looked shaken to the marrow. Because Nanciormis had seen something she preferred to believe did not exist? Because it was becoming clear that the spells of the Witches of Wenshar, so casually tampered with, might contain things beyond her knowledge or control—might even turn her evil against her will? Or merely because someone had survived an attack?

Why Nanciormis? As last scion of the Ancient House of Wenshar, he might know things . . .

Or was there a why? Sun Wolf was uneasily aware that, as a wizard himself, he, too, might know too much, but he had not been attacked.

And the cool, detached portion of his mind retorted, *Yet.*

The cold stars turned against the black sink of the sky. The night circled toward morning. Blazing with lights against the darkness, the Hold towered above him; behind it, black and silent, loomed the bulk of the Binnig Rock. Standing on a platform of crumbled adobe wall, he spread out his arms and sank into meditation once more, tasting, smelling the night. But there was nothing, save the breathing of the serpents and the dreams of the doves.

When he returned in the cool yellow brightness of dawn, it was to find Starhawk, Anshebbeth, and Jeryn all deeply asleep, and Tazey's bed empty.

A note lay rolled on the pillow.

It was superscribed, "Father," but he tore off the pink hair ribbon that bound it. Beside him, Starhawk slumped against the side of the bed, eyes sealed in stuporous sleep—Starhawk, raised to the all-night watches of convent vigils, who had never been known to sleep on guard duty in her life.

The note said:

Father—

I made Starhawk and 'Shebbeth fall asleep, please don't be angry with them.

Incarsyn was right to put me aside. Sun Wolf and Starhawk are right. I am a witch and the Heir to the Witches of Wenshar. It is all my doing— Nexué, and Galdron, and Norbas Milkhom, and Egaldus, and Uncle Nanciormis. I know this now and I swear to you, it won't happen again. Please, please forgive me. And please don't look for me. Don't blame anyone—I'm doing this by my own choice. I don't want to become like the Witches of Wenshar, and I know that's what would have happened to me.

I love you, Daddy; please believe that I love you. I never wanted this. I never wanted to be anything but your daughter and to love you. Please just tell Jeryn that I've gone away, and that I love him very much. I love you and I'm so very sorry.

Good-by,
Tazey

CHAPTER

—— 13 ——

*U*NDER THE CRUEL BRILLIANCE OF THE LATE AFTER-
noon sun, Wenshar lay like an elephants' graveyard of
houses that had somehow crept to the base of the blackened cliffs to die. Wind sneered through the crumbled
stone walls, unbroken even by the buzz of a rattlesnake;
dust devils chased one another like lunatic ghosts. The
few portions of houses still boasting roofs watched the
two searchers from windows like the dark eyepits of
skulls.

Starhawk's mare started for no apparent reason,
throwing up her head, long ears swinging like leaves in a
gale; the woman leaned forward and stroked the sweating neck. But she made no sound.

Listen as he would, Sun Wolf could hear nothing—no
echo from any of those three twisting canyons or the
rock mazes beyond.

But he knew they were there, waiting.

They had been waiting for him since he had left.

Wind thrummed in his ears as he turned his horse's

226

head toward the wide mouth of the central canyon. Starhawk followed without a word; the blue shroud of shadow covered them as they passed the narrow gate of its mouth. In the stifling heat of the canyon, the rocks stank of demons.

Neither spoke. They had ridden together too long to need words; they both knew that whatever happened, she must not lose sight of him.

A short way past the canyon mouth, a narrow trail led up its wall, to a sort of lane above the first levels of the pillared facades fronting it. The last time he'd been here, Sun Wolf had explored it. At points along the main road up the canyon, bones were heaped, where mountain sheep, gazelles, or straying cattle had fallen from above. Near the foot of the trail lay a little pile of horse droppings. A grain-fed horse, Sun Wolf saw, pushing them apart with a twig, not a mustang scavenging on sagebrush. He pulled his head veils closer around his face and began to lead his own mount up the narrow way. Farther up, they found the tracks of shod hooves.

He felt neither surprise nor triumph at having guessed correctly. In a way, it was the only place Tazey could come, even if her only intent was to destroy herself. Though neither her mother, her grandmother, nor her grandmother's grandmother had known the demon-haunted city, she knew herself to be its heir.

"She could be above or below," the Hawk said. Soft as she spoke, her voice echoed hideously from those narrow, gaudy walls.

"There's half a dozen ways down to the bottom of the canyon." Sun Wolf glanced over the edge to the tilted pavement, half-hidden under shoals of pebbles, winding along the parched course of the old stream. "We'll stay up top."

Starhawk nodded. There was no question of splitting up— not in Wenshar.

Afoot and leading their nervous horses, they moved up the trail.

Sun Wolf knew from his earlier explorations that the trail was neither narrow nor intrinsically dangerous. Rose-colored spires and cupolas, cut in openwork like lace, towered above and around them; here and there, stairways arched to pillared doorways under canopies of stone vines. They led their horses to the trail's edge and looked across the canyon to the shadowed folds of rock, the sightless doors, and down to the dead oleanders by the sterile wadi and the white heaps of bones.

"Why?" Starhawk asked softly. "Demons aren't creatures of flesh, are they? They can't eat what they kill, if they kill it."

Sun Wolf shook his head. Glancing back at that calm, immobile face in its white frame of veils, he knew she couldn't be feeling what he felt. She might sense herself watched, but not have that terrible awareness of being known. At the edges of his hearing, he could detect the demons' whispering, like the canyon wind that turned locks of his horse's mane, the words just too soft to make out. He feared to listen more closely. His hand tightened on the reins he held; under the veils, clammy sweat crawled down his face.

"I don't know what they are, Hawk," he replied. "I know there are biting-demons, so they can do some physical harm. Everyone knows demons lead men to their deaths in swamps or in the desert, but . . . no one's ever said why they do it."

The shriek came at the same instant that his dappled gelding flung up its head in panic. The leather of the rein cinched around his hand, and he caught at the cheek piece of the bridle. From up-trail the echo of hooves splintered the close, shadowy air. Fighting to keep his own panicking horse from bolting, he could not turn to see, so the little sorrel mare was upon them before either he or Starhawk could get out of the way.

He saw the mare from the tail of his eye, bearing down on them with flaxen mane streaming and blood pouring from her flanks. It all happened in instants—he barely slid out of the main impact as she crashed into his gelding, white eyes rolling in mad terror, flecks of foam from her muzzle stinging his face, tangling him between the two heaving bodies in a desperate thrash of hacking hooves. With his hands full of bridle and ears and his mouth choked with dusty mane, for a moment he could do nothing but hold on to his own horse's head. Starhawk, who could be capable of great brutality when in peril, had twisted and levered against her horse's bridle and threw the frenzied animal to its knees against the jagged canyon wall to their right. Half-crushed and lifted off his feet, the Wolf could glimpse her through a frenzy of veils and dust. The mare was on his blind side; so was the cliff edge to the rocks below. The bridle-leather cut his hands, and he braced his feet. A second later he heard a skittering crash, rocks falling, the mare's frantic scream, then a crash, somewhere down the canyon below him, and another.

Then nothing.

He released his grip under the gelding's chin, and the beast threw up its head with a wild snort, but made no further moves to fight or run. It stood trembling as he pushed his veils back. He was still on the trail itself, not even near the raised brink. Starhawk came hurrying up to him, still leading her stumbling horse. Had she let go to help him, he knew they'd certainly have lost her mount and probably the mare as well. In spite of the part of him that felt piqued that she hadn't come to his aid, he realized grimly that Starhawk was never one to lose her grasp on essentials.

"You all right?" she asked.

He looked down at himself, covered with dust and filth and, he now saw, daubed with great, uneven splotches of the mare's blood, all mixed with sweat. He wiped his face. "Haven't felt so good since the last time I got mauled by bears."

"Glad to hear it." She led the way to the edge of the cliff.

The mare lay dead on the rocks below. Something like heat shimmer seemed to dance over her twisted body; but even at this time of the afternoon, the canyon's shadows were deep. She lay on her back; a thin sprawl of white veils fluttered out from beneath.

In spite of the fact that he knew that by no stretch of the imagination could Tazey's body be covered by that of the dead horse—even had she not, as any rider would have, fallen clear in the fifty-foot drop onto the rocks—he felt a shudder deep within him. He glanced quickly across at Starhawk.

She shook her head. "The saddle was empty."

He looked back down at the mare. Blood ran down her flanks, lathered by the dust and sweat until her body was almost coated with it. The smell of it rose to them, on the dust-choke and the incongruous dry sweetness of the sage. Then he raised his head and saw Tazey, standing about twenty feet away.

She stood just where the trail turned around a rocky bulge in the amber stone of the canyon wall. Her hands were pressed to her mouth, her honey-colored hair was hanging in unveiled tangles over her faded pink shirt, and her boy's breeches and boots were dusty and scratched. As he saw her, she turned to run.

"Tazey!"

She stopped, her face a blurred white oval in the blue shadow of the rocks. Her voice shook. "Please go away."

Sun Wolf straightened up and handed his gelding's rein to Starhawk. "Don't be stupid."

"I can't . . ." She swallowed hard. Her eyes, in the dust and the circles of sleepless shadows that ringed them, were almost transparent. "I don't want to hurt you."

"I doubt you could, Tazey." He walked toward her, slowly so as not to frighten her, but she did not flee him. The brooding silence of the city pressed on his consciousness, like the dead watching open-eyed from their graves. With it, he sensed the queer, terrible prickling of another warning that he had been aware of since noon. "There's another storm coming late tonight, you know that..."

"I know," she said softly. "I thought..." Her voice cracked. "It started with the storm. I should never have tried to stop it."

"Since you saved the Hawk's life as well as your own, I'm glad you did." He reached her side. He could feel her whole body tremble as his hand touched her shoulders. She was so different, so changed from the beautiful girl who had done the war dance, that his heart ached for her. "Why would you hurt me, Taswind?"

She shook her head wretchedly. Tears tracked slowly down through the dust on her face. "I don't know!" She wiped at them and pushed back the tangles of her hair to look up into his face. "I don't want to, not—not consciously. The Witches of Wenshar..."

"Have you seen Kaletha's books, then?" Starhawk inquired matter-of-factly, coming up with the two horses on lead.

That stopped the girl. Puzzlement took the place of desperation in her haunted eyes. She shook her head. "No. I..." She swallowed, and the fear and grief rushed back; with them came knowledge that no girl of sixteen should have to endure. "The Witches of Wenshar— Uncle Nanciormis used to tell me about them. He knows about them, as Mother did, a little. He said that in the cult, the coven, of the family... They didn't always know it was them, you see. People they hated, people who crossed them, people who got in their way, would die, but they... but they didn't know at first that it was they themselves doing it. They didn't know they had the power. Only later, when they accepted it and used it... But it would start with dreams..."

She drew a deep breath, trying to steady herself, and wiped her face again, smearing the sweat, tears, and dust into brown smudges across her cheeks. Her fingers shook; she clasped them together, locked tight to keep them still. "I was afraid that was what was happening when—when the Bishop...and Father's friend just happened to be with him. I had nothing against Egaldus, nothing at all, but there was such power in the air that night, such...such violence. You felt it. You know. It could have been anyone. I dreamed horrible things..."

Green eyes stared up into his. "I don't want to become like the Witches of Wenshar. I never wanted to. And then Uncle Nanciormis—"

"If you ask me," Starhawk remarked dryly, "Uncle Nanciormis is the only one who deserved what he almost got."

"Don't say that!" Tazey whispered frantically. "Don't—"

Gently, Sun Wolf said, "I thought you liked Nanciormis."

Her voice strangled to a thread. "I do." She pressed her hands to her mouth. "I did. I don't know. He..."

With careful firmness, Sun Wolf put his arm around her shoulders. There were no house fronts at this point on the trail, and, in any case, it would have been unsafe to go into one; but near the vast, jutting nose of eroded rock, a bench had been carved in a niche beneath a garland of stone lilies. He sat down, cradling her against him, until her shaking stopped.

At last she managed to say, "Uncle Nanciormis—came to me after—after Incarsyn—last night." She looked up and shook the hair from her eyes again. "He—he said things to me. He—he—he—" The words choked in her throat.

"About being a witch?" She shook her head violently, *too quickly,* Sun Wolf thought.

"But I—I hated him after that. That same night—just hours later..." She shook her head again, her hair hissing dryly against his unshaven face, tears trickling down her filthy cheeks. "It's growing in me, Sun Wolf, and I don't want to be that way! I'm so afraid. Everybody gets angry at people and hates people, sometimes. I do. But

since the storm, since I've been a mage..." She
clutched at him desperately, sobbing into the dusty head
veils that lay in a tangle over his shoulders. He stroked
the girl's heaving back, rocking her as he would have
rocked a child, waiting while her sobs subsided.

At length he asked, "Tazey, tell me this. Were you
aware of directing your hate? Or do you just think it's
you because you happened to hate some of the people
who died?"

She brought her head up from his shoulder, her eyes
ravaged. "Uncle Nanciormis... You don't have to know.
You don't have to do it consciously. You don't even see
it in your dreams, not at first, he said. It has to be me.
It's only happened since the storm."

"No, it hasn't," Sun Wolf said quietly. "The first
morning I was in Tandieras, I found some dead birds in
the empty quarter. There was something growing even
then, before you'd touched your powers." He looked
down into her face and with one dirty thumb wiped the
smudged tears from beneath her eyes. "It was little then
—it couldn't hurt a human. Later, I think Starhawk felt
something, maybe directed at her, or me—maybe just
wandering loose in the dark. But now it's grown." He
stroked back the tangled curls from her face. "Tell me
one thing, Tazey. Did your mother know about the inner
cult of the Women of Wenshar?"

For a long time, she sat quiet, her eyes never leaving
the brass buckles of his doublet. But his words about the
dead birds and the thing Starhawk had felt by the gate
that night appeared to have their effect. When she spoke,
her voice was very small but calm. "I don't know.
Mother died when I was seven. Uncle told me that—that
girls in the family weren't initiated into the cult until
they'd had their first period. So I don't know."

"Do you think she knew?"

There was another long silence in which the wind
boomed softly down the canyons and the horses
twitched nervous ears. At last Tazey said, "Mother was

—like Father keeps saying—Mother was sweet and good and kind. But . . ." She raised her eyes to his. "I don't know if it's the same way with men as it is with women. But we . . . I know we—women—can be two or three things, I mean really *be* them, sincerely, at the same time. I know what I am deep inside, and it's—it's not how I try to be with people. And the things I think and dream and want at night aren't the things I want in the daytime."

She fell silent. Sun Wolf gathered her to him again and held her like a child, but his mind moved now on other things. The wind bore the burning whisper of dust, the prickle of the far-off storm, and the sweetish back-taste of the dead mare's blood that still blotched his clothes. During the Great Trial, he had seen the depths of his own soul, and the glimpse of what lurked there had been enough to convince him that there was no such thing as an act impossible to conceive.

Curled in his arms, Tazey whispered, "We should be going. We can make it back to Tandieras before the storm comes, if we leave now. I—I don't have a horse . . ."

"You can share with the Hawk," the Wolf said softly. "Whatever is happening, the key to it's here, in Wenshar." He glanced up at Starhawk, who stood silently with her shoulder to the carved sandstone pillar of the niche. "The killing isn't going to stop until we know why it started. I'm staying the night."

The preparations for return across the desert were made quickly. Starhawk and Tazey's going would be slower with only a single horse between them, and the storm would come, Sun Wolf thought, before midnight.

While Tazey was filling the waterskins at the rock tanks near the canyon's foot, Starhawk walked back up to where the Wolf sat on the eroded stump of a broken balustrade, carved like the tsuroka from the sandstone of the cliff. He glanced up at the sound of her boots on the gravel.

"What is it?" she asked softly, and he shook his head, not even certain in his own mind what it was that he had listened to in the hushed-wind murmurs around the rocks. The air already had the feeling of evening to it, though, above the high canyon rims, the sky blazed like polished steel. Perhaps the sounds had been, in fact, only the wind.

She hunkered down at his side. "Chief," she said in her quiet voice, "I have a bad feeling about all this."

He did not glance down at her, keeping his single eye up-canyon, but he felt the touch of her shoulder against his thigh. "My guess is the heart of the storm's going to be south again, over the desert," he said. "Even if you don't make it back to the Fortress, Tazey should be able to keep you both safe."

"It isn't that. You remember the time we got caught in the seige of Laedden, when the plague broke out in the city? You remember the mob in the square, lynching that dim-witted boy who used to draw chalk pictures on the pavement, because somebody said it was his fault?"

Sun Wolf nodded. He'd ordered his men to stay out of the fray when two of them had wanted to rescue the boy, knowing even then that the action could have triggered all their deaths. They'd been staying in a boarded-up tavern. The contents of every bottle on the shelves hadn't helped him much.

Starhawk went on quietly, "It felt like that in the Hall last night. If Nanciormis knows about the Witches, it's a sure bet other people do as well."

The polished glare of the desert came back to his mind, the sandy harshness of the wind flickering around the gatehouse walls, as he, Kaletha, and Tazey stood watching the white dust column advance from the south. *The only witches left in Wenshar*, he had thought: himself, the woman, the girl.

"All the more reason," he said slowly, "for you to keep an eye on Tazey, once you get back."

Starhawk nodded; she'd thought of that already. "When you return," she said after a moment, "don't come to the gates. Work your way around through the empty quarter; there's old gateways through the back. Wait for me in the cell behind the one we've been staying in. It's close enough that, if there is trouble, we can collect our things and the money we've stashed behind the loose brick there and get out."

He turned his head and considered the woman hunkered at his side, ranginess folded compactly to balance on booted ankles, brown hands resting one over the other, as long as a man's, but narrower. Her face was, as usual, expressionless, save for the shift of thoughts behind the pewter-colored eyes. "You think it'll come to that?"

"I have no reason to, no," she replied. "But there's no sense taking chances." She straightened up in one single, graceful motion. She would follow—and had followed—him to the Cold Hells and back, but he had long since given up the notion that she would ever display anxiety for his safety. "You think staying the night here will tell you what's behind this?"

"Maybe not. But it'll sure as hell tell me something."

Twilight came early to the canyons, filtered gloom deepening in the mazes of the split rock walls while the sun still blazed on Starhawk and Tazey's retreating dust. At the foot of the central canyon Sun Wolf found a small temple whose inner sanctuary could easily be barricaded with rubble and thorn. He spent an hour marking it with every spell he knew, the Circles of Light and Darkness and all the Runes of Ward. He did not know whether what he did was correct, but he worked slowly, carefully, concentrating all his powers upon their formation. He felt tired when he was done, as if he had accomplished some physical labor, and it disturbed him, when he looked up at the fading slit of brightness high overhead, to see how much time it had taken. He watered his horse in one of the broken tanks in the westward canyon, fed it, then hobbled and tied it in the sanctuary, barricading the door and scribbling sign after sign upon the barricade—of guard, of illusion, and of light.

In the half darkness of those silent corridors of rock, he walked along the central canyon to the palace at its end.

Nothing whispered to him now from the black sockets of empty doors and windows; only silence waited in the eternal dark under the deformed cypresses. In the deepening shadows, the carved facade that stretched across the canyon's end seemed the color of dried and ancient blood.

He climbed the steps. Here, alone in the silent city, had the conquerors from over the mountains done more than simply break doors to loot. A double line of crouching statues, lions and leopards it appeared, had guarded the stair. Their heads and forepaws had been deliberately smashed off—not only smashed, but pulverized, for no broken pieces littered the sand-drifted steps. One beast still retained part of a paw. Sun Wolf saw that it had been a woman's hand.

There was no question in his mind where in the palace he must go. The small door to the right of the great entry hall beckoned to him, like the mouth of a tomb one sees in nightmares, knowing it for one's own. He had heard Starhawk's voice calling to him from its hoarded night. Now there was only silence, save for the faint reverberance of his footfalls and the distant muttering of the canyon winds.

As a wizard, he could see clearly in the interior darkness of the corridor beyond, but he summoned witchlight anyway. From the faded frescoes on the walls, women's eyes looked down at him—dark, knowing, amused. A room opened before him, and he stopped on the painted threshold as the stench of the evil there smote him in the face.

I shouldn't be here, he thought, as his heart lurched and began to slam heavily into his ribs. *I should go away QUICKLY and draw the Circles around myself . . .*

But it was foolish. If he did that, he would learn nothing, either about Tazey or about that eerie sense that it was him they wanted . . .

Wanted for what?

The room stretched before him. Every foot of its barn-like emptiness lay bare. Under the blue-white radiance of the magelight, it seemed to say, "See? There's nothing to fear here." Yet the smell was there, as sharp and terrible to him as the smell of blood.

His breath fast and light and the instincts of thirty years of war tearing at his guts, he moved slowly into the room.

At the far end, a door was tucked into one wall, barred shut and ruinously old. Halfway down the long chamber, a stone altar had once stood, but only the stump of it was left. Like the statues outside, it had been violently broken; but forcing himself to step closer, Sun Wolf saw that even those who had done the thing had been too afraid to remain in this room long enough to finish. Fragments of its frieze were still visible. He shuddered and looked away.

The Lady Illyra had said nothing of the customs of the inner cults of the shirdar Houses, but, without being told, he knew that this room had been their temple. What they had done had been done here.

In front of the altar a trench, six or seven feet deep, had been cut to the bedrock, though the gravel and debris of decades now littered its floor.

Here, Sun Wolf thought, hating it, drawn to its lip, almost against his will. *Here.*

He knelt and made sure of the strength of the edge. Then he took a deep breath and dropped lightly into the pit.

As if it had been a well filled with invisible water, he felt the presence of the demons. Through his boot soles he could sense them underfoot, could feel them moving like glowing fish within the rock walls all around. When he knelt to press his palms to the gravel on the floor, his soul cringed from it, as from red-hot iron.

Through his hands he felt their whispering in his mind, meaningless noises like the guttural murmur of the wind beneath the earth. His understanding flinched from them, holding back, like a lover holding back from some too-intense ecstasy. Then he bent his head, and his long, thinning hair fell forward around his face. He forced himself to relax, to hear.

As he had suspected, they knew his name.

It was only a touch; he slammed shut his mind against them and stood up quickly, shaking as if burned. Looking down, he could see a filthy glow rising like ground water through the gravel beneath his boots. He sprang up, caught the rim of the pit, and swung himself up and out. Somehow the magelight all around him had failed, but it seemed now that every fissure in the rock of the temple wall and every twisted shadow of the broken altar glowed with what was not light. Below him he could see them clearly now in the pit, seeping up out of the earth, staring at him with cold and empty wisdom in their eyes.

He fell back a few paces to the altar, wanting to run but aware in the calm corner of his mind that it was far too late. No Circle he could make would be strong enough now.

Like the crystal skeletons of ghosts, they drifted into the air above the trench. Gibbous laughter flicked at the edges of his consciousness. It seemed to him he heard in it Kaletha's scornful voice, his father's hoarse bellow, and the drink-slurred mumble of Osgard. Other voices threaded through it—the giggling of Altiokis, the Wizard King, and Sheera of Mandrigyn's caustic laugh. Like black liquid bubbling to the surface from the darkness of his dreams, he felt the old hates, old angers, and past resentments welling up within him at the sound.

The demons glowed brighter. Their ring around him closed.

Other things went through his mind, a pestilent ooze dripping from the walls of his thoughts—dark lusts and the memories of women raped in the fury and triumph of sacking a city in the aftermath of battle. Things came back to him, things that he knew he had done, cruel and stupid and bestial—things he had done because in the fighting he had come within kissing distance of death, and his mind had craved power as a dying man's body craves the water of life. But now he saw these things, not with the horror of what he had done to other human beings, but with an animal's savor at the taste of blood.

Looking up, he saw the eyes of the demons all around him. They were yellow, like his own remaining eye.

They had been cold, but now, as they gathered closer and closer about him, those shrunken, spider limbs glowed with the reflection of warmth. No longer fully transparent, the frail ectoplasm showed pale, bleeding colors, like watered paint filmed on glass. Their mouths opened, and he saw all those ghostly red teeth, as if they had been tearing at living flesh.

Like sound re-echoing from a thousand hollows of polished bronze, he heard them whisper, *Take it. It is yours.*

Power surged like the pulse heat of lust in his flesh—the power to crush and tear, the power to wield the winds. He saw himself smashing Osgard across the face only for the pleasure of watching him cringe; felt the hot desire to take and keep that slut Kaletha's books, not because he wanted them, but because she did; to have her and cast her away like the cheap trull she was; to bring down a city if he wanted it and have its fat bourgeois snivel to him with offers of gold, of women, of more power—power for its own sake, to warm his blood like brandy—the power of the mageborn.

He managed to whisper, "No."

Those fragile fingers touched him. The hunger for power clutched him, belly and loins and mind, and the demons screamed it back at him a thousandfold. They were starved, and their starvation kindled in his flesh like fire in dry tinder.

Feed us, they whispered, *and we will feed you*.

He cried again, "NO!" And this time his hoarse voice, raucous as the broken caw of a vulture, echoed against the stone roof and down all the painted corridors of darkness. He turned from the broken altar stone and fled back into the darkness of the room, smashing blindly through the inner door, stumbling into the black corridor beyond, with the demons rushing in a glowing mist at his heels, like greedy dogs sniffing at the smell of his fear.

He sensed them everywhere in the darkness around him. Even as he fled from them, his heart trip-hammering with terror, Sun Wolf kept that cold battle calm that had more than once saved his life. He was aware that he had to turn left and work his way back to the vast entrance hall; and, as he fled through silent chambers and corridors painted with queer, stiff scenes of animal-headed women tearing apart fawns and rabbits with their hands, he was aware again that he was being herded.

Voices piped at him from the darkness, voices that blended eerily into those that he knew—Starhawk's, Tazey's, Jeryn's. Other voices whispered and laughed to him from the frescoes of the walls, the Queens and Princesses of the Ancient House of Wenshar jeering down at him, with their bare white breasts and streaming hair, from the painted immortality of the walls. There were other things in the darkness as well—evil that clotted in the corners and filled some hallways like a miasma of blood— but he closed his mind and plunged through, knowing that, above all, he must not be driven into a corner. If it cost his life, he must avoid the touch of those skinny, fleshless fingers and the warmed honey of the demons' power.

Gasping, he plunged into open darkness; starlight

gleamed between pillars, barely to be seen in the Stygian gloom. The desert night, usually so cold, was treacly warm on his skin, and dust stung his nostrils.

The storm, he thought, despairing, even as he plunged across the open darkness of the floor. Like a rotten pomegranate spawning flies, the darkness spawned demons around him.

They rose from the floor before him and materialized from the walls. The colors of their flesh glowed as they drank his fears and were warmed by them. Their teeth tore at his hands and face. In the starlight, as he plunged outside, he saw the black glitter of running blood.

He had denied them the right to feed upon his power. To them he was now no more than the mare that they had driven over the cliff to feed on its fear and pain.

They were capable of killing; that much he now knew. The riddle of Wenshar fitted together in his mind with horrible clarity—what it was the women had done in their cult, and how its power had been reawakened. He plunged down the steps, running as he had never run before, with the storm heat of the night burning in his lungs, knowing there was no escape.

Still he ran, stumbling on the broken roadway in the ghostly shadow of the stone needles and the black cypresses, hearing the faint chitter of their laughter at his heels, and breaking every sinew of his body to buy minutes, seconds...

He remembered Nanciormis lying in the shelter at the bottom of the wall and Incarsyn saying, *"The last scion of the Ancient House of Wenshar would know..."*

His mind reached out and found the storm.

It came like a stampede of wild horses, apt to the power of the mageborn and greedy to answer his call. He felt its direction, searing out of the west, and knew he had to make open ground. Here in the canyons it would be only an eddy of wind. The demon glow flickered bright in the tail of his eye, and something ripped his arm like a comb of thorns; the muscles of his thighs and knees burned, his chest seemed filled to bursting with hot salt, and the ground a loose carpet of potholes and rolling rocks beneath his pistoning feet.

The black weight of the storm dinned in his head. He thought of the tearing stones, debris, and choking dust; he thought of what would happen if he missed the shelter of the ruins below the canyon mouths. But Nanciormis had been right to fling himself over the battlement; Tazey had been right; and weirdly, old Galdron, stroking his silky beard in self-satisfied righteousness, had been right. It would be better to die than to do what the Witches of Wenshar had done.

Now was the only chance he had to escape.

The demons were waiting for him in the canyon mouth. He bellowed the ancient battle cry of his tribe as he hit the narrow place at a dead run. He felt the teeth of the demons fasten on his neck and jaw, felt claws clinch around his arm and rip through his sleeve and the flesh beneath. They drew on the heat of his blood, and the shock of it was like falling naked into icy water. His knees buckled, but he forced himself not to fall, as he had forced himself in thirty-one years of battle and carnage. The only thing to do was keep running, running into the sand-laced winds . . .

Pain shot through his leg, and he went down. Gravel tore at his flesh as he buried his face in his arms. Like razors, teeth ripped his shoulder and raked his back; claws scrabbled at the hand he'd clapped over the nape of his neck. Then hot wind twisted at his hair and clothes and the rage of the storm struck him—searing, tearing, choking.

He felt the demons loosened from his back, like burrs ripped from a dog's coat. Almost sobbing with relief, he dragged himself up to one elbow, then to his feet, his legs shaking so badly they could barely obey his will. Wind-blown debris savaged him, adding to the blood already running down his face and arms. It took all the strength he had left to push the worst of the burning dust aside.

Like a blind and wounded animal, he began to crawl toward the shelter of the ruined walls of Wenshar.

The sun woke him, and the pain of his stiffening wounds. He rolled over, aching; sand and debris slithered grittily from his legs, which lay partly outside the shelter of the half-collapsed brick kiln into which he had dragged himself. He looked down at his hands; blood and filth clotted the semicircular tears in the flesh. His whole body hurt. He had remained conscious long enough to twist the worst of the baking shroud of dust from him, but he still felt parched with thirst, feverish, and strange.

He crawled out of his shelter, blinking in the brightness. When he stood up, sand, pebbles, and twigs poured from every crease of his torn shirt and doublet and from his breeches and boots. His hair, the stubble of his beard, his moustache, and even his eyebrows were stiff with grime, matted into place with blood; sand gritted in the empty socket of his left eye beneath its leather patch. He coughed and spat the dust from his throat.

Before him in one direction lay the whitening bones of the city, half-hidden now under gray drifts of sand; beyond them lay the black reg and the ghostly sentinels of tsuroka, already shimmering in the day's heat. He turned. A couple of chimneys and the corner of a wall rose through the sand like the ribs of an animal. Around his shelter, the dune was broken by a dip, the print of the spells which had saved his life. Everything else was buried under ash-colored dust. In the new light, the decayed and blackened cliff face of the Haunted Mountains wore a brooding, waiting look, as incongruous and horrible as a thoughtful frown on the brow of a half-rotted corpse.

He had outwitted them and had learned their secret. But the demons of Wenshar were far from finished.

It took a good deal of courage simply to go up the canyon far enough to get his horse. He was rather surprised to find the beast unharmed where he had left it behind the barricades in the honey-colored temple. In the exhaustion-drugged depths of his unconsciousness, he had felt the storm ebb and had felt the demons go seeking other prey. The echoes of their triumph when they had found it, the terror and the blood of their prey clung in his throat with the back-taste of the dust. He had assumed he'd be walking back to Tandieras. But other than being crusted with dried sweat from a night of terror and half-crazy with thirst, the beast was as the Wolf had left him. Moving slowly, stumblingly, Sun Wolf led him to the rock tanks, where both of them drank and the Wolf washed the numerous shallow gashes that covered his arms and face. Then he saddled up, wrapped on his head veils, and turned the horse's head back toward Tandieras once again.

He reached the Fortress shortly before sunset and waited until it was dark to work his way around through the dilapidated gates of the empty quarter.

But it was not Starhawk who waited for him in the gloom of the abandoned cells. It was Nanciormis, with Kaletha and over a dozen guards and shirdar warriors, to arrest him for the murder, by means of sorcery, of Incarsyn of Hasdrozaboth and all those who had gone before.

CHAPTER

—— 14 ——

"*If you tell us who paid you and why,*" Nanciormis said quietly, "you could spare yourself a lot of pain."

"The hell I would." The shackles that held Sun Wolf's wrists extended out to either side of him clinked faintly against the stone of the wall as he tried to shift his shoulders. About the only thing that could be said for the dungeons under Tandieras—stinking of old excrement, crawling with roaches, foul with smoke from the brazier in the corner of his cell—was that they weren't damp. His single eye glinted in the choking murk. "You know as well as I do that Illyra's going to spare nobody pain who was responsible for killing that wooden-headed brother of hers. Without him she can't go on ruling the Dunes. Confessing would only buy me her hate instead of her suspicion."

The Desert Lord folded his heavy arms, his thick lips pressing taut. "You have more than her suspicion, Captain," he said. "Your bluff is over. We know."

"You *what*?!"

Behind him, Osgard, sober for once, his sweat like pig muck in the close heat of the cell, said, "It wasn't until you came to Tandieras that this started. Nexué didn't die until you'd come back from Wenshar—by the Three, why we didn't realize then it was you—"

"It wasn't me, rot your eyes!" the Wolf stormed. At the angry jerk of his chains, the guards who crowded in the narrow doorway raised their crossbows. Sun Wolf realized belatedly that, as a wizard, his slightest movement could be grounds for death. He sensed already Kaletha's spells on the manacles, like a blindfold over certain parts of his mind. Evidently someone believed in taking precautions, anyway.

Osgard's face reddened at the contradiction, but Nanciormis merely raised one white-gloved hand. "There's no need to maintain the charade any longer, Captain," he said quietly. "I saw you, the night you tried to murder me."

"WHAT?" Even in that first shocked instant, Sun Wolf remembered how Nanciormis had evaded certain questions after the attack, had looked away from his eyes, and had spoken to Osgard afterward. "Dammit, man, I was in the Hall when it happened! A dozen people saw me . . ."

"No one saw you leave," Osgard said, his voice thick. "But a dozen people saw you come running back in, Johnny-Behind-The-Fair, when the screaming started. You seemed to know where it would be, and be damned to the noise of the wind."

"And even had you not," the commander put in, "it is witchery we deal with." He stepped closer, the amber glow of the brazier making pinpoints of fire far back in his somber eyes. "When I felt the horror coalescing in the darkness of my room, when I understood what was happening, I flung the lamp at it. And for an instant, outlined in the flame, I saw it. It had your face, Captain."

Sun Wolf stared at him, shocked into silence. When he could speak, the words came out as a whisper. "It couldn't have." But the demons in Wenshar had had his eyes. And Tazey had said that the Witches did not always know.

Cool even through the shock and horror, he thought, *I would have known*. He shook his head slowly. "No," he began, and Nanciormis struck him across the mouth.

"Do you deny you were in Wenshar last night?" The gloved fingers took him by the chin and forced his head back again; torchlight glanced over the overlapping crescents of dried blood that marked Sun Wolf's face and neck. Close to his own, the Wolf could see the broken veins on that elegant nose, smell wine and mint on his breath. "Do you deny that you had to do with the demons in Wenshar?"

He had to fight the urge to boot the man's testicles halfway up to his solar plexus. "I was in Wenshar, yes. If you'll listen to me—"

Nanciormis struck him again, casually, but with a force that slammed his head back against the wall. Stepping back, he said softly, "They say that all the Witches of Wenshar had such scars, from coupling with the demons in that city. I hope for your sake, Captain, that you were paid to do what you did by the enemies of Wenshar, and that you are not simply a madman acting from his lust for blood. For if you tell us who hired you to destroy all hope of an alliance with the shirdar, you may look forward to the mercy of a slit throat after the torturers are through." He turned and signed to one of the guards.

Exasperated at the man's obtuseness in spite of how shaken he was, Sun Wolf growled, "And don't bother showing me the instruments of torture. I've seen 'em plenty of times, and they don't impress me." *Why?* he thought, his mind racing—*how could that be possible?* But for answer, all he saw were the demons' golden eyes. They didn't always know, Tazey had said. Suddenly, horribly, he understood the girl's secret terror, worse because of what he had learned in the ruins last night.

Nanciormis paused and turned back toward him. "Perhaps not," he said. "You are a strong man, Captain. If you are being paid, I hope it is sufficient."

There was a jostling around the door—the cell had been excavated and lined with stone back in the days when Tandieras was merely the administrative center for the governors of Pardle, and the room wasn't a large one. It was crowded already with Osgard, Nanciormis, two guards with crossbows, the brazier, and the Wolf himself. The other guards who entered, two men and a woman, made it all the worse. The instruments that the woman carried were those of what was called ironically "small torture"—a thumbscrew, an assortment of iron rods, which the woman placed in the brazier to heat, razor-edged pincers, the sight of which always turned the Wolf's stomach, the thin-bladed probe for prying under the fingernails, and tie-frames to hold the hand open while balls of burning cotton and oil were dripped onto the palms.

The two men led Starhawk between them.

Everything within Sun Wolf contracted to a single, cold ball of horror.

Absurdly, he wondered why he hadn't seen this coming. He'd certainly forced enough information from captives during campaigns by the same method. Perhaps because of the hundreds of concubines who'd filed through his bed, there'd never been one for whom he'd have put a campaign, or any one of his men, in danger. Had one of his friends in the troop been tortured in the same fashion, he'd have felt sorry, but he'd have known that whichever of them it was would understand.

This was different.

Starhawk's face was brown with dust through which tracked runnels of sweat; her eyes seemed the color of white ice against that darkness. A bruise covered half her face, running back under the pale, sweat-matted hair of her temple. By the scabbed edges, it looked like the flat of a sword; that was probably what had knocked her out. Her throat, visible through the open neck of her torn shirt, was marked as well, under a choke-noose of chain. It had undoubtedly been one hell of a struggle.

Nanciormis said softly, "Who paid you, Sun Wolf? The King-Council of Kwest Mralwe?"

"Nobody paid me," he said. The words came out queerly level and quiet. "I had nothing to do with it."

But he knew despairingly it would do him no good. He felt paralyzed, as if he had been knifed in some unarmored spot; his only thought was that Starhawk must not suffer for this.

His mouth felt dry, his lips as if they belonged to someone else. "If you'll listen I'll tell you . . ."

"We're not interested in your lies." Nanciormis' silky voice turned cold. "We know what's happening. We want a confession."

Anger flared in him at this man's stubborn stupidity, like the criminal incompetence which had nearly killed Jeryn, the blind selfishness with which he satisfied his lusts for his niece's governess without any thought to its consequences to her. But he held his rage in check. Whatever he did, the Hawk would be the one who paid.

Carefully, he said, "There's nothing to confess. Unless it was without my conscious knowledge—"

"That's a lie!" Osgard surged forward, face crimson. His hands wrenched at the collar of Sun Wolf's shirt, nearly strangling him. "The Witches all knew what they were doing! It's a lie they use to excuse themselves!"

Beyond the King's massive shoulders, Nanciormis watched the scene in silence. *Of course,* thought the Wolf dizzily, he was too much of a politician to contradict a man whose daughter might be accused. "My Lord," the commander stepped smoothly forward and put a hand on the King's arm. "I think we can get the truth easily enough."

Turning, he walked back to Starhawk. With the delib-
erateness of a physician, he tore open her shirt to the
waist, pulling the thin rags of the fabric down over her
arms. Under the bruises, Starhawk's face was as uncar-
ing as a prostitute's. The two guards holding her arms
shifted and tightened their grip; the third, coming up behind her, took hold of the slip-chain and drew it tight
around the flesh of her throat.

Sun Wolf twisted against his own bonds, the manacles
tearing unnoticed at the flesh of his wrists. "She has
nothing to do with this, damn your eyes!"

Nanciormis took one of the metal rods from the heart
of the fire in the brazier, its end cherry-red with heat.
"Of course she doesn't," he remarked, and twirled it a
little in his hands. "A pity, isn't it?"

As the glowing end came near Starhawk's breast, Sun
Wolf saw her relax, turn her head aside and, still expressionless, shut her eyes. She was sinking into meditation,
fast and deep, like a porpoise sounding in the sea, trying
to dive beyond the reach of pain . . .

"Stop it!" The crossbows raised again as he flung
himself against the chains, but he scarcely noticed. All
he saw was the glow of heat near the white skin of the
Hawk's breast, and how the sweat poured down her
calm face. "STOP IT! All right, I did it! The King-Council of Kwest Mralwe paid me—five hundred pieces of
gold! For God's sake let her go!"

He was shaking, his body drenched with sweat, gasp-
ing as if he, not the Hawk, were facing the heated iron.
Starhawk's eyes snapped open, shocked—she hadn't
been so far into her trance that she wouldn't have felt it.
"Don't be a fool, Chief, we haven't been near Kwest
Mralwe."

Even as the choke-chain jerked tight around her
throat, he roared over her, "They contacted me before
we ever left Wrynde, dammit! Shut her up and get her
out of here. She doesn't know a thing about it!"

Starhawk was struggling now, fighting for air against

the strangling loop of metal around her windpipe. The agony of panic and terror the Wolf felt as he watched them systematically club and strangle her into semiconsciousness was nothing he had ever experienced—something for which he had never even thought to prepare himself in all his years of war. He found himself roaring hoarsely over and over, "Stop it! Stop it!" His whole body trembled as they finally dragged her from the room. There were tears as well as sweat running down his face, and he was aware of Nanciormis watching his humiliation with interest, disgust, and a certain smug satisfaction, as if this proved that Sun Wolf was not, in fact, a better man than he.

Another time, the Wolf would have felt fury. Now he was too sickened and shaken to care. He was aware he had broken, as he'd broken other men, and that they'd done it by the simplest of means. Some detached portion of his mind was mildly interested in the fact that he didn't care about even that; the rest of him was thinking illogically that Starhawk hadn't made a sound.

The commander's thick lips curled in a little smile.

"So the Lords of Kwest Mralwe paid you to murder the Bishop Galdron and Egaldus and Incarsyn?"

"Yes." He was panting, sobbing, as if he had run miles. *So much,* he thought, with strange detachment, *for the hardened warrior who can take anything his enemies dish out.*

"Why?" Osgard grabbed him furiously again by the shirt-front and dragged his face close. Green eyes like bloodshot rotten eggs glared into his. "And Norbas Milkom died just because he happened to be with Galdron, is that it?" His breath was like a cesspit; the Wolf fought nausea. "A man who'd never harmed a soul—a man who was my friend and the best friend this country ever had!" His big hands tightened as he slammed the Wolf back against the wall. "You stinking, murdering traitor, I took you into my Household—"

"Get out of the way, you fool!" Nanciormis wrenched

the King's hands free and shoved him impatiently aside. He turned back to the Wolf, speaking quickly, as if to get this over with. "You did this to cause disruption of the alliance between Wenshar and the shirdar?"

"Yes." Sun Wolf swallowed, grasping for what was left of his thoughts. "I don't know," he amended, realizing this was likelier—*anything,* he thought, *to make them believe.* He had seen torture, seen the torture of women. *Anything,* he thought, *to spare the Hawk that.* "They didn't tell me. They knew I was mageborn, knew I could get control of the demons . . ."

The dark eyes narrowed in their pads of flesh. "So that's how it's done," he murmured. Then, with a glance at the King, "And the King would have been your next victim."

Sun Wolf nodded. He felt drained and strange to himself, emptied of the pride he'd once held in his own strength. It had all happened so quickly. He understood then why men who held out through the pain at the torturers' hands would weep after it was over.

"You stinking traitor." The King's breath hissed thickly in his nostrils. "You took my money, you ate my bread—I entrusted you with the life of my son." He spoke quietly, his anger coalescing into a hardness far beyond his usual pyrotechnic wrath. "Witch-bastard— you have no more pride nor honor than a camel-skinner's whore." Stepping close, he spat in Sun Wolf's face.

Sun Wolf was aware, as the spittle ran warm and slimy down his chin, that there had been a time when he would have struck at the man for that, even if they killed him for it. But not even anger was left him—only numbness and fear for the Hawk. *I would never have hurt Jeryn,* he wanted to say, but could not. He'd seen the abject and stupid hopes of men once he'd broken them, clinging to straws of self-deception and the delusion that if they licked their torturer's boots sufficiently clean, no further harm would be done to those they loved. He remembered, too, his scorn of such men and what he'd done to those loved ones out of spite and pique and sheer perverseness, if the victim's pleas had been too fulsome. There was that, too, in Nanciormis' eyes.

But all of it changed nothing. He felt alien to himself, as if soul and body had, in less time than it took to put on his boots, been turned inside-out.

"We'll take his confession and fling it in the faces of those toads in Kwest Mralwe..."

Nanciormis shook his head. "It would do us no good." He fastidiously wiped his face on a cotton handkerchief he'd taken from his sleeve. Even through the stench of the straw underfoot and the King's stained and sweaty puce doublet, the Wolf could smell the aromatic vinegar with which it had been soaked. "They'll only deny it—deny that they ever knew the sources of the power of the Witches. But as the ones who broke that power, they very well could have known how to awaken it again." He glanced back at the Wolf. "As for this one —we have his confession. We need no more."

He signed to the guards. They raised their crossbows again, and Nanciormis put his hand on the King's arm, to draw him back out of the way.

Osgard remained where he was, between the barbed iron points and Sun Wolf's chest. "After the bill for it is signed," he said.

Nanciormis stared at him as if he'd taken leave of his senses. "What?"

The King regarded him for a moment, green eyes slitted. "After a bill is made out and signed for his death and posted in the city from sunrise till sunset tomorrow," he said. "The fact that he's a witch-bastard and a killer doesn't mean I can break the law to kill him without a bill."

Emotionally emptied, Sun Wolf observed with distant interest that this was one of the few times he'd ever seen Nanciormis taken off guard. Between the velvety ropes of the braids, his face turned tallowy yellow with anger, his mouth squaring hard at the corners. Then he recovered himself, stammered, "We have the man's confession! He betrayed you, would have murdered you in your bed. He slaughtered Milkom like a sheep..."

Osgard's voice turned to flint. "Don't talk about Milkom to me," he said softly. "It's only chance my uncle Tyrill named me and not Norbas his successor. It could have been either of us, because we both believed in law. A shirdar lord might have a man's throat slit on his own say-so, in the dark, without anyone's knowing about it, but that isn't how it's done here. I'm the King, but I'm King under laws, something you and your people never got around to making."

"And my people," said Nanciormis, viper-quiet, "are the stronger for it. Among my people, these killings would never have gone on as long as they have."

"Your people," retorted Osgard, his voice equally deadly, "were unable to hold these lands against folk who were united by law, Nanciormis. Remember that."

And turning, the King strode from the cell. Nanciormis stood for a moment, watching his shadow pass across the torch-glare in the stairwell; then he turned back and studied Sun Wolf with considering eyes.

For a long moment he said nothing. Sun Wolf met his eyes through the burning smoke of the brazier that now choked the cell, acutely aware that the two guards still remained, their weapons at the ready. He was utterly weary, body and soul—yesterday's long ride and the horrors of the night mingling with the ache of strained shoulder muscles, the hot, viscous trickle of blood down his arms from the torn flesh of his wrists, and the burn of sweat in his wounds. His only thought was how Starhawk had fought them—silent, desperate—and how in silence she had been beaten unconscious. In the strange, clear corner of his mind that was detached from any personal concerns, he was aware that, though Osgard would undoubtedly promulgate and sign the correct legal bill for his death immediately, by tomorrow there was a good chance he would be too drunk to inquire

whether Sun Wolf had survived the night to be executed
the following sunset. By the commander's eyes, Nanciormis was thinking it, too. Sun Wolf knew he should be
afraid, but somehow was not. He only stood, his head
tipped back against the stone wall behind him, watching
the commander incuriously. In spite of the almost un-
bearable heat of the room, he felt queerly cold.

But something of Osgard's sober and deadly quiet
seemed to have reached through the commander's contempt for his brother-in-law. At length he signed to the
two guards. "Keep watch on him. Remember he's a wizard. Stay alert. If he either moves or speaks, kill him at
once. Understand?"

The men nodded. Nanciormis paused for a moment
longer, studying Sun Wolf's chained figure, stretched between the torches, the light glancing along the crescent-
shaped scabs of the demon bites, gleaming stickily on the
perspiration streaming down his chest and ribs. Then his
mouth hardened with some private thought; turning, he
strode from the cell.

It was a long time before Starhawk found the strength
even to move. The fresh pain blended with the ache of
bruises several hours old, taken in the struggle when
they'd arrested her as soon as the boys on the watchtower had sighted Sun Wolf's horse. Looking back on it,
she wondered with dull disgust at herself why she had
not suspected the very fact that no one had arrested her
upon her return with Tazey. Of course Osgard would be
readier to plant the blame on him or Kaletha, rather than
on his daughter. She wondered what had finally tipped
the scales.

Some circumstance of Incarsyn's murder? She shivered, remembering the screams that had shattered the
terrible silence between the end of the storm and dawn.
Some piece of proof that Kaletha was innocent? Or was
it just that Sun Wolf was a stranger? She cursed herself
for not picking a less obvious rendezvous, for not know-

ing the empty quarter well enough to choose one further in, and for not being ready for a delayed arrest.

She sighed and tried to roll over on the uneven stone of the floor. It was like a cobblestone street, bumpy and filled with little pits and holes where roaches nested under crumbled straw. Its jagged edges cut into her bare arms, and she winced and lay still again.

She had to get him out, if it wasn't too late already. Illyra had threatened the most barbarous and lingering death for the witch whose magic had slain her brother. But in the long hours of the earlier night, while she had waited with hammering heart for the guards to come for her, she had gone over every square foot of the stone-lined room. There was nothing she could use for a weapon or tool.

Sun Wolf had confessed. He might be already dead.

Her body hurt; her soul felt shaken to its marrow.

She had long known that she was willing to perjure her soul and destroy her body for Sun Wolf's sake—it had never occurred to her that he would do likewise for her. Struggling to submerge mind and feeling to the dark silence of meditation, she had heard him cry out, and it had left her stunned. He would not have confessed, she knew, if they'd put the iron to his own flesh.

That he had done so for her sake terrified her. She was used to pain from arrows, swords, and every instrument designed to cut or break human flesh. The tears that slid in such silence down her face were from grief at his humiliation and because she understood now that he valued her above his own pride.

He had said that he loved her. Until now she had not understood that his love was of the same quality as hers.

This is weak, she told herself angrily, *weak and stupid. While you're sniveling over how much he loves you, he could be dying. There has to be something you can do.*

But the tears slid cold down her face. Even had she

not been half-dead with exhaustion, she knew there was nothing she had not already investigated before.

Somewhere behind her, she heard a faint, hollow *scritch*.

Her muscles stiffened.

In the long waiting she had become familiar with every sound of these cells—the queer, hollow groanings of the wind in the walls, and the scrabble of rats who hunted the enormous brown jail-roaches in the corners. This was different.

Very faintly, she heard it again—the unmistakable scrape of wood on stone and the soft squeak of a hinge.

"Warlady?"

An unvoiced whisper, a scout's in enemy territory. She moved her eyes to the judas-hole in the door. The faintest glow of reflected torchlight filtered through, but no shadow of a watching guard. She rolled over—every pulled, burning muscle of her back and belly stabbing at her—and sat up, shrugging her torn shirt back up on her shoulders again.

In the blackness of the rear wall, a small square of more velvety black had appeared and, in it, the white oval blur of faces.

As soundlessly as she could, she edged her way to the back of the cell.

Tazey was wearing her boy's breeches and a man's embroidered black shirt, all smutched and filthy now with mud and slime and what looked like soot. Jeryn's usual prim, formal outfit of hose, trunks, and a stiffly braced doublet were as grimy as his sister's.

Starhawk breathed, "Sorry, but we just had the chimney swept yesterday—come back next week." They both put their hands over their mouths to keep from giggling with relief.

She ducked down and crawled through the narrow black slot in the wall; there was the faint scrape of wood as Jeryn replaced the hidden door. Small hands groped for hers in the darkness, and they led her, half stooping, half crawling, a few paces and around what felt like a corner. Then with a hiss and sneer of metal, a lantern-slide was uncovered to show them in a narrow passage-way with a sharply sloped roof. Roaches longer than Starhawk's thumb scrambled for cover from the light.

Jeryn whispered, "This runs behind all the cells."

Starhawk nodded. "It's an old trick, if a prisoner turns stubborn. Put him in a cell with his partner and station a man to listen to them talk when they think they're alone. Or if he's a Trinitarian, hide a man here when the priest comes to hear his confession. It looks like it hasn't been used in years."

They were staring at her with wide eyes; Starhawk felt her hair, sticking straight up, all stiffened with sweat and blood, and the puffy, discoloring bruises on her face and half-exposed breast. "I'm fine," she added. "The Chief..."

Jeryn whispered, "We heard. We were behind the wall."

Tazey added softly, "Father's gone to sign the bill of execution, but the law states it must be posted from sunrise to sunset before a man can be killed. He—" She swallowed. "He hasn't been hurt."

Starhawk had half guessed, from their lack of panic, that the Wolf had at least a few hours left. Exhausted and shaken as she was, the sudden release from stress made her eyes sting nonetheless and her throat ache. With an impulsive move, she hugged the girl to her, fighting to keep from breaking the armor of her calm. There was no time for it now.

"I—" Tazey hesitated, biting her lower lip. "I can use magic to get the guards away from him. I don't think it will be hard." She spoke swiftly, as if admitting something which hurt her; but once it was said, she relaxed a little. She looked far better than she had yesterday in Wenshar; better even than she had on the silent trip back across the desert—less withdrawn and hagridden. Star-hawk guessed she'd used magic to get out of her own

room—as their friend she had certainly been watched—
even as she had laid sleep-spells on her watchers two
nights ago. *You can sometimes un-be what you are*, the
Hawk thought, *but you can never unknow that you were
it*. Tazey had made her choice. For her there was now no
going back, if indeed there ever had been. She went on,
"We can . . ."

Starhawk shook her head. Her mind was working
fast, running ahead. Her immediate fears for the Wolf
were assuaged. She was thinking like a trooper again.
"No," she said. "Listen, what hour of the night is it?"

They looked at one another, then Tazey said, "About
the third."

"All right." Starhawk drew the children close to her,
keeping her voice low, for the tunnel would carry the
smallest noise. "People are still awake—they're still
alert. We can't make a break-in until two or three hours
after midnight, when most people are asleep, and when
the guards will be tired and stale—not only the guards
on the Wolf's cell, but the guards around the corrals."

Huddled, squatting, in the narrow space beside her,
they nodded, accepting her soldier's wisdom. She could
see Jeryn tucking that piece of information away in his
mind for another time.

"The Chief was right. These killings aren't going to
stop until we know why they started. We need to know
what the Witches of Wenshar knew. We need Kaletha's
books." She looked at them in the upside-down glare of
the shaded lantern, two grimy royal urchins sitting with
their chins on their knees in the stinking spy-tunnel behind their father's dungeon, dark eyes and green shining
through the tangles of their dust-streaked hair. "Are you
kids game?"

"Do you know *every* tunnel and cellar in Tandieras?"
Jeryn glanced over his shoulder at her and flashed her
a shy grin. "Just about." There was a trace of pride in his
soft, treble voice. Broken out of its habitual sullenness,

his peaked face looked more handsome and less pretty than usual. He wiped away the soot that had coated them all on their way through an old hypocaust, leaving a large, pale streak amid the general filth.

Jeryn had crossed the big, musty-smelling kitchen cellar without light, by touch in the dark; he'd flashed the lantern-slide, once, to guide Starhawk across. Long training in night scouting had taught her to take in the cleared pathways at a glance. She'd negotiated the expanse of piled sacks of potatoes and wheat, clay oil jars as tall as Jeryn was, and knobby, dangling fronds of onions and herbs without a sound that might be heard by those whose footsteps creaked over their heads. She could hear Tazey making her way softly now, moving in the dark, as the mageborn could.

The boy's cold, fragile little fingers sought hers. "I used to hide anywhere, when Uncle Nanciormis wanted me for sword practice, or riding. And it wasn't that I was a coward," he added, a crack of hurt suddenly breaking his voice. "That is—it isn't cowardly not to want to do something you can't do if it's dangerous, is it, Warlady? I mean, I'm *not* afraid of horses—it's just I—I can't ride the wild ones the way Tazey does, and I know it. But Uncle..." He hesitated, ashamed. "Uncle told Father I was a coward for not wanting to do it and a sneak for running away from lessons. I tried, I really did, to climb ropes and scale walls and things, but I...I just can't. That's—that's why I had to find the Chief out in the desert in Wenshar. Because he—he's a better teacher. I mean, it's boring, but he's careful you won't get hurt, you know? Sometimes I thought..." He stopped himself, let go of her hand and, by the sound of it, wiped his nose hastily with a sleeve which would leave it blacker than before.

Starhawk felt that knobby small hand in her own, remembered the thin legs, the pipestem wrists. He hadn't the strength that would have gotten him safely through the more dangerous elements of training, and Nanciormis was clearly a teacher who found it easier to blame his pupil's failure on anything but his own careless ineptitude. It was easier, she thought, remembering her own earlier humiliations in Sun Wolf's school for warriors, to hide from the lessons than to be mocked.

"I did try." Then, as if ashamed of the crack in his voice, he turned toward the small door, hidden behind a wall of wine tuns whose wooden sides were thick with dust. "Through here."

Starhawk paused, as Tazey ghosted up beside them in the darkness. "Wait a minute."

She took the lantern from Jeryn and flashed a quick gleam in the direction of the shelves nearby. As she had suspected, remembering her convent days, in addition to red wheels of wax-covered cheese and bags of ground flour, they also contained empty flour sacks, folded neatly for the myriad purposes of the kitchens. She took one of them, removed the lid from a barrel of dried apples, and collected half a dozen, then borrowed Tazey's knife to cut a substantial chunk from one of the cheeses. After stowing it in the sack, which she tied through her belt, she neatly turned the rest of the cheese toward the wall so the cut would not be noticed until someone wondered why all the mice and roaches in the Fortress were converging on that particular shelf.

"When we run for it, the place is going to be like a polo game with a hornet's nest for the ball," she whispered. Shoving two more sacks through her belt, she followed Jeryn to the little slit of a doorway behind the wine tuns. "I'm not going without something to eat."

As Starhawk had suspected, the empty quarter of the Palace was as deserted as the ruins of Wenshar itself. Even had they known she had escaped, she doubted anyone would have searched there before sunup. Moving like a ghost through the bleached skeletons of the decaying walls and sand-drifted cells, she admitted they had a point. From across the deserted compounds, she could smell the faint, nauseating waft of old blood, like the stench of a three-day-old battlefield, and recalled the horror she and the Wolf had found, all that was left of Egaldus—remembered, too, Incarsyn's blood splattered not only over the walls of the room that had been his, soaking the sheets of his bed where the largest part of his body still lay, but the gore that had dripped down from the ceiling as well. The room lay on the edge of the empty quarter, where Nexué and Egaldus had both died.

Beside her, Jeryn whispered, "Uncle Nanciormis said he—he saw the Chief's face. Could—you don't think—"

Starhawk knew what he was getting at, but deliberately misunderstood. "Could it have taken on the Chief's features?" Jeryn, though that wasn't what he'd meant, nodded eagerly at this more acceptable hypothesis. "I don't know. That's why we need to know about the Witches." She halted, the chill of the night biting into her body through the rags of her torn shirt, stinging the bruises on her face and arms and making her wrenched muscles ache. When she turned her head, the short steel slip-chain around her throat pressed cold into the flesh. "The Chief said it was in a corner of a big adobe kitchen with the roof half fallen in and two ovens, catty-corner to each other."

Jeryn nodded. "I know where that is."

Tazey glanced worriedly over her shoulder. The night wind had fallen, and silence seemed to hang over the empty quarter like the darkness of sleep before dreams begin. Her voice barely touched that hideous stillness. "You don't—You don't think we're in danger?"

Deadpan, Starhawk said, "Two out of three, we're safe."

"Two out of three?"

"If it's you or the Wolf behind it, we've got nothing to worry about."

Realizing belatedly she was being kidded, Tazey grinned shakily. "Oh, thanks."

Save for the faint skiffs of wind playing hide-and-seek

in the zebra moonlight beneath the broken roof beams, the dark kitchen was silent. Nevertheless, Starhawk waited a long moment in its doorway before entering. It was in her memory that Egaldus had been killed wandering at night in the empty quarter, and it was probably a safe bet that he hadn't been seeking herbs to harvest in the dark of the moon. But nothing molested her. She raised her hand, signaling the children to come.

When Starhawk and Tazey lifted the grille clear of the pit, scales stirred on sand in the darkness below like the whisper of dead leaves. She slid the cover from the lantern and held it down in that black well. Something twitched in the darkness. As if jet beads had been scattered from a burst sack, the eyes glittered unwinkingly up at them.

Starhawk took a deep breath. Sun Wolf had told her about it; but, as with the fear-spells written on the grille, just knowing was not the same. "Do you think you can do it?"

Tazey wet her lips and hesitated for a long time, staring down into the dark. Then she shook her head. "I don't know how. It's—I know what Sun Wolf and Kaletha say about illusion, but—I can't make them think a stick is something and your body is a stick. I just—I can't feel what they'd feel. I'm sorry, Warlady."

She looked wretchedly at Starhawk, as if expecting to be cursed for her failure—obliquely the Hawk wondered if her father had led her to expect that. She put a comforting hand on the square, delicate shoulder. "I'm certainly not sorry you admit it," she said frankly. "And particularly that you're not willing to try anyway." She squatted on her haunches, hugging her knees, and stared down at the restlessly moving shapes below. The dry buzz of rattlers echoed against the low roof, rising to a harsh crescendo. In spite of herself, she felt her stomach curl with dread. "And even if you could deal with the snakes," she added, "there's still the scorpions."

"Could you make the snakes go after the scorpions?"

Jeryn leaned over their shoulders to look down into the pit, fascinated. "Make them hungry or something?"

Tazey thought that one over, and Starhawk swallowed a grin at the practicality of the suggestion. "I don't think so," said the girl doubtfully. "I don't really know how to make them think or feel anything. I don't know how they—how they think or feel."

"So that puts out just making them fall asleep." Starhawk rested her chin on her knees, considering the matter in the light of what the Wolf had told her of magic. "If scorpions sleep in the first place. I know snakes do—"

"Look," said Jeryn abruptly. "Tazey—you stopped a windstorm or made it blow in another direction. Can you do other things like that? With the air, I mean?"

She frowned up at her younger brother, puzzled. "I—I don't know."

Starhawk cocked her head to one side. "What did you have in mind, Scout?"

"Well, snakes shouldn't even be awake at night—neither should scorpions, because it's too cold. Can you make it colder?"

"Yes," Tazey said, then stopped, looking disconcerted.

"You're sure?" asked Starhawk.

She looked a little uncertain, not at her answer, but at her sureness. "Yes. I—It's like the wind."

Not an answer, Starhawk thought, *that would make sense to a non-wizard,* but she had been around Sun Wolf and Kaletha enough to know that wizards spoke to one another in a kind of bookhand, with minimal clues that both understood for things which could never be explained to those who had not felt them.

Tazey edged closer to the brink and rested her chin on her folded hands. Jeryn stepped back, knowing by instinct that he must remain absolutely silent. The girl shut her eyes.

Starhawk did not pretend to feel, as Sun Wolf could, when magic was being worked. All she saw was a young girl in faded old breeches and a black, too-large shirt, her head bowed and her saffron hair falling over her face, sunk in a self-induced trance of concentration. But she saw in the moonlight the faint, cold mist begin to curl into the air above the inky shadows of the pit, like ground fog on a winter morning, and felt the hair prickle on her scalp. Jeryn stepped back a pace, his thin face catching with a fleeting expression that was not quite fear, not quite grief, as he looked at this enchanted stranger who had once been his sister.

Starhawk's instinct was to throw something down into the pit, to make sure the terrible chill had worked its way upon the things below. But from her own early days of meditation she knew how easy it would be to break the girl's desperate concentration. She knew, too, that there was no telling how long she could keep it up. She handed the lantern to Jeryn and tucked Tazey's knife in her belt to force the locks with. With a whispered mental prayer to the Mother and to whatever of her or Sun Wolf's mythical ancestors might be listening, she lowered herself by her hands down into the darkness.

She dangled for a moment, listening for the telltale swish of scales upon dust. Nothing but silence met her ears. *Would the sound of her dropping*, she wondered, *break Tazey's hold on the spells?*

There was, as the mercenaries liked to say, only one way to find out.

She landed lightly, springily, knees bent. The light wavered and staggered over her head as Jeryn leaned down after her with the lantern. Its gleam reeled over scaled backs—black, brown, patterned in sand-hued lozenges or glistening like oil and pearls. One mamba flicked its tongue stuporously. That was all.

The cold in the pit was incredible, slicing through the rags of Starhawk's shirt and chilling her to the bone. Her breasts hurt with it—she was glad of the small warmth of the hot lantern-metal so close to her fingers. Even in the desert dryness, her breath was a cloud of white steam. Tiptoeing so as not to step on any of the snakes, she made her way across the room and remembered to set the light far enough from the niche so that the heat from the flame inside would not revive any of the sleeping vermin. By the time she reached the niche itself, she was shivering uncontrollably.

Scorpions covered the chest and the rafter above them, like metal plates sewn on a garment. Starhawk paused for a moment, rubbing her bare hands, loathing the thought of what she must do. *It's do it or go back out and think of something else*, she told herself. *After the roaches in the jail and the vermin in some of the inns you've stayed at, it's no time to get squeamish now.* With cringing fingers she reached forward and picked a jointed brown body off the lid and tossed it aside. It landed with a faint *plop* in a corner. None of the others moved.

Starhawk supposed she had done worse things in eight years of soldiering—retrieving the chest of gold pieces one sacked township had sunk in the latrine pit behind the town hall came to mind. But shivering in the cold, ensorcelled darkness as she crouched to force the locks, waiting for the breath of warmth that would tell her that Tazey's concentration had failed and that she herself was, for all intents and purposes, already dead, she couldn't think of too many.

There were thirteen books in one chest, five in the other. Two of them were so large and clumsy she could only carry them one at a time, picking her way back through the loathsome carpet of the pit, to hand them up to Jeryn. Her hands were clumsy with cold, barely able to close around the heavy volumes that she passed up to him in twos and threes, hoping there were no scorpions hidden within the bindings that would revive in the warmer air above. It wasn't likely—the chests looked tight against moisture, sand, and the small, glue-eating vermin of deserted places. When she was finished, she closed up the chests again, picked a six-foot diamond-back off the rungs of the ladder, and scrambled out of the pit, her bruised flesh shuddering with considerably more than cold.

Jeryn was looking at her, eyes enormous with awe. As she gently shook Tazey out of her trance, the boy whispered, "You're braver than Uncle Nanciormis—braver than my father."

"I've just had eight years' more practice as a looter," Starhawk said. "Now for God's sake take a look at my back to make sure none of those things dropped on me, and let's get the hell out of here. We've got a lot more to do tonight."

CHAPTER

—— 15 ——

*F*OR THE FOURTH OR FIFTH TIME, PAIN WAKENED *SUN* Wolf, jerking him back to awareness of more pain. He changed his half-waking sob into a curse and braced his knees once again to take some of the excruciating tension from his burning shoulders and back and his lacerated wrists; the guards, on the other side of the cell, shifted nervously and raised their crossbows. It was the squat, blond young man and the dark shirdar girl again, he saw—he had lost count of how many times they'd swapped off with the other pair sitting upstairs in the guardroom playing piquet. His knees trembling, the Wolf felt like telling them that if they were tired of the routine, next time *he'd* go sit in the guardroom for a change.

It would be something, he thought, if he could only summon up the smallest of go-away spells to keep the roaches and the few big, fat, insolent flies away from the raw flesh of his wounds. But the sorceries in the chains did their job thoroughly. All he could do was shake his

cramped arms weakly and curse. He was growing too
weary now to do either.

It was about the seventh hour of the night. He had the
rest of the night to get through and all the hours of daylight tomorrow. The thought was far worse than that of
whatever death he'd have to endure afterward.

A draft from the corridor moved the putrid air, and his
eyes swam with the smoke. By sunset tomorrow in the
desert dryness, he knew he'd be half-crazy with thirst,
but now it was lack of sleep that tormented him most—
lack of sleep, and the tree of agony rooted in his legs,
growing up his spine to his cramped, searing shoulder
muscles, and branching out to the red rings of bleeding
pain that circled his wrists. Sooner or later his knees
were going to give out. And then, he thought, he'd look
back on this moment with nostalgic longing.

Wherever they'd put the Hawk, he hoped she was
better off than he.

The queer, sinking sensation of panic returned at the
thought of her.

She would never have broken as he had.

That might be, he thought ruefully, because it was un-
likely that, had their positions been reversed, he would
ever have been an innocent victim. But at heart, he knew
Starhawk to be both colder and tougher than he was.
Since he had come to love her—since he had embraced
the magic that was his destiny—he had discovered in
himself a widening streak of sentimentality that his father would have puked to behold—puked first and then
beaten him till the blood ran.

He wondered if she would despise him for breaking
down as he had or if she'd guessed what he knew—that
his holding out would have made no ultimate difference.

Why had the demon had his face?

In the darkness of the corridor outside, something
moved.

Sun Wolf raised his head sharply, and one guard
shifted her crossbow while the other turned, casting a

swift glance through the stone arch. The reflection of torches from the staircase above had long since sunk into smoky darkness, but, like a gauzy brush of fox fire, white light danced along the cracks in the stone. Then it was gone.

Exhausted almost past caring, Sun Wolf wrenched his body back away from the door—and that light—as far as he could, forcing himself not to feel the burning scrape of the manacles on his wrists. As he did so, he let out a gasp and molded his unshaven features into what he hoped was a convincing expression of utter shock and horror, as if the light were some threat as much to himself as to the guards, though in point of fact he felt no sense of danger from it at all. The guards looked at one another, then back at him. He threw them a desperate look and hoped to hell they remembered him sobbing and begging Nanciormis for mercy. *If I had to go through that*, he thought grimly, *at least let me get some good from it* . . . Whatever the hell was happening, it would be better than being shot out of hand.

At least he hoped so.

After a moment's hesitation, one guard signed to the other to keep his eye on the Wolf, then stepped cautiously into the corridor to investigate. He saw the girl's shadow on the wall, the dancing phosphorescence leading her away. The other guard braced himself, crossbow leveled, his eyes never leaving the Wolf.

Thus he didn't even see Starhawk as she stepped lightly through the arch behind him with half an adobe brick twisted into the bottom corner of a flour sack. She caught the man before he fell and held onto his crossbow, too, lowering him gently to the rock floor as Jeryn slipped in like a little shadow at her heels.

The ache of joy flooded Sun Wolf, painful as the rush of blood to a numbed limb, to see her alive and, at least by mercenary's standards, unhurt; it was so intense that he could only whisper as she came close enough to hear, "Where the hell have you been?"

She was pulling free the pins which held the wrist chains to the rings in the wall, the rags of her shirt hanging like a beggar's on her rangy frame and a layer of dust gummed to the bloody filth that coated her swollen face. "I leave the royal ball before the dancing is over to come here and rescue you, and that's all you can say?"

He lowered his arm and swore violently to keep from crying out in pain. Starhawk's arms were gentle, solid, and strong as a man's. For a moment their eyes met. Then he clasped her to him, gritting his teeth against the agony the movement cost him, holding her as hard as his shaking arms would permit, his face pressed to her sticky hair and the crossbow jammed uncomfortably between their two bellies. He tasted her blood and his own as their split and puffy lips met, regardless of the pain. Then he whispered, "Let's go." He knew if he didn't let go now, he never would.

Jeryn slipped past them to the darkest corner of the little cell and pushed low down on the wall. A small section of it fell back, and, without a word, the boy ducked in. Chains still dangling from his lacerated wrists, Sun Wolf slipped after him, and Starhawk, ducking through last, crossbow in hand, pulled the door shut behind them.

Tazey was waiting for them with saddled horses beside the old gate of the empty quarter that led down to the pass. Covered with dirt and soot as she was, Sun Wolf took her in his arms. He knew where that luring light had come from.

"Good-by." Her small hands were cold against his back through the holes in his torn shirt. "I wish you could have stayed. I'll need a teacher..."

"Rot good-by," the Wolf said shortly. "We may be getting the hell out of here, but I'm not leaving until I know what's behind this."

"You don't—" she began.

"The hell I don't." His single golden eye went from her to Jeryn, holding the horses in the shadows of the broken-down gate. "Aside from the fact that sooner or later Lady Illyra or Kaletha's going to track us down, I don't think that thing's stopped killling. We've got no guarantee about who its next victim's going to be. Since we don't even know what the range is, it could conceivably be either me or the Hawk or both."

From the direction of the main block of the fortress came a distant shout, then a rising clamor and torchlight spinning like mad fireflies along the walls. Starhawk remarked, "Either there's a skunk in the Hall or they know we're gone."

Sun Wolf glanced out through the broken-toothed maw of the gate to the chiaroscuro of velvet and ice that the moonlight scattered over the twisted land. An elf-owl hooted once from where ocotillo threw its shadows like a skeleton hand across the sand-drift near an old wall; the moon gleamed like a rim of frost on the spines of the Dragon's Backbone. "There a place we could hole up in the mountains where the horses could be hidden?"

Jeryn looked blank—he might know every underground tunnel and secret passage in Tandieras, but he'd never stepped willingly outside its walls in his life. Tazey said, "There's a deserted chapel high up in the side of the Binnig Rock—up there." She pointed to the dizzying bulk of the half dome. "The trail's pretty narrow, but it can be done on a horse."

He turned to Jeryn. "You think you can find your way up there tomorrow, as soon as you can slip away? I'm going to need somebody to read pieces of those books to me."

The boy nodded, dark eyes glowing.

"Good. Tazey, stay here and keep an eye on things—best you aren't both missing at the same time." He swung into the saddle. If Starhawk alone had been there, he probably would have groaned and cursed with pain; but as it was, he only gritted his teeth. "And see if you can't smuggle us weapons of some kind—and a blanket." He collected the reins and turned away through the

narrow gate to the pewter moonlight of the narrow trail
beyond.

Tazey asked softly, "Will you be all right tonight?"

Starhawk said, deadpan, "I think we'll manage to
keep each other warm."

"Chief?"

He turned his head sleepily to look down at the ivory-
fine features of the woman who lay in the crook of his
arm. The washy dawnlight turned her hair colorless, the
bruises on her face almost black. The air was bitterly
cold, so that even the harshness of the sacking and sad-
dleblankets in which they were wrapped was welcome.
The links of the slip-chain still around her neck jingled
softly as she raised a scarred hand to touch one of the
few unbruised portions of his face, with a gentleness no
one would have guessed who'd seen her brain a man
with a mace in battle.

She said softly, "Thank you."

"Did you think I wouldn't have given them whatever
they wanted, told them whatever they wanted, to save
you?"

She was silent a long time, while buried thought fum-
bled its painful way to the surface. The gray light seeping
through the chapel's narrow door to lie over the two
ragged fugitives silvered her eyes—he saw them flood
with sudden tears. "I never thought anyone would," she
said at last.

When next they spoke, the light had warmed on the
thick tangle of brush and mesquite outside the chapel
door, and wavering gleams of yellow and green reflected
into the shadowy stone room from the catch pools outside. The slit windows above the little stone altar glowed
with the wide nothingness of desert air, five hundred feet
above the level of the crumbling talus and rock below.
The chapels of the Mother were for those who would
fight to reach her, not like the easy, open churches of the
Triple God.

"Why'd you ask Jeryn about his etymology? About the difference between a witch and a wizard?"

Drowsing on the edge of sleep, Sun Wolf almost laughed. Only Starhawk's logical mind would bring a question like that out of the afterglow of lovemaking.

"What is the difference?"

Starhawk considered the two words for a time. "In the dialect of the north it's a difference of—of kind of magic," she said at last. "A wizard is an academic; the word 'witch' implies earth-magic, granny-magic some-times—intuition. In the dialect of the Middle Kingdoms, and here along the cordillera, I've noticed that 'wizard' is masculine and 'witch' is feminine—the way 'God' is feminine in the singular and masculine in the plural."

"Close," he agreed, and sat up, shivering a little at the touch of the chill air. "But in the shirdar there's a differ-ent connotation, a pejorative one—the implication that the magic wasn't yours to begin with. The shirdane is a language of nuances. In it, like in the north, a wizard is an academic, one who studies, a scholar or an engineer. But the shirdane word for 'witch' is someone who buys her power, usually in trade for her soul. When they speak of the Witches of Wenshar, they aren't describing power—they're speaking of how power was acquired." He sat cross-legged under the ragged blanket and pushed back the faded strands of thinning hair from his scabbed, unshaven face.

There was something ironic, Sun Wolf thought, in his utter comfort in this bare stone cell. When he was the wealthiest captain of mercenaries in the West, he'd never have believed he would one day delight in being a ragged, filthy fugitive this way, sitting in a bare stone room with nothing but a half interest in a saddle blanket and four saddlebags full of stolen books to his name. *Nothing like a quick glance down into the Cold Hells to make you pleased with life on damn near any terms.*

"It's the demons of Wenshar that were the source of the Witches' power," he went on. "They traded their power, their service, to the Witches—became their servants."

"Are you sure?" Starhawk raised herself on one elbow and pulled the saddle blanket awkwardly over her bare shoulder. "Demons are—immortal. And immaterial. There are old legends of people controlling them, but why would they allow themselves to be controlled? We have nothing they'd want."

"Don't we?" His hoarse voice was soft in the watery gloom. "Think about it, Hawk. Demons have no flesh, as we know flesh; no blood; no passions. They are cold creatures, ephemeral, entities unattached to bodies. They can never die—and so they never live. I felt their minds all around me in Wenshar, Hawk; I felt their cold, that seeks after warmth." He leaned forward, resting his elbows on his knees.

"They crave heat—not heat as we understand it, or at least not as we understand it consciously, but the heat of the soul, of the blood—the heat of fear, for which they drive beasts and men, if they can trap them, to panic deaths, so they can drink it as it spills out of them; the heat of lust, which leads them to couple in dreams with men and women, feeding their partners the images that they crave, to warm themselves by that mortal fire. And the heat of hate, which is the best of all, because it doesn't fade with time.

"The demons in Wenshar became addicted to hate, the way men become addicted to dream-sugar. The Witches of Wenshar fed them, using their magic to open the channels between their minds and the demons', and the demons found they liked that food. There are earth-demons in many parts of the world, but mostly humankind avoids them, as they avoid humankind. Originally the House Cult of Wenshar may only have sought to control the demons, because their city was built where they lived. But later they sought to bend them to their bidding. Afterward they found there was a price to pay. That was the secret power of the Witches of Wenshar—

that the demons would kill whomever they hated. But in return, they had to go on hating."

Starhawk glanced over at the untouched books, piled at the foot of the bare stone altar. Sun Wolf shook his head.

"It's only my guess," he said. "But the demons knew me for mageborn the minute I entered their city. They tried to get me to take that power, to use it as the Witches did. The Witches gave their hate to the demons, to feed on and to act on, but in doing so they gave them a taste for it. Corrupted them, if you like. Demons are immortal. While Altiokis dominated this part of the world, people would not admit to being mageborn, not even to themselves. Demons have been living in that city for over a century, like roaches, feeding on the piled rot of old hates. They're coming out of a long starvation."

In the glowing blue-green cleft of the doorway, a tiny rock-mouse paused, whiskers aquiver, silhouetted against the colors of leaf and stone. A flurry of doves swept past the entrance like a skiff of blown snow. Starhawk looked down at her hands for a long time.

"The kids say Nanciormis saw your face on the demon that came for him."

Sun Wolf nodded, remembering how, in the darkness of the temple in Wenshar, the demon eyes had glowed golden, like his own. In that moment, when their minds had touched...? He hadn't forgotten the dead birds found after his own first night spent in this country.

"I can't explain it," he said slowly. "But I think I'd have known."

"According to Nanciormis, via Tazey, they didn't, always. That cuts both ways," she added after a moment. "The fact that you found the dead birds before the storm doesn't mean it couldn't have been Tazey herself. She may well not have known. In the north I've heard of knocking-demons, and there's always a young boy or girl somewhere involved. And she is mageborn."

"So's Kaletha," the Wolf said. "And if Kaletha's thir-

tyish now, she must have been in well into her teens
while Queen Ciannis was alive—old enough to have
been initiated into the cult, if Ciannis was its last survi-
vor. Particularly if Ciannis was as frail as Nanciormis
says and might have suspected she wouldn't survive a
second childbirth."

"Maybe," Starhawk said. "It could account for Kaletha wanting as badly as she did to get Tazey into her
teaching, if her own vanity didn't. But there was no
change, nothing new happening with Kaletha that could
have triggered all this. Why now? Why not nine months
ago, when Altiokis died?"

"You're arguing as if the killings made sense. They
may not." Sun Wolf heaved himself to his feet and
gasped at the agony of his back and legs.

Starhawk pushed herself more or less upright also,
moving as if she were in pain but not showing it on her
face. "Don't get excited," she said in her usual calm
voice. "It's going to be lots worse tomorrow. Let's see
what the books have to say about all this."

Of the eighteen books, seven were in various forms of
the old tongue of Gwenth, as it had been spoken in the
Middle Kingdoms in the centuries before. Together,
Starhawk and Sun Wolf limped to the rock-pools below
the chapel and watered the horses and bathed in the
freezing, shallow water. Sun Wolf shaved with Tazey's
dagger and bound the messy, abraded flesh of his wrists
with part of what was left of his shirt. It was fully light
when they returned to the chapel and settled down to
read.

"I don't like this," Starhawk said softly, looking up
from the faded and grubby pages of the Book of the Cult.
"Nanciormis was right. They didn't always know, especially not at first. But their mothers and sisters and aunts
would watch for the signs, if the girl was mageborn, and
would initiate her, teach her to control the demons her
mind had summoned. It was only five or six generations,
you know," she added, settling her bruised shoulders

gingerly back against the wall. "That's not a long time in the history of the Ancient Houses. It looks as if there was a family cult before that time, but the demons probably came in when the mageborn streak surfaced. Unless..." She paused for a moment, frowning to herself at those words, then began thumbing back through the faded, close-written pages again, with their red and blue capitals, their loops and pothooks where words were abbreviated by a hurried scribe, seeking impatiently for something there which she could not seem to find.

Sun Wolf's yellow eye narrowed. "By my first ancestor, that palace must have been a hell to live in," he murmured. "Have you ever dealt with a knocking-demon, Hawk? Even when they aren't throwing things, or making noises, you can feel them in a place, watching you. No wonder no one would come to the defense of Wenshar when Kwest Mralwe sent armies through the passes."

In the forenoon Jeryn rode laboriously up the trail on Walleye, sweating in his ill-wrapped head veils and starting at every unfamiliar noise. He curled up in a corner of the chapel where a dim sun shaft fell through the weed-clogged roof hole of the rock chimney. While Starhawk pursued her own researches, Sun Wolf sat beside him, following the boy's finger along the scribbled black line of brushed writing. The more he heard, the greater his uneasiness grew.

All those who wrote of demons remarked upon the fact that in dreams they might show the features of those who sent them. Nowhere did it say that they could cloak themselves in the forms of those who had not.

They had known his name, in Wenshar. Could that have given them his form as well? Or was there another explanation?

I'd know it, he thought, over and over, while feeling the stir of fear in his veins. *By my first ancestor, I would sense it, in my dreams if nothing else ...*

But the boy's voice droned on, over the names of the

various demons—hundreds of them—and the obscene and hideous spells of their summoning. Sun Wolf remembered, years ago, a man in his troop who, disturbed suddenly in sound sleep, had strangled his mistress to death, taking several minutes to do it. Waking, he had sworn with bitter tears that he remembered nothing of it—that when the men had wakened him, he had been sitting by her corpse—and could not be convinced that it was not they who had done it and put the blame on him.

In the haunted halls of Wenshar, the painted shadows of the women had watched him from the walls, amusement in their dark eyes. They had initiated one another, the elder helping the younger along, cushioning the shock of that terrible knowledge. What was it to one who had not that help?

After Jeryn had gone and he and Starhawk were settling down to the meal of meat, bread, and wine that the boy had brought, along with blankets and a chisel to rid them of the last of their chains, he spoke of his fears. The Hawk thought the matter over, as if they had been discussing some third person whom neither knew well. "Do you hate Nanciormis?" she asked.

Sun Wolf considered. After what the commander had done to him and to Starhawk last night, he realized he should, but he didn't, really. Perhaps, he thought, it was because he'd done the same thing himself. "I don't trust him," he said at last. "He's too strong and too smart for the position he's in, or he thinks he is, anyway. Osgard seems to have been pretty shrewd to keep him where he is. He looks good, but he's irresponsible—he's a decent fighter, but he couldn't teach a dog to lift his leg to a tree. He could have got Jeryn killed one day, if he goaded him into trying a horse too strong for him. He's a schemer and a user and he gossips worse than an old woman. But no, I don't hate him. And I certainly didn't hate him before the attack."

"Or Incarsyn?" she pressed. "You care about Tazey, and you might say he insulted her."

"There wasn't enough to Incarsyn for anyone to hate." The Wolf took a bite of the tough, harsh-textured bread and stared thoughtfully at the canyon wall beyond the door, where the shadow of the rim lay across it in a slanting line of blue and gold as sharp as if it had been drawn with a rule, inked, and gilded. He added, "Tazey might have."

Starhawk shook her head. "She never wanted to marry him," she pointed out. "She just couldn't say so to her father—maybe couldn't admit it to herself. If he'd died before backing out of the match, maybe . . ."

"You think she wouldn't have feared her father would find some way to revive it, in spite of Illyra? Particularly if Nanciormis had told her what he told us about what Incarsyn had said of her?"

The woman's dark brows went up thoughtfully and she looked down into her wine cup, digesting that idea.

"You're still talking as if the killings made sense," the Wolf said. "They might not have. Tazey might have hated Incarsyn, might have hated Galdron for telling her she was damned—evidently she believed she hated Nanciormis enough, after whatever it was he said to her, for it to be her. That still doesn't explain Egaldus' death."

"Unless we're dealing with two killers," Starhawk said quietly. "Kaletha may very well have had reason to hate Egaldus, if he was trying to get her books away from her. She certainly had reason to hate Galdron."

"And Nexué?" the Wolf said. "For all she was a vicious old gossip, Hawk, she was pretty harmless. The way you deal with someone like that is to cast spells to make her hair fall out or her sciatica act up, not strew her guts over fifty square yards of ground."

"If you're sixteen, you might." Starhawk finished a piece of bread, tossed the crumbs to the threshold where three little black wheatears swooped down to fight over them. "And then, we don't know what Nexué knew. She was a spy as well as a gossip. If she'd seen Kaletha and

Egaldus coupling like weasels in rut in the empty quarter, Kaletha might just want her dead to preserve that purity she's always throwing up in everyone's face. It would kill 'Shebbeth to find out her precious teacher is less than perfect. As badly as Kaletha sometimes treats her, she isn't anxious to give up that devoted a slave."

"You've changed your mind about her, then?"

"No." She leaned back against the dressing stone of the lintel. "I'm just arguing both sides. It doesn't sound like Kaletha—but it doesn't sound like you or Tazey, either." She frowned again, scouting the thought, then let it go. "As I said, there was no change in Kaletha's life, except one, which argues more than anything else that it *wasn't* her."

He cocked his head, curious.

"You," the Hawk said. "A rival, a barbarian, a boor. She hated you from the beginning. You should have been the first. A potential book thief..." She gestured towards the dark volumes, stacked at the foot of the altar, threads of reflected light gleaming dully gold and pewter on their bindings. "Also, you're the one with the greatest chance of figuring out what's going on. But there hasn't been an attack directed at you."

"Hasn't there?" The Wolf studied his bandaged wrists for a moment, the flesh around them bruised brown and stained now with the poultices he'd concocted to cleanse the wounds. "You know what was odd about that attack on Nanciormis? It was the only one to take place early enough in the evening for people to be around."

"You know," Starhawk said, "I thought there was something strange about that. Something—I don't know. During the calling of Galdron's spirit..." Her dark brows came together for a moment, as if she searched for some lost thought, then she shook her head. "But not only was the attack on Nanciormis the only one reasonably early enough to expect witnesses, but it was the only one which the victim survived."

Sun Wolf dusted the crumbs from his hands. "I don't

think Nanciormis was the one who was supposed to die as a result of that attack," he said quietly. "I think it was me."

"Could Kaletha have done that?" she asked. "Sent an illusion which felt like the coming of a demon, with your face?"

"She might have," he said. "I can't think of a neater way to get rid of someone in a position to expose her without drawing blame to herself by killing me and narrowing the field still further. If she'd been dealing with demon magic from these books, she would have known what one felt like and put it together. Particularly if she was afraid to send the real demons after me, for fear I'd take them and twist them to my own will."

He got painfully to his feet and limped to the door. Outside, the narrow rock-cleft, sun-touched for only a brief hour at noon, was sinking again into cool green gloom. From here, he could smell the water and hear the sounds of the birds and beasts who came down to drink, so unlike the untouched, sterile catch-tanks of Wenshar. "In the Dark Book our little Scout read us this afternoon it said there always came a point at which the Witch realized her power, realized it was she who was causing the deaths of those she hated. I think Kaletha might have reached that point with Egaldus' death. She certainly didn't shed a hell of a lot of tears over it."

"Not where you'd see them, anyway," Starhawk put in softly.

"But Nexué, and Galdron, and maybe Egaldus, were all her enemies—and when Egaldus died she must have realized there were people who'd guess it. And she had to shift the blame. There was no—no *smell* of evil in Nanciormis' room after the attack. That might just have been an effect of the storm, but I'm not so sure."

"And Incarsyn?"

He glanced back at her over his shoulder, his one eye darkening with concern. "I don't know," he said. "That worries me. Maybe by that time the demons had begun to touch Tazey as well. Maybe . . ." He half turned back, drawing closed the clasps of his worn old sheepskin doublet, which had been part of Jeryn's contribution that afternoon.

The southern-window slit above the altar was dimming now, as darkness settled on the desert. Through it, nothing of the Fortress was visible, nor the town—only the endless planes of air and sand, marching away into a flat infinity, broken by the single whitish plume of dust where one of Nanciormis' scouts cantered back towards Tandieras after an unsuccessful day of search.

"So what are you going to do?"

He sighed heavily. "There's no way I can prove my innocence, or Kaletha's guilt. And if the demons have begun to touch Tazey's mind . . ." He turned back. Starhawk, her big hands clasped around bony knees, sat watching him in the blue glow of the witchfire. "I think if Tazey could get away from this place, she'd be all right," he said. "But I can't see her father letting her go, not to get the teaching she'll need. And untaught, God only knows to what channel her powers will turn." He leaned his powerful shoulders in the stone lintel. "We'll have to stop them both at the source."

Starhawk glanced again at the books. The witchlight, gleaming on the sand-polished jewels and the queer, twisted silver shapes that clasped them shut, seemed to impart a glowing half-life to them, as if they had spent the centuries, like the demons, dreaming in silence of alien longings. "Do you think you can?"

He nodded, though he felt by no means sure. "There are spells in the Demonary that provide for the binding of demons into a rock, or a tree, or an altar stone," he said. "The Book of the Cult lists all their names. If I can make a Circle of Darkness wide enough and draw them into it, it would keep them long enough for me to work such a binding, to hold them to the stones of Wenshar for eternity."

The woman who had been for years his second-in-command and who never failed to pour the cold and lucid water of her logic onto his strategies regarded him with those enigmatic gray eyes for a moment, then said, "If it works."

Sun Wolf nodded and tried to ignore the chill curl of dread at the thought of standing once more in that haunted temple. "If it works," he agreed.

CHAPTER

—— 16 ——

ORDINARILY IT WOULD HAVE TAKEN THEM UNTIL JUST after noon to reach Wenshar from the tiny chapel on the Binnig Rock, but they were delayed, searching for certain herbs and stealing a bull calf from an isolated foothills ranch. By the time they entered the ruined city, the shadows were already beginning to slant over, the sun blinding but curiously heatless in the crumbled mazes of the lower town, a glaring line halfway up the chromatic rocks in the canyons. It took them a few hours to water their horses, stable them in the rear chamber of the temple Sun Wolf had used before, and to barricade them in. As he drew the Circles of Light around the door this time, Sun Wolf was interested to see how close his own half-learned, half-guessed defenses had been to the Circles as described in the Demonaries. Whatever happened, they knew they could not afford to lose the horses.

He thought with brief regret of the small cache of his and Starhawk's money, hidden behind a loose brick in the dusty little cell where they had slept and talked and made love. When this was over and the demons bound to the rocks of Wenshar for all time, they would have to flee; a dozen pieces of silver would come in handy, perhaps make all the difference, somewhere along the road between capture and escape.

But more than that, there was a sharp ache inside him as he realized that it would be years, if ever, before they would see Tazey and Jeryn again. That, too, was a sensation totally unfamiliar to him, as unfamiliar as the pain and terror he had felt for Starhawk's safety—as if, loving her, some wall within him had been irreparably fissured, and he had had thrust upon him the capacity to love others as well. He had come to look upon those two children as if they had been his own; his deceased ancestors were the only ones who might have kept track of the bastards he'd fathered over the years. Odd that the first children for whom he should feel responsible should be some other man's.

But if nothing else, Tazey would be safe. If he could not engineer her happiness, at least he could give her that.

"I don't like this, Chief," Starhawk said softly, as she watched the Wolf trace the final signs of the Circle of Light around her on the smooth-swept temple floor. The bleached smudge of daylight that lay like a rumpled carpet by the nearer door was fading. The gloom seemed thicker beyond the wavering rings of a dozen small fires whose smoke, in spite of the old air shafts hidden in the darkness of the ceiling, stung and burned the eyes. It would soon be night.

Sun Wolf sat back on his knees and used the ragged hem of his torn shirt to daub loose charcoal and ochre from his scabbed fingers. "I don't like your even being here," he retorted. He wiped sweat from his face with the back of his hand, leaving long smudges of black and rust. The vast silence of the dark temple around them picked up the echoes of his broken voice. "But I'd like it a hell of a lot less of you were where I couldn't see you."

"I didn't mean that."

Looking across the lines of the Circle at the thin, strong face, with its old scars and rock-crystal eyes and sun-whitened hair, warmed to honey by the light of the small fire enclosed with her in the enchanted ring, Sun Wolf knew too well what she did mean.

They had both been a dozen times over the rite of summoning in the Demonary and the Book of the Cult of Wenshar. Near the lighter doorway into the entry hall the bull calf lowed plaintively, as if it knew it had reason to fear the slow gathering of darkness.

The central canyon, as they had walked up it, dragging the unwilling calf between them, had been dead silent. The crunch of their feet on the gravel, the slip and scrape of the calf's hooves, and its frightened bawling, had echoed in that horrible stillness, prickling the hair on the Wolf's nape with the sensation of being watched. Now and then, from the tail of his eye, he had glimpsed movement. Several times he had turned his head, knowing there would be nothing when he did so. And there was not. Familiar as he had come to be with the haunted canyons and the not-quite-empty black eyes of the stone-cut houses, still his heart thumped hard against his ribs, and the sweat crawled clammily down his backbone at those soft, scritching movements and the touch of those unseen eyes.

What little light filtered into the temple from the entry hall was fading.

He and the Hawk, working together and as swiftly as the unfamiliar rituals would let them, had swept and ritually cleansed the temple. Sun Wolf had repeated the archaic spells learned from the Demonary as he had drawn the runes in the temple's four corners, first slowly and clumsily, checking the moldering black book to make sure they were right, then with more certainty in his harsh, scraped voice. It would take him longer to

form and consecrate the greater Circle, which was his
ultimate goal, without her help—longer, as the weariness grew on his stiff and aching arms and tired mind;
but he was not having her unprotected once night came.

His back and arms smarting all over again, his mind
fighting the strange sleepiness of concentration held too
strictly and too long, he paced and marked out the biggest Circle of all, encompassing the stone altar and the
pit before it in the floor. Meticulously, he drew the signs
on the stone floor with lumps of charcoal, with sticks of
red ochre, and with thin lines of powdery white sand like
the finest sugar—Circle within Circle, Darkness within
Light, points oriented like a compass rose to the corners
of the universe, long curves sweeping to enclose power
within. Instead of marking the rune circle on the outside
of the defensive points, he marked the runes on the inside, to imprison rather than repel. And deliberately, he
left two of the runes unwritten.

He flinched, and looked up. He'd left his doublet and
head veils crumpled in the corner near Starhawk's small
Circle, and the chill air crept through the holes in his
bloodstained shirt to touch the damp hair on his back. It
was now utterly dark. Repeating the words of the rune-
spells over and over to himself, he had let his mind slip
into the trance of concentration. He had no idea how
much time had passed.

Outside, the canyon lay submerged in chilled obsidian
darkness. Of the half-dozen little fires lit around the temple floor, all had died but the one small blaze in the Circle with Starhawk. By the dim throb of that orange light
he saw the glint of her eyes, the pale blur of her shirt-
sleeved arms still wrapped around her drawn-up knees.
In the utter silence, he could hear her breathing, steady
and calm. Then the calf bleated again, desperate fear in
the sound.

Sun Wolf got to his feet, like a man startled by some
other sound than that. His stiff back muscles stabbed
like a hidden stiletto. He was aware of his own hunger

and thirst, the stink of his unwashed body, and the dark
heavy odor of spent wood smoke, the smell of the rock,
of dust, of . . . incense? Through the darkness, for a moment, it was as if he smelled myrrh burned two centuries
ago, like scents caught in women's hair. Through his skin
he was aware of a sandstorm, building somewhere out in
the darkness of the desert. Though cold, the air felt suddenly stifling, hushed with expectation. In the terrible
silence, he nearly jumped out of his skin at the whisper
of one breath of wind, trailing over the stone like the
hem of a woman's silk gown.

Brimming with shadow, the pit lay before him. He
turned from it, and his own shadow brushed over the
mottled sides of the broken altar. Why had he thought,
for just that moment as he glimpsed it from the tail of his
eye, that it stood whole again? Outside the frail glimmer
of Starhawk's little fire, the darkness seemed thicker,
clotted in the corners of the vast room like the vapors of
old decay which would never be cleared away.

The demons lay in the stone, like sharks below the
surface of the sea, and watched.

The calf bellowed again, desperate with fear.

He hated what he knew must come next.

Starhawk had not understood it and had only been
repelled when Jeryn had read in his cool little alto voice
how the Witches of Wenshar had summoned their
demons. Very few of them had used animals in the pit,
once they'd realized more demons would come if the
victim were a human child. Even back then, it seemed,
orphans were cheap in the poor quarters of the city.
Some of the Witches, the Book of the Cult had said,
could summon the demons without sacrifice; but when
Starhawk had suggested trying to do so, the Wolf had
categorically refused. The book had not said it, but he
had sensed what he would have to be projecting with his
mind—filth and hatred and the unholiest of urges—to
bring them. He'd rather kill a calf, even in the gruesome
way prescribed.

It took more nerve than he'd thought it would to walk to the edge of the pit. He wasn't certain what he feared he would see there, with his wizard's sight, in the swimming blackness below. But it contained only a little sand drifted in the corners, and the skeleton of what looked like a dove, white as a bit of lace dropped upon the loose gravel of its floor.

He wondered why the sudden thought of how deep that gravel might lie over the bedrock repelled him like a nauseating smell.

Turning back, he kindled the little heap of aromatic woods he had left on the bare stump of the broken altar and from it lit two fire-bowls which he set in place of the two missing runes on the inner Circle. Stepping carefully between them, he walked out of the Circle and over to where Starhawk sat beside her little fire.

Without stepping over the protecting barrier, he said softly, "You all right?"

She nodded. She had been silent for hours, watching him, gray eyes inscrutable. He had been totally absorbed in his task and wondered now what she had seen in the darkness as it had closed around him. All his nerves prickled, his mind screaming to him to beware in this vast darkness where the dry rustle of gowns and hair seemed to have only just that moment stopped in the black beyond the fire's light.

"Whatever you see," he said quietly, "whatever you think is happening, don't step out of the Circle. Once it's broken, it will be no protection to you."

She nodded. "I know."

"They shouldn't be able to get in at you." Of that, at least, mercifully, he was now sure. "Once I draw the last two runes and complete the great Circle, they shouldn't be able to get out. With them trapped, I should be able to work the binding-spells to hold them to the rocks of Wenshar forever."

She cocked her head a little. The smudgy firelight deepened the shadows of her hollowed eyes and the lines that fanned backward from them on the unswollen side of her face and scored deep marks from her nostrils to the soft corners of that calm mouth. "How long's that going to take you?"

He muttered a curse at her for seeing what she saw: the marks of fatigue on his face; the dark ring of weariness around his single eye and the bruised look of the lid; the taut mouth beneath its straggly mustache; and the strange pallor under the stubble of his golden beard. He was close to the edge and he knew it, nearing the point where the cumulative stresses of flight and concentration would begin to cause mistakes. Even the smallest break in his mental barriers could be fatal in dealing with the demons of Wenshar. "Until just after dawn, rot your eyes, and what the hell business is it of yours?"

"And the sandstorm? Will that break before you're done?"

The Wolf hesitated. The sandstorms, as he and Nanciormis both had learned, would scatter the demons on their winds—but as they both had known also, where the demons were able to walk during the killer winds, they walked more strongly. They fed upon violence, even the violence of the air.

As if she read his answer in his silence, she said, "Can you send it away? Or delay it?"

He shook his head. He could feel the whisper along his bones, a crawling tingle as if his nerves were being drawn from his flesh one fiber at a time; it was coming and it was strong. His hoarse voice quiet, he said, "I haven't the strength to spare, Hawk. Not from what I have to do. By dawn..." He shrugged and spread his hands. "We may have time. An hour would be all we need."

Dark wind licked the tiny fire; Sun Wolf swung around as the bull calf bellowed again, in despair as well as terror. The poor creature was jerking wildly at its rope, its bound feet bouncing and threshing, its eyes gleaming in the faint reflections of the fire. Sun Wolf was aware again of how dark it was in the temple, how the shadows seemed to creep forward, curious, questing fingers seeking to probe his body and his soul. He shifted his aching shoulders again, his heart beginning to pound at the thought of what lay ahead.

Softly, the Hawk said, "Good luck, Chief. May the spirits of your ancestors lend you a hand."

"The spirits of my ancestors would disown me for messing with demons," he replied, the levity he had intended hushed from the raven-croak of his voice. "They at least had brains." He wanted to reach across, to touch her, like a man drawing luck from some talisman of dark-stained ivory and gold, but even that would have broken the Circle and negated the forces of protection held so tenuously in the tingling air. The little fire before her feet was sinking, and he could not even spare the power to summon witchlight to brighten that ghastly darkness for her. He wondered, as he turned from her and walked toward the terrified calf beside the door, how much of what was going to happen she would even see.

It was going to be a hideously long night.

The calf fought Sun Wolf's grip on its stubby horns as best it could, bracing its bound feet, writhing as he half dragged, half carried it toward the Circle. The ghost-whispers of wind murmuring in the ventilation shafts echoed like an eerie chanting. Had they chanted, Sun Wolf wondered, as two or three of their number had dragged some poor terrified child to the altar? Chanted to summon the demons, to hold their own powers of protection against them?

He remembered again the painted eyes of those worn frescoes and the dark cynicism of their ironic regard. A slashing hoof cut his shin; slobber from the calf's muzzle slimed his hands and stung in the half-scabbed demon bites; its rough coat abraded the skin of his side as it flung its weight against him. In his mercenary days, he'd tortured men and taken pleasure in torturing them, if they'd hurt or betrayed him or some member of his troop. Why did slaughtering this bull calf, who'd have ended up dead at cattle-killing time before the onset of winter anyway, make his soul cringe as it did? Why did those huge brown eyes, white-rimmed with terror, seem so human, staring up into his? He dragged the animal between the two fire pots and the calf bellowed again in fear of the flames...

And from the corner of his eye he saw movement.

A glow that illuminated nothing flickered in the darkness behind him.

They were coming.

He was battered and aching in every muscle of his tired body by the time he got the calf wrestled up onto the uneven altar stone. The beast flopped like a landed fish, its pitiful, frantic bellowing for its mother turning the vast stone darkness into a ringing sound-chamber whose echoes went through Sun Wolf's skull. He roped its hind feet together, and then to its already-bound forelegs; sweat ran down his ribs and back, sticking the torn rags of his shirt to his body and burning in the abrasions of his wrists within their filthy bindings. He worked from the front side of the altar rather than the back, hating the open, silent mouth of the pit at his back, but preferring that, for the moment, to the alternative. Where he stood now, panting, smelling the warm animal smell of the calf, the dirt, and the aromatic woods of the small fire beside the altar steps, he could look between the two fire pots into a Stygian corridor that seemed to run back far past the rear wall of the temple in its concealing shadows, a corridor extending into the blackness of the earth, into realms he had never known and never wanted to know —into time.

He could see them now, far back along that corridor, bobbing like marsh-lights over swamps long dry. He could hear the whisper of their chittering laughter. The fire beside the altar seemed to wink in the glinting reflection of their eyes.

The knife hilt pressed like an arm bone into his hand.

With deliberate brutality, he slashed the tendons of two of the calf's legs, one fore and one hind. The poor beast cried out with pain as well as terror, the smell of the blood on the knife mingling with the smoke, filling the darkness of the room. Something cold brushed Sun Wolf's shoulder. Whirling, warrior's muscles honed by terrors of his own, he almost cried out himself at what he saw, inches from his own face—the skeletal countenance of a demon, its head the size of a calf's, brown eyes bulging from sockets of terror, complete even to the fringe of white eyelashes—the calf's eyes. Under them, the unspeakable mouth smiled.

Turning back swiftly, Sun Wolf slashed open the calf's belly, blood pouring hot and slippery over his hand. He felt the prickle of cold claws in his back, the thin, bodiless muzzling of teeth against the skin of his neck; he forced himself not to look, not to think, not to panic. In the split second before the hot fumes of the blood and the smell of the sagging entrails choked him, he remembered being buried alive in a collapsing sapper tunnel at the siege of Laedden, remembered the torture pits of Elthien the Cruel, and remembered the floating flame speck whirling in the darkness of the dungeons of the Wizard King Altiokis, the pain of it lancing into his left eye...

He hadn't panicked then, and he had lived.

The blood smell pierced his brain. His head throbbed with the frantic lowing of the tortured calf. His mind felt locked, clamped in a crystal grip that he dared not open. *The Women of Wenshar had all done this,* he thought dizzily.

But they had enjoyed it.

As if he were someone else, he watched a demon like the glass skeleton of a serpent twine down his outstretched arm, to lick the blood from his hand with a human tongue. The edges of the altar were thick with demons, seeping from the stone, floating down through the air, and whispering and giggling in straw-frail descant

to the agony cries of the calf. One of them smiled at him
with a mouth like Tazey's, except for the fangs. Another
had breasts like Starhawk's, even to the scar. Their cold
pressed all around him, teeth like chips of broken glass
chewing at the bandages on his wrists. Worse than the
cold was the knowledge, from he knew not where, that it
would only take a slight giving of his mind to feel that
cold as warmth.

He dragged the calf from the altar, demons swarming
and crawling over it, bouncing weightlessly free and
floating in the air, limbs dangling, like monster wasps
over a rotting peach. He cut free the calf's feet and
shoved it over the edge into the pit, averting his eyes
from what he half-saw swarming below. The calf bellowed in agony and terror, staggering from side to side in
the pit, crippled, bleeding, dying, unable to escape the
things that had now begun to tear at it. Through the glittering, crawling swarm of demons, Sun Wolf could see
the dusty hide matted with blood, as Tazey's mare had
been. In the darkness of the pit, demons flashed like
starlight on glass, colors deepening their skeletal shapes,
blood spattering them, and their eyes the dark eyes of
women.

The Witches of Wenshar had summoned demons so
—and not with animals.

From the sticky trail that led from altar to pit, he
daubed up enough blood to mark the last two runes, as
he knelt between the rune circle and the outer boundary
of the Circle of Light. He then traced in the last mark-
ings, the calf's blood mingling with his own where the
demons had ripped the bandages from his wrists.

The Circle was finished. It would hold the demons—
for a time.

And for a time, he could only crouch on his knees
outside the Circle, his blood-slimed hands pressed together over his mouth, shaking so badly he was unable to
stand, like a small child exhausted by fleeing to safety
from that which whispers in the dark. He felt cold,

empty, sick, and weary unto death. Yet he knew he had a night's work ahead of him, to bind the demons permanently to the stones . . . And he must start at once, before the sandstorm, whose approach bit and whispered at his nerves, gave them its electric strength.

He raised his head, and saw that Starhawk's Circle of Protection was empty.

Shock jolted him like a fist driven into the pit of his stomach. He stared for a moment at the tiny glow of its smoky fire and the dark flower of points, curves, and runes on the stone floor, all with the inner glow of magic gone.

"Chief!"

He swung around. She stood beside the darkness of the temple door, face and throat and her one bare shoulder and arm white against those horrible shadows. With her was Tazey.

Somehow, he managed to get to his feet. The two women started to come toward him, and he waved them violently back. In the peripheral vision of his single eye, he could see the cloudy swarm of corpse-light weaving and billowing above the pit, like hornets over a burning nest. The women had no business coming anywhere near.

He stumbled to them across the patterned sandstone of the floor. Reflected in their eyes, he saw how he must look—bloody, scratched, with the filth on his face and the dark line of the eye patch standing blackly against the pallor beneath. Starhawk put out her hand to his neck, and he flinched—for the first time he was aware that the demons had bitten him, shallow scratches, like love bites. He remembered what he had read of the Witches of Wenshar, and the simile turned him ill.

"They came, then."

The Hawk had, of course, seen nothing. Even now he could see her looking toward the altar and the pit; in her eyes he could see no awareness of the evil lights floating above the glow of the pit. He fought a hysterical urge to laugh. "They came."

But by the horror on Tazey's face as she stared toward the pit, he knew she saw something and he wondered obliquely if their forms looked the same to her.

She tore her gaze from it and looked back at his face. "You have to flee," she said quietly. "Nanciormis and his men are coming. Kaletha's with them. They saw Jeryn coming back and followed his trail. I got the fastest horse I could. If you can get even a little ways away from here before the storm comes, it will cover your tracks."

"And you?" Starhawk's arm tightened around the girl's slim, straight shoulders.

"I'll—I'll wait it out here."

"The hell you will," the Wolf rumbled. "That Circle isn't going to hold the demons forever..."

"You could draw one around me," she offered, clearly frightened but not about to obligate him to help her by admitting it. "I wouldn't be in any danger then."

Sun Wolf put his hands on her shoulders, the blood on his fingers leaving sticky red blots on her faded pink shirt. "You'll be in danger as long as you live, if those demons aren't bound to the rocks that spawned them here and now," he said quietly. "So will everyone in Tandieras—everyone in Pardle. Whoever has been calling them..." He hesitated and looked away from that absinthe gaze. "It isn't only danger from them. If the Hawk and I ride on, and there's another killing, you may very well take the blame. I'm sorry, Tazey. I know what they did with the Witches..."

She flinched—evidently Nanciormis had told her that, too. But she only said, "It's what they're going to do to you."

"How long do we have?"

She shook her head. "I don't know. I rode as fast as I could. I could see their dust behind me and their torches after it got dark, but I lost sight of them when I came into the ruins. An hour, two hours, maybe. They'll be hurrying," she added, "because of the storm."

It was close. He could feel it turning, far out in the desert—dust columns like mountains, black-bellied anger holding night and blotting dawn. His struggle to keep his mind locked against the probing lusts of the demons had left him shaky with fatigue; he had little enough power left to complete the binding-spells. Within the enchanted Circle, he could hear the demons chittering furiously over the fading wails of the dying calf.

"I can't turn it," he said softly. "In any case we may need it . . ." He hesitated. They would need it for escape, from Nanciormis and his men, perhaps from the demons, if it came before the binding-spells were done . . .

There were too many variables, pressing upon his aching mind like the collapsing weight of a tunnel roof. He could sense the anger of the demons now, as they began to scratch and whisper at the rune-circle that held them in. The light of Starhawk's little fire, far back in the vast cavern behind them, was going, and he knew he had no strength to spare, either to make witchlight or kindle the ashes again. His hoarse voice low to hold it steady, he said, "Take care of the fire, Hawk. I'll do what I can to finish and get us out of here, but it can't be rushed." If the demons got out, the Hawk and Tazey would be in danger, too.

She said softly, "I know." Tightening her arm around Tazey's shoulders, she led her back toward the dying glow of the flames. Sun Wolf stood for a moment, willing strength back into his numbed muscles and shaken mind, as he had willed it on a dozen occasions in the camps of war throughout the years, rallying his men to fight or his own bruised body to haul himself out of some peril or other . . . They all seemed so trivial now, compared to what he must face.

He could smell dawn coming, hours away. If there was even a little daylight between the retreating hem of night and the coming of the storm, it would help, but he sensed now there wouldn't be. Whatever happened, it was going to be close.

The awareness of the storm grew on him as he dragged out the small pack of implements he had assembled and the battered black Demonary with its crumbling leather cover. The storm's electricity chewed at his bones as he drew further signs on the floor and repeated the words, marking the runes and the great curves of the power-lines, digging strength and the last glitters of magic from the marrow of his bones to summon and fix the power of the ritual in the air.

As he had in the snake pit, he cursed his own sloth in pursuit of Starhawk's meditations, cursed his arrogance in refusing to believe entirely what Kaletha had grudgingly tried to teach him, and felt the power slip with his concentration, even as he cursed. He brought his whole mind back, to center on his work—runes drawn, softly shining in the air, and the sweet resinous smells of the aromatic herbs, the search for which had further delayed their arrival in Wenshar earlier that day. He relaxed into the ritual, willing himself to see the reality of the light-runes that flickered into shape between his hands—the clumsy, heavy-knuckled hands of a warrior, nicked with scars and gummed, like a butcher's, with blood. He forced each gesture to be calm and unhurried and precise, sinking his mind and thoughts into the soft chant of the words, unfamiliar at first, then stronger as his tongue caught their alien rhythm. He forced his mind not to be caught in wondering contemplation of the glowing ritual itself. That was perhaps the hardest of all.

He repeated the names of the demons, as they had been known and written over the years by the women of the cult, summoning each, binding each, holding it to the honey-yellow sandstone beneath his feet with the ritual mix of herbed wine and blood, commanding it never to depart from this place, never to walk upon the air, never to seek surcease of its cravings in the dark warmth of men. He felt their anger and their rage shimmering from the pit as he walked the outer perimeter of the Circle and repeated their individual names. And he felt his own exhaustion twist his sinews as he dredged and scraped power from his heart, like a starving man scraping the scum of rice-boilings from the rim of an empty pot.

He couldn't let himself stumble. He couldn't let his cracking concentration break. The demons were swarming against the glowing barriers of the Circle of Darkness now, their arms edged with color and their cold, chitinous bodies burning with smoky phosphorescence, whispering in thin voices that stole like wind through the chinks in his soul. It had grown hot in the temple, the air close and thick with the coming storm. Gluey wind kissed his cheek as he passed between the Circle and the doors, the hot electricity of dust ... then, sharply, the smell of horses.

Starhawk had gone to the door. It was a small entrance, narrow and tucked away; she'd be able to hold it ...

He dragged his concentration back. He could not even permit himself to speculate on how long the ritual would last, could not let that break the silence he held like perilously friable armor around his heart. The demons; the storm; Tazey sitting near the broken protective Circle, feeding twigs to the little fire, her absinthe gaze dark with horror as she saw the ragged heat-swirl of the demons and sensed the tearing cold of the demons' minds seeking a way into his. The far-off call of voices touched his consciousness, the rattle of weapons, the scuffle near the door, and the smell of new blood. He heard the chittering of demons and the weak groaning—by his ancestors, he'd never have thought the calf would have lived that long in the pit. Arms aching, he traced the signs in the air again, his numbed mind repeating the formulae, thanking all the spirits of his ancestors that the magic took most of its strength from the building power of the rite, not from his own emptied reserves.

There was another cry from the door and the hiss and

clash of swords. He pulled his mind back again as his warrior's reflexes twitched. There were too many of them for her, even in that narrow way. The demons swirled up like rags of fire above the pit—a glowing holocaust breaking against the ceiling—screamed at him in voices he knew he alone could hear, and reached skinny arms for him. He raised his hands again, his back muscles a twisting spine of flame.

Then in the darkness deep at the back of the temple, where the second door was, he saw the glint of a crossbow bolt—not aimed at him. Without turning his head he knew where Starhawk stood, sword in hand, silhouetted now against the black rectangle of the narrow entrance, a dead man and a wounded one at her feet.

He yelled, "DROP!" the second before the iron bow whapped, hideously loud in the echoing temple. Spinning, he was aware of all that fragile creation of magic and light that hung in the air around him shattering like kicked glass. Rocketing iron clashed on stone; footsteps thundered, racing across the temple floor toward him from the inner door. He swung to meet the two men who fell upon him, bearing him backward. The sacrificial knife was in his hand as he made a despairing dive inside the reach of one attacker's drawn sword. At the last second he twisted, springing aside from the second man's sword . . .

And he felt it, when the next thrust drove him backward over the Circle of Darkness.

He screamed, "NO!" as he hit the stone floor, and for an instant the demons swirled like hornets around him, a rending glitter of claws. Then the two men in the green leathers of the Tandieras guards were on him. He tried to get up. The knife fell from his bleeding hand as his back struck the stone of the altar; the weight of human arms and bodies twisted him face down on the stone. Edged metal pressed up under his jaw.

For a moment there was nothing but the smell of blood on the stone where his face pressed it and the thin, sharp push of his pounding veins against the pressure of the razor edge. Then from somewhere Nanciormis' voice said, "Is there anything in the pit?"

The soft vibration of boots through the stone under his cheek. No sound.

Then, "Dead calf, sir. Fair tore to pieces it is. He was sacrificing, right enough."

"Anything else?"

"No, sir."

More footfalls. Closer now, Nanciormis said, "So. It is as we said. He is the witch."

Sun Wolf raised his head from the stone, the blade against his throat giving back slightly as he did so. The commander stood at the pit's edge, looking down into it; his full lips thinned in an expression of disgust and horror, but every line of that thick, muscular back reflected satisfaction like a smirk.

And well he might feel so, the Wolf thought bitterly. His accusations were borne out beyond the shadow of any man's doubt. Beyond in the darkness he glimpsed the shapes of Starhawk, standing between the black-robed Kaletha and half a dozen guards, and of Tazey, shivering tearfully in the uncertain arms of the faithful Anshebbeth.

In all the silent blackness of the temple, there was no other movement. On the floor, his own footmarks and those of Nanciormis and the guards scuffed through the lines of the Circle. The smell of blood and smoke hung on the air like the stink of a battlefield, but the demons were gone.

CHAPTER

—— 17 ——

"Turn the storm?" Kaletha's short laugh reeked bitterness, like sweat in a beggar's rags. "You'd put it to better use if you tied that barbarian thief hand and foot and pushed him out in it. It would save Illyra's torturer the trouble of flensing the meat from his bones." Her white hand, like a spider in the darkness against its black homespun sleeve, stroked the rotting cover of the Demonary that she held like a child to her full breasts. "Both of them," she added spitefully, glancing across at Starhawk, who sat, hands bound, in watching silence. Starhawk met her eyes calmly, without apology. It was Kaletha who looked away. From where he lay Sun Wolf could see her fingers tremble with anger.

He sighed and let his head drop back to the patterned amber stone of the floor. He was glad only to be out of that haunted temple, though this wide oval chamber deep in the center of the palace maze wasn't much of an improvement as far as he was concerned. Most of the doors in the old palace had been battered from their

hinges by the invading troopers of Dalwirin a century
and a half ago; to escape the fury of the storm, whose
voice had begun to rise in the canyons outside, it had
been necessary to come deep in. The absence of drifted
sand and debris had told them that this inner chamber
was a safe refuge.

From the storm, Sun Wolf amended, watching how
the torches flickered nervously in the crossing drifts of
wind from the ventilation shafts. *From the storm.*

Anshebbeth wet her lips and glanced across at the
Wolf. "Are you..." Her voice sank, an exaggerated
whisper above the conspiratorial murmur of the wind in
the shafts. "Are you sure he's *safe*?"

Annoyed, Sun Wolf rolled to a slightly more comfortable position on his back, his shoulders and his arms,
bound behind him, piercing him with sharp pain. He'd
long ago learned that, when one is tied up, there is no
such thing as a comfortable position. "Hell, no, I'm not
safe," he growled. "And none of us is, in this demon-
haunted hell hole."

"Be silent," Kaletha snapped. Everyone was on edge.
The heat and electricity of the storm plucked and teased
at the nerves and set up a throbbing in the brain. Impatient and contemptuous, she went on, "There are no
demons. The only thing to fear is your killer's mind and
your stolen magic, and those, yes, are safely bound."

Anshebbeth, sitting huddled beside the silent Tazey,
looked little comforted, but Sun Wolf could have told her
that even without the spells laid on his wrist chains, she
had nothing to fear from him. He felt emptied, as if after
long sickness or starvation, like grass burned to its roots.
In a way, that troubled him more than the binding of his
powers. The demons had been summoned, their appe-
tites whetted, not satisfied. They were still abroad in the
storm-hot, hazy darkness of the painted halls.

"You've bound my magic, Kaletha, but not my mind.
The demons in this place are real."

"If you are not silent," she said, low and perfectly

steady, "I'll have one of the guards come over here and cut out your tongue. Do you understand?"

One of the little cluster of frightened guards glanced up from their huddle around a small fire directly beneath a vent shaft, then looked quickly away, pretending he had not heard. They might be under Nanciormis' orders to obey Kaletha, Sun Wolf thought, but they weren't at all happy about it.

A gust of wind kicked at the blaze, sending sparks whirling up. Sun Wolf shivered, seeing again how the demons had whirled above the pulsing glow of the pit. The guards drew nervously together—young men and women recruited from the cordillera mining towns, trained to fight, perhaps, but only to fight what they could see. In the unsteady light, their shadows writhed over the honey-colored sandstone pilasters circling the walls and lent to the painted figures on the plaster a subtle and furtive life.

Though the storm winds did not blow here, the air was curtained with fine dust, which lent a ghastly, muted quality to the firelight and made Sun Wolf's head ache. In that hideous haze, nothing seemed quite as it should be. All around the room they watched, mocking, from the faded walls—mother and daughter, grandmother and daughter-in-law, crones and girls with dark eyes and too-knowing smiles. He felt them, like ghosts, listening, staring down at the last Princess of the House who sat head bowed, beside her governess, not daring to raise her eyes. Kaletha, too, seemed to feel the pressure of those ironic gazes, but she remained straight-backed as a queen, as if daring them to show themselves.

And he was troubled with the thought that they might.

Somewhere the wind sobbed in the corridors; Anshebbeth slewed around to face the empty door from which the sound seemed to come, then edged closer to her teacher. With thin, shaking hands she plucked at the red-haired woman's sleeve.

"Please," she whimpered. "Can you—Can you do

anything? This is a terrible place, Kaletha. I know it, I can feel it. We shouldn't be here. The Captain is right, it is haunted."

Kaletha jerked her arm away and rubbed her temples, as if doing so could crush out the splitting pain of the storm-ache within. "You're the one who's haunted," she snapped irritably. Her eyes darted to the door and back again. "Haunted by your own fears, which he plays upon like a common charlatan."

"No . . ."

"There are no demons." Her mouth was suddenly rigid with rage. "Even you believe his lies now, as everyone does."

Anshebbeth stammered, "No—"

"Then why are you afraid?" Kaletha cut at her. "He used my magic, stole it, twisted it to work evil out of his own greed and vice. His greed has given wizardry an evil name that shall never be eradicated, leaving me—*me*— and all who come after to suffer for it. That's all there is. The power comes from the mage, from the mind, not from some—some desert legend or djinn of shirdar superstition."

"But what if he's right?" Anshebbeth's eyes, black and liquid, shirdar eyes, flickered from one empty socket doorway to the next. She was shivering as she tried to draw nearer for comfort, and angrily Kaletha moved away. "There were demons in the temple where we found him: I sensed it, felt it. And I felt them . . . the night Egaldus—"

"Will you stop whining!" Kaletha swung around, blue eyes blazing in the firelight. "Don't you speak to me of Egaldus! What would you know about demons or anything else?"

Spots of red flared on Anshebbeth's white cheeks. "Just because Egaldus was a more apt pupil than I doesn't mean I know nothing—" she began shrilly.

"Apt!" Kaletha's laugh was like a dog's bark, harsh and false. "You don't know what you're talking about!"

"Don't I?" Anshebbeth's thin nostrils flared, her black eyes widening with a long-pent boil of fermented rage as the storm triggered her temper as it had triggered Kaletha's. "And whose fault is that? Because you'd rather have taught him than me..."

"He had more promise—he had the power—"

"He had you!" Anshebbeth almost screamed. "Again and again, for all your talk of purity! I heard you tell the Captain that, through your window—I heard it! You taught him because he was a man, because he'd lie with you and pretend he loved you!" Tears flooded the dark eyes. "*I* love you! *I* could have given you everything he did..."

"When? While you were playing the slut in Nanciormis' bed?"

The tears spilled over, creeping down the blotched, swollen cheeks. Starhawk, sitting unnoticed by the wall, watched the scene with head tipped a little to one side, gray eyes suddenly sharp with interest. Hysterically, Anshebbeth cried, "At least he cares for me for what I am —which you never have—never..."

"Oh, for God's sake, don't snivel!" Kaletha turned away and pressed her hands to her head again. Anshebbeth fell back, her hand rubbing nervously at her throat, her face working with stress and grief.

Tazey reached out to touch her comfortingly. "Don't. She doesn't really mean it. Everyone loses their temper during a storm." But at that moment footfalls rang in the darkened hall. With a sob, Anshebbeth flung herself to her feet and, as Nanciormis came through the dead socket of the door beside her, fell desperately into his arms.

For one second Sun Wolf thought the commander would thrust her off him. His thick face, doughy-looking with strain, twisted in revulsion as Anshebbeth's skinny arms clutched at his shoulders. The two guards behind him went on into the oval room with carefully averted eyes, not wanting to look at their commander and his hysterical, middle-aged mistress; that, too, showed on Nanciormis' face. He patted her heaving back perfunctorily while she ground her flat breasts and running nose into the soft green leather of his doublet, but the Wolf could see in his face only the desire to get this over with and get her off him as quickly as he gracefully could. Sun Wolf supposed he should have thought better of the commander for taking even that trouble, but suspected Nanciormis would have shown less forbearance without the presence of an audience.

He turned to trade a glance with Starhawk and saw her gaze, not on Nanciormis, but on Tazey. The girl was watching her uncle and her governess, nauseated cynicism in her eyes.

"That's right, go to him!" Kaletha jeered viciously. She had not forgiven the public revelation about Egaldus. "You'll never see, will you? If I was never able to touch magic within your mind, it was because your mind wasn't willing—because you had other fish to fry. It was you who lied, not I!"

Anshebbeth was sobbing miserably. "No! No!" Nanciormis, with the exasperation of an insensitive man who finds himself facing a scene, shoved her aside and strode over to the Witch.

Very softly, under the cover of the commander's angry bluster, Starhawk said, "Tazey?"

The girl turned her head. Through the blurred apricot haze of dust, tears glinted in the shadows.

"What did Nanciormis say to you?" asked the Hawk. "What made you hate him so much that you thought it was you who had summoned the demons? *Was* it about your magic?"

Even in that strange gloom, Tazey's face went first scalded pink, then white with shame. In a stifled voice she said, "No. He . . . He tried to kiss me." She moved over closer to them, her face looking old and drawn with fear and shame at the memory. After a moment she corrected, "He did kiss me. I used to think it was sort of sweet, that he would be in love with 'Shebbeth. Now I see it—he only wanted to—to get near me. I—He—" She looked pleadingly at Starhawk and the Wolf, revulsion clear on her face. "He's my *uncle!*"

"He's your uncle," Starhawk said softly. "Your mother's brother. Except for Jeryn, the last Prince of the Ancient House of Wenshar."

Something in the way she spoke, the half-detached, half-speculative tone of her soft, even voice, made Sun Wolf look up at her suddenly. Her eyes looked as they had in a hundred pre-dawn conferences on battle lines and siege camps, adding up a thousand tiny details and coming up with . . .

"Taswind!"

Tazey looked up at Nanciormis' voice. Her uncle strode over to her, his white cloak billowing, his eyes oil-dark and hard.

"Come away from them."

She did not move. The big shirdar lord hesitated for a moment, indrawn breath waiting on his lips, then changed his mind. He came to where she sat, against the wall at Starhawk's side, and squatted before her. She tried to pull her elbow away from his gloved hand, and the silk and leather grip tightened.

"Don't be a fool," Nanciormis said softly. But now, listening for it, Sun Wolf heard the caress behind the hardness of the words. He saw by the angry stiffening of the girl's mouth that she heard it, too, and resented it like a too-familiar touch. "They've played the friend to you, yes. Up to this point men can still be gotten to admire your loyalty, even if it is misguided. Don't you see?" He leaned closer to her, put his hands on her strong, slender shoulders, where the Wolf's grip had left sticky fingermarks of blood. His voice softened further, urging, coaxing. Tazey's face was like stone.

"The proof is sure. If it wasn't with the apparition that attacked me, what more can men need? He's been seen to sacrifice as the Witches of old used to do.

You have to disassociate yourself from them. I can protect you..."

Tazey pulled her body from his grasp. "Get away from me," she said softly. Sun Wolf could see her tremble. "Just get away."

Nanciormis glanced sharply from Sun Wolf to Starhawk and back to Tazey, and the glint in his dark eyes was an ugly one. But he turned, to summon Anshebbeth —and saw that the doorway where she had stood was empty. His brows plunged down over the hawk nose; he muttered angrily to himself, "Damned bitch..."

Starhawk said quietly, "It's a dangerous game you're playing, Nanciormis. It's you she'll be hating next."

The commander slewed around, as if at the sudden whine of a drawn sword. After a second's shocked immobility he lunged to his feet, dragging Starhawk up by a handful of ragged shirt, his hand raised to knock her back against the plaster of the wall. And in that second, as when he had turned his head from the bleeding calf to see the demon grinning over his shoulder, Sun Wolf understood.

He thrust himself back against the wall and so to his feet, oblivious to the stabbing pain in his legs. "I wouldn't," he said, his hoarse voice like the faint scrape of metal on rock. Nanciormis stopped. For a moment he stood, even as his guards, half-risen around the fire at the commotion, waited immobile, fearing to tamper with a wizard even to aid their lord. The firelight glistened along the sweat on Nanciormis' face.

Very softly, Starhawk said, "Magic isn't the key, is it? I think that's what I understood, what I realized and forgot during Kaletha's summoning of the dead—that it didn't have to be magic. And that's what scared me— that if it didn't have to be magic, it could be anyone. No wonder they call the time of storms the season of witches. Because the key isn't magic. It's hate."

"I don't know what you're talking about." He didn't

raise his voice loud enough for the guards, or for Kaletha, to hear.

"Don't you?" Her cool gray gaze shifted to Sun Wolf, as if they sat in a tavern with all the evening ahead of them to converse. "You called Kaletha a fool when you first met her, Chief," she said. "Why?"

Slowly, Sun Wolf said, "Because of her claim to be able to teach anyone magic—to make a mage of anyone. At the time I called her a fool because I thought she couldn't. Now I think it's because she could.

"Magic..." He hesitated, groping for words to explain the core of fire in his soul. "Maybe magic does come, as Kaletha says, from the mind. But the mind is a deep darkness. Magic wells out of depths the nonmageborn can't penetrate, can't even comprehend. It's as if there were a cover over that pit in their minds. In the mageborn, that pit is uncovered. We can control what flows out of it. That pit is where we descend, during the Great Trial."

Nanciormis said nothing, but in his thick face, the dark eyes shifted.

While the Wolf was speaking, Kaletha had come over to them, in her blue eyes an intensity he had never seen there. In the gloom her hair seemed braided out of smoke. "Yes," she said. "It is that cover I sought to remove."

"But removing the cover wouldn't give the person the ability to control what came out, would it?" the Hawk said. "Or what went in, to feed on the power there." In the darkness of the hallways beyond the gaping doors, wind groaned like a soul in pain, and below the wind was a faint chittering that raised the hairs on Sun Wolf's nape. Starhawk went on, "I'm not mageborn—for me, the pit of my soul is covered over. But in meditation, I've been able to listen to the sounds on the other side of that cover and to make guesses about what's down there."

Tazey said softly, "The demons..."

"There are no..." began Kaletha, but another moan of wind silenced her, and she did not finish. Under the cinnamon darkness of her looped braids her face turned chalky, as she faced, for the first time, the possibility that there were indeed matters with which she was not qualified to tamper.

"When we formed the Circle to call up the soul of the Bishop Galdron," the Hawk said, casually leaning her back and her bound hands against the painted plaster of the wall behind her, "I could feel the power moving through it, from hand to hand. You, Egaldus, and Shelaina Clerk, a little, could summon power up out of that pit in your souls at will. I couldn't—not until I sank into a trance from the incense and the chanting. Not until I lost myself in dreaming. And now I remember realizing that all the killings had happened in the deep of night, as if the mind that wielded the demons had to be asleep before they would go free. That meant that the killer might not know who he was, might not even be mageborn. The storms do that, too—make everyone less careful about controlling their rages. Later, when you said you'd never heard of the Great Trial, I knew it couldn't have been used by the Witches. That meant they wielded power without having passed the Great Trial—that like you, they could teach anyone, mageborn or not, to wield that same power. I checked through the books myself, later. Nowhere did it say all the Witches were mageborn—but it did remark that many of the killings took place in the deep of night."

"And just as many took place in the day," Nanciormis snapped. His eyes went from face to face and then darted swiftly to the small knot of guards still warming themselves by the fire. He seemed to feel their curious glances and kept his voice quiet, as they had all kept their voices but for his single outburst of rage. "Everyone in Tandieras was certainly abroad and awake when I was attacked."

"Of course," said Sun Wolf. "You needed witnesses to the fact that you had nothing to do with the killings."

Nanciormis' face flushed. "I don't have to listen to this . . ."

"I want to listen to it," Tazey said unexpectedly. In the tangle of lion-colored hair, her face was pale and set.

"The man's mad—a tramp wizard who's confessed himself in the pay of our enemies. You can't—"

The girl's voice was cold. "As Royal Princess of Wenshar, I *can*." She turned back to Sun Wolf. "Go on."

There was a moment's deadly silence, during which Nanciormis stared at his niece with hate in his dark eyes —hate, and considerable surprise.

"That must have grated on you like a broken tooth, mustn't it?" the Wolf said, his hoarse voice low. "Knowing you were born of the house that had ruled Wenshar and seeing it in the hands of a blustering drunkard whose parents were outlanders and slaves? Knowing it would pass to a scholar brat who could barely lift a sword, for all that he knew the language and customs of the shirdar as no king had for three generations? Osgard never trusted you enough to give you real power—he kept that for his friend Milkom. And if I'd been jumped coming home by a bunch of shirdar, I'd be a little careful, myself. You know, that attack on the road the night we met Osgard never did seem quite right to me, but as a Prince of an Ancient House, you'd be able to arrange with the shirdar to do it. And as the Prince of an Ancient House, you'd have known about the demons. And you'd have known there was no way it could be traced back to you."

"Naturally it can't," Nanciormis said derisively, but his hand, still closed over Starhawk's shirt, clenched nervously, a ripple of tendon and bone beneath the embroidered leather of the glove. "Because it was nothing to do with me. It's a good try, my barbarian witch," and the Wolf heard the shirdar inflection in the word, the meaning of one who copulates with devils to buy power. "But your attempt to discredit me will be no more successful than your attempt was upon my life. I certainly had no reason to hate half the people who died."

"No," Starhawk agreed calmly. "But the ones you did hate, you made damn certain Anshebbeth did as well."

In the terrible silence that followed, Sun Wolf could hear the storm winds groaning like souls trapped forever in the haunted labyrinths of the palace. Within, eddy and counter-eddy scurried through the halls, stirring the murky curtains of dust on the air in the dark rooms where the painted frescoes stared open-eyed into the eternal night. He was aware of them now—a shrill skitter of sound, a skeleton flicker of light far down a corridor that none of the others seemed to see. Sweat crawled down his arms to the manacles and the chewed, dirty bandages on his wrists.

Starhawk went on, "We always thought it sounded like two killers, didn't we, Chief? Not counting, of course, the attack Nanciormis faked on himself, which even at the time looked like just a means of getting you out of the way. But it was only one man wielding a weapon—a weapon that sometimes went and killed on its own."

Kaletha's lips moved; though she made no sound, Sun Wolf could see she whispered, "Anshebbeth..."

Starhawk's gray eyes went to her ashen face, and something softened a little in her voice. "She never was mageborn, was she? And you were never able to wake magic in her at a conscious level. That meant that she couldn't see what was happening. But you broke that cover over the pit of her soul, nevertheless—and it was to her that the demons spoke. There was a cauldron in her of lust and hate that refused to look at itself..."

"No." The word came out strangled and dry, but Kaletha's eyes suddenly swam with grief and utter horror. As if to convince herself, she stammered, "There are no demons. Only the mind, the powers of the mage... It was my destiny to teach, to help others realize... Dear God, what have I done?"

"Nothing." Nanciormis thrust Starhawk from him and turned angrily to face the Witch. "You've done nothing. Neither this bitch nor her demon lover can prove anything. They're lying to save their skins."

"How else would you explain Nexué's death?" Starhawk asked, catching her balance easily. "You knew the signs before that time, though, didn't you, Nanciormis? The signs the Witches used to look for, when one of their adepts was first becoming acquainted with those dark dreams of power and hate. Did she tell you of them? Was that when you went to her room on the balcony that first time, woke her out of that first dream of hate against me and the Wolf? She was the ideal weapon. You fed her lies and gossip, played on her love for Tazey, her fears for Kaletha's safety, knowing Milkom would be riding with Galdron—Milkom who would never have countenanced your offer for Tazey's hand. And you did offer, didn't you, as soon as Incarsyn was out of the way?"

Nanciormis said nothing, but Tazey's smoldering green eyes answered as clearly as words could have.

Starhawk went on, "At that point Incarsyn should have been safe. But you'd already planted the seeds of hate for him in Anshebbeth, with your gossip of what he'd said of witches, and how he'd treated Tazey. Whether any of it was true or not—the poor bastard always seemed pretty harmless to me and he had the decency to be kind to her—that hate couldn't be erased. And besides, he still might have wanted the Kingship of Wenshar enough to have gone against his sister's bidding."

"Kingship?" Tazey's dark brows startled down over her eyes. "But I'm not the heir. Jeryn..." She stopped. In the hush, Sun Wolf heard it again: the whispered chitter, a slither like a woman's gown passing over stone. He looked quickly around the oval room, wondering if he had truly seen a shadow moving retrograde across the restless jitter of the flames.

Tazey's face darkened with rage from which all fear of

her uncle had departed. She said quietly, "You pig. No wonder he was afraid to take his sword lessons with you. No wonder he spent all his time hiding. No wonder he'd risk his life to get another teacher."

He put a firm hand on her arm, and she wrenched away from it as if it had been smeared with dung. "You're letting this man's lies run away with you."

"Am I?" Tazey said harshly. "I know my brother's not a coward. He knew it, too, until you started telling him —and telling my father—he was one. Until Sun Wolf came, he would have done anything to prove it, like riding the horses you gave him which were too strong for him, or going out in the desert. You told him to do that, too, didn't you?"

"As the last Prince of the Ancient House," Starhawk said, "your marriage to her would have made you the logical heir, when the inevitable accident finally did happen. But I'm sure you know that."

"What I know," Nanciormis said, "is that you and this man, by his own confession, were sent as agents from Kwest Mralwe to spread confusion and dissension in Wenshar, and now you have succeeded beyond even the King-Council's wildest hopes. You have shattered the alliance between the shirdar lords and the Lord of Wenshar; you have discredited me, the only man capable of ruling in the stead of that pathetic sot on the throne"

Furious, Tazey lashed out at him. With a warrior's quickness, he caught her wrist before her palm connected with his face. His grip like steel on the slender, browned flesh, he went on softly, "You have spoiled all chance for the only logical union that would save the kingdom." He turned his head back to look at Sun Wolf. "You've earned your pay well. As for that slut Anshebbeth..."

He looked around. The guards, who had been huddled in low-voiced conversation over their fire, looked up now, as if at some sound. Their faces, male and female, bearded and unbearded, were drawn and strained in the jittery light, their eyes darting nervously from door to black and gaping door. Neither Kaletha nor Anshebbeth was anywhere in the room.

Starhawk's face went white under the bruises. "She's gone after her." She twisted past Nanciormis like a cat through a half-closed door and started for the rectangle of peaty darkness. "Kaletha!"

Furious, Nanciormis caught her arm, and flung her back against the wall with all his strength. With the nearness of the demons like acid on his nerves, Sun Wolf lunged at him, kneeing him in the groin even as Nanciormis twisted to avoid it. The commander went down, white-faced with pain, and Sun Wolf made a dash for the empty eyepit of darkness.

Galvanized into belated action, the guards were upon the Wolf like a dog pack, bringing him to the stone floor even as he writhed and kicked against their grip. A boot connected with his ribs, and he felt at least one break, stabbing like a knife in his side. He twisted in time to catch another brutal kick on the outside of his thigh and heard the sharp whine of drawn steel, and Nanciormis' voice, thick with pain and rage, yelling "Kill him!"

Sun Wolf turned his head as much as he could in time to see Starhawk drop through the grip of the single man who held her, somehow grab his knee with her still-bound hands and rise again to dump him backward. Her roundhouse kick broke the wrist of the woman guard whose sword was sweeping down toward Sun Wolf's neck. The weapon went ringing, the guard cursing in pain as others dragged Starhawk back and Tazey's voice sliced through the confusion. "I forbid it! Let them up!"

"Don't listen to her!" shouted the commander. Sun Wolf could see him, staggering to his feet and fighting with all his strength not to hunch over. "She's under this wizard's spell."

"I thought Kaletha's bonds rendered his spells harmless," Starhawk retorted, and Nanciormis slapped her with furious brutality. Blood trickled from her lip, but she raised her head to meet his eyes nevertheless.

"Kill them both."

"No!"

He caught Tazey as she tried to spring forward and held her in a grip of iron. The guards hesitated, weapons in hand, their edges glinting in the shaken firelight. Sun Wolf, panting, his every breath now as if a knife were being driven into him, tried to move, and one of the several guards on top of him twisted his arm and ground his cheek against the stone of the floor. Through his agony, even then, he sensed the demons, whispering a name.

Nanciormis said, "Do it."

Sun Wolf felt a knee crush his back and a hand take a killer's grip of his thin, sweat-soaked hair. Then he felt it, like fire along his mind, driving out even the death that would come in the next instant—the rush and whisper of the demons, the surge of horror and power. A woman screaming—for an instant he believed he was the only one who heard.

The weight pressing his body to the floor flinched, then slacked, frozen. The knife dropped past his face, clattered unnoticed on the stone.

The screams went on, reverberating through the mazes of that haunted labyrinth, but no one in that firelit hall moved. Above the shrieking he thought he could hear other things: the shrill chittering of the demons, a soft whisper of terrible laughter like an echo from the end of a lightless corridor. He wasn't sure, but he thought he could hear a second voice, somewhere distant, screaming, too.

Then Tazy said softly, "Let them up. Cut them loose. We're going to need whatever magic we can get."

CHAPTER

—— 18 ——

*T*HEY FOUND ANSHEBBETH, SITTING ON THE ALTAR within the fragments of the broken Circle of Darkness. The air here was hot, thick with filtered dust, and reeking of smoke and fresh blood. Anshebbeth's gown was matted and dabbed with it where she sat on the stone, and, by the faint witchlight he and Tazey were able to summon between them, Sun Wolf saw finger-runnels of it marking the woman's white cheeks under her half-uncoiled tangle of hair.

She turned her eyes toward them, huge and luminous in the shadows, as they stopped in the inner doorway of the temple. Sun Wolf saw that she was mad.

"Come in," she said, and smiled, as the demon had smiled when Sun Wolf disemboweled the calf. "Come in."

Nanciormis and the guards hung back, but Sun Wolf walked forward into the shadowy temple, his steps putting soft fingerholes in the silence. With a cat's fastidious tread, Starhawk followed him. A moment later, Tazey shook free her uncle's staying grip and moved out also, her breeches and boot tops, like the stained rags of the Hawk's shirt, mere blurs of white in the gloom. Everywhere now, Sun Wolf could sense the demons, smell them, and feel their greedy expectancy, half-slaked but craving more to satiate. The dust caught the bluish-white glare of the witchlight, filtering it into a ghostly fog; in places it seemed to glow, though he could see nothing further—reds and a certain shade of blue that reminded him of Kaletha's eyes. Beyond the altar, the pit radiated a rotted light which permeated the darkness and dust; against it, Anshebbeth's thin, dark shape stood up like a corroded spike.

"She's dead, isn't she? Kaletha."

The blood trail, sprayed over walls and floor, had wound for almost a hundred yards among the twisting corridors and painted rooms. "Yes," the Wolf said. "She's dead."

Anshebbeth moved convulsively, clapping her hands over her face. When she took them down, tacky-dry blood smudged her eyelids and the sides of her thin nose. "I had to," she said in a strangled voice. "She was jealous of me. She only wanted me to—to follow after her. She said I should come to help her carry her books back. She didn't trust anyone else. She didn't care that there was danger here, that I'd be afraid. But I'm not afraid anymore."

She smiled again, like a skull. "Now I can make other people afraid."

"If that's what you want," he said. He stood with his arms at his sides, the rough golden hair on them prickling with the hot weight of evil in the room. They'd taken the chains from his wrists, but the magic in him was kitten-weak. He was aware of that more than of anything else, staring into the madwoman's dark eyes.

"Now Nanciormis will have to love me." She dangled her feet from the altar, kicking them back and forth, as a child might, and twisted a lock of her straight black hair into a sticky ringlet with her forefinger. "I can give him whatever he wants. I saved him from Galdron's hate and plotting. Now he doesn't have to marry Tazey. Now he'll marry me."

"Anshebbeth..." Tazey began, and her governess turned toward her, pointy face blazing with spite.

"I will marry him!" she insisted furiously. "You don't want him! I saved you from having to marry Incarsyn, after all those cruel things that Nanciormis told me he said about you! You're just jealous of me!"

"No," the girl said quietly. The witchlight slipped like electrum along her thick curls as she shook her head. "No, Anshebbeth, I'm not jealous of you."

"Well, you should be!" The thick air sifted with the dry whisper of demons. Light flicked in the corner of Sun Wolf's vision—he turned his head quickly, but there was nothing there. At the same moment Nanciormis and his small knot of guards stepped quickly away from the dark door, as if they had heard something in the blackness of the corridor behind them that they feared more than they feared the haunted temple ahead.

Anshebbeth stretched out her hands, thin and white as bone. "Nanciormis," she whispered, and the sibilance of it was picked up by echo and shadow.

Sun Wolf could see the white rim of terror all around the irises of the shirdar lord's dark eyes. The last Prince of the House of Wenshar knew the tales of what had taken place on that altar and what had happened to the men afterward.

Anshebbeth's face clouded. "What's the matter?" she asked softly. "You don't need to be afraid. I won't hurt you."

In the corners all around her, the demons stirred. Sun Wolf moved his head again, sharply, but that skeleton flick of light was gone. *They know your blind spots,* he thought, *and stand in them...*

He saw Tazey whirl like a startled fawn and look back

at him with frightened eyes. Still Nanciormis did not move.

"I love you," Anshebbeth insisted, hurt in her voice. "I did it all for you." Then the note in her voice changed, and there was a sliver of anger there. "It was all for you."

The glow behind her changed into a kind of shivering glitter, and the Wolf thought he saw bright flecks of color begin to swirl in the air above the pit like sparks over a fire.

"Come to me!"

His face a mask of marble, Nanciormis stepped forward. He stopped, swallowed hard, and cast a quick glance of terror and pleading at Sun Wolf.

All his life, the Wolf thought, Nanciormis had never thought of long-range consequences to himself or anyone else, except where they served his ends. Now he was like a man wading in the ocean who steps off the underwater cliff to find himself suddenly struggling in deep water, fearing the things that swim in it beyond his knowledge. He whispered helplessly, "Please . . ."

"You're afraid of me," Anshebbeth said softly. "You don't need to be afraid of me." In the frame of her disheveled hair, her blood-marked face was horrible, the rage that had come easier and easier to her in the last weeks flaring suddenly in her eyes. "Say you love me!"

He was fighting desperately to keep face and to grip his slipping hold on even the pretense of self-command. Barely audible, he whimpered, "I—I love you, Anshebbeth."

Her face contorted again. "Liar! You lied to me!" Terrified, Nanciormis fell to his knees, raising supplicating hands. *He knew,* the Wolf thought through the pounding of his head and the dagger-thrust of each indrawn breath, *just what she could do.*

"You all lie to me!" Anshebbeth swung around, staring with wild, mad eyes at them all. "None of you loves me! You all love each other." Tazey had stepped almost unconsciously into the protective circle of Sun Wolf's arm, sensing the horror that was gathering in the corners of the temple. Starhawk, typically, had moved off to the left, widening the target distance between them and giving herself more room.

Anshebbeth's voice broke with self-pity. "But no one loves me! And no one ever will."

Hands uplifted, Nanciormis gabbled, "Of course we love you, 'Shebbeth. We all love you."

"It's hard to love hate, Anshebbeth," the Wolf said, like a thin swirl of sand in the darkness. In the face of her rage, the blue glow of witchlight over his head had dimmed to a small, flat pearl, like the sun on a foggy day; he could see the demons now, melting out of the ghostly blur of dust. Their eyes were the dark eyes of shirdar ladies, their lips like women's lips running with blood. "You've become addicted to hate, even as the demons are. It warms you, as it does them."

"It isn't my fault!" she screamed. Her skinny finger jabbed out, and Nanciormis shrank back from it, his fat face tallow-colored, as if he were about to vomit with terror. "It's his! He did this to me! He made me like this! And now no one will love me ever!"

She buried her face in her hands again, the white fingers twisting her hair as her whole bony body shook with sobbing. His nerve breaking, Nanciormis turned on his knees and crawled, scrabbling over his stained white cloak, for the dark doorway back into the labyrinth of the palace. But as he reached it, he stopped, and the sickly magelight showed the sweat pouring down his face between his hanging braids. The guards were already crowding farther from the door, pressing into the wall in a tight little group, back to back, their weapons pointing outward. The fat man scrambled ungracefully to his feet, stumbled toward them for protection, and the corpse-light glow flashed on the sword points as they turned toward him. The wrath of the demons clung like the stink of plague to his flesh and his garments. None of them was willing to let him come among them. "Sun Wolf, help me!" He turned his tear-streaked face back toward the dark figure on the altar, fighting for an echo of his former mastery. "Anshebbeth, I—I didn't mean to. Truly. I'm—I'm sorry..."

"You made me do it!" she screamed. "I wanted to be mageborn, so Kaletha would love me, would treat me as her equal! But you made me hate people! You whispered to me and whispered to me about this person said this and that person said that. And then I'd dream about them—dream about their deaths, and when I heard about it the next morning I'd be glad..."

Nanciormis covered his face, giving at the knees and crumpling, as if his whole body were rotting with terror. Anshebbeth rose to her feet, her face working, the winds stirring the eldritch shimmer of dust around her, flicking the darkness of her dress and hair. The adepts did not always at first know their power, Sun Wolf remembered, but there was always a moment when they did. What ritual had they used, what final twisting of the soul, what dreadful self-justification, to temper and seal and harden the girl into their numbers? Had many of them had resisted and cried out as Anshebbeth was crying now?

Tears were streaming down her face, tears of fury and utter wretchedness tracking through the gummy blood. Shrill and barely human, she sobbed, "I feel them here —I hear them whispering. It was like my dreams, but I wasn't asleep! Kaletha—Kaletha—"

She turned on Nanciormis like a rabid weasel, and he buried his face in his arms and groaned. "You made me be this! You made me hate!"

The air seemed to burn around Sun Wolf's flesh. Wind that came from nowhere knifed in his hair and the rags of his shirt and fingered Nanciormis' cloak and long braids as he lay groveling on the stone. Tazey gasped, her hand tightening on Sun Wolf's bare arm, as glowing shapes began to pour up out of the pit, flowing along the stone floor, around the altar, and over Anshebbeth's feet. They drifted dangle-footed in the air, like monster wasps with Anshebbeth's eyes. Nanciormis scrambled to his feet and started to back away, batting blindly at the air around him, then screamed as one of them laid his arm open to the bone.

"No!" he shrieked. "Sun Wolf! Anshebbeth! I'm sorry! I'll do anything—please, help me!"

Hate doesn't stop, Sun Wolf thought, strangely calm. *When it's done with him, it will take us all.*

Swiftly, he disengaged Tazey's hands from his arm and strode empty-handed toward the altar where Anshebbeth sat. He felt the tiny slip of light that glowed above his head die. Only the dim glint of Tazey's power shimmered across on those blue, skeletal backs, and on the halo of greedy fangs surrounding the dark shape of the Witch.

Nanciormis screamed again, running desperately as the demons began to harry him around the room as they had harried the calf in the pit. Flesh gleamed opal white, bulging through claw-rents in his clothes, bouncing almost comically as he ran; blood oozed, glittering down his trouser legs and boots. He was sobbing, tears of terror pouring down his cheeks.

Sun Wolf seized Anshebbeth by the arms, and she looked up into his face, startled, so intent upon her hatred that she had not seen him come. Her countenance was scarcely human, streaked with tears and snot and blood; from a frame of coarse black hair that flowed down over his hands, she stared unseeing. "No one makes you hate, Anshebbeth. They can only ask you to. You can always say no."

"It isn't like that!" She was gasping, clutching at her throat as if it were strangling her. "I love him, and he did this to me, made me like this . . ."

Darkness closed on them, a vortex of power and terror whirlpooling into those stretched black eyes. Sun Wolf shook her, violently, furiously, trying to break that rigid centeredness of hate, and her head lolled on her shoulders, her mouth open in a soundless shriek. In the blackness, he knew the demons were around him and he felt the soft nibble of fangs against his neck. "Do you love him?" he demanded. "Or do you love your hate more than him?"

"I don't!" she sobbed. Then something broke in her, and she gasped, "I don't want to!"

Pressed to the stone of the wall, Nanciormis was screaming, begging as he fought with the bleeding air.

"Say it!" the Wolf commanded.

Anshebbeth stared up at him like a hysterical child, unable to speak or draw breath. He shook her again, her neck snapping back like a white, corded stem in the black wrack of her hair. A sob ripped her, as if it would tear her body in two. He saw the madness retreat from her eyes and knowledge take its place—knowledge and horror at what she knew she had become.

As though torn from her with a knife, her scream rent the air. "I don't want it! Let him go! I don't want this!"

Nanciormis shrieked again, huddled against the wall as the glowing ring closed around him. In Sun Wolf's grip Anshebbeth's body felt as fragile and skeletal as theirs.

Despairing, Anshebbeth screamed, "I can't let it go! I can't let it go! I want to but I can't . . ." She twisted away from him, burying her face in her skeletal hands.

Then she screamed—not the tense, tight shrillness of her strangled shrieks before, but loud, aching, louder and louder as the torrent of freed sound seemed to rip apart the containing flesh. Like startled hornets the demons rose from Nanciormis, shining horribly in the dark air. Sun Wolf flung himself aside as they descended upon the altar in a whistling swarm, knowing he had been too late. Anshebbeth did not raise her head, but screamed on and on, rocking like a hurt child, as if some last rag of sanity had slipped finally from her grip. He caught a glimpse of Starhawk running toward him, as he turned back weaponless, magicless, to face the phosphorescent storm of death.

Anshebbeth's scream scaled upward, twisting the darkness as the demons settled over her. In a flash of terrible enlightenment, Sun Wolf understood that she had regained, rather than lost, her sanity. She knew what she had done.

Blindly, striking with her hands at the glowing fangs that ripped her flesh, she ran forward, the demons driving her into the pit. Starhawk reached the Wolf's side at the same moment that Anshebbeth fell, the glowing ghost shapes swirling down after her, shriek after shriek ripping the air.

It took her twenty minutes to die. When it was over silence settled on the dark temple, as it had lain for a hundred and fifty years.

"You awake, Chief?"

Sun Wolf started to roll over, then ceased with a gasp of pain. Vaguely, he remembered Starhawk wrapping a makeshift field dressing over his cracked ribs as he was sliding into sleep in the sickly yellow post-storm light, but the recollection was cloudier than the dreams that had followed. He felt chilled, sticky, and bone-tired, hurting in every limb, with dust gummed in his eyelashes, moustache, and the stubble of his beard.

He felt someone bend over him, light and very swift, and lips touched his. Opening his eye, he saw Starhawk just straightening her body where she knelt beside him.

"Well, that fairy tale does work after all," she remarked.

She was wearing the dark-green leather doublet of the Tandieras guards over a black shirt which made her sungilded fair skin shine like ivory. She had bathed and looked clean, calm, and, except for the black handspan of bruise on her face, utterly unruffled. Squinting past her, he saw over the broken wall of the ruined house in which he'd slept, the cliff faces of Wenshar, blackish maroon in the polished sunset light, guarding their treasure of rose and apricot within. Like strange and far-off music, he heard the hushed voices of Nanciormis' guards and the comfortable nicker of horses.

The storm had ended shortly after noon. In spite of an exhaustion so deep that he could barely stagger, Sun Wolf had insisted on moving down from the canyons to the piled debris and crumbled walls of the Lower Town before he would sleep. It had taken him and Tazey two hours to work all the binding-spells to hold the demons forever within the rocks of Wenshar; exhausting, nerve-wracking hours, while he had listened, with as much of his mind as he could spare, to hear the demons wakening again from the pit where Anshebbeth's mangled body lay.

They had not wakened. Like drunkards, they were satiated, wallowing in the afterglow. He hadn't wanted to expose Tazey to the full knowledge of what the demons were and of the terrible powers necessary to hold them to the stones, but he had had no choice. He had been simply too weary, too drained, to pass through the ritual a second time alone. Later, the girl had been very silent as she had walked beside him down the sand-drifted canyon in the after-hush of the storm, but he suspected that she was less shocked by the vileness of the demons than she would have been even twenty-four hours ago.

With the demons bound to the rock that had given them birth, it would have been possible to sleep safely, even within the temple, but Sun Wolf had not wanted to risk the dreams that might come.

He mumbled, "What is it?" By the color of the light, he knew he'd slept four or five hours.

"Riders on their way," she said. "Still a couple hours out on the desert, but my guess is it's reinforcements."

"Good." He sat up. Starhawk, as usual, refrained from helping him; he didn't know whether he should be miffed or pleased with the implied compliment of super-human stamina. The jab of the hardened dressing was almost as bad as the cracked ribs underneath. "They can take Nanciormis back."

Starhawk shook her head. "He's gone," she said. "You'd started the binding-rites already when his guards took him out of the temple. He was cut to pieces, you know, and bleeding like a flayed steer. For a long time he just cried in a corner. . . ."

"Don't tell me," the Wolf said wearily. "They thought the poor bastard was pretty harmless where he was."

Starhawk shrugged. "After what went on in the temple, they weren't anxious to search the canyons for him. I'd have the lot of them flogged, myself, but it's not my business."

Sun Wolf sighed and sat quietly, his back to the crumbling house wall. Dry wind curled across his naked chest, bearing the smell of dust and horses.

He wondered why, in spite of everything—the memory of his humiliation at the commander's hands, the beating they'd given Starhawk, the pain in his wrists and side—his only anger toward the man stemmed from what he had done to Anshebbeth and what he had tried to do to Jeryn—not even so much trying to murder him, but planting in his mind the fear that he was a coward and turning his father against him.

He still found it difficult to hate Nanciormis. After seeing Anshebbeth's death, he found it difficult, at the moment, to hate anyone.

Thinking back, he realized that he always had—and in that he was like Nanciormis himself.

"He was only playing the game, you know," he said after a time. "It was only selfishness and greed, with no hate in it. He couldn't have summoned the demons if he'd wanted to, and maybe he knew it. There was nothing personal in it at all. None of them, not Tazey nor Anshebbeth nor Incarsyn, was real to him. Only himself and his wants."

"It's what tipped me off, you know." The Hawk settled back on her heels, a bar of sunlight slanting through the broken roof, turning her hair to platinum but leaving that cool, scarred face in shadow. "You saw Nanciormis as a man, but I saw him as a woman sees him. He was a man who used women. He used other people, too—their hates, their loves, their fears—and their magic. In a way, his evil was deeper than Anshebbeth's hate or Kaletha's vanity and irresponsibility with what she'd found in the books that had lain forgotten for centuries in the library. And, of course, poor Ciannis knew less of the cult than Nanciormis did. If she had known, she might have warned Kaletha about it—if she ever knew Kaletha had found the old books at all. But Nanciormis simply didn't care."

Sun Wolf nodded. "The worst of it is," he said quietly, "that it was my evil as well. That was what being a mercenary was all about. Like killing that poor calf—you do what you have to do, like an animal eating. I don't know how many people I've killed, not for a kingdom or for love or pride or for anything, really—just because some politician was paying me to take a city they happened to be living in."

The corner of her mouth moved slightly, less ironic than simply rueful. "Yes, I know," she said. Their eyes met. In hers he saw the understanding that he had done evil and that she had known it for evil at the time and had still followed him into battle as his second-in-command. It was, he understood then, what Nanciormis had done to Anshebbeth. It was how she had known.

It was some time before he could say anything. When he did, it was only, "I'm sorry, Hawk." In her eyes he saw that she knew for what.

She only shook her head. "It's history," she said, meaning it. "Like Anshebbeth, I had the choice. Unlike her, I don't hate myself for the choice I made." He remembered that she had remained Kaletha's friend.

"You understood that?"

"Oh, yes. She knew in the end what she had become —and the one she most hated was herself. I suppose it's what happened to all the girls, when they came to an understanding of what was happening to them." She un-

coiled her whipcord body and rose to her feet, watching
with her usual mild detachment as Sun Wolf agonizingly
followed. "It was only the evil ones that survived."

"I can't say that I blame those that didn't," he said.

They passed through a gap in the wall, which might or
might not once have been a door, and walked across the
trampled, dusty side of a sand dune toward where one of
the old rain tanks hid in the niche of a rock, away from
the prevailing wind. "Would you have done the same in
her position? If you learned it was you?"

Sun Wolf glanced up at the dark, eroded cliffs of the
Haunted Range, guarding their rainbow labyrinth of evil
within. "I'd like to think I would."

There was water in three of the old tanks; Sun Wolf
bathed in the shallowest of them; Starhawk joined him
there and later on the spread-out blanket that he'd worn
flung over his shoulders like a cloak. "No wonder sol-
diers' women have to be versatile and creative," she
commented, when he flinched at the pain of his ribs.

In time they both dressed in the clothes that were part
of the bundle Tazey had brought to Wenshar with her to
further their escape. The bundle also contained some
food, their weapons and mail, but not the little cache of
money. "Cheer up," Starhawk said, slipping various
hideout daggers into her boots with the air of one resum-
ing a much-loved garment. "With the demons laid for
good, they'll have to give us *some* reward—an exorcist's
fee if nothing else."

"Bets?" the Wolf grumbled.

They rode out of Wenshar as darkness began to fall
and met, an hour and a half later, the oncoming party
from Tandieras in a circle of torchlight on the pebbled
desolation of the wind-scoured reg.

As they got close, Sun Wolf could see Osgard's coarse
blond-gray hair by the torchlight and, beside his great
horse, the fat, trotting figure of Walleye and his small
rider. Tazey cried out, "Daddy!" and spurred her buck-

skin gelding, riding like a mad antelope to throw herself into her father's arms.

"It seems I've you to thank that I'm not going to find scorpions in my blankets some night." By the campfire's windblown light, Osgard looked sober and better than he had since the Wolf had come to Tandieras. The veils that swathed his coarse, stubbly face were pushed back, falling over his sand-colored cloak behind. With his rough shirt and battered boots, he might have been just another range hand, as he had been before his warrior-uncle had made him King. "Oh, I knew he was dangerous, but . . ." He hesitated, then looked into the amber heart of the fire, his thick mouth pursing with embarrassment. "I suppose I was like the owner of a dog trained for killing. You get careless."

Sun Wolf nodded. "I know." On the other side of the campfire, a guard told a joke, but the laughter was subdued. Out on the asphalt blackness of the reg, it was less easy to dismiss the demons and djinns of desert lore as mere superstition, no matter what the priests of the Triple God might say. "He did, in a way."

"He always was careless," Osgard said. "He was a good fighter, but irresponsible—he never thought anything could touch him. I'm not sure being publicly broken and turned out like a beaten dog in the desert wasn't something to which he'd have preferred death. He had a conceit of himself, besides liking his pleasures. But I wouldn't have let him put a hand on Tazey . . ." He paused, and the bluster died out of him again. Off by the other campfire, Tazey and Jeryn sat together, conversing quietly with Starhawk, their arms around her. Past Osgard's shoulder, the Wolf could see Jeryn's dark eyes shining with a boy's gruesome enthusiasm as Tazey spoke of what had happened in the temple.

The King sighed. "But God knows I'd have sworn I'd never have let matters go this far. Damned witches with their stinking magic . . ." He stopped again, looking over at the Wolf, as if he'd spoken slightingly of sand in the tents of the shirdar.

Sun Wolf shook his head. "Magic had nothing to do with it," he said. "Nanciormis was the kind of man who'd have used any weapon. He'd made attempts on your life—and Jeryn's—before he learned Anshebbeth's mind had been touched by the demons. Her power was just the readiest weapon at hand. If she'd been mageborn and not simply the victim of her own and Kaletha's vanity, she'd have understood what was happening to her and been able to control it. I felt it—I think Tazey did, too. If you have power, you must face it, touch it, and learn to use it, or it rots within you like an abscessed wound." He fell silent, regarding the King across the campfire, and Osgard, knowing his thoughts, looked away again.

He muttered, "I—I know." Unwillingly, his eyes returned to the Wolf. "But you can't blame me, can you? I wanted a daughter I could be proud of . . ."

"Good God, man," Sun Wolf said angrily, "you've got one of the finest natural wizards I've ever heard of for a daughter and a son who'll politic and finesse and treaty-make rings around the shirdar and the Middle Kingdoms, and all you can do is complain because they're not a brainless brood mare and a beef-witted ox like you and me? I can only think of two things in my life that I wouldn't trade for those children of yours. Can't you be proud of them for what they are and not for what you want them to be?"

Osgard stared into the fire, rubbing his big, sword-scarred hands over one another, as the Wolf remembered his own father used to do. Then he looked up again and grinned, a little embarrassed to admit it. "Jeryn is a clever little bastard, isn't he?"

"It's men like Jeryn," Sun Wolf said, "who hire men like me. Let 'em be what they are, Osgard. They're going to get hurt bad enough swimming against the stream as it is."

The King sighed and rubbed his stubbly chin. "I know it," he said quietly. Then, after a long pause, "Where should I send Tazey?"

She'd been willing, Sun Wolf remembered, to give up everything she wanted to please him. He remembered the fauve torchlight on her hair as she danced the war dance and the pride that had glowed so visibly from Osgard as he'd spoken of her—*the sweetest daughter a man could want.* Beside the nearby campfire, she and Jeryn sat huddled in their quilted jackets and head veils, their eyes bright as they talked to Starhawk, reunited for this last brief time.

"You could send her to Yirth of Mandrigyn," he said at length. "She's just about the only wizard I know qualified to teach." He added, seeing her father's face thicken at the thought of how far away Mandrigyn was, "But if Tazey prefers, I could stay here for awhile first, teach her what I know. It isn't the teaching she'd get from Yirth, but it would tell her what to look for later. And it would give her more time here."

"No." Osgard sighed. "Tazey can't stay here. And neither can you." A half-burned log broke in the fire; he picked a branch from the slender bundle of wood they'd brought in from the far edge of the reg and pushed the fallen chunks back together. The spurting flame showed deep lines in his unshaven face—annoyance and shame.

"You don't know the temper of the people in Pardle, Captain. They're a superstitious bunch, when all's said, and the mageborn have always had a foul reputation in Wenshar. I wouldn't have cared if you'd been lynched on the way back, but when I heard Illyra's men were out hunting your blood, I thought I'd better come and make sure Tazey got back all right. The miners and the Trinitarians being on one of their witch hunts is one thing, but Illyra..."

Sun Wolf felt his face flush with anger. "I didn't have a damn thing to do with the murders."

The King held up his hand. "That doesn't matter," he said. "And I think you know it doesn't matter."

The cruel vulture-eyes of the Lady of the Dunes returned to Sun Wolf, and the keyed-up tension in the Hall, the night Nanciormis had staged his attack. And it was gold pieces to little green apples that Nanciormis had spread the story of his confession from the Fortress to the town. Anger surged like a core of heated iron in him, but he knew Osgard was right.

"I think you'd better ride on tonight."

Osgard collected all the spare food and water from his troop of guards, and Jeryn and Tazey helped them load it on their horses. "We can hold off Illyra for a while," the King said, as Sun Wolf finished tying the latigos that held the slender bundle of his possessions to his dapple gelding's cantle. "But you'd better ride straight north and get across the Backbone as soon as you can."

"Easy for him to say," Sun Wolf growled, as the big monarch went striding off to give some direction or other to the little knot of dark-clothed guards. "You know every copper we have is still behind that brick in our cell in the empty quarter?"

Starhawk regarded him, amused, by the faint glow of the ball lightning that flickered over his head. "You want to risk meeting Illyra to go back for it?"

Sun Wolf grumbled an impious wish concerning Illyra's future sex partners and tightened the gray's cinches. He added, "I never should have promoted you from squad captain."

"You always said a warrior had to be versatile."

"I wasn't talking about sweeping floors and feeding pigs from here to Farkash."

"Chief?" The bright flicker of magelight danced in the night; the black gravel of the reg crunched underfoot as Tazey and Jeryn came back from the baggage piles, carrying sacks. It was not lost on the Wolf that the guards looked askance at the soft light that surrounded the girl, and gave her wide berth. "These are all the Demonaries and books of magic that weren't in the shirdane."

Sun Wolf hefted the sack experimentally, then opened it and removed the three largest volumes. These he handed back to Tazey. At her inquiring look, he explained, "They're too big to grab up in an emergency. I'm not going to have them destroyed by accident just because I want them with me on the road. Take them to Mandrigyn with you, along with the others. You and Yirth between you can work out translations of the shirdane ones."

She nodded, hugging the books to her breast. Her mouth flinched a little, and she looked away; he saw the witchlight glisten in her eyes.

Gently, he reached out and put a hand on her shoulder. "You'll like Yirth," he said softly. "She's a good lady." Then, grinning, he added, "You say hello to Sheera of Mandrigyn for me, too."

"And be prepared to have her spit in your face if you do," Starhawk added irreverently.

Jeryn, who had been doing something over by Sun Wolf's horse, came back into the double ring of fox-fire light, and the Wolf could see in his face, too, the grief of parting.

Tazey asked hesitantly, "Will I meet you again?"

"Not if we keep getting thrown out of every kingdom we visit."

Sun Wolf ignored his second-in-command. "One day, yes." He hugged them both, the daughter and the son that he would never father, and felt Jeryn's thin arms around his waist in a tight clutch and the sting of Tazey's tears against his unshaven chin. Neither mercenary captains nor wandering wizards could afford to raise children. It was the first time he had been conscious of regret for what he had been or for what he was.

It was the first time he fully understood what it was he had given up.

The wan glow of Tazey's witchlight was visible for a long distance across the reg as they rode away.

"It's going to be hard for her," Starhawk said after a time. "Hard for them both. But she never really wanted to be mageborn, you know. She really wanted to be what her father wanted her to be—a beautiful girl who dances well, rides anything with four legs, and eventually marries some handsome man and lives happily ever after. There was a time when she could have turned aside from what she has and gone back to lying to herself about it. She gave that up for us."

"No." Sun Wolf glanced back over his shoulder at that will-o'-the-wisp, a marsh light in the flat, black desert of stone. "You can never turn aside from it, nor lie to yourself about it. Not ever."

The moonlight dusted her uncovered ivory hair as she moved her head. "Do you want to?"

He thought about Tazey and Jeryn again, their years of learning to be what they would be, years in which he could have no part. "Sometimes."

His horse stumbled a little on the harsh gravel, making him curse as his cracked ribs pinched him, and something tied to the saddle horn jogged against his knee. Curious, knowing he had hung nothing there, he reached down and brought up a little wash-leather bag that jingled softly as he opened it and dumped its contents into his hand.

"Well, I'll be go to hell."

Starhawk drew her rangy bay mare closer, to look over his shoulder at the handful of silver gleaming softly in the dusky moonlight. "It has to have been Jeryn," she said.

Sun Wolf laughed, with relief and triumph and delight. "Nine years old and already he knows you don't turn your hired troops off without pay!"

"Yeah?" Her eyebrows went up. "And how long do you think his daddy's troops are going to cover our tracks against Illyra once they realize he's gone through and rifled every pocket and saddlebag in the camp?"

Sun Wolf shuddered and shoved the money into the pocket of his sheepskin jacket. "Kid's going to be hell on wheels when he takes over Wenshar," he said. "Let's ride."

"And just think," Starhawk mused as they nudged their horses into a canter, north to the distant, jagged line of the mountains under the sand-colored moon. "The next teacher you find may be even worse."

ABOUT THE AUTHOR

At various times in her life, Barbara Hambly has been a high-school teacher, a model, a waitress, a technical editor, a professional graduate student, an all-night clerk at a liquor store, and a karate instructor. Born in San Diego, she grew up in Southern California, with the exception of one high-school semester spent in New South Wales, Australia. Her interest in fantasy began with reading *The Wizard of Oz* at an early age and has continued ever since.

She attended the University of California, Riverside, specializing in medieval history. In connection with this, she spent a year at the University of Bordeaux in the south of France and worked as a teaching and research assistant at UC Riverside, eventually earning a Master's Degree in the subject. At the university, she also became involved in karate, making Black Belt in 1978 and competing in several national-level tournaments.

Her books include *Dragonsbane*; *The Ladies of Mandrigyn*; *The Silent Tower*; THE DARWATH TRILOGY: *Time of the Dark*, *The Walls of Air*, and *The Armies of Daylight*; and a historical whodunit, *The Quirinal Hill Affair*, set in ancient Rome.

From the lairs of darkness comes...

THE DARWATH TRILOGY

Barbara Hambly